"A must-read author . . . her [stories] are always full of emotional situations, lovable characters, and kick-butt story lines."
—*Romance Junkies*

"Heated . . . romantic suspense . . . Intense, transfixing."
—*Midwest Book Review*

"Grabbed me from page one and refused to let go until I read the last word . . . When a book still affects me hours after reading it, I can't help but Joyfully Recommend it!"
—*Joyfully Reviewed*

"An excellent read that I simply did not put down . . . A fantastic adventure . . . covers all the emotional range."
—*The Road to Romance*

"Searingly sexy and highly believable."
—*Romantic Times*

PRAISE FOR

SHAYLA BLACK

"Orgasmic."
—*Publishers Weekly*

"Wickedly seductive from start to finish."
—Jaci Burton, national bestselling author

"Intense, erotic, and sizzling hot."
—*Fresh Fiction*

"Searing . . . A must-read!"
—Lora Leigh, *New York Times* bestselling author

"The first word to come to my mind . . . is Wow! Others are amazing, terrific, fantastic, and outstanding! . . . richly drawn, fascinating, and utterly irresistible."
—*Romance Junkies*

FOUR PLAY

MAYA BANKS | SHAYLA BLACK

HEAT | NEW YORK

THE BERKLEY PUBLISHING GROUP
Published by the Penguin Group
Penguin Group (USA) Inc.
375 Hudson Street, New York, New York 10014, USA
Penguin Group (Canada), 90 Eglinton Avenue East, Suite 700, Toronto, Ontario M4P 2Y3, Canada
(a division of Pearson Penguin Canada Inc.)
Penguin Books Ltd., 80 Strand, London WC2R 0RL, England
Penguin Group Ireland, 25 St. Stephen's Green, Dublin 2, Ireland (a division of Penguin Books Ltd.)
Penguin Group (Australia), 250 Camberwell Road, Camberwell, Victoria 3124, Australia
(a division of Pearson Australia Group Pty. Ltd.)
Penguin Books India Pvt. Ltd., 11 Community Centre, Panchsheel Park, New Delhi—110 017, India
Penguin Group (NZ), 67 Apollo Drive, Rosedale, North Shore 0632, New Zealand
(a division of Pearson New Zealand Ltd.)
Penguin Books (South Africa) (Pty.) Ltd., 24 Sturdee Avenue, Rosebank, Johannesburg 2196,
South Africa

Penguin Books Ltd., Registered Offices: 80 Strand, London WC2R 0RL, England

This book is an original publication of The Berkley Publishing Group.

This is a work of fiction. Names, characters, places, and incidents either are the product of the authors' imagination or are used fictitiously, and any resemblance to actual persons, living or dead, business establishments, events, or locales is entirely coincidental. The publisher does not have any control over and does not assume any responsibility for author or third-party websites or their content.

PRINTING HISTORY
Berkley trade paperback edition / October 2010

Library of Congress Cataloging-in-Publication Data

Banks, Maya.
   Four play / Maya Banks & Shayla Black. — Berkley trade pbk. ed.
      p.   cm.
   ISBN 978-0-425-23669-7
   I. Black, Shayla   II. Title.
   PS3602.A643F68   2010
   813'.6—dc22
                        2010022839

PRINTED IN THE UNITED STATES OF AMERICA

10 9 8 7 6 5 4 3 2 1

CONTENTS

PILLOW TALK

MAYA BANKS

CHAPTER | ONE

*Zoe Michaels climbed on top of Chase Hilliard, their sweat-*slicked bodies humming with arousal. She lowered her head until her mouth hovered over the shallow indention of his navel, and she flicked her tongue out, rimming the edge.

She smiled when he shuddered beneath her lips. He was highly sensitive in that area. It drove him crazy when she touched his belly button.

The tips of her breasts grazed his abdomen when she moved higher. She straddled his hips, and his balls rested against the juncture of her thighs. If she moved even the teeniest bit, her clit pressed against his sac.

Chase groaned, "You are such a damn tease."

He reached for her, but she playfully dodged him, taking his hands and guiding them instead to her breasts. He eagerly complied and brushed his thumbs across her nipples, bringing them to rigid points.

She closed her eyes as he played. She loved having her breasts touched. So much of her sexuality was wrapped up in her breasts. It seemed silly, but she'd rather have a man's mouth on her nipples than her pussy any day.

And her neck. Oh God. She went positively weak whenever Chase nibbled at her neck. Hell, all he had to do was touch her there and she became a gelatinous blob. And to his credit, he loved to stroke her nape. They'd sit on the couch watching movies, and he'd idly pet and caress her neck until she put an end to her torment and jumped him.

Sort of like she was jumping him now. Only she'd already jumped him, and now she had every intention of revving him up again.

Her hands curled around his cock, and she purred in contentment as she caressed his length.

"Quit making that sound," Chase grumbled in a strained voice. "You know it makes me crazy. What guy doesn't get off on knowing his girl is satisfied by his equipment?"

She grinned and leaned down, her hair falling like a curtain over his chest. She kissed the hollow of his chest and lapped at the salty taste of his skin.

She rose up just enough to get his cock underneath her. As soon as she tucked the head to her entrance, they both caught their breath. His hands gripped her hips, his fingers digging into her ass. Then she lowered, taking him inch by delicious inch.

"Holy hell," he breathed. "You feel so damn good. I should be worn out and have a serious case of shriveled dick after you worked me over, but I swear you look at me and I get hard again."

She straightened, sending him even deeper, and smiled down at him. "You say the most gorgeous things. It's a good thing you say them when we're not having sex too, or I'd think you only love me for my body."

He slid his hands up her sides and then cupped her breasts in his palms. "Who says I don't?"

She laughed and planted her hands on his chest as she arched up and then moved down to sheathe him.

"Tell me your deepest, dirtiest fantasy," she challenged.

He closed his eyes for a moment as she clamped down around his cock, milking him with her internal muscles.

"You already know all my kinky fantasies," he said raggedly. "I'm an open book."

"I don't believe that for a minute. There has to be something you've fantasized, something so outrageous you'd never admit it to me."

He looked up in amusement. "And you think I'd tell you now?"

She leaned forward until her mouth was just a breath from his. "Tell me. Give me the inside scoop on that tawdry mind of yours."

"Okay so it's not exactly the kinkiest thing in the world. It just sounds . . . strange I guess."

She raised an eyebrow. "Oh do tell. I'm dying of curiosity now."

He grunted and pulled at her body, lifting her until her nipple rested against his mouth. He'd pulled her nearly free of his cock, and just the head rimmed her entrance. He slid his tongue over one nipple, and her vision went all blurry. Damn the man, but he knew all her buttons.

To make matter worse, he slid a hand around to rest on her nape, and then he simply squeezed just as he sucked her nipple hard between his teeth.

She went wet around the tip of his cock. She drenched him, and then he ran his hands quickly down her waist, gripping her and ramming her down onto his dick.

"Oh God," she breathed. "Oh shit."

"Not yet, Zoe. Not yet, baby."

It was all she could do not to give in and slide over the edge.

"I'm at a strip club."

His husky voice washed over her, eliciting a deep shiver. She loved it when they talked about their fantasies. There was something intensely sexy about his voice when it dropped and he spoke to her in low, hushed tones as if he were afraid for anyone else but her to hear.

"I'm there with the guys. The other firefighters. Everyone from the station. The lights go down and the music starts. This really gorgeous woman strolls onto the stage like she fucking owns it. She has killer legs, hips that make a man ache to touch, and an ass that inspires some dark fantasies."

She watched as his eyes grew dark and he got into the spirit of the game. His body tightened, and his cock pulsed deep inside her pussy.

"She throws off her top, and she has a set of tits that make every man in the place drool. Just right. Not too big, not too small and they're firm. Her entire body is just tight."

He began to move slowly within her, stroking in and out. She let him dictate the pace, and she just sat astride him as he worked her hips with his hands and thrust with his.

"She's you," he whispered. "And every guy in the place knows you're mine, and they're jealous as hell. You're dancing and watching me with this mysterious smile. There's not a guy in the entire club that doesn't have a hard-on the size of a tree trunk, but they know you're mine, and they hate me because they know you're going home with me. But you put on a show for them and I watch, loving every minute of it."

She moaned softly and undulated her hips over him. "You like the idea of other men watching me?"

"Oh hell yeah," he breathed. "I love them watching, knowing they can't touch what's fucking mine. I love that they're jealous, and they're all wondering what you see in me and they think I'm the luckiest son of a bitch alive."

"Mmmm."

She let out a breathy sigh as she imagined herself doing just the things he fantasized about. Dancing in front of a room full of men all focused on her.

The possession in his voice, the pride in his ownership tightened every nerve ending until she gasped for breath. She loved that he was so into her, so proud of his relationship with her.

"Not yet, Zoe," he reminded her.

Shit. She was close. So close. She squirmed as she tried to hold her orgasm at bay.

"And what if they touched me," she whispered. "What would you do?"

He rolled, tucking her into his arms and coming to a stop, him still buried deep, their positions reversed. His eyes glittered as he stared down at her.

"Do they touch you in *your* fantasy, Zoe?"

She swallowed and slid her hands up his arms to his broad, muscular shoulders. She loved touching him. It was something she never got tired of doing. He'd worked hard for his body. He stayed in tip-top shape. His job as a fireman demanded it. And she enjoyed the benefits. Oh hell yeah, she did.

She normally wasn't shy about imparting her fantasies to Chase. They often enjoyed naughty pillow talk during or right before sex. But this particular fantasy . . .

He leaned down and kissed her, licking over her lips then delving inward to slide his tongue over hers.

"Tell me," he demanded.

Her hands curled around the back of his neck, and she arched into him, wanting him deeper. His strokes were firmer now, more powerful, and he touched a part of her that sent fiery shards of intense pleasure blowing through her body.

"I fantasize about being captured—by you . . . and others. You capture me when I'm not expecting it and you take me away and you take turns making me . . ."

"Making you do what?" he asked huskily.

His pupils were dilated, and his lips parted. His breaths came out in jerky little puffs.

"It's weird because in reality . . . it's not something I'd want to ever happen. But with people I trusted . . ."

"What do we make you do, Zoe?"

She touched his face, her fingers trembling as the excitement from the mental images bombarding her coursed through her veins.

"You make me pleasure you. You pleasure me. You bend me to your will. You fuck me over and over. And while they fuck me, you watch. Sometimes you tell them what to do. Sometimes you let them do whatever they want. You watch and you enjoy seeing other men take what's yours and completely take me over."

"Ah shit," he breathed.

He tightened all over. He swelled within her, and they both teetered precariously on the edge.

"Don't move," he said harshly. "Not an inch. Give me a minute."

She obeyed because if either of them moved, she would explode. She was so tense, so buzzed on sexual excitement that she tingled from head to toe. Her clit swelled, and she ached to reach down and touch herself. Just once. It was all she'd need, but she waited, wanting them to go together.

"You like my fantasy?"

She was genuinely curious. They were pretty open about their sexual kinks, and Lord knew they had a very active sex life. Their motto was they'd pretty much try anything once.

"Fuck yeah," he gritted out.

She ran a finger over his lips, easing some of the strain as he fought against the urge to come.

"The idea of you stretched out between two other men? Or maybe you're riding one while another takes your ass and another is fucking your mouth? While I watch? Holy shit. That's hot."

She trembled. His words buzzed over her skin, evoking erotic images of her being taken over and over as he watched. She arched helplessly into him, no longer able to control the rising tide.

Chase withdrew and then slammed hard into her, his muscled thighs pounding the backs of hers. His balls slapped against her ass, and he leaned forward so his angle was sharper and his entry deeper.

She curled her fingers into his shoulders and then raked her nails over his back. He loved it when she did it, said he loved wearing her mark.

Their mouths fused hotly, in rhythm with their bodies. Over and over he thrust, taking them closer and closer until every inch of her body was one big balled-up jumble of nerves.

"Chase, please!"

He reached down, knowing what she needed. His thumb brushed over her clit, and then he pressed harder, rubbing it in a circular motion. He thrust again, and she lost it.

She came unglued in his arms. Her cry echoed across the room, and then his mouth came down over hers, silencing her. His hoarse shout was swallowed up by her inhalation.

Faster and harder. Pleasure razored across her body, a thin edge of pain and ecstasy. Sweet, sweet ecstasy.

She spun out of control, and for a moment lost all sense of herself, only that she floated on a hazy cloud of oh-my-God good.

Slowly she became aware of Chase kissing her. He kissed a lazy line up her jaw and to her mouth, nibbled on her bottom lip before continuing on to the other side of her jaw and down to her neck. Ah shit, her neck.

She shivered uncontrollably as soon as his lips touched the column below her ear. He chuckled and sucked lightly. Tremors overtook her, and a second orgasm raced over her like a quick thunderstorm in summer.

"Not fair," she croaked as she collapsed underneath him.

"You love it and you know it."

There was that.

He kissed her one last time before carefully withdrawing from her body. She lay there as he rolled out of bed to get a towel. She loved not using condoms and was happy they'd been together long enough that trust was established and they could enjoy spontaneous, mind-bending sex without latex. She didn't even mind the cleanup afterward because Chase always took care of that.

She was a lucky, lucky woman.

After taking care of the sticky parts, he slid back into bed with her, and she snuggled into his embrace. Another thing she loved about him is he didn't seem to mind her need for postcoital cuddling. How cliché was that?

Not that they didn't have their share of quickies—half of which were instigated by her. There were plenty of times they had sex on the run and cuddling was definitely out. But times like tonight when they had all the time in the world, lying in his arms after spectacular sex? There wasn't anything else like it.

He kissed her forehead and smoothed her hair away with gentle fingers.

"So tell me another fantasy," he said.

She shifted until she looked up at him. "Oh no, it's your turn. I confessed last."

He grinned. "Hard-ass."

A door shutting across the house had her looking up. "Guess the guys got home. At least this time they weren't around to hear me scream," she muttered.

Chase snorted and reached over to pat her behind. "They're used to all the noise you make. It's a regular joke down at the station."

She rose up on one elbow and pounded his chest with her fist. "Get out! Tell me that's not true!"

It was bad enough that their roommates Brody McNamara and Tate Winslow were an inadvertent audience to their noisy sex—okay, so she'd tried really hard to be quiet, but sometimes it just wasn't possible!—but now the entire firehouse knew she was a screamer?

Chase had that smug shit-eating grin that told her the other firemen definitely knew and that Chase took it as a personal badge of honor that he could satisfy her so thoroughly in bed.

"You probably brag about it," she said in disgust.

"Of course I do. I'm a guy."

She flopped back onto the pillow and sighed. "You're not getting out of telling me another fantasy. You owe me two now."

He chuckled and cupped her ass possessively. "It's sort of like your fantasy, only I walk into the house one day to see another man bend you over the counter in the kitchen and fuck your brains out while I'm watching."

Her eyes went wide. "Are we talking like cheating here? I mean you catching me with another guy?"

He shook his head. "No, babe, I don't mean it that way. I know you wouldn't cheat. It's just sort of a fantasy of seeing you, bent over and fucked six ways to Sunday while I watch and me knowing you're completely helpless."

"Mmmm, I like the helpless part. It's sort of like one of my favorite fantasies I think about when I use a vibrator. You know, when you're working forty-eights and I'm all alone," she pouted.

He tweaked her exaggerated lip pout, then nipped at her full bottom lip. "What's this fantasy?"

Heat rose up her neck.

"You're blushing!"

It came out as a hoot, and his eyes twinkled with laughter.

"Oh shut up," she grumbled. "I feel like such a slut."

He snorted. "You're my slut and I like you that way."

She thumped him again for good measure.

"So? Fess up. What's this vibrator fantasy you have?"

She closed her eyes and conjured up the image. "You're holding me down. My arms above my head while other guys take turns fucking me. I'm all stretched out, and you're holding my wrists so I can't move."

"How many are there?" he asked huskily.

She blushed again. She just knew it.

"I don't really know. Several. Two hold my legs apart and I look down to see one step between my legs and he just thrusts. It's so wicked. He fucks me down and dirty and hard and then he moves and another guy takes his place."

"I'd like that one if you were on your belly so I could fuck your mouth while they're fucking your pussy," he said thoughtfully.

She rolled her eyes. "Trust you to turn my fantasy into yours. I'm more comfortable on my back. I don't want to have to do any work, and giving you head is work."

He grinned. "Are you saying I'm a chore?"

She arched an eyebrow at him. "It takes concentration to suck you off. You're not exactly small."

"Poor baby," he murmured. "Would it surprise you to know I'm not very small right now at all?"

She glanced down to see that he was indeed very erect again. "Holy hell. You trying to set a record?"

"It wasn't intentional. I fully intended to retire him for the evening after going two rounds with you, but all this fantasy talk has him revved up and ready to take off again."

"As long as I don't have to do the work this time," she teased. "I'm tired!"

He rolled over onto her, parting her thighs and settling between them. He leaned down to kiss her.

"Don't worry. All you have to do is lay there."

CHAPTER | TWO

Zoe whipped into the parking lot—or what served as the parking lot—for the community baseball and softball fields. The town of Cypress had banded together a few years back to build the fields for the Little Leaguers, but in the fall, the adults used them for mini leagues.

She'd barely had time to get home after her shift in the ER and change and get to the ball field before the game started.

Today the guys from the Cypress fire station played the EMTs and paramedics from the ambulance service. The winner got to play the sheriff's department in the next game.

She hopped out of her sporty mini SUV and bent down to tie the laces of her tennis shoes. She eyed the bleachers and saw that a large number of supporters had shown up for both sides. She smiled. Good times followed by beer and barbecue. Life didn't get much better in the South.

Toni Andrews drove up and parked beside Zoe, and Zoe got a

glimpse of the toddler in the car seat. Little Samantha was as cute as a button wearing her MY DADDY'S A FIREMAN shirt.

"Hey Toni," she called when Toni got out of her car.

"Hey Zoe. You just get off work?"

"Yeah, busy shift. Almost didn't get out in time. I'd hate to miss the game."

Toni walked around to get Samantha out of her car seat, and Zoe smiled and blew kisses at the grinning baby.

"Is Simon playing today?" Zoe asked.

Toni wrinkled her nose. "No, but Matt and A. J. are. Simon's working. I couldn't miss the two boneheads, and plus Sam loves her uncles to pieces."

Zoe walked toward the bleachers with Toni, but her thoughts drifted. She hadn't been able to get last night's fantasy conversation with Chase out of her mind. An idea had taken root and now it refused to go away.

She shook her head, wondering how she'd manage to pull this off.

She was about to take a seat with some of the other wives and girlfriends when she heard her name. She looked up, holding a hand over her eyes to shield the sun.

Brody stepped out of the dugout and loped over to where she stood.

"Hey, glad you made it. We need you to play shortstop."

"Where's Chase?" she asked. She turned to the parking lot. Now that she thought about it, she hadn't seen his truck when she pulled up.

"He was called in. Captain has one out sick. We drew straws. He lost."

Zoe rolled her eyes. "How badly did you and Tate cheat?"

Brody gave her an innocent look, his blue eyes twinkling with mischief. Before she knew what was happening, he was tugging her toward the dugout.

"Brody, wait! I can't play." She glanced down at her tank top and denim shorts. "I'm not dressed, for God's sake."

Brody paused long enough to send an assessing look down her body that had heat climbing over her ears.

"You're perfect! Besides, if we start losing, we can use you for distraction purposes."

She glared at him.

"Come on, Zoe. You're a kick-ass shortstop. We need you."

Tate Winslow stuck his head out of the dugout. "Come on guys, we're taking the field."

She eyeballed her two best friends in exasperation. "You could have called so I could have at least worn a decent top."

"Why the hell would we do that?" Tate asked.

She walked toward him, and Brody grinned because he knew she'd caved.

"If I come out of this top, I'm going to kill both of you," she muttered.

Brody smirked down at her as they rounded the corner to duck into the dugout. "Honey, if you come out of that top, we'll be your slaves for life. And so will the rest of the team, no doubt."

The other firemen held up their hands to high-five Zoe as she made her way by. Tate tossed her an extra glove.

"Head to short, short stuff."

"Kiss my ass," she grumbled as she shoved past him onto the field.

She squinted as she trotted toward shortstop. Damn sun was killer today. Before she could turn around to take position, a cap settled roughly over her head, and a firm hand shoved the brim over her eyes.

She tipped the bill back up to see Brody slap her on the ass as he walked past to left field.

"Thanks," she called.

She repositioned the cap until she was satisfied with the result, and she took position as the first batter came up.

The first three innings went quick. Lots of fun and laughter and plenty of horseplay. It was obvious neither team took the competition very seriously. Until one of the paramedics bet the firemen's team captain a case of beer that the paramedics would wipe the field with the firemen in the last three innings.

"Oh it's fucking on," Mike Sanders growled as the firemen returned to the dugout at the bottom of the sixth inning.

The score was tied four to four, and the firemen had last bat. They only needed one run. The problem? Zoe was up in the batting order.

No pressure. None at all.

"Come on, Zoe," Matt Langston called as she selected her bat.

"Just get on base, darlin'," A. J. Spinelli said. "We'll bring you home."

Brody and Tate walked out of the dugout with her, and they flanked her as she stood in the on-deck circle waiting for the catcher for the paramedics to come out of his dugout.

"Right field's weak, and they're playing you shallow, Zoe," Tate murmured. "Sail it over his head and you've got a double at least."

She fidgeted, transferring the bat from hand to hand. "Shit, guys, you know how long it's been since I played?"

Brody put his hand on her shoulder. "You can do it. Oh, and show a little more cleavage. They'll be too busy staring at your tits to watch the ball."

"Asshole."

Tate snickered. "He'd be the first one out of the dugout to throw a shirt over you if you had a wardrobe malfunction, and you know it. Unlike me, who'd get an eyeful and *then* throw something over you."

"What a pal," she muttered.

"Batter up!"

Brody patted her on the ass. "Come on, Zoe girl. You can do this. Piece of cake."

She drew her shoulders up, then let them fall as she walked toward the plate. Oh well, it was only a case of beer, right? Only she'd known the fire crew to murder for less. This was all Chase's fault for not being here. He was their strongest bat by far. And he had a competitive streak that bordered on vicious. The firemen would have never gotten away with fucking around in the first three innings if Chase had been there hounding them.

She fouled the first one back, which was just as well. She hadn't liked her swing and had been too indecisive. She turned inward just a bit and lined up, ready for the second pitch. Tate was right. They were playing her shallow, and the right fielder was a hefty guy who would never have the speed to run back for something over his head.

The pitch came in perfect. Slightly low and down the middle. She connected with a sweet smacking noise, and the ball drilled hard over the right fielder's head. She took off running, trying to ignore the way she bounced in her tank top. She'd wanted to look good and show off her tan. She hadn't planned on exerting herself.

She toed first base and shot to second, determined to get at least a double. When she got to second, Tate, the third base coach, held her up.

She stopped and bent over to catch her breath while the firemen and their bleachers cheered loudly.

"Come see me, sweetheart!" Tate called from third base.

She held up her thumb, and the dugout roared in approval.

Matt Langston was up next and flied out to center. His teammates groaned and ribbed him as he returned to the bench. Mike Sanders was up next and hit a hard ball between third and shortstop into left field, enabling Zoe to get to third while Mike held up at first.

"We've only got one out, so stay put on the fly," Tate reminded her. "Anything out of the infield, get your ass home."

Brody went up to bat and Zoe mentally cheered. He'd get her home, no doubt.

He let the first pitch go by only to get ribbing from the opposing team. The second went off his bat with a solid crack and Zoe took off, head down.

"Slide! Slide!"

She vaguely heard Tate hollering behind her, and she lined up for her slide. The catcher stood in front of the plate, his glove out to make the catch.

It all happened so fast she still wasn't sure what the hell happened. One minute she was about to slide, the next the catcher initiated a flying tackle, nailing her in the jaw with his glove.

They both went flying. The catcher landed on top of her, knocking the breath from her chest. Her foot skidded across the plate and through the buzz in her ear, she heard, "She's safe! Catcher dropped the ball!"

She tried to get up, but the damn catcher was still struggling on top of her. Then suddenly he was yanked up by an irate Brody.

"What the fuck, man?"

Brody shoved him back until he hit the fence, and suddenly Tate was there, every bit as angry as Brody.

"There was no call for that shit," Tate bellowed. "This is a friendly goddamn game. You could have seriously injured her. You don't tackle a woman like that."

The dugouts emptied, and the firemen and paramedics alike pulled Brody and Tate off the catcher. Tate knelt on the ground, his green eyes worried as he ran his hands over her body.

"You okay, Zoe? You hurt anywhere?"

"I'm good," she wheezed. "Seriously. Just need to catch my breath."

"Son of a bitch," Brody bit out. "I'm going to kick his dumb ass for that stunt. What did he think this was, a freaking wrestling match?"

"Help me up and quit planning the poor guy's funeral."

She extended her hand up, but Tate curled his arms underneath her and lifted.

Several of the paramedics came over to ask her if she was okay, and she waved them off. "I'm fine. Really. Put me down, Tate."

He let her slide down until she was on her own two feet again. Mercifully she could draw a full breath now even if her head was spinning.

"Christ, Zoe, I'm sorry. I didn't mean to hit you that hard, I swear."

She looked up to see the very contrite catcher standing in front of her, his glove still on.

"It's okay, Mac. Really. I'm okay. And hey, we won. You dropped the ball."

"Don't remind me," he grumbled. He reached over and ruffled her hair, which earned him a growl from Brody. "Sorry, kiddo. I forgot you weren't one of the guys."

She smiled and nodded, then promptly groaned at the pain that splintered her skull.

Tate swore. "Come on, Zoe. We need to get you home and get some ice on that head."

"And miss the beer?" she asked in mock horror.

"I'll make Brody buy a six-pack on his way home."

"Why do I get stuck buying the beer?" Brody protested.

"I hate to remind you but it's your turn to cook too," Zoe said.

Brody looked at them with a hopeful expression. "I don't suppose you guys are up for a grilled cheese?"

Both Zoe and Tate eyed him balefully.

"No? Damn. All right, all right. I'll make a run by the grocery store and meet you guys at home."

Tate squeezed her shoulder. "Come on, I'll follow you home if you think you're okay to drive."

She looked at him in exasperation. "Tate, I'm fine. Let's go. I look like I've gone three rounds and lost." Then she looked down at her tank top that was most definitely not covering everything it should. "Shit. Did I flash everyone?"

"Huh? Sorry, baby. I wasn't looking at your tits. I was too worried about other parts of your body."

"I'm strangely insulted by that."

He laughed and smacked her ass. "Come on. Let's go."

Zoe pulled up in front of Tate and got out of her car. Not waiting for him to catch up, she headed into the house, anxious for a shower to wash off the layer of dirt caked to her body.

Fifteen minutes later, she walked into the living room in a clean pair of shorts and a T-shirt to find Tate waiting for her with an ice pack.

"I'm good, Tate."

He ignored her and sat next to her on the couch, tilting the bag of ice over her head. After a few seconds he removed it and then started thumbing through her hair.

"What are you doing?" she asked.

"Wanted to make sure you weren't bleeding or something."

"And?"

"No blood, but you have a hell of a lump."

He stuck the bag back on her head and held it there while they sat on the couch. He reached for the remote with his other hand and turned on the TV.

"College football, bass fishing, or a movie?"

"Football," she said. "LSU is playing this evening."

"Don't see your fixation with LSU," he grumbled. "Have you no loyalty to Texas teams?"

"I might if they didn't suck," she said sweetly.

"Oh, damn, that hurt."

She laughed and he grinned good-naturedly. Tate was a lot of fun. Laid back, playful. Sun-streaked, muddy blond hair that was more brown than blond in winter and more blond than brown during the summer. He had playful green eyes and a killer tan, and he lived in cutoff jeans and bare feet.

Brody, on the other hand, was dark-haired and smart-assed and could be surly as hell when provoked. He had his moody times when she, Tate, and Chase left him alone, but he was as good as gold, and the four of them had been friends a long time. He tended to be overprotective when it came to just about everyone he considered a friend or loved one. She teased him and called him a growly bear, and he took it in stride.

Fifteen minutes later, the bag had drooped precariously as the ice melted, and Brody walked in the door with a six-pack in one hand and two bags of groceries in the other.

"You okay, Zoe?" he called from the kitchen.

She could hear him rummaging around and then opening and shutting the fridge.

Tate took the bag off her head and felt her bump with his fingers again. "Looks like the swelling has stopped. Is it still hurting?"

"Nothing some ibuprofen won't cure. I'm fine, Brody," she called back to the kitchen.

"I'll go get you some and see what Brody's digging up for dinner. I don't know about you but I'm starved," Tate said as he got up.

After he left, she promptly commandeered the remote and went in search of her football game that Tate had conveniently forgot to tune in to.

It was kismet that Chase was gone and she was alone with Tate and Brody. Her idea had been percolating the entire day. While she was at work, it rolled around in her mind until she could literally see the scene as she'd set it. Now she just had to work up the courage to talk to Tate and Brody about it and hope they didn't think she'd lost her mind.

Tate didn't immediately return, which meant Brody had wrangled him into helping with dinner. Half an hour later, she was primed for kickoff when the guys walked in each holding a plate. Brody had two, and he set one of them down in front of her on the coffee table. Tate plunked the six-pack of beers down beside the plates, and they took seats on either side of her.

"Hey, this looks great," she said as she sniffed appreciatively at the mound of pasta.

"I can cook," Brody mumbled around a mouthful of food.

"Yeah, but we usually get burgers or hot dogs on your night," she pointed out.

"You deserved a good meal. You won the game for us and took a hard-ass hit. That was fierce!"

"Ah, the things I do for beer."

Tate laughed. "Girl after my own heart."

They ate in silence, with Zoe stopping every once in a while to either cheer a good LSU play or yell at the referees over a bad call.

Afterward, Tate took the plates into the kitchen while Brody and Zoe kicked back on the couch. Nervousness scuttled around her belly, and she suddenly wished she hadn't eaten so much.

She sipped at her beer and wondered the best way to broach the subject of her plan with Brody and Tate. It wasn't that she had any problem with getting up in front of the guys and doing a topless dance. Fact was, it was a huge turn-on. Who knew she was such an exhibitionist? She was more worried that Brody and Tate would veto the idea before she could get it out of her mouth, and there was no way she'd go to anyone else for help with this kind of thing.

"Hey guys, I have a favor to ask."

Both guys turned curiously in her direction. "Shoot," Brody said.

"Well, you know Chase's birthday is next week. I sort of have something planned. A surprise. But I need your help pulling this one off. It's, um, unorthodox."

Tate grinned. "I think I'm loving it already."

She drew in a deep breath and plunged ahead. "He has this outrageous fantasy, and I want to give it to him."

"Whoa. Define *outrageous*," Brody said.

"Picture guys' night out. Strip club. It's him and the guys from the firehouse. This hot chick comes out and she's shaking it. Only it's me. Everyone's staring and Chase is loving that I belong to him and that other guys are watching his girl."

"Holy shit," Tate breathed.

"Uh, I have to ask the obvious here, because I'm afraid the image of your tits is now branded on my eyeballs."

Zoe burst out laughing. Leave it to Brody to make light of it and ease the tension.

"You want to actually pull this off? And where exactly do Tate and I come in?"

"Yeah. I want you two to arrange guys' night out at the strip club in town, only I'm going to try to rent out the place for the night so I can be the evening's entertainment. I want it private, with only the people you guys invite. I don't want Chase to suspect a thing, and I plan to tell him I have to work."

Tate threw her a skeptical look. "And you really think Chase will be all right with this?"

Her lips lifted into a smile. "Oh yeah. I think he'll be blown away."

"Dude, don't talk her out of it. We get to see her naked. Finally," Brody said.

She shoved at his arm and glared him into silence. "A few ground rules. No married guys from the station, okay? That means Simon and Matt are out. I don't want that kind of awkwardness if this gets out. I'd prefer that it remain private, but I figure that has a snowball's chance in hell of happening."

"You're serious? You want to do this?" Tate asked.

"Yeah, I mean it's hot."

"You're telling me," Brody muttered.

"So will you do it? Think you can get the guys on board?"

"Are you kidding?" Tate asked. "Mike would give his left nut to see you naked. The guy's been lusting after you for months. If Chase hadn't already threatened to kick his ass, he would have made a pass. I'm sure the others aren't going to complain about seeing a beautiful woman shaking her ass onstage."

"You can't tell them anything more than they're celebrating Chase's birthday with guys' night out at the strip club."

Brody snorted. "We won't have any problem getting a group together. They'll be more surprised Chase is being allowed out to play."

She rounded on him, her mouth wide open. "What's that supposed to mean? He does what the hell he wants. You say that like I keep him on a tight leash or something."

"Down, girl," Tate soothed. "What he's saying is that the other guys will be surprised you're cool with him hanging out on his birthday at a strip joint. They'll think he's a lucky son of a bitch. When they see it's you dancing, they're going to *know* he's a lucky fucker."

"That's sort of the idea," she said ruefully. "He wants every guy in the place to be insanely jealous of him."

"Vain bastard," Brody said with a chuckle.

"Thanks, you two." She leaned over to kiss Tate on the cheek and then bobbed back to kiss Brody. "You're the best."

Brody's goatee brushed across her chin, and a light shiver worked down her spine. She ignored it and sat back, determined not to let the fact that she'd be dancing naked in front of her best friends cause any weirdness.

CHAPTER | THREE

Chase entered the house and tossed his keys on the counter. It was quiet; everyone was already asleep—something he needed to be doing because he started a forty-eight tomorrow morning. Sucked being called in today and missing the game, especially in front of a shift.

He walked through the bedroom and smiled when he saw Zoe curled up in his spot, her head on his pillow. Cracked him up. She was fiercely possessive of her pillow, but the minute he vacated the bed, she always took over his.

He quickly showered, eager to get in some time with Zoe, even if it was only a sleepy snuggle. A few minutes later, he slid into bed, nudging her over with his body until she stretched, mumbled in her sleep, but complied with his silent request.

Man, she felt good. He wrapped his arms around her and pulled her into his chest.

"Hey, you're home," she said in a sleepy voice.

He dropped a kiss on her forehead. "Yeah, for a few hours anyway."

"If I didn't hurt so much, I'd make the most of those few hours."

He frowned. Then he pulled away, staring at her in the darkness. "How come you hurt?"

"Game. Made me play for you. Got laid out by the catcher."

Zoe never was the best conversationalist when she was half asleep. It wasn't the optimum time to ever get straight answers from her, but he rolled back and reached for the lamp.

She buried her face in his chest when the light flooded the bed.

"Damn it, Chase."

"Look at me," he growled.

She raised her chin, blinking at the light. A bruise marred her jaw, and he touched it gently. She winced.

"Ow. That hurts."

"What the fuck happened? Are you hurt anywhere else?"

"Sore. Feel like I got hit by a wheelbarrow full of bricks. Mac tried to tag me out at home."

"With what, his fists?" Chase demanded.

She put a finger over his lips. "Don't snarl. Tate and Brody already crawled all over his ass. He didn't mean to. Besides, he dropped the ball and we won."

He leaned down and brushed his lips across her bruise. "He should have been more careful. I'll kick his ass when I see him."

Zoe snorted. "Leave him alone. He felt bad."

He cuddled her to him, then reached back to turn off the lamp. He didn't like seeing her bruised and was surprised by his reaction to it. He wasn't used to feeling so possessive of any woman. If asked, he would have classified his relationship with Zoe as fun, extremely hot, but very laid back. She wasn't demanding—a fact he loved. And she didn't pressure him to get serious too quickly—another thing he loved. In short, she was the perfect girlfriend.

But this dark feeling that possessed him the minute he knew she'd been hurt—by another guy—wasn't comfortable. It wasn't fun and it wasn't light. His mind screamed that she was his and no one better lay a fucking hand on her. How messed up was that?

"Want me to cook breakfast?" she mumbled.

He smiled and stroked a hand down her back. "No, baby. Sleep in and catch up on your rest. You've had a busy few days in the ER. Aren't you working evening shift tomorrow?"

"Mmm-hmm."

"Sleep tight, then. I'll see you in a couple days."

She nuzzled closer and kissed his throat. "Night."

Nervous bubbles scuttled around Zoe's belly as she checked her appearance in the dressing room mirror. She's been careful not to use so much makeup that her identity wasn't discernible. After all, that was the point. For everyone—especially Chase—to know who she was.

But now that it was nearly showtime and she was as scantily clad as a stripper—hello, she *was* a stripper for the evening!—she was having some serious cold feet. Oh not about the idea in general. She was still a big fan of knocking Chase's socks off, but she hoped to hell she didn't trip onstage. Or fall off it. Or that the guys didn't laugh her into infinity.

Renting out the club hadn't been cheap, but it beat having the entire town see her naked and gyrating.

A knock sounded on her door. "You're up," the manager called.

"Oh holy hell," she breathed.

She stared back in the mirror, cinched up her top so that a little more cleavage was shoved forward, and then ran her hands over her lean belly to her hips, where the sparkly little tassels flickered in the light.

She wore only a G-string underneath and so with every movement, her ass was exposed beneath those shimmery little tassels. She wasn't taking off more than her top. Not that she wasn't proud of her wax job, and she knew damn well Chase loved it, but some things were too private to be flaunting. Her girly proclivities being one of them.

With a deep breath, she walked into the hallway and headed in the direction of the stage. She paused at the curtain and then nodded toward the DJ.

Showtime.

Chase laughed at something one of his buddies said and snagged another beer from the waitress.

"Is it me or is it dead in here tonight?" Mike asked.

"You would know," Brody said in a dry voice. "Not all of us have lifetime memberships."

The rest of the guys hooted in laughter and threw pretzels and nuts in Mike's direction.

"Hey, before the show starts, I want to propose a toast to the birthday boy," Tate announced.

He stood and made a show of clearing his throat.

"Speech! Speech!"

Tate grinned, then tipped his beer in Chase's direction. "May this birthday be the best ever."

The others raised their bottles in response, and Chase's ears were drowned in a chorus of *Happy Birthdays*.

He raised his beer good-naturedly as he stared at the dozen friends gathered. They'd think he was a pussy if they knew what he was really thinking. If Zoe hadn't had to work, they could have spent a quiet night at home.

They would have watched a movie while he played with her neck. She would have been so hot by the end she would have jumped his bones there on the couch, and then they would have retired to the bedroom and made love the entire night.

Yeah, he was keeping that thought under his hat. The guys would never let him live that one down.

The lights dimmed and the spotlight hit the stage. Whoops filled the air as everyone focused their attention on the small stage. The music began, a frantic, high-tech bumping and thumping.

Then the curtains flew open and there she was. His supposed birthday present.

The guys surged to their feet as she strutted forward in a pair of heels that were designed to make a man drool. Chase followed the line of her legs up to an ass that jiggled with every step.

Hell, he might be attached but he wasn't dead. She had an ass to die for.

She turned around, sticking that ass out, and began to shake it in time with the music. Around him the air exploded in whistles and catcalls.

She undulated, working herself back to a fully upright position. The light wasn't on her face, but then who came to this kind of place to look at a chick's face?

When her hands hovered teasingly at the clasp of her top, the roar got louder.

"Take it off, honey!"

"Oh hell yeah!"

Strangely, Tate and Brody stood back, their arms crossed, and they had peculiar expressions on their faces. Brody took a swig of beer and then drained the entire bottle as if he needed fortification.

He'd have to give them both shit later because it looked like they were wary as hell to see the lady in question disrobe.

She strutted to the very end of the catwalk until she stood directly in front of the group of men. Then her top flew open, and her breasts bounced free.

Chase nearly swallowed the tip of his beer bottle and put it

down before he embarrassed himself. Brody and Tate looked strangled, and both reached for another beer simultaneously. The other
guys pushed forward, crowding the stage.

Then the light flooded her entire body, and Chase forgot to
breathe. Hell, it felt like someone had kicked him right in the balls.

"Zoe," he whispered.

She smiled a sexy, disarming smile and pointed directly at Chase.
Then she crooked her finger in a come-hither motion about the time
the other guys recognized her.

At first there was deafening silence that was obvious even above
the din of the music. Then a chorus of "Holy shit!" went up.

Chase was paralyzed at first. This was his fantasy. She was playing out his fantasy. He caught a flash of uncertainty in her eyes, and
he knew he had to act fast or this was going to be a disaster.

With a broad grin, he shoved his way through the crowd of guys
and came to a stop in front of her. He looked up at her with an
arched eyebrow.

"Are you my birthday present, sugar?"

A slow sultry smile lit up her entire face. She bent down until
her breasts swayed precariously close to his mouth, and she kissed
him just once.

"Just sit back, cowboy, and enjoy the show."

She straightened and the music changed to a slower, more seductive beat. Her gaze never leaving him, she began to dance, her body
writhing in time to the music.

Around him, the guys stared up at her in awe. They looked back
and forth between her and Chase as if they couldn't quite believe
what was going on.

Then he saw the jealousy and the lust in their eyes. It hit him
with more power than he'd ever imagined in his fantasy. This was
his girl onstage, giving him the performance of a lifetime, and his
friends were watching, envying him with their every breath.

He glanced back at Brody and Tate and realized then that they must have been in on it. It explained their unease. He almost laughed. They looked a little green, and every time one of the guys yelled something to Zoe or made a motion like he wanted to touch, he thought they were going to resort to violence.

But he saw something else in their eyes. Something they probably didn't want anyone to see. He saw desire and yearning.

"Goddamn it, Chase, you are the luckiest son of a bitch," Mike said over the music. "I've never had a girlfriend willing to do this for my birthday."

His statement was met by a round of guffaws.

"You don't keep a girl long enough to be called your girlfriend," A. J. said with a snort. "Taking them to bed, then sending them on their way doesn't a relationship make."

"Fuck you, Spinelli," Mike said rudely. But he grinned in acknowledgment even as he flipped A. J. off.

The rest of the firemen crowded round and finally it was too much for Brody and Tate. They pushed to the front and glared at their fellow firefighters.

"You don't touch and you better damn well be respectful," Brody growled.

Chase chuckled and looked back up to see Zoe lower herself to her knees in front of him. She crawled to the edge where he stood, reached for his shirt and pulled him roughly to meet her lips.

Her kiss was scorching and he felt the sensation all the way to his toes. Hot, sweet, intensely erotic. He burst into flames, and he sported wood that threatened to ruin his jeans.

"Happy birthday, baby," she murmured.

He reached to cup one breast and rubbed the pad of his thumb over her nipple. She smiled a devilish little smile that told him this wasn't all she'd planned for him.

She kissed him again, then rose to her feet and continued her sexy dance—topless and not enough to cover her ass—but Chase wasn't complaining. She'd go home with him afterward while everyone else would go home cursing Chase's luck.

A chorus of whistles rent the air.

"Son of a bitch!" one of the firemen yelled. "She's freaking hot!"

Chase settled back on his heels and stared at her as she gracefully danced, her breasts bobbing, her face flushed with exertion—and excitement—and that delectable ass bouncing enticingly close.

He knew they all wanted her.

And then he remembered the fantasy she'd imparted to him.

A slow grin traveled across his face.

She'd taken the initiative and given him something he'd only fantasized about in his dreams. He could do the same for her, and furthermore he'd have a fucking awesome time doing it. Her fantasies were hot. They were as much a turn-on to him as they seemed to be for her.

He glanced sideways at Brody and Tate. Who better to ask to give Zoe her fantasy than two guys who cared about her every bit as much as he did?

CHAPTER | FOUR

*Zoe ducked behind the curtain and stood there for a long mo-*ment, catching her breath and still riding the adrenaline high. Wow. It was the only word that came to mind.

Seeing Chase's face when he saw her for the first time, seeing the lust and desire that burst into his eyes, had sent a set of flurries loose in her belly that were still making their rounds.

She glanced down at her bare tits and then up at the DJ. Oops. She hastily covered herself and started down the hallway to the dressing room.

Footsteps behind her—quick, hurried footsteps—had her turning nervously around, her hands still cupped over her breasts.

She relaxed when she saw it was Chase but tensed again as he strode forward, his eyes glittering with purpose. She didn't even have time to open her mouth to say anything.

He swept her into his arms and backed her against the wall. She hit with a resounding smack, and his lips went immediately to her neck.

As soon as his teeth sank into her tender column, her knees buckled, and she would have slid to the floor if he hadn't been holding her up.

"You were. So. Fucking. Hot."

His breath blew over her ear as he kissed a path to her lips. She moved her arms to twine around his neck, and her breasts pressed into his chest.

"Jesus, I want you, Zoe. Right here. Right now."

Without waiting for an answer, he ripped at the cheap thong, rending it into two pieces that fluttered to the floor between her ankles. She was completely naked, and she didn't care.

He fumbled awkwardly with his fly. The sound of his zipper coming undone excited her. Then he reached in and pulled out his cock.

He leaned away from her long enough to reach down and wrap his muscular arms around her thighs and then he lifted, spreading her, slamming her back against the wall again.

Deep and hard, he pushed into her with one devastating thrust. His mouth found her neck again, and he was merciless. No light tease. No tender smooching or nibbling. He went for it all.

She heard a noise but Chase was in her so deep, so full, that he was all she could focus on.

"Ah hell, get back," Brody ordered. "He's fucking her in the hall."

A chorus of laughter rang out.

"Lucky bastard. I never get birthdays like this."

She didn't know who said the last. She didn't care. Chase's arms were around her, holding her, as he plunged deeper and deeper.

"Are they watching, Zoe?" Chase murmured next to her ear.

She turned her head, her vision fuzzy as she struggled to focus. Brody was at the end of the hall, his expression tight. Tate stood behind him while the other guys were obviously straining to see over his shoulder.

"They're watching," she whispered.

"Good."

He slammed into her again, taking her breath.

She moaned and he rammed into her again. God, he was so big, so aroused. She was already teetering so very close to explosion.

"Do you have any idea what it did to me to see you rocking that stage?"

"I think I do," she gasped out.

"You're fucking amazing, Zoe."

She threw her head back, ignoring the fact that it slapped the wall. Closing her eyes, she grabbed hold of his shoulders, her fingernails digging deep.

Then his mouth descended, and his lips fluttered over the pulse in her neck. He nipped, then went for the kill. His teeth sank deep, and she yelled as she came apart in fifty directions.

Her body convulsed. She went wet around his stroking cock. Her back hit the wall as he thrust wildly.

She lost herself for a moment because the next thing she knew she was straddling Chase's waist, her head resting on his shoulder while he stroked his hand up and down her back.

"Shhhh, baby," he soothed.

Had that whimpering noise been coming from her? Holy hell but she was destroyed.

"Damn, he was right. She *is* a screamer," Mike said in amusement from the end of the hall.

She groaned and banged her head against Chase's shoulder as he chuckled.

"Come on," he said as he eased away from the wall. "Which one is your dressing room?"

She raised her hand to point and buried her face in his neck as he carried her farther down the hall. She loved his arms. So strong. She made him carry her at least once a week, because hello? Hunky fireman with bulging biceps? Not to be wasted.

He shouldered his way into the small changing room, then kicked the door shut behind him. There was a tiny love seat along the left wall, and he deposited her gently onto the cushions.

He knelt in front of her, gathered her hands in his, and brought them to his lips.

"You are diabolical and an evil planner of debauchery, and I loved every second."

She smiled. "So you weren't angry that more than half a dozen of the guys you work with on a daily basis saw me naked?"

"Oh hell no," he growled. "My stock just went through the roof at the firehouse."

"You're a nut."

"Baby, my *nuts* are about to burst."

Her eyebrows shot up. "I thought they just did?"

He grinned. "They're ready to go again."

She glanced back and wrinkled her nose. "I'm not having sex on this couch. The wall in the hallway was bad enough, but I do *not* want to know what's been on this couch."

"Then I suggest you get some clothes on so I can take you home and fuck you for about the next six hours."

She scrambled up and reached for her clothes strewn over back of the couch.

His smile broadened. "Damn, I love it when you're so eager."

To say he walked around with a smug, shit-eating grin was the absolute truth. As soon as he hit the firehouse the morning after Zoe's dance routine, he was greeted by a chorus of whistles and catcalls. He was lauded as the man and while immature, it was total male arrogance at its best.

Chase grinned and took the good-natured ribbing in stride. He took it better than Tate and Brody did. His two friends scowled every time one of the guys mentioned Zoe.

It wasn't until noon that Chase got a moment alone with Tate and Brody. The three were in the small kitchen taking their turn at dinner duty while the others washed the two fire trucks in the garage.

What he wanted to ask them wasn't something he could just blurt out. Every time he opened his mouth to say it, he hesitated and kept quiet. Which started him examining why he couldn't just bring it up.

After five minutes, Brody was the one to bring an end to the awkward silence.

"Are you really cool with what happened, man?"

Surprised, Chase turned around to look at Brody. Tate stopped what he was doing as well and tuned in with keen interest.

"Yeah, I'm cool with it. Were you worried I wasn't?"

Brody lifted one shoulder in a shrug. "You seem a little tense. I wanted to make sure Tate and I hadn't stepped in it by going along with Zoe's surprise for you."

"Everything's cool. I actually wanted to talk to you . . . About Zoe."

Tate frowned. "Is everything okay? I mean you're not mad at *her*, are you?"

"No, things are fine. I swear. You two need to chill out. I'm not sure how much or what Zoe told you about why she did the dancing thing."

"She said it was some fantasy of yours," Brody said.

"Yeah, we sort of traded fantasies one night. I want to talk to you about hers."

Tate groaned and held up his hands in surrender. "You gotta give me a second here. I'm still trying to get over seeing Zoe in the buff and having to listen to you two fucking in the hallway, and now you want to lay her fantasy on us?"

Brody just frowned. "Isn't that shit supposed to be private or something? I mean, would she be okay with you telling us this stuff?"

Chase chuckled to himself. Trust Brody to be all protective of

Zoe. They'd all been friends for a long time, but Brody had always been super protective of Zoe. Even back in high school. Chase had occasionally wondered, if he hadn't asked Zoe out, whether Brody would have worked up the nerve.

That was something they didn't discuss, though. They talked plenty about Zoe in the casual sense, but they never discussed Chase's relationship with her or whether things were serious. Maybe Brody didn't want to know.

"I can't very well make her fantasy come true if I don't talk about it," Chase said dryly.

"Oh shit," Tate breathed. "I had a feeling we were coming to this."

Chase cocked an eyebrow at his friend. "You don't know what I'm going to ask."

"Ask?" Brody echoed. "This involves a request?"

Chase rubbed a hand down the back of his neck. "Well, yeah. I mean there's not anyone else I'd trust with this sort of thing."

"Jesus Christ, tell me we're not going to have to see you do some striptease for girls' night out because there ain't enough money in the world," Tate said.

Chase burst out laughing. "Oh hell no. Although you and Brody would make cute girls."

"Fuck you," Brody muttered.

Chase looked out the window to make sure the other guys were still washing the trucks out front and then turned back to Tate and Brody.

"Look. Zoe has some capture fantasies."

Brody's brow crinkled, and Tate just looked confused.

"You know, being spirited away, ravished, that sort of thing."

"Oh." Tate still looked confused, though.

Chase blew out a breath. Christ, but this was more difficult than he'd imagined. Better if he just came out with it instead of dancing around the subject like a moron.

"She fantasizes about being abducted and made to pleasure multiple men. She imagines being made to submit to whatever they want. It's not a light and fluffy fantasy by any stretch. She wants to be fucked and bent to their will."

Brody looked like he'd swallowed his tongue. "Men? As in more than one?"

Chase nodded. "This is where you and Tate come in."

"Holy shit, you aren't really considering that, are you?" Tate asked.

"Let me get this straight." Brody's frown deepened. "You're asking me and Tate to . . . fuck your girl? Zoe? Our best friend Zoe? And you're okay with this?"

He might as well have been asking Chase if he'd lost his goddamn mind. And it was probably a good question.

"I'm still trying to get over seeing her naked," Tate muttered.

They were fast approaching territory Chase didn't really want to get into. The last thing he wanted was to get all touchy-feely with his best friends and admit that he thought her fantasy was hot with a capital *H*. Not that he wanted to see either of them naked. But seeing them fuck Zoe six ways to Sunday? Yeah, he could get into that.

He almost groaned. He was obviously a deviant, and he was probably going to hell for this.

Both Brody and Tate were staring at him expectantly, and he realized he hadn't said anything in response to their questions. Hell.

"This is Zoe's fantasy," he began lamely. "I'm okay with it." And when his two friends continued to stare at him like he'd been set on fire, he finally added, "All right, so I think it's pretty fucking hot. Sue me. The idea of watching someone else fuck Zoe does it for me."

"You're serious about this," Tate said. "You'd actually set something like this up? You'd arrange for us to kidnap Zoe and fuck her brains out? Bondage and the whole nine yards? Forgive the skepticism here, but I wonder if you've thought this through at all."

Chase's lip curled. "Look if you're not in, just say so. I'll find someone else." Okay maybe not, but damn he felt all defensive now.

Brody stiffened and straightened to his full height. "Oh hell no," he said softly. "I'm not about to allow you to round up some goddamn strangers to go abduct Zoe and . . . and . . ." He shook his head and didn't finish the statement. "That's just crazy," he finally added.

"Oh, for fuck's sake. You know me better than that," Chase said irritably. "I'm not about to do anything to hurt her. We talked quite a bit about this. I'd never do anything that I wasn't positive she wanted."

Tate held up his hands. "I get that. I don't think that's what either of us were insinuating. We know you're crazy about her."

"I shouldn't have brought it up," Chase said. "Let's just forget it. I don't want any weirdness."

Brody started to say something, but they were interrupted by loud footsteps and voices coming toward the kitchen. They all clammed up just as the other firemen came in and headed for the table.

"Where the hell is the food?" Mike demanded. "We left you guys in here a half hour ago to start on lunch."

"Cool your jets, Sanders. We're working on it," Tate said as he went back to his task.

The subject was effectively dropped as they finished the lunch prep, but Chase could feel Tate and Brody looking at him every once in a while. He hoped to hell he hadn't screwed up by bringing up the thing with Zoe. The last thing he wanted was awkwardness between them, and he didn't want Tate and Brody thinking any differently about Zoe just because Chase had wanted to give her her fantasy.

It had seemed like a good enough idea when he'd seen the way his friends looked at Zoe in the strip club. Now, however, he wasn't so sure.

CHAPTER | FIVE

"Hey, thought I'd find you out here," Tate said as he closed the door behind him.

Chase stood outside the back door of the firehouse, a place he often went for some fresh air. He'd just gotten out of the shower after an early-evening accident call, and he'd retreated for a few minutes alone so he could try to grab Zoe at work. Or not. He put his cell phone away as Tate came out and looked up at his friend.

"What's up?" Chase asked. Tate didn't usually come out when Chase was back here. It was an unspoken agreement among all of the fire crew that the backyard was for privacy.

Tate shoved his hands into his pockets and leaned against the brick wall. "Zoe," he said after a moment.

Chase's lips twisted, and he started to tell Tate to just forget about it, but Tate continued on.

"How much of this is Zoe's fantasy and how much is yours? Don't take it the wrong way, man. I just want to know how on board Zoe is with something like that."

"Well hell," Chase muttered. "She's the one who brought it up. But I mean it was pillow talk stuff. We were in the middle of sex, and we were both saying some erotic stuff."

"But do you think she was really serious, or was she talking about stuff that turned her on in theory?"

"You're asking me to dissect the mind of a woman and get into her psyche?"

The two men stared at one another for a long moment before both burst into laughter. They were still laughing when Brody came out of the house. He stared suspiciously at them as he ambled over.

"What the fuck are you two laughing about?"

"The female mind," Chase replied.

Brody physically shuddered.

The three stood around for a bit longer, chatting about the call they'd taken earlier. Then Tate cleared his throat and glanced back at Chase.

"So? About Zoe? How serious were you, man?"

Chase sighed. "I wouldn't have brought up something like that if I weren't sure about it. I get the impression you two don't think I gave it any thought at all. But I also understand if it's not something you're comfortable with. I know Zoe means a lot to both of you."

Brody nodded. "Yeah, she does."

"I'd be a lying son of a bitch if I said I'd turn down the opportunity to be with her," Tate said. "She's . . . Well, let's just say I'd be willing to do a whole lot to make her happy."

Brody toed his shoe in the dirt and remained silent. Chase was content to wait. He kept his mouth shut and let Brody stew. Tate seemed aware of Brody's mulling as well, because silence fell once again among the three.

Then Brody sighed and ran a hand through his hair. "Look, you both know I'd do anything for Zoe, but I'm not looking at this as something just for her. It'd be a hell of a lot simpler if it were. I won't lie. The whole damn scenario is pretty hot. I mean, Jesus. I just don't want anything to change between the four of us, and this has the potential . . . If something went wrong, it could really fuck up something I value a whole hell of a lot."

Chase nodded. "I get it. I understand completely. I probably shouldn't have asked you guys. I was looking for a way to fulfill her fantasy, and you two are the only ones I trust with something like this. And, I'll admit, it was something that appealed to me too."

Brody held up a hand. "I'm not saying I wouldn't want to do it, just that it's not something I'd go into lightly. I want to. I doubt you know how much I'd love to have sex with her."

"I'd do it," Tate said quietly. "As long as the three of us agreed that nothing changes for us. I know we can't, to a degree, control how Zoe feels, but we can make a pact not to act like buttheads."

"You're worried I'm going become a jealous asshole," Chase said.

Brody nodded. "Yeah, something like that. She's your girl. We all live together. You have to admit, things could get . . . awkward if we let it."

"Yeah, I hear you."

"When did we become such fucking girls?" Tate grumbled.

Chase grinned. "That's a good question. I'm not the one talking about my feelings." He jerked his thumb in Brody's direction. "Apparently B is getting in touch with his inner woman over here."

"Fuck you," Brody growled. But he grinned as he said it.

Chase cast a casual glance in their direction. "So . . . y'all up for it or what?"

"I'm in," Tate said.

Brody took a deep breath and then nodded. "Yeah, I'm in."

Zoe pulled into the driveway and frowned when she saw that the house was completely dark. She'd been looking forward to seeing Chase tonight and kicking off two whole shared days off. It didn't happen very often that their schedules aligned, and she wanted to make the most of every second.

She parked in the garage, then reached for her cell as she got out. She was punching in Chase's number when an arm curled around her waist and a hand closed over her mouth.

Her pulse exploded, and she drew in a breath to scream when Chase murmured next to her ear.

"It's me, baby. Don't be afraid. Relax and enjoy your fantasy."

For a moment she couldn't even process her thoughts. Ridiculous excitement surged and pumped through her veins. Her stomach fluttered nervously. Her cheeks heated, and goose bumps raced across her skin.

Chase went silent. His hand stayed clamped over her mouth. Material slid over her eyes, and the world went even darker around her.

More hands joined Chase's. She was picked up, her arms bent behind her and then secured with soft binding. A vehicle roared up in the drive, and she heard doors open and slam shut. Then open again.

Chase tossed her inside. Not a seat. Back of a van? One of those utility jobs. Holy crap, where did he score a van?

She lay there, her pulse pounding in her ears. Rough hands pulled at her scrubs until cool air blew over her ass. Her pants were only down around her knees when a cock prodded and pushed at her pussy. Fingers separated her flesh, lifted her thigh just enough for access and then the cock drove deep and hard.

She flexed her fingers, but her bonds held tight. On her side, her legs curled toward her chest, she was deliciously helpless to move.

Strong, blunt fingertips dug into her hair and pushed at her head, angling it back. A thick cock pushed at her lips. At her gasp of surprise it surged forward, lodging deep in her throat.

She knew it was Chase in her pussy, but who was in her mouth? The sheer decadence of not knowing, of being fucked so crudely had already put her close to the edge. A warm buzz settled in her ears and hummed over her body.

If there was any doubt that the real thing wouldn't excite her as much as the fantasy, it was gone now.

Her orgasm worked hard and fast, spinning low in her abdomen and tightening every one of her muscles. She panted around the cock shoving back and forth over her tongue.

Chase fucked her hard and without mercy. There was an urgency to his movements that he'd lacked in the past. He was big and hard, and her swollen tissues clasped him tightly, reluctant to let go when he withdrew.

Her body rocked as he thrust into her again. The man at her head began gently. Almost tentative. But then his hands curled into her hair and held her head in place as he began to fuck her mouth harder and deeper.

His taste wasn't unpleasant in the least. Wholly masculine. Strong. Who had Chase chosen to partner with in her fantasy?

She relaxed and gave herself over to the experience. This was hers, and Chase was giving her what she'd given him.

Chase's hips smacked against her ass. His movements were frantic. It was quick, down and dirty. With a gasp around the cock invading her mouth she tensed, trying with everything to hold off her impending release.

It was too much. Pleasure bloomed deep. She pictured what it must look like, her on the floor of the van with two men working her over, controlling her, taking her, over and over. She immersed herself in that image and surrendered to the rising swell.

She cried out, the sound muffled by the thick cock in her mouth. The man fucking her face paused as she shuddered and quivered with the force of her orgasm. Chase pounded into her and gave a shout of his own just as he came deep inside her.

He came to rest against her ass, his hips twitching as he emptied himself inside her. His hands skimmed across her flesh and then he issued an order in a low, guttural voice.

"Suck him off, Zoe. Make him come."

The man at her face began to move again. Slow at first, gradually faster. Then harder. She relaxed her jaw and took him deep, sucking with each thrust.

A low hiss escaped. Fingers tightened painfully into her scalp. The wet sounds of her lips smacking around his cock filled the air.

He made fists in her hair and pulled her to meet his forward motion. Her lips stretched around the base and his hair tickled her nose.

There was so much strength in his hands. In his movements. It overwhelmed her and excited her until she twisted restlessly underneath his assault.

Hot fluid shot to the back of her throat. His release coated her tongue, filled her mouth until she swallowed reflexively. More spurted and the spicy taste burst over her tongue. He continued to thrust until finally he gave a huge shudder and the last drops shook from the tip of his erection.

For a long moment he remained in her mouth, his fingers still tangled in her hair. And then slowly he withdrew.

She sucked in mouthfuls of air and lay there, her heart thudding painfully against her chest as she tried to gather her shattered senses. It was an experience like she'd never had before. She couldn't have imagined the reality no matter how many times she might have closed her eyes and fantasized.

It was . . . incredible.

The van slowed, and she heard the crunch of gravel beneath her. Then it came to a halt and the engine shut off.

A shiver worked over her when the back door opened. There was a third man. She hadn't thought of it before, but obviously someone had driven them. And now they were stopped.

The van shook, and she felt the presence of the third man close.

She inhaled, searching for some clue to his identity. She heard the slam of doors and the van started up again. It lurched forward and she rocked onto her other side, the side of her face pressing against the rough carpet of the floor.

They'd switched on her.

Her pulse thudded erratically. They were taking turns. Chase was gone. She knew he was driving now. She couldn't smell him. Couldn't sense his presence in the back anymore. She was alone with two strangers, one of whom had already fucked her mouth and come down her throat.

Fear and uncertainty snaked down her spine. It excited her, this nervousness. She wasn't afraid in the sense that she thought Chase would place her in a situation where she'd be harmed. Her fear was born of the unknown.

Hands gripped her knees and rolled her to her back. It was an awkward position, given that her hands were still bound behind her back. She shifted and arched up, and as soon as she did, her thighs were spread wide.

Her newest mystery man wasted no time. His movements were urgent, like he couldn't wait to get inside her. The tip of his cock brushed over her entrance, and she sucked in her breath, at first in shock, and then she let it out in excitement.

He was big.

He pushed, and she felt the smooth, clean feel of latex sliding easily through her tissues. The remnants of Chase's orgasm eased the second man's way, and a decadent thrill tightened her nerve endings at the sheer naughtiness of Chase's semen acting as a lubricant.

He curled his hands around the tops of her thighs and yanked her hard to meet his thrust. She gasped at the sensation of him stuffing that huge cock inside her pussy. Her body resisted, hugging tight and pushing back. She panted and blinked against the blackness caused by the blindfold.

He withdrew an inch, but before she had time to register the relief over the lessening pressure, he rammed forward, his thumbs digging into the back of her thighs.

Her knees buckled under his weight and bent back toward her chest. His hips pumped against her ass. Forceful. There was an edge of pain mixed with the heady excitement coursing through her veins. His hands left her legs, cupped underneath her ass, and held her up so his angle was sharper.

Part of her was in denial that this was happening. She'd fantasized a scenario where she was captured, fucked, and completely dominated. Those thoughts had fueled more than one explosive orgasm. She'd enjoyed whispering those naughty thoughts to Chase while his cock was deep inside her.

She'd imagined so many down and dirty scenarios. She'd imagined lying helpless under strange men while Chase watched. She'd imagined situations where he willingly gave her to other men and forced her to pleasure them.

But for it to happen?

There weren't words to describe it.

Her fingers sought purchase against the floorboard. They curled into the worn carpet as he moved farther up her body until his shoulders met the backs of her knees. He rose over her, pushing harder, deeper, his hips slapping loudly against her flesh.

She was a receptacle for his pleasure. She couldn't move, couldn't protest, even if she wanted to. She lay there, sucking in each breath as her body sucked his cock deeper.

He tensed against her, made a groaning sound, and then he began pummeling her. Her body jiggled and bounced, driven into the floor until she was sure she'd have carpet burn on her back.

Faster. More desperate. He went wild, his body thumping against her until she was sure she could take no more.

Her orgasm flared wild and out of control. A quick flash. On her before she even realized she was working up to one. He shuddered and then went still, his hips pressed flush against her.

She couldn't get air fast enough. Her lungs were squeezed, and she huffed spasmodically as she tried to catch up. Then he ripped himself from her pussy and rolled off her, landing with a thump to the side.

Immediately, the other man took his place. This was the one who'd come in her mouth. There was no finesse to his movements. She wondered if watching her being fucked so brutally had sent him beyond control.

One moment he bumped against her and then he was inside her, thrusting and humping in quick jerky motions. Her breath escaped in a long hiss when he found his depth. Though not as big as the previous man, he was long and she was taking all she could. To the hilt. He thrust like he wanted her to take more, but it just wasn't possible.

Then he pulled from her. Her womb clenched and her pussy tightened. She wanted him back. Wanted the delicious friction by his frenzied thrusts.

Rough hands pulled at her and turned her onto her knees. Her forehead bumped against the floor, and she turned so her cheek rested against the carpet. Her knees dug painfully into the floorboard as the van rocked over a series of bumps. Her ass jutted upward, and already possessive hands were claiming it, spreading her.

He ran his fingers over the opening to her pussy and then his cock stabbed deep. The van slowed abruptly, sending the man behind her painfully forward. She yelped as he lodged deep inside her and then gasped as he continued riding her with fierce, hard pumps.

Her skin prickled. Felt alive, like a thousand ants were crawling just below the surface. Her blood chugged sluggishly through her veins, and her pulse beat wildly at her temples.

Never before had she entered such a state of absolute euphoria. It was like being on a drug high. The air was dense around her, and she processed things in slow motion.

Her senses were shattered. All she could process was the intense pleasure that mingled with the pain of his rough assault. It was a pain she liked—liked very much—and she wasn't sure what to do about that knowledge.

He was relentless in his taking of her. The sheer savagery shocked and aroused her in equal measures. She felt restless. Like a wild thing captured and fighting extinction.

Over and over, he took her, owning her. He pounded against her ass until she lost awareness of everything but the feel of his cock punishing her.

A dreamy smile took over her lips. She closed her eyes against the soft blindfold and let go of the tension boiling inside her. She went limp, her surrender complete.

This time her orgasm wasn't sharp. Wasn't a painful build-up to a tumultuous explosion. It began soft. A warm glow that slowly spread through her groin. Her pussy clenched around the cock battering her and then she dissolved, no longer able to fight the inevitable.

She vaguely registered him pulling out of her, heard his harsh rasp of breath, then felt his fist bump against her ass. He jerked at his cock and hot semen splattered across her ass and onto her back. She arched up, wanting more.

Fresh air spilled into the back of the van. They'd stopped and she hadn't even realized it.

"Nice," Chase drawled. "I wish you could see yourself, baby. All tied up, ass in the air and covered with cum."

Then he gripped her ankles and yanked her backward. She slid along the floor until her legs hung over the back of the van.

"I've got to have you again. Right here, right now," Chase growled.

She heard the rasp of his zipper, and then he thrust into her. No warning. No workup. There with the doors of the van open, God only knew where, where anyone could see, he fucked her fast and hard.

The van shook with the force of his thrusts. His hand tangled in her hair, and he pulled her head back as he continued to pin her against the van.

It was fast and furious. Almost over before it started. He rammed into her and held himself deep, then arched forward until his body was molded tight to hers. He continued to push, straining deeper, rising up and arching over her.

He trembled as his release pulsed from his cock and into her body. Then he pulled out abruptly in a warm rush. His hand tightened in her hair, and he pulled her sharply up. Her feet hit the ground outside and he forced her to her knees.

His cock hit her cheek as his other hand went to cup her chin.

"Open," he ordered. "I want you to lick every bit of the cum off my dick, Zoe."

He wasn't precise as he shoved into her mouth. He smeared the sticky remnants of both their bodies over her chin and lips before finally sliding over her tongue and deep to her throat.

Dutifully, she licked and sucked until he seemed satisfied. He cocked her head back as he withdrew, and she could feel the weight of three stares. Did they like what they saw? Was this as huge a turn-on for them as it was for her?

How indelicate she must look, half dressed, disheveled, semen coating the insides of her thighs and smeared over her lips and face.

"We're not finished, baby. Not by a long shot," Chase told her.

Excitement fluttered through her stomach. What else did they have planned? And where were they?

He hoisted her up and into his arms, then walked several steps away from the van. A door creaked open, and a slightly musty smell flared in her nostrils as they walked inside a building. Or a house. At this point, she had no clue.

His footsteps echoed across a wooden floor, and then she was unceremoniously dumped onto a bed. The springs creaked under her weight and bounced a little as she righted herself.

And then he ripped off her blindfold. For a moment, the light blinded her. She blinked, and gradually the room came into focus.

Hunting camp. He'd taken her to the hunting camp he shared with Brody and Tate. And then her eyes locked onto the two men standing by Chase just a few feet from the bed. Brody and Tate.

Hunger and lust glittered in their eyes. These weren't the usually easygoing expressions of her best friends. There was no indulgence or affection in their eyes. These were the looks of two very hungry males. Her nipples tightened, and a throb began low in her groin.

She'd just been worked over in the back of a van by her boyfriend and her two best friends. One had face-fucked her and come down her throat. The other had come all over her ass. God, it was hot.

She licked her lips. The taste of his semen was still in her mouth. Which one had fucked her mouth? Her gaze shot to Chase, an automatic gesture to see what his reaction was to all of this.

His features were drawn into a harsh line. He was incredibly aroused, and though he'd just fucked her hot and heavy, he was hard again and straining at the fly of his jeans.

They were *all* aroused.

Her mouth went dry as she remembered Chase's words just a few moments ago. They weren't finished. She hoped to hell they weren't. She hoped they were just getting started.

CHAPTER | SIX

Zoe spared a quick glance down her body and blushed. It seemed ridiculous to expend any time feeling self-conscious after what had just happened, but she was extremely vulnerable in her position.

Her hands were still tied behind her back, and she was indelicately sprawled on the bed, leaned back at an angle, legs spread and her scrub top gathered around her belly.

The vulnerable part intensely excited her. She was nervous, more than a little scared, but adrenaline buzzed through her veins like a hacksaw.

She had plenty of excitement in her job as an ER nurse. Adrenaline was nothing new to her. She faced challenges every single day. But this. This was new. It was different.

It was on the tip of her tongue to ask them what they were waiting for, but that ruined the part of her fantasy where she was in no way in control. So she waited and squirmed under their heated gazes.

Chase made the first move. She watched from underneath her lashes and huffed in a quick breath at the look in his eyes. Gone for now was her gentle, affectionate lover. In his place was a man who wasn't afraid to take things too far.

He reached behind her to tug at the binding around her wrists. As soon as her hands fell free, he pulled her scrub top over her head and tossed it across the room. Before she could react, or think to cover her breasts, Chase pulled her arms to the front and began winding the cloth strip in a figure eight around her wrists.

She stared down as the bond tightened. The image did more than she'd have dreamed. Her wrists pushed closer together with each pass he made until they were locked and her palms were flush.

He tied a firm knot and then another, checked the strength of the tie, and then lifted one hand to brush across her cheek.

The gesture was such a contradiction to the force and power they'd exerted so far that she reacted far more than she would have in other circumstances.

His palm skimmed gently across her jaw until his fingers nudged at the hollow beneath her ear. She closed her eyes and nuzzled into his hand, enjoying the sudden tenderness he displayed. And maybe it reassured her. She hadn't realized she needed it, but more than excitement pumped rapidly through her body. She was nervous and a little afraid.

"Look at me, Zoe."

The command was quiet but firm, and she complied immediately, her gaze lifting to his, to the darkness of his eyes. There was danger lurking in their depths. An adrenaline-inducing mixture of mastery and of answering arousal.

"This is the only time I'll say it. I don't want to ruin your fantasy with the intrusion of reality. This is for you. All of it's for you. If at any time you don't want what we're offering, if you want us to stop for any reason, just say so. We'll push. We're more than willing to push you as far as you want to go, but you get to say *when*, okay?"

She swallowed and nodded, and then he leaned in and kissed

her. His tongue swiped gently over her lips and delved inside, tasting her, offering reassurance for what was to come.

She loved him for this. For being secure enough in their relationship to give her something she'd only fantasized about and for taking such care in the execution.

When he drew away, she unconsciously drifted forward, seeking him even as he left. He took several steps back and finally settled into an armchair a few feet from the bed. Her gaze drifted to Brody and Tate, who'd stood silently as Chase talked to her, and then back to Chase.

It was then she understood. Her heart leapt to life and beat so fast her cheeks tightened, and the room grew fuzzy around her. He would watch, at least for now, while Brody and Tate fucked her.

She licked her lips and turned once more in the direction of Brody and Tate only to find they'd moved. Her breath caught and held when she saw Tate purposefully unbuttoning his fly. The rasp of the zipper sounded loud in the silence, and it sent a shiver straight up her spine until the tiny hairs at her nape stood on end.

Brody put his hand on her shoulder. His fingers curled into her skin, firm and commanding. Without a word he turned her, then put both hands on her shoulders and guided her down onto the mattress. Her head hit the edge of the bed with a soft bounce.

Above her, he shrugged out of his shirt. Muscles rippled across broad shoulders. A flame tattoo snaked up his arm and over his shoulder. It extended down the left side of his back. She'd seen it many times, admired it—and him. Of the three guys, he was the most muscular. He spent a lot of time in the gym and in the garage of their house lifting weights.

Then his hands lowered, and he pulled at his pants. His cock jutted forward, so close to her face. He was the one who'd fucked her after Chase. The one who had been hard for her to take. His length and girth mesmerized her. He was all male, beautiful. She lifted her bound wrists, wanting to reach back and touch him.

His fingers closed around her hands and pushed roughly so they once again rested on her belly. Then he slid a palm underneath her neck and pulled until her head leaned over the side of the bed.

He fisted his cock then aimed at her mouth.

"Open for me, Zoe."

The shock of hearing him speak for the first time momentarily threw her off balance. Yes, she knew she was being fucked by her best friends, but it hadn't seemed real. Until he spoke.

She trembled even as her lips slowly parted to accept him.

Chase leaned back in his chair and watched as Brody thrust into Zoe's mouth. The angle of her head was perfect. Brody didn't have to bend or maneuver her. He just stood against the bed and fucked her. Only he was sliding deep into her throat and not her pussy.

Tate took the other side and got onto the bed between Zoe's spread thighs. He stared down at her body like a man about to sit down at a feast. He ran his hands up Zoe's slim body until he cupped her breasts. He toyed with her nipples until they hardened and stood upright in pouty points.

Chase had to shift in his chair. The position was becoming rapidly uncomfortable. The sight before him was more erotic than even he'd imagined. Hearing her soft sighs of pleasure mixed with the wet, sucking sounds she made as Brody relentlessly fucked her mouth was about to send him crawling out of his skin.

Mesmerized, he watched as Tate leaned over her, put his hand down to guide his cock to her pussy, and then rammed his hips forward. Zoe bowed up under the force of his assault, her back coming off the bed. Her breasts thrust outward, and the silhouette of her perfect body made him want to go over and put his mouth around her nipples while his friends went at her from both ends.

Later. Later, he promised himself. He'd incorporate his part of the fantasy where he fucked her mouth while one of them fucked her from behind. He'd come down her throat while her body shook and swayed from the force of Brody or Tate's thrusts.

Hell, maybe they could both take her at the same time. One could fuck her ass while the other took her pussy. And he'd have her mouth.

His groin tightened painfully. The bulge in his jeans was becoming unbearable, but he felt a little weird about pulling his dick out when he wasn't an active participant.

Brody pulled away, then motioned for Tate. Tate backed off the bed, leaving Zoe deflated. She sagged downward, and Chase could see her chest heaving as she sucked in her breaths. The two men switched positions. Tate tore off his condom and Brody rolled one on.

Tate cupped the side of Zoe's face and then leaned in, no finesse, no warning. His cock slid inside, and Chase could see her throat work to accommodate him. Holy fuck but it was hot to see her stretched out like that.

Brody got onto the bed and hauled her legs over his arms. He doubled back her knees and then thrust into her. Zoe gave a strangled cry from around Tate's cock. For a moment, his friends seemed unsure. Tate withdrew, giving her a chance to breathe while Brody shot Chase a quick look.

Chase merely nodded for them to continue. It was what Zoe wanted, and she could call a halt at any time. And the truth was, Chase was enthralled with the spectacle before him.

Still, Brody gentled his movements. He leaned over Zoe and began moving slower, his big body covering hers as Tate continued to fuck her mouth.

The slim beautiful woman lying bound on the bed as two much larger men made use of her body evoked powerful lust within Chase. He was riveted to the undulating bodies, and he didn't miss the enjoyment his friends took from the experience.

Tate touched the side of her face in a tender gesture that belied the strength of his thrusts. His face was drawn in intense pleasure, but there was also satisfaction, as if he were finally obtaining the one thing he'd wanted most.

Brody's hands skimmed up and down Zoe's sides and then to her breasts, where he thumbed her nipples. Then he leaned down and took one of them in his mouth. The same thing Chase ached to do. Zoe had fantastic breasts. They were a source of endless fascination to him, and it was one of the two spots on her body guaranteed to drive her wild.

Predictably she arched up, and her entire body went rigid as Brody sucked strongly at one and then the other.

Chase grinned. He'd give her five seconds tops before she orgasmed.

Zoe's entire body tightened as soon as Brody's lips surrounded her nipple. She gasped and convulsed, then arched up, straining for more. Her legs shook, her thighs spasmed, and her orgasm caught fire in her womb.

"Whoa," Brody murmured as he pulled away from one breast. "I'm guessing you like that."

An inarticulate sound tore from her throat even as Tate plunged forward, cutting her off.

For one horrible moment, she thought Brody wasn't going to touch her breasts again and she'd be left teetering on the edge of explosion.

Then he powered his hips forward, sending his huge cock into her depths just as he sucked her other nipple between his teeth and nipped.

It set off a chain reaction so fierce that she lost awareness of anything other than the intense fire blowing over her. She bucked wildly. The action tightened her mouth around Tate's cock, and she sucked hard as Brody stoked the fires even higher.

"Oh Jesus," Tate groaned.

Tate gripped her face between his hands, held her firmly in place, and began fucking her hard and fast. She couldn't breathe, couldn't process. She couldn't think. All she could do was lie there and allow them to do as they wanted.

Tate began coming, the hot spurts exploding into her mouth and hitting the back of her throat. His thumbs dug into the side of her face, and she heard the hiss of pleasure tear from his lips.

Brody leaned farther over her now, and her hands were trapped between their bodies. She turned her hands as much as she could, wanting to touch him. Feel the hardness of his chest and the muscles ripple underneath her fingertips.

How long she had known this man, admired his body, but she'd never touched. Not intimately. Until now.

Tate stilled against her, allowing the last of his release to leak into her mouth. Then he pulled away, his cock smearing fluid on her cheek. He leaned down until she could see his eyes so close to hers, and he pressed a gentle kiss to her forehead.

Just as when Chase had touched her a short time ago, she was buoyed by Tate's reassurance. Even amid the full-on assault they'd launched, this reminder of their regard for her was something she needed.

As he moved away, she lifted her head so she could see Brody. The fierceness in his eyes, the wild spark that smoldered back at her sent a wave of satisfaction through her. There was no doubt she was enjoying the deepest, darkest parts of her fantasy come to life, but here was proof that she wasn't the only one.

Their gazes connected, and she was powerless to look away. His body rocked against her, and still he didn't drop his gaze. His jaw clenched and his lips tightened and she felt him, so hard and powerful tunneling into her body.

Finally, as if the strain were too much to bear, he closed his eyes, threw back his head. An agonized sound escaped those tightly held lips, and then he dropped his head and slowly lowered himself to her body.

He lay there, his chest heaving, her bound hands trapped tightly between them. His heartbeat thumped against her breasts, and his back rose with the sharp breaths he drew in.

She closed her eyes as exhaustion settled over her. She was sore—deliciously so. Her jaw ached, her hands were numb, and she wasn't sure she could even feel her legs. She let her head fall back and lay there, Brody sprawled on top of her, as they both attempted to recover from the night's events.

CHAPTER | SEVEN

Zoe stood in the shower, eyes closed and head turned up into the spray as hot water cascaded over her body. It had taken her more than a few moments to collect herself and drag herself off the bed and into the bathroom after Chase had given her the terse order to "clean up."

He and the others had left the bedroom, and her mind was still too fuzzed to imagine what they were planning next.

She was ridiculously loose and limber, so much so that it took all her concentration to stand and wash the tender parts of her body. Each brush of the washcloth brought back memories of how *they'd* touched her.

Her clit still tingled. It was swollen and excruciatingly sensitive. Her breasts were heavy, and her nipples seemed to be in a permanently erect state.

Even amid her fatigue, anticipation whispered a seductive promise. There was more. She wanted more. She wanted to be pushed to her limits and beyond.

She stepped from the shower, wrapped in a towel, and she quickly combed through her wet hair. After looking through the drawers, she found an old hair dryer that to her surprise worked.

A few minutes later, clean, hair dried, she walked nervously into the bedroom, still clutching the towel around her breasts.

Chase had been clear. Take a shower and then meet them in the living room. And she wasn't to wear a single thing.

God, it was one thing to have had power taken from her, to have had her clothing stripped from her body by others, but it was quite another to walk of her own accord—naked—into the living room where Chase and her best friends waited. Best friends that had just fucked her six ways to Sunday.

She sat on the edge of the bed and attempted to collect her scattered wits. Okay, she was being ridiculous. After all, she'd dragged both Brody and Tate to a strip club where they saw her take it off in front of the entire fire crew. Walking out naked in front of them was nothing. Right?

Only this time they were going to lay claim to her. She didn't have Chase to hide behind. For all she knew Chase would be content to watch from the sidelines while his friends got down and dirty with her.

Ohhh but that image made her shiver with excitement. She liked having sex while Chase watched. Loved the sensation of his eyes burning over her body, watching in satisfaction as another man took what was his.

They'd acted on a lot of their fantasies in the past, but this was a new chapter in their relationship. It displayed a boldness she loved. Never had they gone beyond the confines of their personal intimacy. And as she sat here examining her feelings on the subject, all she could think was that she was *exhilarated*.

Taking a deep breath, she rose and let the towel fall to the floor.

She hesitated at the entrance to the living room, her gaze seeking the occupants before she took another step forward. The guys were sprawled on the couches watching television. It looked very much like days off at their own house. Only she wasn't normally about to walk in naked and tempt them to do their worst.

Tate looked up and saw her first. He froze and stared unabashedly up and down her body, his eyes lingering first at her pussy and then her breasts. Then he simply crooked his finger in a clear come-here motion.

Brody and Chase turned when she took a step forward. She had the instant urge to cover up everything her hands and arms would cover up, but given that they'd just spent the last hour touching all those places, her urge was pretty damn silly.

She'd always been proud of her body, and she damn sure hadn't minded flaunting it in the strip club. No reason to become a shrinking violet now. If Chase had any inkling of the ridiculous thoughts floating through her head, he'd laugh his fool head off at the absurdity.

When she reached Tate, she was surprised by his directness. Maybe her fantasy brought out the latent caveman in all of them. He was by far the most easygoing of the group, and she had trouble picturing him as this blunt, forceful man who'd ravaged her body.

He loosened his fly with one hand and reached up with his other to jerk her down to her knees. She landed between his knees and braced her hands on either side of them. His hand left her long enough to pull his jeans down around his hips, and she stared at his cock lying at an angle over his thigh.

He was by no means fully erect, but he wasn't flaccid either. This was the first chance she'd had to really study the beauty of his body, the size of his cock and his muscled thighs. She imagined stroking every inch of his flesh, cupping him and guiding him to her mouth. Would he want her to seduce him, or did he prefer the control?

She had her answer when he fisted his cock, stroked up and down as it lengthened and grew more rigid. He cupped his other hand behind her neck and pulled her roughly toward him.

As her mouth closed over the tip, she inhaled his scent and savored it. Forgotten for the moment was the fact that Chase and Brody watched. She was caught up in her fascination with Tate. Lovable, loyal Tate. Who would have ever thought she'd have him in her mouth, his strong hand cupped around her neck so that she was powerless to do anything but obey his silent commands.

She was more focused now. She'd had time to adjust to the idea of being fucked by three different men. Now she wanted to enjoy the sensation instead of just having it thrust on her. So she took her time, lavishing attention on Tate's cock, working with her hands and her mouth as she sucked him to full erection.

She heard a noise behind her, but she paid no attention until firm hands grasped her ass and a cock nudged at her pussy. She tried to turn, but Tate grasped her jaw and held her firmly in place.

The question of who was quickly answered when Brody pushed into her from behind. He had her in one hard thrust, his cock wedged so tight she couldn't move. She felt deliciously pinned between two gorgeous cocks. If she could purr, she most assuredly would at this point.

She pushed back against Brody, wanting all he could give. He in turn thrust into her, pushing her against Tate's cock so that it lodged at the back of her throat.

When Brody pulled out, she made a sound of disappointment that was quickly quelled when he ran a finger over the seam of her ass. She caught her breath. Was he going to fuck her ass?

He was big. Bigger than Chase. Chase had fucked her ass plenty of times, but she'd never taken anything bigger than Chase, and Chase had a difficult enough time getting in.

She twitched when the cool slide of liquid spilled down the cleft of her ass. Brody caught it with his fingers and smeared over her opening, up and down and then pushing inside.

Her body fought even his finger, but he persisted, pushing against her until finally she surrendered and took the tip.

"That's it, Zoe," Brody murmured. "Let me in. I'm going to fuck that ass and fuck it hard. It will be a hell of a lot easier if you're ready for me."

The implication was that he'd fuck her whether she was prepared or not. A decadent thrill washed over her at the thought of Brody forcing his way into her resisting body. Oh yeah. Nice. It obviously didn't pay to be too accommodating. She'd stop that nonsense right now.

She clamped down and pulled away, causing his finger to slide out of her ass. He let out a growl of reprimand, and she smiled around Tate's dick. When he tried to ease his finger back in, she clamped down once more and flinched away.

"Zoe, goddamn it."

Then, as if realizing her game, he gripped both hips and held her in place. He slid his cock up and down the cleft of her ass, spreading the lubricant, but then he stopped at her tight little hole and pushed. Hard.

Her mouth flew open around Tate's cock and she gasped, loud and rushed.

"I told you what would happen," Brody said, but he didn't sound very sorry at all.

Then he shoved again, forcing his way into her resisting ass. Oh God, he was big and it hurt and she loved every second. She wiggled and squirmed, trying everything she could to unseat him. He issued a sharp slap to her ass cheek before gripping her hips again to hold her down.

"Stop fighting or I swear I'll push you down to the floor and I'll give you an ass-fucking you won't forget."

If he'd said it to make her stop, he obviously didn't realize just how dark her fantasies ran. Or maybe he did and he was offering her a choice in how far to go. Whatever the case, she went wild, bucking and fighting the incredible pressure pushing against her ass.

A hand curled into her hair, yanked her away from Tate's cock, and then shoved her hard to the floor. Her cheek pressed against the carpet and her ass hung high in the air. Brody was still mounted over her, his cock half shoved into her ass, and now he held her head down while he pried her legs farther open with the other.

"Hold her down," he ordered roughly.

She wasn't sure who the order was for. Didn't care. Another hand dove into her hair and held the back of her neck down while Brody's hand left her. He palmed both cheeks, spread her wide, and then rammed into her.

She cried out as he sank the remaining way. Her ass throbbed. Her nerve endings screamed in protest. Intense pleasure mixed with pain tied her insides into a tight knot.

He began fucking her with forceful, long strokes. His cock powered through her tight resistance with ease now that he'd fully breached her body. His hard abdomen pressed into her ass with each thrust. She'd never felt so opened, so absolutely helpless in her life.

She lay there, motionless while he took his pleasure. It was humbling. She couldn't move, could barely do more than take what he dished out. This was what she'd fantasized about. The moment of complete powerlessness. The moment when she realized there was nothing she could do to prevent him from taking her in any manner he wanted.

He owned her. He took her. He punished her.

He slowed now, withdrawing carefully, dragging his cock over her stretched opening until he nearly popped free. Then he sank deep again, pushing against her natural resistance, showing her she had no power to keep him out.

In and out, slow, so very slow. He withdrew then fed his cock back, inch by inch, until his balls pressed against her pussy.

For several minutes, he sawed back and forth, methodical, making sure she knew and accepted his dominance. Only when she went completely and utterly limp beneath him and closed her eyes, did he pull out. His lesson was obviously over.

Or maybe it was just beginning.

He slid his finger into the still-wide opening and laughed softly as her ass clutched at the tip.

"You like having me in your ass, don't you, Zoe?"

She didn't answer. She doubted he required it. It was pretty damn obvious she liked it.

He helped her up from the floor, and she struggled to get her jelly legs underneath her. He guided her toward the couch, where Tate had already taken position. He sat down on the far end right against the arm. But he'd scooted to the very edge, then leaned back so he was nearly flat on the cushions. Only his head rested on the back cushion, tilted forward so he could see her.

"Come straddle me, Zoe. Come for a ride. I want you on top of me."

Her ass still aching from Brody's treatment, she moved toward Tate and came to a stop between his knees.

He patted his lap. "Hop up."

She straddled his body. Tate slid one hand through her damp heat while he grasped his cock with his other hand and positioned himself at her entrance.

"Slide down, babe. Take me all the way."

She took him, inch by delicious inch. He was long and hard, but her persistence paid off and she didn't have the difficulty taking him as she'd done with Brody.

She rose up and then let herself fall down his cock until her ass smacked against his thighs.

"Oh yeah, just like that," Tate ground out. "Now lean forward, baby."

He tugged at her arms, pulling until her breasts dangled over his chest and her ass lifted just off Tate's body. When Brody stepped between Tate's spread legs, Zoe realized what they were doing and why Brody had had a warm-up session with her ass.

They were going to take her at the same time.

"Be real still, sweetheart," Tate warned. "It's going to be tighter than even before when he gets inside you. Just stay here with me and take it."

She laughed. "Do I have a choice?"

Tate arched a brow. "Given that I currently have you on my cock and have no intention of letting you get up, then no, you don't have a choice. Just lie here against me and take it."

"Won't be so bad," Brody said in an amused tone. "It'll only hurt when I try to get back in. And if you fight me."

She snorted. "You guys are all heart."

Brody spread her buttocks, then lodged his cock against the opening that had shrunk to normal size again. Which meant he was going to have to reopen her all over again. She nearly groaned even as she trembled in anticipation.

"Kiss me, Zoe," Tate whispered. "Kiss me now while he fucks your ass. You can scream all you want."

She leaned as far as she could, as far as Brody's grip would allow. Tate met her the rest of the way and pressed his lips to hers. Their tongues tangled just as Brody pressed against her anus. As soon as there was any give, he thrust forcefully, splitting the seam on either side to accommodate his cock.

Tate swallowed her desperate cry, held her shoulders to keep her from writhing uncontrollably.

"Shhh," Tate whispered into her mouth. "We'll both be in soon and then it'll feel good, Zoe."

The sensation of having both men inside her ass and pussy at the same time just wasn't describable. She felt stuffed at both ends, like neither could possibly fit, and yet they'd made it happen. The thin layer of tissue between her vagina and anus did little to cushion the two cocks. They rubbed back and forth over that thin skin with delicious results.

Never had she felt so full. Never had anything felt so erotic. Naughty. Deliciously bad girl.

Brody provided most of the force, since she was astride Tate and his movements were limited. But Brody thrust back and forth with exuberance that moved Zoe up and down Tate's cock.

She'd been so absorbed with Brody and Tate's attentions that she'd blocked Chase's presence from the room. But now he pushed back into the picture. He shoved his hand into her hair as he stood to the side of the three on the couch.

With him standing and Zoe sitting on Tate's lap, her mouth was at the perfect level for Chase's cock. A fact Chase planned to take full advantage of.

He cupped her jaw, fisted his cock, and then guided it toward her mouth. She opened, and he was inside her deep and hard, just like the other two men in her ass and pussy.

The three men began fucking her in unison, their bodies buffeting hers. They came together, a series of gasps, soft cries and groans escaping into the air.

Flesh met flesh. Wet, sucking sounds filled the room. The slap of thighs meeting ass spurred the others on to find their fulfillment.

It was erotic not just in sight. Nor was it just the intense sounds, the soft whispers and sighs. The light moans. It was erotic as hell because here she was, surrounded by three men, all of whom were giving her everything she could possibility want. They were taking the things they wanted. They wanted her. They desired her and they wanted to make her happy.

Their touches, their regard, the simple act of a reassuring kiss. It made the entire series of events, and not just the actual sex, erotic as hell.

Her body was the receptacle for not one man, but three. Three sexy-as-sin men who knew precisely what to do with a woman when it came to sex.

"I told you I'd fuck your mouth while they fucked your ass and pussy," Chase said in a satisfied tone.

Zoe held up her middle finger for him to see. He chuckled and thrust hard into her mouth as punishment. She choked and shot him a dirty glare. He tweaked her nose and resumed fucking her mouth.

Brody pounded her ass while Tate pushed upward, sliding back and forth into her pussy. It was the perfect trifecta. Mouth, pussy, and ass. Three gorgeous, rock-hard cocks diving into all three.

While Zoe sucked Chase's cock and the other men worked their cocks in her pussy and ass, Tate rubbed his thumbs over her nipples, pulling outward and then pinching lightly.

Chase lowered his hand to cup the back of her neck and then he massaged, squeezing and working the sensitive area.

She shuddered and began moving restlessly. Chase's cock nearly fell from her mouth, but he caught her jaw and turned her back so he could thrust back in.

Brody let out a shout, rammed as far into her ass as he could. The action pressed her so far onto Tate that he was lodged into her pussy. Both cocks were stuffed to capacity. They twitched deep inside her and Brody and Tate bucked their hips as they came almost violently.

Chase cupped her face with both hands and began fucking fast and hard. Race to completion. His cock swelled larger, moved harder and deeper. Semen filled her mouth, coated her tongue and slid down the back of her throat as she swallowed.

Brody and Tate were still locked inside her body when Chase finally eased from her mouth. While Brody and Tate watched, Chase made her clean the semen from his cock with her tongue.

The fact that they twitched inside her body when they were already spent told her the sight was a turn-on for them.

Then Brody carefully pulled from her ass. She flinched at the soreness his exit caused. Then Brody reached down and picked her up from Tate's lap. Tate's cock fell free, and Brody set her on her feet next to Chase.

She would have gone down flat on her face if Chase hadn't grabbed her and hauled her against his chest.

"Whoa, baby, careful. I've got you."

"Tired," she managed to say.

He squeezed his arm around her shoulders. "I know. We're going to put you to bed now so you can get some rest. I think we've roughed you up enough for the night."

She smiled and leaned up on tiptoe to kiss him. "Thank you. It was perfect. All of it was perfect."

"You're welcome, babe."

She turned to Brody and Tate, unsure of how they'd receive her thanks, but she wasn't going to ignore their very large part in fulfilling her fantasy.

She hugged Tate first and then leaned up and kissed him. Not a little brush like she might have given him in the past, a peck as a friend. No, she kissed him hot, with passion and all the lust she'd felt for him while he and Brody fucked her.

She was gratified when he kissed her back with every bit as much enthusiasm and heat.

"Thank you," she whispered as she pulled away.

Tate smiled. "You're welcome, sweetheart. You know I'd damn near do anything for you, but this might have been the best thing yet."

She turned to Brody and pushed herself into his beefy embrace. At first he stiffened and very gingerly put his arms around her, but she wasn't letting him get a corncob up his ass over this. She loved him to pieces. Absolute pieces. He was one of her favorite people in the entire world and nothing—definitely not sex—was going to change that. In fact, she hoped sex between them made things even better.

She all but crawled up his chest since he wasn't exactly helping her. She wrapped her legs around him and hauled herself up his body until her arms were locked around his neck and her legs locked around his waist.

"You finished scaling me?" he asked balefully.

She giggled. "You're a hard tree to climb, Brody."

His expression eased, and amusement glinted in his eyes. "All right. Kiss me and get it over with then."

Her eyes narrowed. "Is that what you think's going to happen? I've got news for you, Brody McNamara," she muttered.

She yanked him to her mouth and covered his lips in a burning hot, carnal kiss to end all kisses. Heat sizzled up her spine and damn near set off fireworks in her head. Her tongue swept over his, licking and then dueling. There was no way he was indifferent to this.

They were both sucking some major wind by the time she let him go and slid back down his body.

"Don't pull that shit with me again," she scowled.

He raised one brow. "I didn't realize I was pulling anything. For God's sake, Zoe. You damn near mauled me."

"Don't pretend you can be all indifferent to me now and you don't want to get close. You're stuck with me, dumbass. If things are awkward, it's because you'll make them so."

He drew his brows up in confusion and then shook his head as if he had no idea what the hell she was talking about. And maybe he didn't. He was a man, after all. She'd probably given him too much credit in the thinking department.

She started for the bedroom but turned and put her palms in the air and let her eyes widen innocently. "So who's going to bed with me?"

CHAPTER | EIGHT

When Zoe awoke, her first instinct was to lie there and sleep for the next year. She was bone tired, and her muscles felt like jelly. And there were certain parts of her anatomy that were extremely tender.

She sighed and snuggled a little deeper into her pillow until it occurred to her that she was in bed with more than one male, and now curiosity niggled at her because she wanted to know who she was cuddled up with.

She pried her eyes open and found she was facing Brody's back. The flame tattoo covered his left shoulder and tapered off near the middle of his back. If she hadn't been afraid of waking him, she'd have traced the edges with her fingers. It was beautiful, like him, and it fit his personality to a *T*. Whoever had done his ink had done a spectacular job. It looked alive, like a blaze soaring up his back and over his shoulder.

She glanced over her shoulder to see Tate sound asleep on the other side of her. They weren't completely naked. At some point they'd retrieved their underwear, which amused her for some reason. Maybe men didn't want their dangly parts observed at full rest.

So where was Chase?

A distant sound told her he was probably in the kitchen, which meant he was probably fixing breakfast. She could eat a cow right now, she was so hungry. That much of a sexual workout would give anyone an appetite.

After the episode in the living room, they'd gone to the bedroom, and the rest of the night was a blur. She'd had sex with Tate. She'd had sex with Brody. She'd had sex with both of them. They'd finished off the night with a foursome on the bed, and she still couldn't remember who went where, but she could still remember how their hands and mouths felt on her skin and how their cocks felt in her body.

A delicious shiver skirted down her arms. It had been a spectacular experience. She was just sorry it was over.

With a rueful smile, she eased up and crept down the middle of the bed so she wouldn't wake the guys. She had no idea where her clothes had gotten to, so she snagged Brody's T-shirt and pulled it over her head. Then she went off in search of Chase.

As expected, she found him in the kitchen working on breakfast. She sneaked up behind him, wrapped her arms around his waist, and rested her cheek against his back.

"Morning, sleepyhead."

"Good morning," she mumbled against his back.

He turned in her arms until they faced each other. He smiled down at her and then lowered his mouth to kiss her.

"How are you this morning?"

"Sore," she admitted. "I may not want sex for a week."

He grinned. "If you go a week without sex, that'll be a record."

She blinked up at him with mock incredulity. "Are you saying I'm some kind of nymphomaniac?"

His eyes widened innocently. "Would I say something like that?"

She gave him an oh-please look in response.

He leaned back against the counter and pulled her with him so she was nestled in his arms.

"So give me the verdict. Was it everything you expected? Were we too rough?"

His face had grown more serious, and there was a distinct edge of worry in his voice. She smiled and ran her hands up his muscled arms and then looped them around his neck.

"Have I told you lately how fantastic you are? Have I told you how lucky I am to have a guy who understands me so completely and who busts his ass to please me?"

"Hmm, maybe, but I'm not opposed to hearing it a few more times," he said in a husky voice.

"If I weren't so tired and sore, I'd totally take you over to the couch and jump your bones," she said regretfully.

He laughed and squeezed her a little tighter. "You need to take it easy for a few days, baby. That was one hell of a workout you got last night."

She leaned into his chest and rested her forehead against his chin. "We still have today and tomorrow off together."

"Yep."

She leaned back to look at him again. "Do we have any plans beyond being couch bums?"

"Oh, I don't know. I thought about taking you to dinner tonight. Maybe a movie."

"Ooooh, date night!"

"And tomorrow I thought we'd have some guys over from the station for a barbecue. Or if you prefer, we can keep it to just you, me, Brody, and Tate."

Remembering her teasing Brody the previous night, she frowned and nibbled at her bottom lip.

"Something wrong?" Chase asked.

She met his gaze, unsure of how to say what was on her mind.

"You don't think . . . You don't think things will be weird between us now, do you? I mean with Brody and Tate?"

"You're wanting to know if your having sex with them changes things."

She nodded. "Well, yeah . . . and between you and me."

As if sensing the very real worry in her voice, he cupped her face and ran his thumb over her lips.

"I can't speak for Brody and Tate. But I can most assuredly tell you that this changes nothing between you and me. In some ways . . . I think it's better. Right now I swear I just want to sweep you into my arms and hold you for the next two days. I can't explain it, but what happened was so absolutely awesome. I don't even have words. It went beyond a simple fantasy fulfillment. Maybe a part of me worried you wouldn't be into it. Maybe I worried I wouldn't be into it. But right now I feel really damn lucky that I have a woman who understands my kinks and fantasies, has a set of her own, and doesn't mind acting on mine or hers. That freaking rocks, Zoe. Maybe I'm a little relieved because I feel like we're being more honest with each other than ever. I'm not saying I could have never not shared this kind of stuff with you. I think we would have been just fine and our relationship would have been as incredible as it's always been. But now? I feel like I've been given a bonus on top of everything else."

She stared at him in shock. This was the most talkative Chase had ever been when it came to the two of them. Their relationship had always been a study in fun, comfortable, and great sex. She'd been willing to go along with the status quo because she wasn't someone who ever liked to rock the boat. And why fuck up something good by demanding more?

Her heart squeezed when she saw the absolute conviction in his eyes.

God, but she loved this man. She'd loved him for a long time. No, it hadn't been some overnight revelation. It had been more like a gradual awareness, something that grew day by day until she hadn't been able to imagine her life without him.

It bloomed and grew, continued to grow each day they were together. It was comfortable. It was steady. Like him.

Shouldn't she tell him? Shouldn't she say the words? Somehow she imagined a better place than the kitchen of a deer camp after a night of hedonistic debauchery. For now, it was enough to know that it was there. He wasn't going anywhere, and neither was she. She'd find the right time. She wanted it to be perfect.

CHAPTER | NINE

To her relief, things hadn't gotten weird between her, Brody, and Tate. It had been a constant worry on her mind the few days following the night at the deer camp. They looked at her differently, but then she looked at them a whole lot different too.

On an emotional level, nothing had changed. She'd always cared very deeply for her two friends. Oh, she'd always thought they were hot. What normal female wouldn't? She'd even had her moments of imagining what they'd be like in bed.

Now she knew, and when she looked at them, she remembered every detail.

"Hey, Zoe, you ready? We're going to be late," Brody bellowed from the kitchen.

She grinned, finished lacing her tennis shoe, and headed out of her bedroom to meet him and Tate.

They were standing in the kitchen when she walked in. Brody had the keys in his hand and was waiting by the door. He made a show of checking his watch, and she rolled her eyes.

"I'm not playing this time," she reminded them.

"You will if one of ours doesn't show," Tate said. "Where else are we going to get a sub?"

"Ask one of the wives to play."

"We like your breasts better," Brody teased.

A hot flush worked up her neck. Damn it. In the past, not only had that sort of remark been common, but she damn sure wouldn't have blushed like a moron—or remembered his mouth around her breasts.

She glanced down at her plain T-shirt. "I came better prepared this time. No way can I come out of this one."

"Pity," Tate said. "That was the high point of the last game."

She scowled up at him.

Tate put his hands on her shoulders and herded her out the door. "Besides, Chase is going to be there. He had some paperwork to finish at the station, but he said he'd meet us there."

Her eyes narrowed. "Uh-huh, provided he doesn't meet with an untimely delay."

Brody chuckled as he got into the truck. "We'd never sabotage the team captain."

Zoe climbed into the back and shoved over Brody's pile of stuff so she could have room on the seat. Thank goodness he kept the house cleaner than his truck.

She leaned up between the two seats as Brody backed out of the drive. "So what's on the line today? Beer? Barbecue? Glory?"

"Yeah, yeah, and yeah," Tate said. "Loser has to throw a barbecue—complete with beer, lots of beer, for the winner."

She frowned. "Is it bad of me to hope we lose then?"

Tate whipped his head around and looked at her aghast. "Traitor!"

She gave him a smug smile. "C'mon, Tate. Nobody cooks barbecue better than Chief Maxwell. Do we really want to eat whatever the sheriff's department comes up with?"

"She has a point there," Brody said.

"Well, hell, now we have to throw the damn game?" Tate asked.

"Maybe you should renegotiate the winner's terms," Zoe suggested. "That way you don't forfeit all your manly glory and you still get something good out of the deal."

Brody's face twisted in thought. "Beer . . . and what?"

She laughed. "As long as the beer's covered, do you care?"

He grinned at her in the rearview mirror. "Weeell, I suppose we could have a side wager. Just between us."

She raised an eyebrow and stared back at him. "Oh? Do tell."

"Since we'd be deprived of decent barbecue if we won, it seems like Tate and I should be amply rewarded if we prove our manhood on the ball field."

Tate snorted and covered his mouth as he began laughing.

"Oh Jesus," she muttered. "What did you have in mind?"

Brody glanced over at Tate, and she could see the mischief gleaming in both the men's eyes. Then Brody looked back at her in the mirror again. His eyes were all wide and innocent.

"You in a bow? Like a really small bow?"

She almost swallowed her tongue. Then she recovered enough to tease back. "Just a bow? So all I have to do is parade around in a bow and you'll be happy."

"That's not what he's saying at all," Tate growled. "It begins with you in a bow. A fantasy of ours. But that's only the beginning. It ends with you, sans bow, bent over the arm of the couch while we fuck your brains out."

"Speak for yourself," Brody shot back. "My fantasy involves her on her knees, between my legs, her mouth around . . ."

"Okay, okay, I get it!" she said, throwing her hands over her ears. Then she dissolved into laughter. "You two are terrible."

Then she had a thought.

"Uh-oh," Tate muttered. "I don't like that evil gleam that just appeared in her eyes."

"So what do I get if you lose?" she smirked.

Brody's brow wrinkled in thought. "Is our losing even an option? What do you have in mind?"

"Well," she began, "it seems to me if you guys get rewarded for winning, you should have to pay up if you lose."

"We're listening," Tate said. "What do you have in mind?"

Now she scrambled to come up with something. Her brain was fried, damn it.

"Okay, if you lose, I get a full-body massage from both of you, and I want the works. Oh, and dinner. A really yummy dinner. And," she added, warming to her topic, "I want my chores done for a week."

Tate shot Brody a disgusted look. "She's such a girl."

"Couldn't you come up with something good?" Brody asked.

"Hey, to a guy sex is the ultimate reward. To a woman? Having a man do the cooking and cleaning is better than an orgasm any day."

"That's not what you were saying a few nights ago," Tate muttered.

Her cheeks warmed again, but this time she was determined not to let embarrassment take over. She loved that they could joke and kid around about what had happened. Her biggest fear had been about residual awkwardness. As it stood, she was the only one acting stupid.

"Okay so maybe after you cook and clean, you can give me a screaming orgasm," she said cheekily.

Brody grinned. "Works for me."

Hours later, Zoe traipsed into the house with three very smug males. Having been told all about the wager between Zoe, Brody, and Tate, Chase had added his own to the mix.

If the firemen won, Zoe had to serve them dinner—naked. If

they lost, well, since Chase was so sure they wouldn't lose, he'd never offered anything to Zoe. Smug bastard.

And since they'd handily defeated the sheriff's department, Zoe now had to pay up. Three times.

"Cheer up, baby," Chase teased.

She shot him a glare and kicked off her shoes in the doorway. "And when, pray tell, am I expected to pay up?"

The three men exchanged looks.

"Uh, now would be good," Tate suggested with a grin.

Well hell. They were really going to make her pay up.

"If I've got to cook, then get the hell out of my kitchen. I'll serve it up in the living room."

She made shooing motions with her hands. Chase caught one of them and brought her fingers to his lips.

"Don't forget the most important part of serving dinner," he said. "Make sure you're naked."

Brody and Tate burst into laughter but hurried out of the kitchen before Zoe could retaliate.

She shook her head but grinned as Chase disappeared behind them.

She made quick work of dinner because quite frankly she was more interested in what happened after dinner. If Brody could get away with making burgers for his turn at supper, so could she. It beat Spaghetti-O's out of a can, at any rate.

Twenty minutes later, she had the burgers on a platter complete with drinks and a bag of chips. Hey, they couldn't be picky if she was serving food naked, right?

She set the tray on the counter and then sucked in a deep breath. She stripped out of her clothes and left them in a pile on the kitchen floor. Lord, she felt ridiculous, but a bet was a bet.

Balancing the tray and mindful of the drinks, she set off for the living room. As soon as she entered, whistles rent the air and the television was promptly turned off. Good to know she commanded more attention than the TV.

"Your dinner," she said, bending over in front of Brody to allow him to take a plate from the tray.

He fumbled with the plate, his eyes never leaving her breasts. He was such a guy.

She moved on to Tate, who was also staring unrepentantly as she delivered his food. She offered him a sugary-sweet smile and then straightened when he'd scooped his offering from the tray.

Lastly she delivered Chase's food, since this had been his fool idea. His eyes glimmered with laughter, and he copped a feel, palming one breast when she bent over.

She shook her head and started back for the kitchen.

"Where you going?" Chase called after her.

"To get dressed," she said over her shoulder.

She was treated to three male protests. She stopped and turned to look at them with a raised brow.

Tate shrugged. "Not a lot of sense in getting dressed when Brody and I have yet to collect our winnings."

Brody snickered and took a drink to cover his smile.

She rolled her eyes. "So you want me to stay naked while you eat?"

Tate nodded. "Well, yeah. Think of it as ambience. And it'll save us the trouble of undressing you afterward."

She laughed and went back to the kitchen to get her plate, returning a moment later, still naked. She felt utterly ridiculous, especially when she had to ask Brody to shove over on the couch so she could sit.

Instead of moving over toward Tate, he patted the space between them, which meant she had to step over his long-assed legs to get to her seat.

She settled in and began to eat, although eating when naked—definitely a new experience.

Brody leaned over and whispered, "Don't worry about spilling. I'll be more than happy to lick it off you later."

Ah hell. Images of him doing just that exploded in her brain. Her hands shook as she put her hamburger down on the plate that rested on the coffee table. Deciding to get back at him just a little, she turned and cocked her head and murmured in a low voice, "Mmmm, sort of like I'll be licking your cock in a little while."

His eyes narrowed and he swallowed. She let her gaze drift downward to where the bulge in his jeans had just gotten quite a bit more noticeable. Then she smiled and went back to her burger.

Chase chuckled from his chair, and she looked over at him to see his eyes full of amusement. Strangely he hadn't asked for any sexual favors, but then he didn't have to. And maybe watching Tate and Brody's "reward" would be reward in of itself.

She finished half of the burger and then licked each and every one of her fingers, letting her tongue linger over the tips.

Seeing that the others were finished, she stood and began to collect the plates and the empty cans. With a saucy smile, she disappeared into the kitchen and immediately began to wonder just how soon they planned on collecting.

She delayed as long as she could. Part of her couldn't wait to go back in. The other part was a little apprehensive. In the end, giddy won out over apprehensive and she walked back into the living room only to see Brody standing in the middle of the room, his hands at his fly.

He smiled when she stopped in the doorway, and then he crooked his finger in a come-hither motion. A little dazed, she complied. When she was directly in front of him, he put a hand on her shoulder. Then he pushed until she went down on her knees in front of him.

"Perfect," he murmured.

He unzipped his fly and shoved his jeans down just far enough that his cock came free. Not waiting for her to take the initiative, he threaded his hand through her hair, gripped the back of her head, and guided her toward his fisted cock.

The broad head pushed past her lips and onto her tongue. She reached for his legs, something to hold on to as she leaned forward to take him deeper.

His breath came out in an audible hiss when she took him to the back of her throat.

"Yes, baby, just like that. God, I love your mouth. It's so hot and sweet."

His words spurred her excitement. She wanted to please him, wanted him to gain the ultimate satisfaction from the act.

She slid one hand from his thigh to delve into his jeans, pulling them lower so she could cup his balls. The crisp hair rasped over her knuckles. She gripped his sac, rolling it as she sucked back and forth over his cock.

He was long and thick and stabbed into her mouth, gliding roughly over her tongue, touching the roof of her mouth and the sides of her cheeks. There wasn't a place in her mouth or throat he didn't touch, didn't explore as he rocked back and forth, stroked long and deep.

He loosened his grip at the base of his dick and reached gently for her fingers, twining them with his. Then he took her hand and positioned it where his had been, signaling his desire for her to work the base.

She gripped his cock, but his hand didn't leave hers. It worked with hers, back and forth. He squeezed when he wanted more pressure and let off when he wanted less.

It was hot. She loved that he guided her, that he showed her how he wanted it and that his fingers lay over hers. She liked that connection. It made it more personal.

His fingers gathered the strands of hair and then danced across her scalp in a gentle, loving motion that belied the urgent way his hips shoved toward her.

He sank deep, held himself there for a long moment, and then eased back out, allowing her a moment to catch her breath. Then he repeated the action, his hand covering hers, moving both his hand and hers up and down his rigid erection.

"Do you want me to come in your mouth, Zoe?"

She tilted her head back, allowing the head of his dick to rest on her bottom lip. He stared down at her, his gaze so intense it raised goose bumps down her arms.

She nodded and sucked the tip farther into her mouth again. He closed his eyes and groaned and then pushed forward with his hips until her mouth met their joined hands.

"Then do it, baby. Make me come."

He released her hand and delved his fingers into her hair so that both his hands were holding her head. She gripped his cock and sucked him deep. She began to move faster, gripped him harder, moving in rhythm with her mouth.

His fingers tightened in her hair, and he strained forward, going up on tiptoe. No longer was she doing all the work. He fucked hard, going as deep as he could. She jerked harder and began swallowing as soon as the first hot jet of semen splashed over her tongue.

He filled her mouth again, and she had to swallow rapidly to keep up. He came and kept coming until some of the semen spilled down her chin. He slid one last time to the very back of her throat and held there as his entire body trembled against her.

Finally he let go, withdrawing from her mouth. Some of the liquid dripped onto the floor as she gulped for air. She reached up to wipe her mouth with the back of her hand, but Brody stopped her.

He put his fingers under her chin and tipped her up so he could see her. He smiled. A predatory male smile that screamed satisfaction. His eyes gleamed with an unholy light that almost scared her.

"Now *this* is my fantasy," he rasped out. "You on your knees and my cum all over your mouth."

She smiled faintly. It was all she could manage. She was out of breath and if she tried to stand right now, she'd hit the floor.

He reached down, holding both his hands to her. She slid her fingers into his grip and let him help her up. Then he turned her in Tate's direction and gently urged her forward.

She took an unsteady step, but Tate was there to help her. His jeans were drawn tight at his groin, and his hands trembled against her flesh.

He took her by the shoulders and led her to the couch, to the big, fluffy arm at the end. Without a word, he pushed her down so that her belly cradled the arm. She wiped her mouth with her arm before putting both hands down on the cushions for support. Her feet left the floor as she got into a more comfortable position.

Again she heard the sound of a zipper, and she tensed as Tate's hands palmed her ass. He caressed the cheeks and then slipped one hand below, his fingers sliding through her wetness.

"Oh yeah, you're ready for me," he breathed.

The head of his cock bumped against her before he found the spot and thrust deep. She closed her eyes and surged forward as he rippled across swollen tissues.

If she expected him to go at it like a dog after a bitch in heat, she was wrong. He was surprising—achingly—gentle.

He withdrew slowly, and the sensation across her super-sensitive flesh was amazing. Then he inched forward, stopping and then pushing, working back to his depth with slow, measured movements.

She tried to push back against him, wanting, needing something more. It was driving her insane and she was already so aroused from Brody's blowjob that it wouldn't take much to get her off.

Tate seemed to know that, and it also seemed he was determined to torture her.

She groaned helplessly. "Tate, please."

His palm smoothed over her buttocks, to the small of her back and then up her spine in sweet, reassuring caresses. God, it felt good to be touched by this man.

Then he leaned down and kissed the area between her shoulder blades. Just one gentle kiss, but it evoked powerful longing inside her. She liked being so treasured by these men. She loved the care they took with her even when they were being rough and raunchy.

Their last escapade had been hot and breathless. A thrill ride that never stopped until the very end. This . . . this was slow, sweet lovemaking, and it unhinged her.

"I love your ass," Tate murmured as he moved his hands back to cup her buttocks. "It's absolutely perfect. Full, lush. I love to watch you walk. I especially love fucking you and watching it move every time I thrust into you. I love fucking you, Zoe. It's absolutely, goddamn perfect."

A knot formed in her throat. Swelled rapidly until it was all she could do to breathe around it. What was he doing to her?

He pushed forward again, still in no hurry, his strokes gentle, but he filled her. He leaned down to brush his mouth across her back again and she moaned.

She wanted his mouth on hers. She wanted to taste him, feel his tongue duel with hers. She wanted him to run his lips over her neck, especially her neck, and then she wanted him to suck her breasts in those slow, gentle movements he was showing her now.

She didn't want sex with him. She wanted to make love with him.

He rocked against her a little faster now, his hips pressing against her ass with each thrust. He'd grown quiet, and she could hear the harsh sounds of his breaths escaping onto her back.

"I want you to come with me, Zoe. Tell me what I need to do," he bit out.

"Kiss me again," she whispered. She was already so close. So very close.

He thrust hard into her and then leaned down to run his tongue up her spine. Near the top he kissed her again, his mouth exceedingly gentle against her flesh.

She tightened around him, gripping his cock as her orgasm started as a light flutter and then floated through her with wicked, sweet intensity.

"Ah, Zoe," he groaned out. He pulled back and then thrust again, harder this time. His movements picked up speed and force until the couch creaked underneath them.

She closed her eyes again and let out a cry as she unraveled from the inside out. Heat bloomed in her pussy and fanned outward, racing through her body like an inferno.

He pushed into her one last time and stood there shuddering against her, his hands gripping her ass. Gradually his grip lessened and then he rested his cheek against her back, his breath blowing over her skin.

"I'm crushing you," he said apologetically as he stepped back.

He carefully pulled out of her body, and the release of his cock sent another aftershock of pure pleasure singing through her body.

She started to push herself up, but Tate leaned over and pulled her into his arms. He eased her over the arm of the couch until her feet hit the floor and she was facing him.

Their eyes met, and as if he had heard her innermost thoughts, he leaned in, hesitantly at first, but when she didn't pull away, his lips met hers.

She melted into his arms. She wrapped her arms around his neck and leaned into the kiss. It was everything she imagined it would be.

Gentle, yet demanding. His tongue brushed her lips, a request for her to open to him. She parted her lips and met the slide of his tongue with hers.

She sighed and let him deepen the kiss until her mouth was fused solidly with his, their tongues tangling in a warm rush. Man, but he could kiss.

When he finally pulled away, she stared up at him, her sight a little fuzzy. She swayed, and he smiled as he put out a hand to steady her.

"Yeah, me too," he murmured. "You do that to me, Zoe."

Remembering they had an audience, she turned in search of Chase. What would he think? What had he thought?

But it wasn't reproach she found in Chase's warm gaze. It was approval and desire. And love. For her. Like her, he might not have said it, but she could feel it reaching over the length of the room. There was no doubt in this moment that he didn't love her. The question was what the hell she was going to do about her feelings for Tate and Brody.

CHAPTER | TEN

Zoe returned to the nurses' station and stifled a yawn. Things had been crazy all week. Every crazy known to man, and a few undiscovered species as well, had turned up in the ER.

They'd had a record number of MVAs, at least a hundred sick, sniffling kids and an equal number of bitchy parents, and even two pregnant women who presented to the ER in active labor and fully dilated. Yeah, it had been a fun week. She'd twice been named a godmother. All because the other nurses suddenly found other patients to manage when the pregnant ladies checked in. The experience had been enough to put her off motherhood for at least a decade.

She'd barely seen the guys on account of pulling double shifts to handle the overflow. She hadn't even had much time to talk to Chase on the phone because she hadn't caught a long enough break to do it.

She missed them. All of them. She sighed as she checked the physician's orders for one of her patients. Another late clock-out was in her future. On the upside, she had two consecutive days off, and this time, she was turning her pager off. The downside was that Chase and the guys had started a forty-eight just that morning.

Her hair fell over her face, and she tiredly shoved it back behind her ear. She had two patients to admit and another to discharge and then maybe she could head home, get something decent to eat, and catch up on some sleep.

An hour later, she clocked out, collected her purse from her locker, and headed back by the nurses' station on her way out. She was so absorbed in getting to the exit that she nearly walked past Chase, who was leaning against the desk talking to one of the techs. He looked up and grabbed her by the waist. Before she could react, he crushed his lips to hers.

She managed to pull away. "Well hello, fancy meeting you here." She glanced down, expecting to see him in fire gear, but he was wearing street clothes. "Catch a break?"

He smiled. "Something like that. You out of here for the night?"

"Yeah, thank God," she breathed. "I was just on my way out. Want to walk me out?"

He fell into step beside her. "I'll do you one better."

"Oh?"

They hit the automatic doors at the main ER entrance, and she was further surprised to see Chase's truck parked in the ambulance bay.

"Yeah, come on, I'll give you a ride home so you can pack a bag."

She stopped and stared at him in confusion. "Bag?"

He smiled and pulled her into his arms, tipping up her chin to kiss her on the nose. "You, my baby, have been working way too hard, and I haven't seen nearly enough of you. I intend to rectify that right now."

A smile rippled over her lips and tightened her cheeks. "Bag?" she repeated. "Where are we going?"

"Nothing too fancy. I thought a weekend in Houston. Good food. Our favorite bars."

"I thought you had to work."

"I did. I called in a favor."

She threw her arms around him and hugged him fiercely. "Can I just say how much I love you?"

He stiffened and then slowly pulled away from her grasp. Utter seriousness and a little shock reflected in his eyes. Eyes that bored into her with intense scrutiny.

"Say that again," he said hoarsely.

Oh hell. This hadn't been the way she'd wanted to tell him. She gathered his shirt in her fists and let her head fall forward.

"Stupid, stupid, stupid," she muttered as she beat her head against his chest.

"Hey," he said. He tucked his knuckle under her chin and nudged until she looked up at him. "What's going on?"

She sighed. "This isn't the way I wanted to tell you."

He smiled and ran his thumb over her cheek. "But you meant it."

"Yeah, I meant it. I've loved you for so long, Chase." She leaned into his body and kissed the hard line of his jaw. "But I wanted to tell you when things were perfect. But I can't seem to get a time when we're together and not working lately."

"I can't think of a more perfect time or place," he said huskily.

He found her lips and covered them with his. Heat snaked down her spine as he hungrily devoured her mouth. Their breaths grew more strained, and her chest tightened as her oxygen-starved lungs begged for mercy. His tongue pushed inward, coaxing her to return his advance. She licked the tip of his tongue with hers and then sucked it farther into her mouth.

He pulled away, his eyes blazing. He palmed her face and stared intently down at her. He trailed his fingers down the line of her face, stroking and caressing.

"I love you too, Zoe. So damn much."

She smiled until her lips hurt. "What a pair we are."

He reached down and took her hands in his. "Come on. Let's blow this joint."

She laughed and let him pull her toward his truck.

They stopped at the house first. While she showered, Chase packed a bag for her. In a half hour, they were on the road to Houston.

Two hours later, Chase parked under the hotel awning. "Want to come in with me to check in?"

He came around to open her door, tucked her hand into his, and they walked into the spacious lobby.

"Gorgeous hotel," she whispered as they approached the front desk.

He shot her a curious look. "Why are you whispering, babe?"

She laughed. "Sorry, it just seemed the thing to do. Everything looks so . . . regal."

"You're a nut."

He tucked her hand into his as he gave the clerk his name and got the keys.

"Tell you what," he said as he handed her a key. "Why don't you go up to the suite and wait for me and I'll get the luggage and meet you there."

She leaned up to kiss him. "Deal."

Chase and Zoe left the restaurant hand in hand and walked down the street toward a trendy bar they frequented when in Houston. The day had been fantastic. The previous night as well. They'd made love and whispered the words that felt so squeaky new and clean. In the morning, they'd ordered room service and eaten in bed. Then they'd made love again and gone shopping at the Galleria.

Full from a delicious dinner, they entered the bar and headed over to get a drink. Zoe rested against Chase's hip as he placed their orders and sighed in contentment as he dug his fingers into her hair and stroked through the tresses.

"I had so much fun today," she said when their drinks were shoved across the counter.

Chase kissed the side of her neck, causing her to shiver in delight.

"You've worked way too much lately. You needed the break, and I was getting tired of never seeing you."

She smiled and leaned farther into him. "I've missed you, too. I've missed Brody and Tate, too. The house is quiet without you guys."

"They're missing you, too. They get all grumpy and surly when you're not around," Chase teased.

They settled onto chairs by the bar and watched the colorful array of people buzz around the small dance floor and the bar area. It was nice to get out after being cooped up in the ER all week. If she had to see one more sick person, she was going to be on sick leave herself.

"You ever fantasized about picking up a stranger in a bar?" he asked casually.

She cocked her head and considered it. "Yeah, I guess. I mean I don't know if it has to be a bar exactly, but meeting a hot stranger in a public place is always titillating."

Chase tipped his beer bottle in the direction of the door. "What do you think about him?"

Zoe turned and surveyed the tall, well-built guy who'd walked into the bar. He had on jeans that cupped him in all the right places. The T-shirt he wore stretched across a broad chest and muscular shoulders. Tattoos ripped down his arms in colorful patterns she couldn't discern from the distance.

"You mean Mr. Bad Boy?" she murmured. "What do you mean what do I think?"

"Would you fuck him?"

She laughed. "You mean would he replace anyone on my current to-do list?"

Chase grinned. "I'm thinking he wouldn't overtake The Rock or Oded Fehr."

Her lips twisted into a dreamy smile. "Nope."

"But would you fuck him? He's looking at you right now. I'd say he's definitely interested. He's looking at you, then looking at me and trying to figure out what my status is."

It took all her restraint not to whip her head back around to look.

"I guess I'd fuck him if you weren't available," she teased.

"Go talk to him."

Her eyes widened. "What? Are you crazy? What am I supposed to talk to him about?"

Chase smiled. "You talk to him about fucking you. Take him back to our hotel room. I want to watch."

He was serious. Behind the easygoing smile, his eyes glittered. Was the purpose of the unexpected trip? Had he done it to set up another sexual fantasy? But whose was this, his or hers? Both?

She glanced over at the stranger to see that he'd made his way to the far end of the bar. He was talking to the bartender. When he got his beer, he turned to survey the room, one hip resting on the scarred wood of the bar. He sipped idly at the beer, his interest seeming to be on scanning the occupants of the crowded pub.

Then he turned his head and met her gaze. She almost ducked guiltily away, but something in his eyes made her remain steady, staring back unabashedly as his gaze drifted up and down her body.

His eyes were dark. Either really dark brown or maybe hazel. His hair was black as midnight and hung to his shoulders in unruly stands. He wore a tan that said he spent a lot of time outdoors. He could be twenty-five or thirty-five. He had a timeless look he'd probably carry with him into his fifties. Rugged, masculine, mouth-wateringly handsome. His arms were made to touch, and his chest to lick. If his cock was as impressive as the rest of him, he'd be one hell of a package.

He cocked one eyebrow as if in question, then tipped his beer bottle in salute.

"Probably has a small dick," she muttered. "Too much perfection."

Chase choked on his laughter. "I don't hear you complain about my dick size."

She broke her fascination with the stranger and turned back to Chase. "That's because you *are* the perfect package. Unusual. I count myself lucky I don't have to settle. You have a great dick, but you aren't one," she added cheekily.

Chase pulled her into his arms until they circled her waist. He leaned in to nibble at the side of her neck, and her knees buckled.

Oh sweet, merciful God.

"Stop that," she hissed. "I'm not going to orgasm in public."

He chuckled and kissed the soft pulse underneath her ear. "Go talk to him, Zoe. Ask him to dance. Invite him back to the hotel."

She gulped nervously. "Are you sure?"

"If you're sure. Tell him where to meet you. I'll drive you back over. I want to make sure you're safe."

"Is this your fantasy or mine?"

"For now, it's mine. Later it can be yours," he said with a hint of amusement.

She twisted in his arms, then reached up to trace the line of his jaw. "And what do you want him to do to me?"

"Whatever he wants to. Whatever you want him to."

She shivered under his hands as he stroked down her arms.

"In that case, I'll be right back."

She pushed away from the bar, swallowed the butterflies, and started resolutely in the direction of her target. She stifled a giggle at the idea that she was *targeting* a man who was twice her size. He could probably snap her like a twig.

Trying not to focus on that particular thought, she stopped beside the guy and motioned for the bartender. Her mystery man slid his gaze sideways, then turned so he faced her.

He didn't say anything at first. He studied her with a lazy gaze that seemed to peel every piece of her clothing off. One piece at a time.

She leaned closer to the bartender as he came over, and she caught a whiff of her guy's scent. Mmmm. He smelled good enough to eat. Or at least pounce on and do her best to lick every inch of him.

When she would have extended her credit card to the bartender, the man beside her put his hand on her arm.

"Whatever the lady wants, put it on my tab."

His low, husky voice washed over sensitive nerve endings. The hairs at her nape prickled and stood up. Her nipples puckered, and a delicious twitch between her legs had her squirming her discomfort.

Was this supposed to turn her on as much as it did? She wondered if she should feel guilty but quickly shook off that notion. Chase had always encouraged her fantasies, and since this particular one was his suggestion, she could hardly be blamed for taking him up on it.

"Thank you," she murmured. She cocked her head to the side and allowed her gaze to drift over his chest and down to the bulge in his jeans. "What's your name?"

"Dillon. Yours?"

She extended her hand and smiled. "Zoe. Glad to meet you, and thank you for the drink."

He closed his fingers around her hand and instead of shaking, he gripped it, turned it up, and rubbed his thumb sensuously over the top of her knuckles.

"Zoe. It suits you. And you're quite welcome."

The bartender slid the amaretto sour across the counter, and she picked it up to sip at the tart drink.

He watched her drink, watched her swallow. His gaze never left her, and her internal body temp had just skyrocketed.

"Do you like to dance?"

She set her drink down. "I do. With the right partner."

He moved in, cupped her jaw, then slid his fingers down the column of her neck and over her shoulder.

"I don't think you'll find me . . . lacking."

"No," she whispered. "I don't suppose I will."

Her drink forgotten, she allowed Dillon to guide her toward the dance floor. His hand burned the skin of her waist, and when they reached the center, his palm slid over the bare skin of her belly as he turned her to face him.

She had no knowledge of what played—fast or slow. The only thing she was aware of was strong arms enfolding her, pulling her against a hard body, and a warm spicy scent that filled her nose.

His hands drifted downward to cup her ass. He paused a moment and stared down at her as if gauging her reaction. She liked his directness. He'd seen something he liked, and like her, he was going after it.

His fingers spread wide, possessive, and he pulled her into his groin so she could feel the hard bulge straining at his fly.

"See what you do to me?" he whispered into her ear.

"What are you going to do about it?"

"What are you proposing?"

She looped her arms around his thickly corded neck and cocked her head back to stare into his eyes. She'd definitely been right. Dark with just a few flecks of gold and green. He was exotically handsome. His face held a hint of wild, and it excited the hell out of her.

"One night, no strings. You show me that magnificent body of yours and everything you know about pleasing a woman."

His nostrils flared and his arms tightened at her waist. "I'm liking your idea."

She leaned in close so he'd be sure to hear what she said next. "There is one condition."

He arched a brow questioningly.

She nodded toward the bar where Chase lounged on a bar stool, his back to the bar. He was nursing a beer and watching Zoe and Dillon with hooded eyes.

"See that guy?"

Dillon nodded. "What about him?"

"I came with him. He's my boyfriend. He gets to watch."

Dillon paused, then turned his gaze back on Zoe. "And he's okay with this. You and me, I mean. He's just going to be okay with me taking his girl home to fuck?"

She shook her head and allowed her hands to wander down his chest, enjoying the dips and lines. It was all she could do not to lean in and kiss him. A man who looked this good had to taste divine.

"We go to my hotel. Separately. Chase will be there to make sure I'm . . . safe. He wants to watch. What happens between us is up to you. No interference unless you cross the line."

Dillon glanced back at Chase and then turned her into his arms as they moved across the dance floor. He backed her to the far wall, trapping her between the surface and his chest.

"So you and I fuck. He watches. Tomorrow morning we go our separate ways. No strings."

She nodded. "If that's acceptable to you."

His grin was slow and so damned sexy. "Sugar, I don't know a man alive who wouldn't think he'd just been handed the keys to the kingdom. Where are you staying?"

Her excitement growing, she leaned up on tiptoe and let her lips brush over his ear. She whispered the name of the hotel and her room number.

"Meet me there in an hour," she said as she drew away.

She started to move around him to return to Chase, but he caught her arm and pulled her back between him and the wall.

"Not so fast. I want a little appetizer to tide me over."

Before she could respond, he lowered his head and crushed his lips to hers. He placed both hands on her belly then pushed upward to the underswells of her breasts.

She tasted beer on his tongue and lips. It mixed with the fruity sweetness of the sour she'd drunk. He delved deeper, his mouth moving possessively over hers. He rubbed his thumbs over her nipples, and she tensed as intense pleasure radiated through her belly.

Not willing to let him get away with winding her up, she lowered her hands to his groin and cupped him intimately. She let her fingers wander over the growing bulge and heard him swear against her lips.

She smiled and pulled away. "See you in an hour?"

His eyes blazed with desire, and harsh breaths spilled from his mouth. He looked like he wanted to devour her whole. She was more than willing to let him. He could eat her piece by piece just as long as he had that sinful mouth on her body.

"Bet on it."

She cupped his cock in her palm one last time before finally pulling away to walk back toward Chase. Her eyes found Chase, but he was looking beyond her to Dillon. She turned to look over her shoulder to see Dillon's gaze locked with Chase. There seemed to be some weird male communication going on. Maybe Dillon was making sure it was okay with Chase or maybe he was saying he simply didn't care.

When she returned to Chase, he pulled her into his arms and found her lips in a fierce, possessive kiss. She wrapped her arms around her neck and returned his kiss with equal fierceness.

"You okay?" Chase asked when he finally pulled away.

She smiled as she dragged deep breaths into her lungs. "I was scared to death at first, but he's an okay guy. Not an asshole at all."

"And he turns you on."

She nodded. "Yeah, he does."

Chase thumbed her swollen bottom lip. "It turns me on to see you turned on. Watching the two of you all but go at it against the wall over there was incredibly hot. I wasn't the only one who thought so, judging by the number of guys checking it out."

She grinned. "Maybe you should ask them over to watch."

"You're turning into quite the exhibitionist," he murmured. "I think I like it."

"I told him to meet us at the hotel in an hour."

Chase tossed a few bills onto the bar and then stood, circling her waist with his arm.

"Then let's get out of here."

CHAPTER | ELEVEN

When Chase and Zoe entered their hotel suite, as soon as the door closed behind them, Chase pulled Zoe into his arms. Their lips met in a heated rush that had them both gasping for air.

When his mouth worked down her jaw, she tensed and put her hands on his chest.

"Don't you touch my neck, Chase. If you so much as breathe on it, I'll go off like a rocket."

He pulled away and grinned. "You all hot and bothered tonight, baby?"

Her eyes narrowed. "You know damn well I am. The bar scene was hot. Knowing you were watching while I picked up another guy was a lot more exciting than I would have ever imagined."

He kissed her lightly on the lips and then pulled her toward the bedroom. There was a pricey-looking boutique bag on the bed that she saw as soon as they entered. She glanced in Chase's direction, but he just smiled, then picked up the bag and held it out to her.

She glanced in to see a mound of silky material. White and lacy. Her fingers delved into the softness and she pulled out a gorgeous, sexy-as-sin set of lingerie.

"Oh, it's beautiful," she breathed as she held up the top.

It was sheer with spaghetti straps and the waist was high so that a strip of her belly would be bared. The bottoms, wow. The bottom was a tiny triangle with thin little strings to hold it around her waist. It might cover the *V* of her legs. If she held really still and didn't do much walking.

Suddenly suspicious of the timing, she glanced over at Chase and arched her eyebrow.

"You planned this, didn't you? I mean you planned to scope a guy in the bar. I wondered what this impromptu trip was about. Not that I'm complaining, but I figured it had to be more than some wild hair."

He smiled. "I might have had hopes as to how the evening would end."

Holding the lingerie in one hand, she rubbed her other hand up her arm in a nervous gesture. "I've got a thousand butterflies running wild in my stomach."

"In a good way?"

"Yeah," she said. "A very good way."

He leaned in to kiss her. It was light and reassuring. "Why don't you get undressed. I'm going to get comfortable on the couch and get ready to watch the show."

Chase sauntered over to the sofa and reclined, putting both arms along the top. His eyes narrowed to slits when she began undressing. Since he was consigned to watching, she decided there was no harm in a little teasing. Since she had to get into that lingerie some way . . .

Watching from underneath her lashes, she slowly peeled away her jeans. She turned so her ass was pushed into the air in Chase's direction while she stepped from the legs. She took her sweet time rising, and she rotated again so he had a prime view of her breasts as she pulled her shirt over her head.

"You are such a damn tease," he said hoarsely.

Satisfaction tightened her cheek at the frank appraisal in his eyes. With a saucy wiggle, she hooked her thumbs in the band of her panties and inched them down her legs until she let the material fall gently to the floor between her feet.

Inspired by his accusation of teasing, she sashayed across the floor in just her bra until she was standing directly in front of Chase. With wide, innocent eyes, she said, "I could use some help with my bra."

Not giving him time to respond, she slowly turned, then backed the one step between his legs and lowered herself to perch on the edge of the couch, her ass cradled in his groin.

Clumsily, his fingers glanced over the clasp of her bra. It took him three attempts before he had the hooks free. She let the straps fall down her shoulders and she rose, holding the cups to her breasts before she walked back toward the bed.

Then she turned, looked him in the eye and let the bra fall to the floor.

The flare of pure male satisfaction in her eyes fired every one of her cylinders.

She reached for the silky scraps of the lingerie and sighed in contentment as the satin fell over her skin. More than the way it felt, she loved the way she looked. Ultra-feminine. Sexy and desirable. It was all there to see, reflected in Chase's burning gaze.

She was debating whether to crawl onto the bed and relax or continue teasing Chase when a sharp knock at the door sounded. Her heart leapt into her throat, and she whirled around in the direction of the bedroom entrance.

With a quick glance back at Chase, she steadied her nerves and then went to let Dillon in. A check of the peephole confirmed his presence in the hallway. He stood idly, hands shoved into his pock-

ets as he stood back away from the door. He was moving forward
to knock again when she gripped the handle and opened it.

Now she wished she'd worn a robe, or a T-shirt, or something
to cover the lingerie. By greeting him at the door in the scant
getup, she'd set the tone—and the speed at which things would get
kicked off.

Dillon's gaze smoldered. Raw appreciation glittered in his eyes
as he seemingly took in every inch of her body.

"Going to invite me in?" he drawled.

She released her knuckle-white grip on the door frame and
stepped back to allow him entrance.

Dillon looked around as he stepped inside. "Where's the boyfriend?"

"In the bedroom," she said.

"Well, before we go in there, you need to tell me the lines."

She looked at him in confusion.

"As in the lines I'm not supposed to cross."

"Oh. Well, there aren't many. As long as you don't hurt me or
do something freaky."

Dillon hooked his thumbs in his belt loops and rocked back on
his heels. "Define *freaky*."

Her cheeks bloomed with heat, and she self-consciously looked
away. "Um, well, maybe the question should be what are the lines
you won't cross?"

"I don't hurt women," he said bluntly. "Not even if they want
me to. I'm not into bisexual games with the boyfriend. Thought we
should get that out of the way."

Zoe nearly choked and struggled to keep laughter from spilling
out. "Neither is Chase. He just likes to watch."

Dillon nodded. "I understand. Watching can be hot."

"What else?" she asked, curious now about this man and his
personal boundaries.

"Not into scat or pissing."

"Oh God, me neither," she blurted out.

He smiled. "Good. Looks like we're on the same page. Anything you don't want me to do while we're talking boundaries?"

"No," she said softly.

"So anything else goes. You sure about that."

"If I don't like it, I'll tell you to stop."

He nodded approvingly. "That was next on my list."

"Okay, well, looks like we're all set."

"Yeah, it does. Now come here."

She started forward, drawn to the command in his sexy voice.

He tipped her chin up and lowered his mouth to hers. He was surprisingly gentle, his lips melting over hers. Their tongues met, danced, and retreated, their tastes mingling.

She gasped in surprise when he swept her into his arms and carried her into the bedroom. From the corner of her eye, she saw Chase focus his attention on her and Dillon as soon as they cleared the door. Dillon, however, solidly ignored Chase's presence. She was grateful for that. She didn't want it to be awkward.

Dillon tumbled her onto the bed and began to undress. He discarded his clothing in a no-nonsense fashion that had nothing to do with teasing. But the very act of him stripping out of those jeans made her heart pump in anticipation. She couldn't wait to see him naked. She wanted to see how far his tattoos went over his body.

He was a boxers guy, which really didn't surprise her. He looked like he was into comfort with minimal fuss. When she saw the size of his erection straining against those boxers, she understood why he needed as much room as possible.

He stripped out of his T-shirt, and she stared unabashedly at the colorful tattoo that splashed over the right shoulder. He had tats on either arm but the one on his right was one big pattern that stretched the length of his arm onto his chest.

"Turn around," she murmured.

He complied, turning slowly until his back was to her. As she'd expected, the tattoo covered most of the right side of his back as well. It was an intricate design, one that told a story. It fascinated her. There was a battle. Dragons, mythical beings, an assortment of "interesting" characters. Daggers, swords. He'd turned his body into a battlefield.

"You done?" he asked as he turned back around.

She smiled and nodded. "I love the tattoo."

"Glad you approve. It turns a lot of women off."

"Not me," she murmured.

He reached for his boxers and shoved them down his legs. His cock jutted outward, long and thick. Her fingers itched to touch him, caress his length. He was very nicely proportioned.

He moved forward until he stood against the bed. Her gaze roved eagerly over his body, examining every muscle. His thighs were monstrous. His waist was narrow and he had a six-pack to die for.

And that cock.

Deciding there was no reason at all she shouldn't touch him right now, she rolled to her hands and knees and reached for him.

He went tense but quickly leaned into her caress the moment her fingers circled him.

Smooth, silky soft. But rigid as steel. She rolled her hand up his length, watching as he got harder. The broad, blunt head darkened to a dusky shade. She mentally calculated just how much of him she could take. She hoped it was all of him.

She palmed his heavy sac and rolled his balls in her grasp. Oh yeah, balls deep, pounding into her without mercy.

"Undress for me," he rasped.

She pulled her hand away and knelt up on the bed so they were nearly eye to eye. Then she slowly pulled the thin straps of the top over her shoulders. The material slid downward, catching momentarily at her breasts before finally sliding down to her waist.

"You have gorgeous breasts."

She smiled. "Glad you approve."

He cupped both of the full mounds in his hands and in a sudden movement, he pushed her down so she was on her back. Then he yanked impatiently at her bottom, taking it and her top down her legs.

"I find I'm running out of patience," he said.

"I find I don't mind."

He lowered his body to hers, and the first electric shock of contact sizzled over her skin with amazing speed. He felt so damn good. She turned her head so she could see Chase in her periphery. He sat quietly, merely watching, his avid gaze taking in the scene before him.

Zoe found herself wanting to make this every bit as hot for him as she hoped it would be for her.

Dillon nibbled at her jaw and then followed with his tongue, soothing the place his teeth grazed. When he got to her lips, he ravaged her mouth. Rough, then tender. There was so much wild trapped in this man. She could feel him holding back, and she didn't want him holding back anything.

Patiently, he kissed each part of her skin, working down her neck to her shoulder and then to her breasts. She shuddered uncontrollably when his tongue licked over her nipples. He played with her breasts a long while, alternating between the two. He lightly teased the points and then sucked them hard between his teeth.

She was desperate, her hands flying over his back, to his neck, down to his ass. She couldn't control the wicked pleasure snaking through her body. Didn't want to.

He chuckled around her breast as he sucked forcefully.

"I wonder if you'll go as wild for me when my mouth is on your pussy."

She closed her eyes and arched helplessly into him as he kissed and licked his way down her belly toward the juncture of her legs.

He slid off the bed, kneeling now, and he hooked his hands underneath her knees and jerked her to the edge so that his mouth was level with her pussy. As he spread her legs, he pressed his lips to the inside of her thigh and gently kissed a path upward.

Fingers pulled carefully at the delicate folds, parting them as he revealed her clit to his seeking mouth. First he just touched the tip of his tongue to the taut bud. She tensed and clamped her legs around his head.

He laughed and carefully pushed her legs back down. "You like that, I take it."

"Mmm-hmm."

"And to think, I'm just getting started."

"Oh God . . ."

He slid his tongue over her entrance and back up to her clit. He was exceedingly gentle with his mouth. She loved a guy who knew how to go down on a woman. It really was an art, and unfortunately, not enough guys ever got any good at it.

He teased her clit, licking lightly and then sucking ever so gently with his lips. Using his fingers to keep her open to him, he lapped at every part, tracing a path down to her opening.

He pressed his tongue inward. He rimmed her entrance and then slipped inside, stroking until she was arching spasmodically to meet each thrust.

Her knees shook. The muscles in her legs twitched uncontrollably. The amazing thing was he hadn't touched her neck, and he hadn't devoted an extraordinary amount of time to her breasts, and yet she was seconds from coming.

She panted and strained upward. Her fingers balled into fists at her sides and she squeezed her eyes shut, teeth ground together as she fought the sharp rise of release.

He seemed to know precisely when to stop so that her release was delayed. He'd bring her to the very brink and then pull away to let her come back down.

"You taste and smell amazing," he said as he lifted his head from her pussy. "I could do this all night."

She groaned and hooked one leg over his broad shoulders. "I'm not sure I'd survive."

His husky laughter thrilled her senses. The man was just too sexy for his own good.

"I want you inside me."

He got to his feet and leaned over her, sliding his chest up her body. He hooked one arm under her leg and pulled upward until she was open to his probing cock.

"I think I can arrange that."

Her eyes widened. "Condom. If you don't have any, there's some in the nightstand."

He smiled again. "Already taken care of, sweetheart. I told you I wouldn't hurt you. That included protecting you."

He released her leg long enough to guide his cock to the mouth of her pussy, and then he returned his hand to her leg and pushed, opening her wider.

With one thrust, he lodged himself firmly within her. She groaned. He made a strangled noise. Their eyes flew open and they stared at one another as he fought to keep his control.

"Don't be easy," she murmured. "You won't hurt me."

His eyes narrowed and his nostrils flared as he sucked in deep breaths through his nose. "Be sure what you're saying, Zoe. I don't have a lot of control right now. You're telling me that doesn't matter. But be real damn sure what you're saying because I'm going to have you. I'm going to fuck you hard. Your pussy, your mouth, and your ass."

"What are you waiting for?"

With a growl, he withdrew and hammered forward. He rose over her, until he was in a more dominant position. Then he hooked both arms under her legs and yanked upward until she was wide open and vulnerable to his advances.

He began fucking her with ruthless precision. The man was a machine. He chased one orgasm from her and then continued fucking her until the beginnings of another stirred deep within.

Through it all, he watched, his eyes coolly assessing her. He was the epitome of control, and his staying power was nothing short of amazing.

She turned her head and fuzzily looked in Chase's direction. Their eyes met and she savored the connection with the man she loved as another man worked in and out of her body.

Chase stared back at Zoe and saw eyes clouded with intense pleasure. He wanted to be over there, stroking her hair from her eyes, kissing her, offering her his touch and reassurance as this big man rode her hard.

The entire evening had been a haze of heightened anticipation and sexual awareness. He'd sported a hard-on from the moment she'd crossed the bar and came on to Dillon. He'd watched as they danced and watched as Dillon had slammed her against the wall and devoured her. He understood the urge because it was one he fought every time he was around her. Chase couldn't get enough of her. He doubted he ever would.

Chase watched as Dillon covered Zoe, his much larger body blanketing her as his hips powered back and forth. The loud smack of bodies meeting sounded erotic in the room.

Then Dillon reared up, stepped back off the bed, and flipped Zoe over onto her stomach. Not wasting any time, he positioned himself between her legs and thrust hard.

Her buttocks flattened under his weight, and she turned her head so she faced Chase. Her eyes were wild and her fingers curled into the comforter. Her body shook with each thrust, and still, she held Chase's gaze, reached out to him over the distance.

Chase was so damn hard that he was going to bust a nut. And the evening was just beginning. He cupped his groin and squeezed, trying to assuage the ache in his balls.

Dillon was paying him no attention whatsoever, which suited Chase just fine. He'd prefer the man forget he was even here. And given the fact his sole focus seemed to be Zoe, Chase reached down and freed his cock.

He nearly wilted in relief as his cock sprang into his open hand. He rubbed up and down, enjoying the sensation as he watched his woman get fucked by another man.

Dillon pushed her hard into the mattress, leaned over to press his hands on either side of her body, and began fucking her in long, brutal strokes.

Each time his hips slapped against her buttocks, she flinched, closed her eyes, and let out a breathy gasp that had Chase's balls drawing up.

Dillon pushed into her, flattened her ass against his hips, and then went still. "You have KY?" he asked Zoe.

It took her a moment to respond, and her voice was shaky when she did. "In the nightstand."

He pulled away and then urged her up onto her knees.

"Keep your head down, get comfortable. I'm going to fuck that sweet ass of yours."

Chase could see the shudder work over Zoe's small frame. The image of her being ass-fucked was a powerful one. He squeezed the head of his cock and stopped his up-and-down motion to stave off his release. He wanted to see this.

Dillon rummaged in the nightstand and then pulled out the tube of KY. Chase watched as Dillon squeezed some onto his hand and then rubbed it up down the length of his latex-sheathed cock. When he was done, he squirted more onto his fingers and tossed the tube aside.

He came back to the bed and slipped his fingers over Zoe's opening. He circled the tight ring and then pressed inward until she opened for the tip of his finger. Back and forth, he worked patiently, until finally he pulled away, reached for one of the towels lying by the bed, and wiped his hand.

"Are you ready for me, Zoe?" he asked when he returned and gripped her hips. "You were so tight around my finger, I don't know how the hell you're going to take my cock, but damn if I can't wait to feel you try."

"God, yes," Zoe ground out.

He spread her ass cheeks and fitted his cock to her tight opening. Chase sucked in all his breath when he watched the other man push forward, ruthlessly opening her.

Zoe made a sound that sounded like a cross between pain and intense pleasure. Dillon paused, allowing her time to adjust to his size.

The sight of her opening stretched around another man's cock nearly had Chase coming in his hand. He breathed in harsh, short spurts of air, his nostrils quivering. His oxygen-starved lungs screamed for more air, but his chest was squeezed too tight for him to comply.

And then, with one hard thrust, Dillon shoved forward and his hips met her ass.

She yelped and tried to lean forward, but Dillon wouldn't let her escape. He gripped her waist and held her firmly in place. She wiggled and squirmed, but he followed her every movement, staying locked deep in her ass.

Still holding her tightly, he withdrew, allowing his cock to slide nearly all the way out. Then he thrust hard and disappeared into her ass again. Then he pulled completely out and held her cheeks apart so that her opening gaped, and Chase got a prime view.

Chase stifled the groan, not wanting to intrude. Dillon seemed perfectly happy to pretend Chase wasn't there, and Chase was just fine with that. The last thing he wanted was for the man to look over and see Chase with his dick hanging out.

Dillon positioned his cock and drove inward again. Zoe gasped and cried out. Dillon palmed her ass and dug his fingers into her flesh as he rode her. The sound of his hips smacking against her ass was the only sound in the room. Each thrust was harder than the last until she began to slide downward, no longer able to hold up under the strain of his body.

He followed her down to the bed, spread her legs with his knees, and began to ride her furiously, his body humping over her ass like a machine.

"I'm going to come all over your ass," Dillon growled.

He reared up, withdrew, and tore at the condom. It went sailing across the room, and then he jerked frantically at his cock just inches above the pale flesh of Zoe's ass.

Chase's grip tightened around his own cock at the sight of her lying there, ass spread and still open. As the first splatter of Dillon's cum landed across her cheeks, Chase erupted too.

Dillon worked his cock back and forth. The semen splashed over her skin and dribbled downward into her opening. Some of it landed in the small of her back and across the backs of her thighs. There wasn't a part of her ass that wasn't decorated.

When his body gave one last jerk, Dillon rolled to the side of Zoe and kept one arm flung over her shoulders. Neither said much, but their heaving bodies told the story all too well.

Chase closed his eyes and worked the last of his orgasm. He sagged against the couch, still replaying the erotic image of Dillon curved over Zoe's body, fucking her for all he was worth.

Leaving them on the bed, he quietly got up and went into the bathroom to do a quick cleanup.

When Chase returned a few minutes later, Dillon was gently wiping the semen from Zoe's body while she lay motionless on the mattress. For the first time, Dillon looked directly at Chase.

"Mind if I use your shower to clean us both up?"

Chase nodded. "Go right ahead."

Dillon picked Zoe up in his arms and strode out toward the bathroom. A second later, Chase heard the shower come on. Chase resumed his position on the couch to the side of the bed and waited for what came next.

CHAPTER | TWELVE

Zoe came out of the bathroom first while Dillon remained behind to dry off. Wanting the moment alone with Chase before Dillon returned, she went immediately to the couch where Chase sat.

Chase's heated gaze warmed her to her toes. She slid onto his lap and cuddled into his embrace. He kissed her affectionately on the temple as she nuzzled closer to him.

"What did you think?" she whispered against his neck.

"It was incredibly hot. Did you enjoy it?"

"Mmm-hmm."

She drew away so she could look at him. She touched his face, then leaned in to kiss him.

"Did *you* enjoy it?"

He smiled. "Very much. You up for more, or is he leaving?"

She stretched, working some of the lethargy from her system. "Do you care if he stays the night?"

He touched the tip of her nose with his finger. "Enjoy yourself. I'm content to sit right here and watch."

She regarded him seriously. "I love you, you know."

His smile deepened. "Yeah, I know. Now go have fun."

He patted her on the rear as she got up to return to the bed. With one quick look back at him, she crawled onto the bed to wait for Dillon.

She didn't wait long. A few moments later, Dillon came out of the bathroom, a towel wrapped around his waist. She ate him up with her eyes as he strode purposefully toward the bed. He paused a foot away and ripped the towel from his waist.

His cock hung from the nest of dark hair, thick and long even at rest. The bed dipped as he got up next to her and stretched out.

"Use your mouth," he said. "Make me hard and then straddle me. I want you on top this time."

She crawled over to him and turned so she'd face him. She draped herself over one of his muscled thighs and carefully curled her hand around his cock.

It came to life, immediately stiffening as she ran her fingers up and down the silky, soft skin. She cupped and caressed his balls, rolling them between her fingers before gripping the base of his penis and working up again.

Finally she lowered her mouth so that the tip brushed over her lips. Her tongue swept out and circled the blunt crown. He smelled and tasted faintly of the soap he'd used to wash himself. She inhaled deeply, enjoying the contrast between the clean scent and his natural masculine smell.

When she closed her mouth over the head and sucked him inside her mouth, he groaned and strained upward to seat himself deeper.

While she sucked, she looked up to watch his face. His eyes glittered as he in turn watched her. He touched her hair and stroked over her head to her face, and then he let his fingers wander down her body until they came to a stop on the curve of her hip.

She was curled like a kitten next to him, her body lying at a slight angle with her feet resting on the pillow next to his head. She enjoyed his sensual caresses as she sucked him to rigid erectness.

A part of her wanted to prolong his blowjob as long as possible. She loved watching the myriad of expressions blow over his face as she made love to him with her mouth. But the other part of her couldn't wait to throw her leg over him and let him slide deep into her pussy.

He grew larger, filling her mouth with each downward slide. He swelled until it was difficult for her to stretch her lips around him.

Determined to give him as much pleasure as he'd given her earlier, she pushed him to the very back of her throat, keeping him lodged there as she swallowed around the tip.

His fingers tangled roughly in her hair, his movements becoming more frantic and less practiced.

Finally he pulled her away. He panted harshly, and his eyes gleamed with satisfaction.

"If you don't stop, I'm going to come before I ever get you on top of me."

She smiled, then reached over him for one of the condoms in the nightstand. "Can't have that."

She tore open the wrapper and then rolled the condom over his cock, stretching the latex around his broad width. Satisfied with the result, she hiked one leg over him and held him in place with her hand as she positioned herself above him.

With infinite care, she lowered herself, closing her eyes when the head breached her opening. She stretched to accommodate him. It was nearly painful but so intensely pleasurable that she huffed in short breaths to control her erratic pulse.

When he was halfway in, she realized she was going to have to work at getting him fully lodged. She let go and braced herself on his chest, enjoying the roll of muscles underneath her fingertips.

"Help me," she whispered.

His hands gripped her hips, holding her in place, and then he thrust upward. Her natural reaction was to arch up and away from him, but he held her in place and thrust again.

Her fingers dug into his flesh and she leaned forward, allowing him easier access. He curled his fingers into her ass and spread her wider. Then he thrust hard and deep.

She sank down onto him, felt his balls roll underneath her ass. She had him. All the way, and now she didn't want to let any part of him go.

His hands left her ass and he reached up to pluck lightly at her nipples. They stiffened and reacted, puckering into hard little knobs that throbbed in time with the throb between her legs.

"You're all the way there. Now ride me."

His guttural command spurred her to action. She rocked forward and then back. Hard. The sensation of him sliding through her pussy made her go cross-eyed. She hugged him tight and each time she moved, his cock dragged across tissues that sucked at him.

"Faster. Harder."

She obeyed and began to ride him. Her arousal eased his passage and with each downward slide, she took him to the balls.

"Can you come this way?" he murmured. "Do I need to do anything?"

"Mmmm," she moaned. "Touch me. My breasts. I'll come, just touch my breasts."

He cupped the mounds and brushed his thumb across the stiff points. "Like this?"

"Just like that."

"I'm not going to last long. Tell me what you need."

She closed her eyes, dangerously close to preceding him. Then she smiled. "Don't worry about me. Just come. As long as you keep touching my breasts, I'll be there. Probably before you."

He chuckled and then captured her nipples between his fingers, tweaking and pinching lightly.

She rose up and down, slamming down onto his cock, her breath squeezing torturously each time he came to rest deep within her.

He tensed and suddenly his fingers became more forceful at

her breasts. She reached down and slid a finger over her clit, then threw back her head as pleasure exploded through her body.

His shout sounded in her ears, but the world was one big fuzz ball around her. She was lost in her orgasm, in the incredible, mind-blowing sensation of her fingers at her clit, his fingers twisting and pulling at her nipples.

She went unbelievably slick around him so that he slid easily through her pussy now. He bowed up off the bed until her knees left the mattress. And then she fell forward, collapsing against his broad chest.

For a few seconds he continued arching gently into her until finally he stopped and they both lay there, ragged breaths tearing from their chests.

"That . . . was amazing," he croaked out.

She remained silent, eyes closed as she rested against his chest. He made a very nice bed.

He lifted a strand of her hair and idly played, letting it twist between his fingers as she came to her senses.

"Do something for me, Zoe."

She lifted her head to look at him.

He nodded in Chase's direction. "This whole setup was so he could watch. Now I want to watch while you go suck him off."

She eased off Dillon and let his cock slide from her pussy. When her feet hit the floor, her knees shook and she nearly sagged. She awkwardly made her way to where Chase sat. Glancing back at Dillon, she saw that he'd rolled to his side where he could easily see her and Chase. Then she looked at Chase to gauge his reaction to Dillon's request.

The bulge at his jeans told her he was anything but put off by the idea. She knelt in front of him, placed one hand over his groin, and leaned up to kiss him.

She took him hard, running her tongue over his lips in a demand to let her inside. Hot. Completely carnal, she ravaged his mouth, putting every bit of her desire into that simple caress.

He pushed impatiently against her hand, his erection hot and pulsing through the rough denim.

Rocking back, she hastily unbuttoned his fly and then carefully unzipped until she could reach in and pull out his cock.

Before she had it fully in hand, he was pushing at her head, guiding her down. Neither of them were smooth. He couldn't wait to get into her mouth, and she couldn't wait to get him there.

Her mouth closed hot over the head, and she swallowed him whole, taking as much of him as she could manage in one suck. It was hard to say who did the most work. She worked her hand over the base, pulling him up to meet the downward rush of her lips. He bucked upward, both his hands tangling in her hair as he held her tightly.

Already she could taste the sips of pre-cum that seeped from the slit. She allowed it to slide over her tongue and gave a sound of appreciation she knew would drive him straight over the edge.

"Ah shit, Zoe."

Those words signaled his surrender. He wasn't going to last. He was too aroused from watching Dillon fuck her. She smiled around his cock and took him deeper, sucking and swallowing. She wanted him deep when he came. Wanted him to come all over the back of her throat. She wanted to taste every drop of his release.

When she felt the betraying quiver work through his hips, she took him all the way and held him there as he began spurting into her mouth. She swallowed and took more, gently working her mouth over his trembling cock. She continued to suck carefully as he jerked one last time against her.

His hands gentled in her hair, and he began stroking lightly, his hands working lovingly over her head and then down to her jaw.

Finally she let him slide from her mouth, and she turned her face up so she could look at him. He wore the expression of a completely sated male. Lazy eyes drifted down her body, sparking with satisfaction when they lighted on her mouth where the remnants of his cum lingered on her lips.

She swiped her tongue over her mouth, removing the last, and then she reached up to push her hair from her face.

"Come here," he said huskily.

She crawled onto his lap and into his waiting arms. He hugged her to him and kissed the top of her head.

"Are you tired, baby?"

She nodded wordlessly and snuggled a little deeper into his embrace.

"Let me pull my jeans up and I'll hold you while you get some rest, okay?"

She pushed lethargically away from him, sliding to the side while he arched his hips to pull his jeans back up. Her gaze caught Dillon's, and he smiled lazily in her direction.

When Chase was done, he reached for her again, and she went willingly into his arms. He felt warm. Strong. Like everything she'd ever wanted in a man. She nuzzled against his neck and pressed a kiss right over his pulse.

"I love you," she whispered.

She was sure he smiled. Could tell by the way he went limp against her and the satisfied roll that went through his body.

"I love you too, baby."

Chase was awakened by the rustle of clothing. He pried open his eyes and stared over Zoe's head to see Dillon dressing by the bed.

Dillon looked over and when he saw Chase was awake, he said, "Hey man, I'm going to get on out of here so you and Zoe can have the bed."

Chase looked down to see Zoe still solidly asleep against him, her soft breathing whispering over his chest. Gathering her carefully in his arms, he eased to the edge of the couch and then stood and carried her to the bed. After he settled her in the covers, he turned back to Dillon and extended his hand.

"Thanks for coming. No way I was going to let Zoe bring a complete stranger back to the hotel, and this was the only way I knew to make the fantasy work."

Dillon grinned and reached out to shake Chase's hand. "Hell, no sweat. I knew your girl was hot. I've seen her picture enough times, but damn, I had no idea she'd be that awesome in bed."

"We still on for next week?"

Dillon raised one eyebrow. "What do you think? I'll be there. It sounds fucking hot. I have to say, you're a lucky man to have a woman who is so uninhibited in bed. Are you sure you're okay with all this?"

Chase smiled. "Yeah. We're both cool with it."

"And you don't think she's going to wonder when I show up again?"

"Judging by her reaction in bed to you, I don't think she'll have any complaints. She knows I wouldn't do anything to hurt her, and the fact that I set up the bar scene will be a relief. I don't want her to have any lingering recriminations if she starts thinking about the fact she picked up a stranger in a bar and then fucked his brains out."

Dillon nodded. "Okay, then I'll see you next week."

Chase watched as his friend left the hotel room and then turned back to Zoe. He smiled as he watched her sleep. He pulled off his clothes and then crawled into bed next to her. She sleepily murmured his name and then snuggled into his arms.

He wanted to turn her over and slide into her body while she was still warm and sated. He wanted to fuck her while those sleepy eyes came alive with answering desire. But she was tired, and there was always the next morning.

For now he was content to hold her close to him and revel in the fact that she belonged to him.

CHAPTER | THIRTEEN

Zoe shivered as she got into her SUV. The weather had turned chilly as a cool front had moved through, dumping copious amounts of rain the entire day. The result had been yet another pileup of MVA victims in the ER and her clocking out late. Again.

She cranked the engine and turned on the heat, then pulled out of the parking garage of the hospital. It was at least a thirty-minute drive home on a good day. Add in the rain and diminished visibility and she was looking at forty-five. Which meant she'd pull into the house at three A.M. If she was lucky.

At least the traffic wasn't bad in Beaumont at this hour of the morning, and she did get down the interstate quickly to her turnoff.

She sighed morosely as she turned the wipers up. Chase wasn't home even though it was his scheduled day off. He'd switched with another crew member so he could take off for their trip to Houston. She'd give a lot to be able to crawl into bed with him tonight. Weather was perfect for a night of cuddling.

She'd turned onto the back-road shortcut to Cypress and had gone about a mile when her SUV lurched and began to slow. Everything turned off: her headlights, her dashboard, even the heater.

Panicked, she pulled over to the shoulder and coasted to a stop. What the ever-loving hell? She stared openmouthed at the steering wheel and then reached for the key to crank the ignition again.

Nothing. Not a click, no sound, absolutely nothing. The truck was deader than a doornail.

Her wipers were stuck in the upright position and rain continued to slash down over the windshield. And damn, but it was dark!

She tried the ignition again and cursed when she got the same result.

She curled her fingers around the steering wheel and slapped her forehead down on the backs of her hands. Great. Just great. Still several miles from home. Whether she walked to or from, there was nothing on this stretch of highway but woods.

Chase was at the firehouse, and she really hated to call him. He'd come get her no doubt, but if they'd had a hard day—and they no doubt had with all the rain and accidents—she hated to wake him up at almost three in the morning. Plus his crew would be short for the time it took him to get her and get back to work.

Brody and Tate were at home—asleep—but hopefully the phone would wake one of them up.

She punched in the number to the house and put the phone to her ear. It rang. And rang.

"Come on, come on," she murmured.

After the fifth ring, voice mail picked up, and she jammed her thumb over the end button in frustration. Then she hit redial and let it ring again.

Having no luck, she punched in Brody's cell number. It rang several times, and then finally his sleepy voice came over the line. Her stomach folded in relief.

"Hello?"

There was question in his voice. Obviously he'd been too asleep to check to see who was calling.

"B-Brody, it's me, Zoe."

Damn but that came out all quivery. Her hands shook, and it wasn't just from the cold.

"Zoe? What's wrong?" he asked sharply.

"I broke down on Old Bridge Road, just before the first bridge."

"Are you all right?"

"I'm fine. I managed to pull over."

"Stay put. Tate and I'll be there as soon as we can."

She let her hand fall to her lap and ended the call. Thank God. She was fast getting in touch with her inner wimp here.

She glanced anxiously around, but it was hard to see through the fogged windows. The instructor of the self-defense course Zoe had taken at the hospital a year back had said a lone woman should never remain inside a disabled vehicle. It had made perfect sense at the time, but when faced with the reality of getting out in the rain and hiding behind a tree until help arrived, she wasn't sure which was scarier.

But remembering the examples the instructor had given— including a few grisly murders—was enough to have Zoe throwing open her door and stepping into the cold rain.

She shivered when water slid down her neck, wetting her back. Making sure to collect her purse and her cell phone, she walked around the front of the SUV and crossed the ditch into the woods. There was a nice, sturdy pine tree that would hopefully also provide a little cover. She just hoped Brody hurried.

Ten minutes later, she was huddled against the tree, shivering, with her hair plastered wetly over her head. She looked—and probably smelled—like a drowned cat. She hopped up and down in an attempt to infuse warmth into her numb legs, but the result was just jiggling more water down her neck.

Finally she heard a vehicle approach and then saw the beam of headlights coming from the opposite direction. Only the memory of that grisly murder kept her from dashing out of the woods.

The vehicle pulled over in front of her truck so that its headlights washed over the SUV. She squinted, trying to make out the color. Really, who the hell else would it be?

The door opened and then slammed.

"Zoe? Zoe? Where the hell are you?"

Brody's bellow spurred her to action. She dashed from the woods and hurried in his direction. He turned and frowned when he saw her approaching. Tate stood in front of Brody's truck, hands shoved into his pockets and his head hunched over to keep the rain out of his face.

Zoe flew into Brody's arms, wrapped herself completely around him, and hung on for dear life. Her heart beat wildly against his chest, and she tried to calm down.

"For the love of God, why didn't you stay in the truck?" Brody demanded.

He wrapped his arms around her, plucked her off her feet, and walked the few steps to his truck. He yanked open the door and thrust her inside.

"I know you think I'm an idiot," she stammered out. "But I was scared out of my mind. It's so damn dark on this road I can't see anything, and I couldn't get my truck started, and my self-defense instructor said a woman should never stay in a disabled vehicle, and I know you think I'm being a total girl, but I'd rather be wet and cold than wet, cold, and dead."

Brody put a finger over her lips to quell the babble fest, and then he hugged her and kissed her on the forehead.

"You did good, honey. Now let's get you home so you can get dried off and warm. We can come back for your truck tomorrow, okay?"

Tate opened the door on the other side and climbed in. He held out his arms to Zoe, and she dove for him, cuddling into his chest as her teeth chattered.

Brody got in and turned the heater on full blast. He backed up enough so he could make a U-turn and then roared off in the direction of home.

"You okay, Zoe?" Tate asked as he smoothed the wet hair from her forehead.

"Yeah, now that you guys are here," she mumbled against his chest. "I hated to get Chase from the station at this hour. They've probably had a busy day."

"If you're ever in trouble, I don't give a damn how busy a day any of us has had, you call," Brody demanded. "Chase would have a kitten if you were stranded out here and didn't call him."

"I'd have called him if I couldn't get you guys," she said.

Tate leaned down and kissed her forehead. "What happened with your truck?"

She frowned, her brow crinkling. "I don't know. The damn thing just quit on me. Engine shut off, lights went off, everything went dead."

"Sounds electrical," Brody said. "We'll get it into the shop for you first thing tomorrow."

She snuggled farther into Tate's embrace. "Thanks, you two. Don't know what I'd do without you. I was scared out of my mind."

"I wish you didn't have to work so damn late," Tate muttered. "You shouldn't be driving home so late by yourself, and especially not in this kind of weather."

They pulled up to the house a few minutes later and dashed inside to the kitchen.

"You go get changed, Zoe. I'll heat you up some soup," Brody said.

She didn't argue. A hot shower might thaw her out and stop the shaking in her legs.

When she returned, Brody and Tate were standing at the counter, a bowl of steaming broth to the side. Brody held out his arms, and she went into his embrace. He hugged her fiercely and stroked her still-damp hair.

"You okay now?"

She nodded against his shoulder. "Thanks for taking care of me."

He smiled and to her surprise bent his head to kiss her. Really kiss her. Not on the cheek or forehead. He sealed his lips over hers, and she melted into his warmth.

She let out a breathy sigh that he caught in his mouth as his tongue laved over her lips. Man, he tasted good and felt even better.

Tate cleared his throat and then shoved the bowl toward her. "Let's go into the living room, where you can get warm on the couch."

Brody snagged the bowl and walked ahead of her. He set it down on the coffee table, and Tate handed her a glass of tea.

She spooned the hot broth into her mouth, sighing in contentment when the warmth traveled to her stomach. By the time she was finished, the shaking had stopped, and she felt human again.

She put the bowl back onto the coffee table and reclined on the couch between Brody and Tate.

"Come here," Brody said, extending his arm so she could snuggle underneath it.

She burrowed into his warmth and laid her head on his chest.

"Sorry to have gotten you guys up at this ungodly hour."

"It's not a problem, Zoe," Tate said. "I'm glad we were home so you weren't stuck out there scared and wet on the highway."

"Or in the woods," she said dryly.

Both men chuckled. Tate slid his hand down her leg and squeezed affectionately. "We like that you're such a girl."

Heat burned into her thigh where his fingers rested possessively. She glanced over to see mirroring heat in his gaze. Her breath caught and held as she continued staring. Then she looked up at Brody to see the same blaze in his eyes.

They wanted her. And God, she wanted them.

"Come here," Tate whispered.

She pushed herself awkwardly from Brody's hold and slowly leaned toward Tate. He pulled her onto his lap, and before she could ponder what he might do next, he cupped her cheek and kissed her.

She closed her eyes and then slid her arms around his neck. Kissing Tate was a study in feel-good. Comforting, natural, and so damn hot her toes curled.

His tongue feathered over her lips, licking at the line and then the corner until it delved inward, finding hers and playfully flicking at the tip.

"Do you have any idea how much I want you right now?" he whispered. "I wanted you back there on the roadside, you all slicked down with rain and those big eyes looking at me like I'd just saved the world."

She smiled and touched his cheek, tracing the line of his jaw and then running the tip of her finger over his full mouth.

"You *had* saved the world. You saved mine."

She turned to Brody, who was watching with unabashed interest. She extended her hand and he caught it, tangling their fingers together.

"I know one way y'all could get me warm," she husked out.

Brody's eyes lit with a savage light. Tate went still against her, and then his hands smoothed up her waist to her breasts, cupping the soft mounds through her shirt.

Suddenly Brody pushed himself off the couch. He stood over her, eyes blazing, his erection bulging the fly of his jeans. He held a hand down to her. Tentatively she reached up to grasp it, and he pulled her to stand in front of him. Tate stood behind her and she was trapped between two very hard, male bodies.

"My room," Brody bit out.

He tugged at her arm as he headed toward his bedroom. As soon as they entered, he turned and pulled her into his arms. Even as he pulled at her shirt, Tate had her sweats down around her ankles.

When she was naked between them, Tate knelt and kissed the cheek of her ass. He licked and then nibbled at the plump flesh. She twitched and squirmed as he worked his way to the other side. His tongue on her ass was exciting and a new experience for her. She shivered when he licked over the seam, ran it lightly up the sensitive skin until he reached the dimple at the top.

Brody palmed both her breasts, plumped them up in his hands, and bent down to flick his tongue over her nipple. He alternated between them, feasting on the hard points.

The dual assault wreaked havoc on her already frayed nerves. Her knees shook, her thighs quivered, and she had to reach out to brace herself against Brody.

She wanted them as naked as she was. Not waiting for Brody to undress, she tore at his shirt, pushing, pulling until finally he broke away to help her. As he raised the shirt over his head, she dove into the waistband of his jeans, unbuttoning, unzipping, impatient to have him in her hands.

His jeans fell, and Brody stepped away to kick out of the legs. When he moved back toward her, his heavy cock swung and then jutted upward, straining and erect.

She placed both palms on his taut abdomen and slid them upward, over his chest wall and to his broad shoulders.

"You have such an amazing body," she murmured.

"Yours is pretty damn fine too," he growled.

She turned, presenting her back to Brody. She stared at Tate and reached for his clothing. He was only too willing to help and in a few seconds, he stood naked before her, his cock pushing outward like he couldn't wait to get it inside her.

Brody pressed into her from behind while Tate stepped into her until their heat encapsulated her. Her breasts pressed against Tate's chest, and she marveled at the feel of such solid male bodies surrounding her.

Hard, unrelenting. Muscular. Taut. She felt small and delicate and very cherished. Tate leaned in to one side of her neck, and she gasped when his mouth gently found the flesh below her ear. Oh God, how had he known?

Brody bent and pressed his mouth to the other side, and they simultaneously began sucking and nipping.

Her knees buckled, and if they hadn't caught her, she would have gone down. Flames blazed through her body. She was on fire. Her nipples hardened against Tate's chest, digging into his skin like twin daggers. Her pussy clenched as pleasure stoked and built higher.

They dragged her to the bed, somehow keeping their mouths fused to her neck. They went down in a tangle of bodies. She landed on top of Brody, and she turned immediately, her need fierce and overwhelming.

She straddled him and leaned down, kissing and licking over his rigid belly and then up to his shoulder where his tattoo fanned out down his arm. She'd always fantasized about having him under her while she licked every inch of that tattoo.

"Ride me, Zoe. Take me inside while Tate fucks your ass."

Brody's guttural words hit her like a blowtorch. She reached down, fumbling clumsily with his cock. In the end, he had to help her by grasping the base and guiding her hips down with his other hand.

She closed over him, wet and hot, sucking him deep. They both groaned.

He grasped her hips with both hands, his fingers digging into her skin. He lifted and then pulled her back down, pushing to her very depths.

The bed shook under Tate's weight as he got up behind her. It took some maneuvering. They were clumsy and desperate and frantic to complete the act.

Brody finally twisted and brought her with him so his legs dangled over the side of the bed. Tate got down and got between Brody's legs, tucked his cock to her ass, and began to push.

Oh God, he was hard and big and she was tight. Too tight.

"I need some KY," Tate bit out. "You're too small this way. I don't want to hurt you."

He retreated, and she heard his steps lead away from the bed. Brody arched into her again, and she closed her eyes, throwing back her head as his hands left her hips to cup her breasts.

"Do you have any idea how many times I've fantasized about having you on top of me?"

"Do you know how many times I've imagined you under me?" she whispered.

She leaned forward, spreading her hands over his chest. She bent to kiss him, devoured his mouth. She was hungry and insatiable. She wanted him.

"God, Zoe, slow down, honey. I'm never going to last."

She smiled, wicked, flashing her teeth as she sat up, going still over him. She reached for his hands and pulled them to her breasts, molding them over the sensitive mounds.

Tate's hands spread over her back, smoothing up her skin, eliciting a deep shudder. She closed her eyes and arched back into him, wanting, needing his touch.

"Lean forward, baby. Let me get you ready."

She bent and as his fingers found her, sliding the lubricant over her opening, she crushed her lips to Brody's, taking his gasp of pleasure deep inside her, filling her.

He slipped in a finger and then two, stroking and easing her passage. Then he retreated and his cock nudged impatiently at her ass.

She went tense and Brody's hands gripped her shoulders.

"Easy, honey. Be still a moment and let him in. Let him do the work."

Her opening stretched around his persistent intrusion. The head slipped in and she gasped into Brody's mouth at the intense, stretching sensation. Tate halted and she whimpered her protest. She wanted him. Inside her. Now. Any way he had to do it.

Tate's hands gripped her hips. Brody held her shoulders. Then Tate pushed. Hard.

She cried out. She wiggled and squirmed and four hands held her down. Brody leaned up to kiss her and murmured soothing words that blew over her ears, but she was too hyped to hear what he said.

Every muscle in her body trembled as she fought the overwhelming sensation of both their cocks so deep in her body. They hadn't moved. They just waited for her to adjust.

Slowly their hands began to move over her, petting and caressing, soothing her ragged nerves. Then Tate pulled slowly out, his cock dragging over her stretched opening with excruciating pressure.

He was nearly out, and her body started to close around his retreat. He thrust forward again, opening her wide. She went crazy and began to buck between them. Brody cursed. Tate muttered something unintelligible and then they both began to pump into her body with ruthless precision.

She hadn't a prayer of holding off her orgasm. It lit up her insides like fire to dry kindling. She exploded around them, shaking spasmodically. It rolled and continued to roll, tightening her womb, tightening around their cocks, demanding their release.

Hot liquid spilled into her ass and pussy. With each thrust, more pumped into her, until she was slick around their cocks and the tension eased. They moved quicker and smoother now, continuing to thrust through their orgasm.

No longer able to keep herself up, she sagged against Brody and felt Tate come with her, his chest pressed against her back. Sandwiched between them, she felt their bodies tremble and quake.

Brody cupped her jaw and lifted until their lips met in a breathless embrace. He and Tate were both still wedged tight in her body. Warm fluid leaked from her ass and her pussy. She lay there, relishing the feel of both of them in her, around her, their skin against hers, their strength surrounding her.

Finally Tate eased off her and withdrew. Brody put his arms around her, cupped her ass, and then rolled her underneath him. His hips lifted and he slipped from the clasp of her body.

He pressed one last, breathless kiss to her lips before moving off her.

"We made a mess," he murmured. "Let me grab a clean sheet, okay?"

She lay there, waiting for them to return. Tate came back a moment later with a warm washcloth and tenderly wiped the semen from between her legs and from the back of her thighs.

When Brody returned, Tate scooped her off the bed and held her up close to his chest while Brody stripped the sheet and hastily threw the other one back on. When he was done, Tate laid her back on the bed, and she immediately cuddled into Brody's embrace.

The bed dipped on the other side as Tate climbed up beside her. He spooned up behind her and kissed her shoulder.

"All better?" he murmured.

She smiled. "Yeah, I'm not scared anymore."

Brody chuckled and tucked her head underneath his chin. "Get some rest. You've had a long night."

CHAPTER | FOURTEEN

Zoe woke all tangled up with Brody and Tate. She faced Tate but was spooned against Brody. He had one arm and a leg thrown possessively over her body. Tate slept with one hand cupping her naked breast.

She closed her eyes again as a sick feeling washed over her. Last night had been magic. She'd been caught up in the moment, and she'd let things go too far.

Chase had been at work. Chase hadn't been here. He hadn't been watching, and he damn sure hadn't known what was going on.

And he'd be home shortly.

In agony over how to face him with this, she carefully pried herself away from Brody's grasp. He mumbled something in his sleep but turned over, and soon his soft, even breathing filled the room again.

She scrambled from the bed, picked her clothing up off the floor, and hurried across the house to her room. Hers and Chase's room.

How was she going to tell him? There were no secrets between them, and there damn sure weren't any lies. She detested lying and so did Chase. This wasn't something she'd ever hide, but what the hell would it do to the friendship the four of them shared?

She dressed and sat on the edge of the bed. A glance at the clock told her Chase would be here any minute. She buried her face in her hands. If only . . .

She couldn't even bring herself to regret it.

She flinched when she heard footsteps in the hallway. Chase.

"Zoe? Baby, what's wrong?"

His concern made her flinch all the more. She raised her head to look at him. He looked tired and disheveled, like he hadn't gotten much sleep the night before. She closed her eyes again. How could she tell him? How could she *not* tell him?

"Zoe, talk to me," Chase demanded as he came over to the bed.

He sat down and pulled her into his arms, but she went stiff as a board.

"There's something I need to tell you," she said quietly.

Chase loosened his hold and pulled away. His gaze was worried and seeking. He opened his mouth, closed it, and then looked away for a moment.

Finally he turned back to her and reached for her, tucking away a strand of hair behind her ear.

"Whatever it is, just tell me, baby."

"Last night . . . last night I broke down on my way home from work. It was dark, cold and raining. It happened out on Old Bridge Road—"

"Why didn't you call me?" he demanded.

She held up her hand to stop him. "Just listen, Chase. I knew you were at work, so I called Brody and Tate. They came out to get me. I was soaked and cold. They took me home and made me some soup. We were sitting on the couch and . . ."

Her voice trailed off. She swallowed nervously but kept her eyes on him. She owed him the unvarnished truth. She wouldn't be a coward.

"And?" he prompted.

"I had sex with Brody and Tate."

He kept staring at her as if he expected her to continue, like there was something else to add. She remained silent.

"That's it?" His features relaxed, and relief spread into his eyes. Relief? Her brow furrowed in confusion.

"I slept with them both, Chase. You weren't here. It shouldn't have happened."

He blew out a long breath and then, to her further amazement, he smiled. The smile grew larger, and then he yanked her into his arms, crushing her against his chest.

"For God's sake, you scared the shit out of me."

She struggled to loosen his hold on her, and she pulled away, staring at him in astonishment. "Is that all you have to say?"

He chuckled softly and touched her cheek. "Tell me you haven't tortured yourself the entire night over this."

"No," she mumbled. "Only when I woke up this morning."

He sighed. "Did you expect me to be angry? Feel betrayed?"

"Well, yeah. I guess."

She was truly bewildered by his reaction. She wasn't sure what she'd expected. Anger? Disappointment?

He took her hands in his and rubbed his thumbs over her wrists. "I'm not any of those things, Zoe. If I were, I'd be a flaming hypocrite. I opened that door, not you. I'm the one who asked them to participate in your fantasy."

"But—"

"Let me finish."

She shut up and waited for him to continue.

"I guess if it had been someone else, some random guy you decided to hook up with, then yeah, I'd be pissed. Brody and Tate are different. They live here with us. They're friends. Good friends. They care a lot about you, and I know you care a lot about them. I thought about what might happen if I opened the door to them having sex with you. I had a lot of thoughts. Things might get awkward. Or things might go really well. I even considered the possibility that one or both of them would have sex with you away from me."

"That didn't bother you?" she asked.

He seemed to consider it a moment, and then he shook his head. "I can't explain it. The thought didn't bother me. Don't get me wrong, if it had been someone else, then yeah, I get pissed even thinking about it. I know we didn't talk about this. Maybe we should have, but I figured things would evolve or not evolve and we'd take it as it came. But if you're wondering if I feel threatened or jealous because you had sex with them, the answer is no. I don't see the difference whether I involve them in a fantasy and they have sex with you, or they have sex with you outside that fantasy. The result is the same."

She bit her bottom lip. "I didn't feel bad about the night with Dillon because it was a decision we made together. And it didn't mean anything. But this . . ."

"This?"

"It meant something," she said softly. "And you weren't involved. I feel like I cheated on you, and you have to know Chase, I love you. I'd never do anything to purposely hurt you."

He leaned in and kissed her. "I love you too, baby."

"But Chase, it meant something," she persisted. "It was different than it was with Dillon. With him it was hot sex. Playful and fun. I loved teasing you and the idea that you were watching. Last night . . . last night I just wanted to be with them. You weren't here and I wanted to make love with them."

"If I had to guess, I'd say it meant something to them too,"

Chase said quietly. "You have to know how much they care about you, Zoe. And if you reach down, I think you'll see how much you care about them too. Loving me doesn't preclude you loving other people. It's just a different kind of love."

"How the hell did you get so philosophical?" she blurted.

He smiled. "I've had a lot of time to think about it."

She closed her eyes. "So what do I do? I can't pretend it didn't happen, but I don't want it to fuck things up either."

"Just see how it goes," he said. "It doesn't change things between us. I love you. You love me. Whatever happens, we'll face it together, okay?"

She went into his arms and circled her arms around his waist. His heart thudded reassuringly against her ear, and she sighed.

"How can you be so perfect? It must be damn exhausting."

He shook against her cheek as he laughed. "As long as you think I'm perfect, that's all that counts."

She picked up her head again and kissed his jaw. "You need a shave. Rough shift?"

He sighed. "Yeah. You?"

She nodded. "I didn't get out until past two."

"Damn, and you broke down on the way home. That sucks."

"Yeah, Tate and Brody said they'd take my car to the shop today."

"Where are they, speaking of?"

"I left them in bed," she said lamely.

"Together?"

She nodded.

Chase burst out laughing. "I'll have to go wake them up. Would be worth it to see their expressions when they figure out they're in bed together."

"Maybe that's not such a good idea," she hedged.

If she felt as guilty as she did, would they feel the same way?

Chase squeezed her hand. "The best way to handle this is to go on, business as usual. I don't want you beating yourself up over something that in the end I'm responsible for. If it weren't for me, they would have never had sex with you in the first place."

"And if it happens again?" she asked softly.

"Are you asking my permission?"

Slowly she shook her head.

"Good, because that's not what this is about. It's a little ridiculous, the idea that I somehow control the actions of three other people and that sex is only okay if everyone involved has my permission. In actuality I gave it when I asked Brody and Tate to participate. It's not reasonable that I'd have to be present or that somehow you have to ask me beforehand if it's okay."

Her mind buzzed with the implications of what he was saying. He couldn't be saying what she thought, and that not only did he expect that it would happen again, but he was okay with it. It was just too . . . weird.

But at the same time, the relief she felt was unmistakable, so what did that say about her?

"This is stupid," she muttered. "They might not ever want to have sex with me again anyway."

Chase smiled. "Somehow, I don't think that's going to be the case."

Despite the fact that Chase was obviously tired, he and Brody and Tate drove out to get her car and tow it to the garage. She made their favorite lunch so that when they got back, they'd have a decent meal for their efforts at least.

All the while they were gone, she worried over the fallout from the night before. Chase had shocked her with his acceptance. And on the surface, she agreed with him. It wasn't any different from her having sex with them before. But somehow she couldn't quite convince herself that it was the same. It felt different.

All her worry wasn't reserved for how it affected her and Chase either, and maybe that was what bugged her the most. She was in agony over trying to figure out how Brody and Tate would react to it.

She was being a total girl and getting all emotional over sex. But she knew it wasn't just sex. Not with Brody and Tate. With Dillon she'd been able to easily separate the act and the emotion. Not so with Brody and Tate. She cared about them too much, and she didn't want to lose them. She couldn't lose them.

The table was set—something they didn't often do. Most of the time they ate at the bar or just ate in the living room. How positively domestic of her. The guys would give her shit when they got home.

She hoped. Because if they didn't, and things changed, it would kill her.

Half an hour later, she put the finishing touches on the potato salad and draped a towel over the container of fried chicken. Chase had called her a few minutes earlier, and they should be rolling in any minute.

She sweetened the tea, filled glasses with ice, and put everything out on the table just as she heard a truck pull into the drive.

Her stomach promptly took a nosedive.

Chase came in the door first, followed closely by Brody. Tate brought up the rear. They all stopped inside the kitchen and Chase sniffed appreciatively at the air. "Tell me that's what I think it is."

She smiled. "Lunch is on the table."

Brody's eyes widened. "Table? As in a place to sit at and eat?"

She relaxed. Yeah, they were going to give her shit.

They sauntered into the dining room and Tate whistled. "Damn woman, you cooked, set the table, and everything. Oh hell, is that potato salad?"

She shot over and smacked his hand just as it darted into the bowl. He drew back with an injured look and held his hand like she'd broken it.

"I figured you guys deserved a decent meal for taking care of my truck."

Chase tucked an arm around her and kissed her temple. "Not that we don't love being cooked for, but that's what we're here for. To help."

She smiled up at him and then gestured for them to sit.

They all took their seats and promptly dug into the food.

"This is kind of nice," Brody said. "We should do it more often. Beats eating in the living room."

"How long will it take them to fix my truck?" she asked Chase. "And did they say how much it would cost?"

Chase winced. "We need to talk about that. The electrical system is shot all to hell. They could fix it, but honestly I think you should consider getting something new. You've had it forever, and at this point, it doesn't make sense to sink a lot of money into something that's likely to break in another week."

Tate and Brody studied her closely. They were staring. Why? She scowled at them and turned back to Chase.

"New?"

Brody made a brave attempt to stifle his laughter. Tate did no such thing. He laughed and continued laughing when she turned her murderous stare on him.

"What the hell is so funny?" she demanded.

Brody chuckled. "You are. We were just waiting for you to squeak at the idea of buying a new car. You're such a tightass when it comes to money."

"I am not!"

Chase managed a straight face. "Baby, you are so. When was the last time you bought anything new?"

"Just because I save money and don't throw it away on shiny new toys all the time does not make me some miser."

"So go buy a new truck," Tate challenged. "Come on. It'll be fun. We'll help you pick out something."

Okay, so the idea of a bright new vehicle with that delectable new-car smell did appeal on a certain level.

"Oohh, we have her," Brody said triumphantly. "I can see that calculating gleam in her eyes. She wants it."

"I have no idea what to get," she said faintly.

"Leave that to us," Chase said with a grin. "We're guys. That makes us expert auto shoppers."

"So, um, when can we go?"

"As soon as we finish with lunch. We can go into Beaumont and check out the dealerships there," Chase said.

Excitement bloomed in her stomach and fanned out until she grinned a little idiotically. "Okay, I'll go. But I'm not promising to buy anything. There's research to do."

Tate rolled his eyes. Brody just gave her a patient look, and Chase leaned back and smiled warmly in her direction. Maybe he was telling her that things were okay and that they were still the family they'd always been. Family.

As she looked around the table at the people who meant the most to her, she realized they truly were a family.

After lunch, they cleared away the dishes. Chase and Tate attacked the dishwasher, and Zoe took a dish towel to wipe off the table. Brody came in as she was finishing her wipe-down and stood just a few feet away.

"Hey," he said as she started to return to the kitchen. "Can I talk to you a second?"

Dread formed in the pit of her stomach. She glanced back toward the kitchen, but Chase and Tate were preoccupied with the dishes.

"Don't look so worried," he said softly. "I wanted to talk to you about what happened last night. I mean not about what happened but . . . I didn't use a condom. It was stupid. I've always used them with you, but last night wasn't planned. I wanted to make sure things were okay, I mean with birth control."

"Oh," she breathed. "Yeah, I mean Chase and I don't use condoms. I use birth control, and Chase is the only person I've been with. Without condoms I mean." Heat bled into her face at her admission.

"Hey, don't worry. I wasn't saying it because I was worried about you. I know you and Chase have been together awhile. You should be more worried about me. I'm clean, though. I worried about you getting pregnant. I didn't want us to make a mistake, because last night was incredible."

She smiled at his discomfort, which seemed to mirror her own. Then she went to him and wrapped her arms around his waist.

"Thank you for caring so much about me."

He hesitated for only a moment before enfolding her in his embrace. "I'll always care about you, Zoe."

"Hey, you guys ready to go?" Tate asked from the doorway. "Chase is chomping at the bit to go find Zoe some wheels."

Zoe grinned. She was a little excited about it herself.

CHAPTER | FIFTEEN

Zoe zipped into the driveway in her new black SUV and grinned at how the moonlight reflected off the shiny paint job. Okay, so she hadn't been that hard to convince when it came down to it. Truth be told, the guys had had to corral her because she'd been a little too eager to seal the deal.

But hey, that's what guys were for. All the wheeling and dealing and the things that made them feel all manly.

As soon as she entered through the kitchen, she tossed her keys onto the bar and frowned at how dark the house was. Wasn't anyone home? Before she could reach for the light switch, she sensed another presence.

She whirled around, but Chase's hand clamped over her mouth. This time he didn't offer the assurance he had the first time he'd abducted her, but then he didn't need to. From the first touch, her blood pumped furiously through her veins.

He hauled her up, her back pressed against his chest as her feet left the floor. He carried her into the living room, where she saw what looked like a padded exam table. She didn't even want to know where he'd scored that—or what he was going to use it for.

Okay, maybe she did, because her mind was swarming with the possibilities. And she loved each and every one.

He tossed her down on the table and yanked at her bottoms. Her underwear came with them, and she was naked from the waist down. He dragged her down the table until her ass was hovering on the edge. And easily accessible.

The sound of his zipper scoured her ears, and before she could think anything further, he pushed into her, shocking her with his entry.

She was unprepared, and it took him more effort to get inside her. The rough sensation of him shoving through her pussy made her pulse soar. Her belly contracted, and she clamped down around him, making it even more difficult for him to gain entry.

"Don't fight me," he growled. "I'll get inside you, Zoe. Make it easy on yourself and accept me."

Her heart sped up at the rough words. Though she didn't want to make it easier—she liked the sensation of him so full inside her too much—his words made her go damp, and he slid in another inch.

The friction was too much. She couldn't hold him off. He powered to the hilt, and they both made deep sounds of contentment when he bottomed out.

He didn't pause long, though. He withdrew and forced himself in again, and then he took off, working rough and fast in and out of her body.

It was quick and brutal in intensity. She came in the next breath, the orgasm knifing through her with power that shocked her. He powered in again and then found his own release, pouring himself into her.

He let her legs go immediately and pulled out, leaving her gasping for breath. He quickly moved around her and pulled at her top until it came over her head, leaving her in just her bra.

Her legs dangled over the edge of the table, and she sagged as he pushed the bra straps from her shoulders. He pushed her over so he could unhook it in the back and then let her fall back to the table.

Her breasts jiggled when he took her hands and pulled her arms over her head. What on earth was he doing?

He curled his fingers around her wrists and trapped them against the table so that she was completely vulnerable, her body laid out like a feast.

And then she had her answer when she heard footsteps on the hardwood floors. Footsteps from more than one person. Her mind flashed back to the night they'd unveiled all their secret fantasies, and she could only think of one that fit the bill here.

Oh my God.

Surely not.

Tate and Brody stepped into view, their hands going to her legs. They pushed until her knees bent and then they spread her wide, holding her in place.

Which meant . . .

She swallowed, and for the first time felt uncertainty and a little fear wash up her spine. She heard the unmistakable sound of a zipper, heard the crinkle of a condom wrapper. She tried to raise her head to see, but Chase pressed her head back down and held her firmly in place.

A thumb pressed to her clit and then slid down her seam to her entrance. Just one brush and then a cock replaced the thumb and pushed into her. She gasped at the instant fullness. If Chase hadn't come inside her, she would have never been able to take this man.

And then he leaned into her and she caught the outline of his face. *Dillon?*

Stunned, she stared down as he began fucking her with long, ruthless strokes.

It was her fantasy come to life, just as she'd pictured it, just as she'd described it to Chase. Brody and Tate held her legs, held her open to Dillon's savage fucking. And oh God, it felt good. She loved their hands on her body. Loved the way Chase held her to the table, her wrists trapped underneath his hands.

Brody held her leg with one hand, but his other caressed up and down the back of her thigh, his touch soothing and sensual. Tate pressed a kiss to the side of her leg as he held her open to Dillon.

And Dillon. Just like in her fantasy, it was down and dirty. Crude and nothing soft or romantic about it. He fucked her like she was an instrument for his pleasure and nothing else. Only she knew better. She could see his eyes, see how he looked at her. She could remember how tender and demanding he'd been that night in the hotel.

His expression grew fierce, and he pulled away from her, leaving her pussy clenching with need. He hadn't come. She looked at him in bewilderment, but when he took Tate's place and Tate took position between her legs, she understood.

Tate unzipped his pants, put on a condom and stabbed into her, his cock sinking deep. She sucked in a steadying breath and prayed she could hold on. She felt light and a little unhinged. If she gave in to the orgasm that rose, she'd never enjoy the rest of this experience. She wasn't even sure she would be aware of what happened.

Need clawed at her, demanding release. Her body shook with the force of Tate's thrusts. Her breasts jiggled, and her head rose up the table, precariously close to the wrists Chase had trapped just above.

Too soon, he too pulled out, and Brody stepped away, releasing her leg to Tate. As she glanced down her body, she saw him shove at his jeans, pushing them just down his hips so that his cock sprang free. Then he stepped between her legs, positioned his cock, and with one fierce push he was deep inside her.

The room began to spin. She looked up, trying to focus, but the ceiling blurred and contorted. She clenched her jaw and closed her eyes, determined not to go over the edge. Not yet.

A whimper escaped, and she struggled against Chase's hold. Not that she was afraid. Not that she truly wanted free. She just didn't know how to handle the overwhelming sensations that bombarded her so relentlessly.

Her skin felt alive and she was wild underneath it, like a butterfly trying to free itself from the cocoon. She went a little crazy, arching, twisting, and undulating.

Dillon replaced Brody and began fucking her all over again. It was more than she could bear. Her orgasm sliced through her, a sharp blade that shredded her senses.

She flew in a thousand different directions. Her release was a vicious, living thing that bloomed and exploded, swelled again and sparked an inferno.

Dillon cursed and stiffened between her legs. The veins in his neck bulged as she writhed against him. He sagged, then stepped back only for Tate to take his place.

She whimpered again when Tate thrust into her hypersensitive body, but her orgasm was still gaining momentum. There was no mercy for her, no letdown after the storm. How could it last so long? Be so intense?

In the midst of Tate's release, every muscle in her body tightened, and she screamed from the sheer agony of it. Somehow, some way she had to be released.

Chase leaned down over her, his lips crushing hers in a sweet, desperate kiss. Tate pulled out of her only for Brody to take his place. No, she couldn't take any more. Could she?

Two mouths, warm and so very sensual, closed around her nipples. She hadn't thought she could push herself up that mountain any higher. She'd been wrong.

Brody pounded at her pussy, each stroke sending fierce streaks of pleasure through her belly, and now the two mouths around her nipples sucked and nipped, sending an equal measure of pleasure streaking down to her pussy.

The two sensations collided in the middle and the result was nothing like she'd ever experienced in her life.

She gasped, but the sound was swallowed by Chase. She tried to scream, but his mouth remained solidly fused to hers. And then he slid his lips down her jaw, pushing so that her neck was exposed. He sank his teeth into the tender column below her ear just as Brody pumped into her again.

She lost awareness. She came completely apart. The room blurred and went black. No longer could she see anything. She could only feel. Mindlessly she writhed, arched, and fought. Not against the pleasure, but she fought to control it—and herself.

She wasn't successful. As Brody sank into her again and held himself against her as he came, she slipped away, borne on a tide of mind-numbing pleasure. She let go, quit fighting, and quite simply, she surrendered.

Going limp, she closed her eyes, feeling them roll back in her head. Her mouth sagged open and she reached for oblivion.

It was a long time—or at least what she thought must have been a long time—before she came back to awareness. For all she knew it could have been a matter of minutes, or maybe just seconds.

Gentle hands petted and caressed her. Stroked her hair, her legs, her belly, and her breasts. Warm mouths brushed over her skin, stopping to suckle tenderly at her breasts or to nip lightly at her neck.

The warm haze built and surrounded her. It was better than the best alcohol buzz. There was nothing better, she was sure of it.

She opened her eyes to see four men surrounding her, each touching and caressing her almost reverently. Chase was closest to her, his lips against her neck and then her ear.

"You're back," he whispered.

"Mmmm."

It was all she could manage, but then she remembered that Dillon was here. She pried open her eyes one more time and stared down her body to see him holding one of her legs, straightened this time, as he kissed just below her knee.

Brody and Tate were at her breasts, one of them suckling a nipple and the other kissing the hollow of her belly. She'd never felt more treasured and so very precious than at this moment.

"Dillon," she murmured. "Fancy seeing you here."

He looked up at her, a gleam of amusement in his eyes. "Chase and I are old friends. I work for a firehouse in Houston."

She chuckled. "Somehow I knew he wouldn't go for picking up a complete stranger and taking him back to our hotel."

"A guy's gotta look out for his girl," Dillon said with a grin.

She looked up to find Chase so close, his eyes locked with hers. She reached up to touch his face, letting her fingers slide down his jawline.

"Yes," she whispered. "He looks after me so well."

Chase smiled and kissed the tip of her nose. "So what did you think?" he murmured. "Everything you thought it would be?"

She shook her head, and he frowned. "Were we too rough? Did we hurt you?"

She smiled. "No, it was perfect. It was far more than I'd ever imagined. And maybe it was because I was with men I trust. Men I know wouldn't hurt me or take things too far but weren't afraid to play rough either."

"I'm pretty sure we're your slaves for life," Chase said in amusement.

Her grin grew wider. "Be careful what you say. I might like the idea of having four very devoted slaves in my harem."

"Want to play some more, or are you done?" Chase murmured.

"Mmmm, what did you have in mind?"

"Me, you, a few of my friends. You could dance for us in the living room and we could take it from there. Anything you want. Anything we want."

"Now that sounds pretty damn awesome," she whispered back. "If you could feed me first and give me a little time to recover, it'll sound even better."

CHAPTER | SIXTEEN

"I'll take Zoe into the living room," Brody said. "You get her something to eat."

Chase raised an eyebrow at Brody's terse voice. Brody shouldered past Chase and gently gathered Zoe into his arms. He curled her against his body, shielding as much as her as possible as he strode into the living room. Tate followed, zipping his pants on the way.

Dillon met Chase's gaze and shrugged. The two men went into the kitchen, and Chase pulled out the sandwich fixings from the fridge.

Dillon hovered, hands shoved into his pocket, and then a sigh escaped him. "Look, man, maybe I should leave."

Chase glanced up at him. "Is there a problem?"

"You tell me. When you approached me about being a part of Zoe's fantasy, I thought why not. She's hot. That night in the hotel was fantastic. She's not the problem here." He hooked a thumb over his shoulder in the direction of the living room. "Big guy in there doesn't like me being here. I think he's pissed."

Chase dropped the ham on the counter and turned to Dillon. "What makes you say that? I admit, my attention was focused on Zoe during the whole thing. I wasn't exactly paying attention to what the rest of you were doing."

"All I'm saying is that he didn't want me touching her. Period. You could have broken a rock on his face when Zoe mentioned the whole bar thing. I'm all for great sex, but I'm not going to step into a shit storm."

Chase frowned. It would certainly explain Brody's protectiveness of Zoe at the end when he all but shoved Chase out of the way to take Zoe into the living room.

"Yeah, I understand. Sorry, man."

"Hey, not a problem, though you might want to check on the fact that another guy is going all He-Man on your girl."

He wasn't about to tell Dillon that he didn't mind, nor was he going to get into the dynamics of the relationship—what relationship? He shook his head. Things were getting complicated. He knew Zoe had some issues where Brody and Tate were concerned, and it was likely they did too. But damn.

"I'm going to head out. Kiss Zoe for me and let her know I had a great time. I don't want her thinking I left because of her, okay?"

"Will do," Chase said. "Later, man."

The door shut behind Dillon, and Chase returned to the sandwiches with a frown. He hadn't imagined that bringing Dillon in would piss Brody off. Maybe he should have planned better. Or maybe it was time to step out of the realm of fantasy for a while.

It was easy to get carried away, that much was obvious. When you had a girl as responsive and open to kink as Zoe was, it was easy to take things too far. Was that what he'd done? Gone too far?

He'd told himself that he was fulfilling a fantasy for Zoe, but what if it was just that? A fantasy. Something sexy to talk about in private and never meant to take into the real world. Or maybe he was living out his own fantasies and rationalizing them by saying he was doing it for Zoe.

Or maybe he just needed a fucking reality check.

He piled the sandwiches on a plate and walked into the living room. Zoe was curled onto Brody's lap. Brody had wrapped a blanket around her so that no part of her body showed. His arms were wrapped protectively around her, and her face was burrowed into his neck. Brody had one hand in her hair, stroking absently as he rested his cheek on the top of her head.

The knot in Chase's stomach grew larger.

Tate sat across from the couch, slouched in a chair, his legs sprawled out in front of him. He watched Zoe, his expression indecipherable.

When Chase put the plate down on the coffee table, Brody looked up.

"She's asleep," Brody said in a low voice. "She's tired."

He said it almost accusingly, and Chase flinched.

"Where's your friend?" Tate asked.

"He left," Chase said as he sat down.

"Good," Brody said bluntly.

Chase sighed. He really didn't want to get into the *why*s and *wherefore*s. It was probably a good idea if they dropped it and called it a night.

"Why don't you take Zoe to her bedroom?" He purposely didn't say *my* or *our* in conjunction with the bedroom even though it *was* their bedroom. "I think we'll call it a night."

Brody nodded and then repositioned Zoe on his lap so he could stand. The blanket started to slip, but Brody caught her closer to his chest so that it didn't fall completely down.

As soon as he left the living room with Zoe, Tate stood, his eyes shuttered as he glanced toward Chase.

"Listen, I think in the future if you want to do something like this again . . . I'd prefer you leave me out."

"I'm not planning for there to be a next time," Chase said.

Relief shadowed Tate's eyes. He nodded and then turned toward his bedroom.

"I'm going to hit the sack. See you guys in the morning."

A few moments later, Brody reappeared in the living room. He nodded toward Chase but didn't say anything as he headed toward his room. Chase stood and stared after Brody for a long time after he disappeared.

Then, blowing out his breath, he went into his bedroom.

Zoe was snuggled into bed, the covers pulled over her shoulders. She was, predictably, on Chase's pillow, a fact that made him smile as he stripped down to his underwear.

He crawled into bed with her and pulled her warm body into his. She stirred and draped her arm and leg over him and then opened her eyes.

"Everyone go?" she asked sleepily. "I didn't mean to crap out like that."

He touched her cheek, letting his fingers glide over the silky skin to her neck. For a long moment he didn't say anything as he looked down at her.

Some of the sleep faded from her eyes and her brow crinkled. "Is something wrong?"

He shook his head. "No, nothing's wrong. Was just thinking."

"About?"

"You and me. And our fantasies."

Her look was still questioning.

"The things we've done have been amazing. I've enjoyed it all. But maybe it's time we called a halt. Maybe we're getting a little too carried away."

She frowned and pushed up to her elbow. "Did I do something wrong?"

He quickly put a finger over her lips. "Shhh, baby. Let me explain. This is not about anything you've done. Quite the contrary.

I'm a lucky guy to have such a fantastic girl. I mean you're so open. I love that you're so honest about your sexuality, that you're not ashamed to talk about your kinks and fantasies and even indulge in them with me. I've loved every minute of it. I just think once we got started, we tried to cram everything into a short amount of time. Like we tried to one-up ourselves with each ensuing experience. I'm to blame for most of it. Apart from the night at the strip club, I've instigated everything else. And I'm not saying we should never play our fantasies out again. I just think for the time being we should slow it down and enjoy each other. I feel like we haven't had a lot of time lately where it's just you and me."

She relaxed and let herself back down onto the pillow. She put her hand on his shoulder and let her palm slide down his arm.

"Were you getting jealous? I mean, did it bother you to see me with other men? Because . . ."

There was a thread of anxiety in her voice and once again, he shushed her gently.

"Zoe, honey, there was nothing you did. My feelings haven't changed. I just think maybe some of the mystery can be taken out of a relationship if we make every erotic thought a reality, you know? Maybe some of the things we whisper about should be kept between you and me."

She smiled and linked her arm around him to pull him closer. He hugged her to him and stroked the soft skin of her back.

"I love you," she said.

"I love you too," he said seriously. "Now tell me about tonight. Was it good for you? I mean, was it as exciting as when you fantasized about it?"

She was silent for a moment and then she pulled away, her expression thoughtful. "It was hot. Dillon showing up was a little weird at first. I guess because I hadn't expected it. I worried . . ."

She broke off and bit her lip, her gaze skating away from his.

He nudged her chin so that she looked at him again. "You worried what?"

"It sounds silly."

"Try me."

"I wasn't worried about you, I mean I knew you were okay with it, but I wasn't sure about Brody and Tate." She sighed. "This is difficult for me because I have such conflicting feelings for them. I guess in the same vein as my initial worry over what you'd think watching another man have sex with me, I worried about what they would think about me being with someone other . . . than them."

"You thought they'd be jealous."

"Well, yes," she said anxiously. "Chase, what's happening here? The only person I should be worried about is you. I don't know that I like this. I feel like something special was breached tonight, but that's so messed up. My relationship is with you, not Brody and Tate, but I'd die if I inadvertently did something to hurt them."

He kissed the lines of her brow, trying to ease some of the worry from her face.

He knew where this was going. It was like watching an inevitable train wreck and he was powerless to stop it. He knew, or he had a damn good idea, of the potential ramifications when he'd asked Brody and Tate to participate. He knew and it hadn't stopped him. But then he'd only been thinking of what *he* was open to and what was acceptable to him. He'd never given thought to the three other people involved and how they might struggle to accept the situation.

He felt like the worst sort of ass. And worse, he wasn't sure he could fix it. Or if it could be fixed.

"You're tired and right now you're upset. I think we should both get some sleep and see what tomorrow brings. I don't want you to worry, Zoe. We'll fix this. I promise."

His gut knotted at the zealous declaration. He hoped to hell it wasn't too late and that things hadn't gone too far. What the four

of them had was very special, and it would kill him to see it dam-
aged in any way. Worse, the worst-case scenario was losing Zoe.
And there was no way in hell he was going to let that happen.

   She snuggled deeper into his arms, but he could feel her tension.
He had a feeling she was going to lie awake tonight. Just like he was.

CHAPTER | SEVENTEEN

He couldn't take the tension a minute longer. Chase curled his fist and had to control the urge to smash it into the wall.

For the last week things had been unbearable in the house. On the surface, it was the same. Lighthearted bantering. Same old kidding. Business as usual.

But below the surface things were very wrong.

Tate had been unusually quiet. Brody had avoided them all for most of the week. And Zoe had haunted shadows in her eyes that made Chase ache.

Even now, on Zoe's day off, she was at work. She'd called to say she was taking an extra shift for someone who'd called in sick, but Chase knew she was avoiding being at home. When all the guys were off.

Which was laughable because Chase was the only one home. He could only imagine that Tate and Brody, assuming Zoe was going to be home on her day off, had found other things to go. That didn't include being home when all four of them would be together.

The entire situation sucked, and Chase was tired of it. Something had to give.

It might not be pretty, but he was about to take the bull by the horns and hope to hell he didn't fuck things up worse.

Having a pretty good idea where Brody might be, Chase hopped into his truck and headed toward the bar and grill where the firemen and police personnel regularly hung out. As expected, when he pulled into the lot, he found Brody's truck parked near the entrance.

He took a deep, fortifying breath and walked in. Brody sat on a stool at the bar, his hands loosely clasped around a beer bottle. He was alone and appeared to be ignoring the world around him.

Chase slid onto the bar stool next to him. "Hey, man."

Brody glanced sideways at him and frowned. "What are you doing here? Thought it was Zoe's day off."

"She's working an extra shift."

Brody's frown deepened. "She seems to be doing a lot of that lately. She shouldn't work so much."

"You want to tell me what's going on?" Chase asked bluntly.

Brody stiffened and stared down at the beer he'd barely taken a drink out of.

"I'm thinking of moving out."

Fuck. This was bad. This was really bad. Chase wasn't going to patronize Brody by acting surprised or asking why. Neither one of them was stupid, and neither liked to play games. They'd always been straight up with each other, and now wasn't the time to change that.

"I wish you wouldn't," Chase said. "I don't think that's what you want. I know it's not what I want, and I know it's not what Zoe would want. This is going to hurt her."

Brody turned then, his eyes glittering. "I can't stay there any longer. I can't do it, man. If you think about it, you know I can't, and you know why."

"I do," Chase admitted. "But why don't you explain it to me so there's no misunderstanding."

Brody sighed and then thumped his fist down onto the bar. "You have to know I'm in love with her."

Chase slowly nodded. "Yeah, I know."

Brody made a sound of frustration. "Did you hear what I said? Really? I just told you I'm in love with your girl and you sit there looking at me like I'm talking about the weather."

"What do you want me to do, Brody? Hit you? Curse at you?"

"Jesus," Brody muttered. "This is a mess."

"Yeah, it's my mess," Chase said evenly. "Look, I knew you—and Tate—had feelings for Zoe. I've known it a long time. I always wondered what would have happened if I hadn't asked her out first."

Brody's face tightened and his eyes went flat. "I can tell you. She'd be at home, with me, in my bed. That's what would have happened."

"Out of curiosity, why didn't you ever make a move?"

"Because you're my friend. Zoe's my friend, and I'd never have done anything to fuck that up."

"So what changed? Other than the obvious. Why move out now?"

Brody's nostrils flared as his breaths came out harsh. "What changed is I wasn't sleeping with her before. Before that, I could play it cool, remain friends, and not have my head involved. But the minute I touched her, things changed. And even then I could deal, you know? Because in my fantasy world, it was just the four of us, living together, and I felt like I had a small part of her, you know? It was easy to pretend."

"Yeah, I get the fantasy thing," Chase muttered.

"But if you want to know when it all changed for me, it was when your friend entered the picture. And I know this sounds fucked up, but when it was you or even Tate touching her, I could deal, because it's always been us. We've always been friends, and I know Zoe loves you and she loves Tate. So I could deal with sharing her . . . with you. But it pissed me off when you brought in the other guy because that's when I felt betrayed. I didn't want that son of a bitch even looking at Zoe, much less touching her. Hell, I didn't like the other guys looking at her the night at the strip club.

"And the bitch of it is, I don't get a say. I was jealous—not of you and Tate—but of that other guy, Dillon or whatever his name is. And it hit home to me that I've been living in a fantasy world where Zoe belonged to me—or at least partly to me.

"But the thing is, Chase, this isn't what I want. I don't want to have sex with her because you said it was okay. I don't want to have sex with her because you're watching and you think it's hot. I don't want permission every time I want to make love to her, and I damn sure don't want her feeling guilty because she made love to me when you weren't in the picture. Yeah, I know she told you. She's too honest and straight up to ever keep that kind of thing from you, but I also know it tore her up because she felt like she betrayed you, and damn it, I don't want to feel like I betrayed you. So the only way for me to win is to walk away, because I'd never do anything to break you two up, and I can't have what I want unless that happens."

"Fuck," Chase cursed. "Look, I have a lot to apologize for, starting with the fact that I knew when I asked you and Tate to participate in Zoe's fantasy that you both had feelings for her. I also knew what might happen between the four of us as far as our relationship, not that it would fuck things up, but maybe I wanted to test the waters and see where things took us."

Brody shot him an incredulous look. "What did you think would happen? That we'd fuck her and go on our merry way?"

"No, that's not what I thought at all. God, this is twisted."

"Try me," Brody challenged.

"Look, it started as a fantasy but deep down I wondered what would happen if we did have some sort of permanent arrangement.

I don't know what the hell you call it. But the four of us together, Zoe having a relationship with all of us. It was arrogant. I was messing with the lives of three other people without thinking it through. I admit that. But I also knew that you and Tate had some serious feelings for her, and I suspected that she had deep feelings for the two of you."

"So why bring in the other guy? I don't get it."

"Because I got carried away," Chase bit out. "It was a mistake, okay? Zoe and I talked about our really hot fantasies. In mine I watched her being fucked by another guy, but at the time I never imagined it being anyone other than you or Tate. She admitted she had fantasies about being me holding her down, you and Tate holding her legs while she was fucked by other guys. In hindsight it was probably just a fantasy, a fleeting thought that turned her on. I should have left it at that, or just kept it to the four of us. But I didn't. I made a mistake. One I genuinely regret because it pissed you and Tate off, and now Zoe is dying because she's worried how you and Tate looked at it all."

"Shit, tell me she isn't worried that Tate and I are angry at her."

"I can't tell you that," Chase said honestly. "She's upset. She admitted to me that night that she'd die before ever inadvertently hurting you or Tate. She's worried that her fantasy put the two of you in a bad position."

"Fuck." Brody rubbed a hand over his face. His eyes looked bleak and tired. "Goddamn it. What a mess."

Then he looked back up at Chase, his eyes narrowed.

"You're telling me you entertained the idea of a relationship between me and Zoe? How the hell is that supposed to work?"

Chase rolled his hand over the back of his head and rotated his neck. Damn but he was tired, and he didn't have all the damn answers.

"I'm saying I thought about it, yeah. As to how it would work, I don't know. I haven't even mentioned it to Zoe. I have no idea how she would react. This isn't even a conversation you and I should be having. We should be talking about this between the four of us before everything goes to hell between us and things are done and said that can't be changed. Like you moving out."

"Are you saying you want me to say all this to Zoe? In front of you and in front of Tate? You want me to unload all this on her this way?"

"Yeah, I do. We've always been honest. Always. It does us no good to talk about this because we're leaving out the one person who is most important to the equation. Zoe. This has to be her choice. It has to be your choice. I'll tell you right now, I'm not giving Zoe up. I'm not being noble and stepping out of the way just because you and Tate have feelings for her. I love her and I know she loves me. The thing is she loves you too. But if you expect her to make a choice, just let it be known that I'm not going to stand aside and be the better man. Fuck that. I'll fight for her with every breath in my body."

"So you're saying if I want a relationship with her, I'll have to share her with you and Tate, provided Tate is even down with this."

"That's exactly what I'm saying," Chase said.

"Christ," Brody whispered. "This is crazy. How does something like this even work?"

"Does it matter? Tell me this, Brody. If Zoe wants it. If she wants the three of us, are you going to give a damn about anything other than the fact you'll have her?"

"No," he said bleakly. "No, I won't."

"Then I suggest you get your ass home so that when Zoe gets home we can talk about this with her so she'll stop hurting. Right now, no matter what happens, whether she kicks me to the curb or she goes along with this, I just want her to stop hurting."

"Yeah, me too," Brody said quietly. "When does she get off?"

"Three today. She's pulled a double, and she's going to be tired, but I want us all to be there when she gets home."

"Have you talked to Tate?"

Chase sighed. "No, I have to find him first."

It took Chase the better part of an hour to track Tate down, and by the time he drove up to the batting cages, Chase was tired and ready to get it the fuck over with.

He watched from the truck as Tate cracked ball after ball. When Tate finished the current rotation, Chase got out of the truck and headed his way.

"Hey, hold up," Chase called when Tate pressed the button for another turn.

Tate lowered the bat and stepped away from the plate. "What's up?"

The guarded way he looked at Chase told him he was going to a tough nut to crack. Maybe even harder than Brody. Although Brody never had qualms about laying it out in the open, Tate tended to be a lot more private. It was anyone's guess as to whether Tate would open up. Unlike Brody, who'd announce to everyone he was leaving, if Tate decided to move out, he'd just be gone one day.

"We need to talk."

The ball smacked the back of the fence. Tate hesitated a moment before opening the gate and leaving the batting area. He didn't say anything to Chase as he walked toward his truck to put his gear away. Chase followed, not disturbing the silence.

Finally Tate closed his truck door and turned to Chase. "What do you want to talk about?"

"Zoe."

Tate flinched and averted his gaze. "I don't think that's a good idea."

"Look, I've already had this conversation with Brody an hour ago. I'm tired and impatient so I'll apologize up front for my bluntness. Brody's thinking of moving out. Any chance you're thinking along the same lines?"

Tate didn't look surprised by Chase's announcement. Not a good thing. Maybe Tate and Brody had discussed it, although Chase doubted Tate would have discussed his personal feelings for Zoe with anyone.

Tate shrugged and his lips pressed together in a firm line. "I've considered it, yeah."

Chase ran a hand through his hair and wished he didn't have to get into this all over again with Tate and then go home and rehash it all when Zoe got there. Part of him wished he had the balls to just say fuck it and only focus on his relationship with Zoe. But Zoe was miserable, and he wanted her happy. Tate and Brody were his friends, and he wanted them happy.

"You're going to get an abbreviated version of what I told Brody, okay? Then you can decide what to do. I can't make a decision for you."

Tate frowned and his brow crinkled in confusion as he stared back at Chase. "Okay. Hit me with it."

"I made some mistakes. I'll apologize up front about the night with Dillon. It shouldn't have happened, and it only clouded the issue and made everyone involved damned uncomfortable. I've already had this conversation with Zoe. I went too far.

"The other thing I have to apologize for is the fact that I knew before I ever asked you and Brody to participate in Zoe's fantasy that you both had feelings for her."

Tate's gaze narrowed. "You knew?"

"Yeah, I knew." Chase shoved his hands into his pockets and took a breath. "Look, Zoe has feelings for you too. She's avoiding us all because she's worried she hurt you and Brody with her fantasy, that somehow she messed up because of Dillon. Dillon is my fault. Not hers. But I can't fix this with her without you and Brody. This has to be something that comes from the three of us."

Tate shook his head and rubbed his palm over his jaw. "You've lost me, man."

"Are you in love with her?" Chase asked bluntly.

Tate's expression grew impassive. It was like iron bars rolled over his eyes. He was a hard son of a bitch.

"Now that would be pretty damn stupid, wouldn't it?" Tate asked softly. "Falling for my best friend's girl?"

"I didn't ask you if it was stupid. I asked if you were in love with her."

For a moment Chase thought Tate would deny it. He wore a pinched, pissed-off look that usually meant someone was in trouble. Hell. The last thing he wanted was a fight with his best friend.

Then to Chase's surprise, Tate's shoulders sagged, and he leaned back against the truck frame.

"Yeah," he said quietly. "For all the good it'll do me."

"Bear with me, okay? Because Zoe gets off soon, and we need to be at the house when she gets there."

Tate's brow wrinkled again. "We?"

"Yeah, we. This is going to sound bizarre, but I'm just going to lay it out there. What if . . . What if you could have a relationship with Zoe?"

Tate started to scowl, but Chase held up a hand to silence him before he got started.

"This is a conversation we're going to have to have with Zoe because in the end it'll be up to her, but the fact is, the three of us all love her and she loves us. I'm simply proposing that things stay the same. We all live together. Recently we've all been making love to her."

Tate held up both hands, his head shaking in denial. "That's crazy, Chase. You're saying you'd be okay with me and Brody having a relationship with Zoe while you are? I'm not even sure what the hell you're saying because it's nuts."

Chase looked down at his watch and blew out his breath in frustration. He knew he wasn't handling this right. He'd dropped a bomb on Tate, and he didn't have time to sit here and go through it like he had with Brody. Furthermore he didn't want to. Not when they were destined to have the conversation all over again when Zoe got home.

"I don't have time to explain. Think about what I said. If it's something you're open to, meet me at the house. Zoe will be home soon, and Brody and I intend to be there when she walks in the door."

Knowing he'd probably just made a giant clusterfuck of the entire situation, Chase turned and walked over to his truck. Maybe he couldn't solve the problem for all parties involved, but he damn sure wasn't going to screw up things between him and Zoe. And maybe that's all he could control.

CHAPTER | EIGHTEEN

She was a live coward. An exhausted, bone-weary coward, but a chicken nonetheless. Which was stupid, really. No one had said anything to her after the night of the . . . Hell, she didn't even know what to call it. Gangbang?

She winced. Bad word choice. It might be apropos, but she didn't have to like it. And the thing was, she enjoyed it. It was sexy and she'd definitely orgasmed long and hard. It was the aftermath where reality caught up to her that squeezed her insides.

Some things . . . Some things just weren't worth the end result. Something had changed between her and Brody and Tate that night. Something that made her afraid. Like maybe they'd turned a corner they couldn't go back on.

She needed to talk to them about it, but she was too worried about what they'd say. So she'd avoided them for days, hoping . . . stupidly hoping that if she ignored the problem it would go away.

Add *dumb* to *coward* and you got a stupid chicken.

When Zoe realized she'd been sitting in the driveway for five minutes now, she shook her head and got out of her vehicle. From the looks of things Brody and Chase were both home. Tate was not. Well, two out of three wasn't bad, and it was a start.

Just before entering the house, she rubbed her damp palms nervously down the legs of her scrubs. What the hell was she afraid of?

Well, she knew; she just didn't know if her fears were founded or not.

When she walked into the kitchen, she found Chase waiting for her. Or at least she assumed that was what he was doing since he was in the center of the room staring directly at her.

There was a seriousness to his expression that unsettled her. She couldn't read his eyes, didn't know if he was angry or upset, or if he was anything at all.

"Hey," he said softly. "Tough day at work?"

She tried to answer, but her throat was so tight that the words died before they ever hit her tongue. She swallowed and tried again.

"Just tired. Usual stuff. Nothing out of the ordinary."

She hated this awkwardness between them. They weren't the type to indulge in meaningless little small talk. And yet here they stood, feet apart, talking about mundane shit. Next they'd actually be discussing the weather.

"We need to talk," he said in a somber voice. Again, nothing in his expression betrayed what his intent was. So she nodded because they *did* need to talk.

She just wished she weren't so afraid of the outcome.

He reached out and picked up her hand, his fingers curling around her palm. "Before anything else is said, I need you to know I love you. That's not going to change no matter what."

"You're scaring me," she whispered.

His eyes softened. "There's nothing to be afraid of, baby. I just need you to know I love you and nothing's ever going to change that. Tate . . . Brody and I have some things we need to say to you."

She glanced around Chase to see Brody leaning against the doorway to the kitchen, his expression tense . . . but hopeful.

The door opened behind her, and she swung around to see Tate standing in the doorway, his eyes dark, his features drawn tight. He looked past her to Chase.

"I'm here," he said in a low voice. "Am I too late?"

Her brow furrowed as she looked between the two men. What in the hell was going on?

"No, Zoe just got home," Chase said.

Tate walked in and shut the door behind him. Without another word he walked up to Zoe and surprised her by pulling her into his arms.

"Don't look so worried," he murmured against her ear. "We'll work things out, okay?"

Before she could respond, he tilted her chin up and kissed her, his fingers tangling in her hair as he pulled her closer to him. When he stepped back, she stared at him in bewilderment. He smiled, touched a finger to her swollen lips, and then walked past her toward the living room.

She turned back to Chase, looking for his reaction to what had just occurred.

"Chase, what is going on?"

He held out his hand, palm up. It was a request for her trust. He wanted her to come with him into the living room where Tate and Brody had retreated. As she slid her fingers over his hand, butterflies took wing in her stomach.

Fear and uncertainty gripped her as Chase led her toward the living room. She sensed this moment was huge. Bigger than anything else that might happen in her life. How she handled it would have an impact, not only on her, but on the lives of the three people she loved most in the world.

Neither Tate nor Brody was sitting. They stood in different parts of the room. Tension emanated from them until she could feel their discomfort as keenly as her own.

Had their friendship come to this? Awkward moments where they couldn't even look at each other without uncertainty? Where they couldn't talk without some grand production? Had she done this with her avoidance? Had she gone too far with fantasies that should have been confined to pillow talk with Chase?

She didn't want to lose Tate and Brody. She didn't want to lose Chase. She took heart from his declaration just a few moments ago. No matter what, he loved her. That wouldn't change. Right?

But he didn't speak for Tate and Brody. Only they could do that. And now she was afraid to hear what they had to say.

"I'll start by offering you the same apology I've already offered Tate and Brody," Chase began in a low voice. "You all need to hear it together because it builds the foundation of everything else we need to discuss."

Her head swiveled in Chase's direction. "Apology?" What did he have to apologize for?

Chase nodded slowly. "I had a good idea of what might happen if I asked Tate and Brody to participate in your fantasy. It's not that I wanted trouble. Quite the opposite, actually. I thought . . ."

"He thought there was a possibility that the four of us could share a unique relationship," Brody said.

She turned in Brody's direction to see him staring at her, his eyes so intense that she shivered under his scrutiny. "Four?"

"He suspected that we . . . I . . . was in love with you," Tate said.

"And me," Brody added quietly.

Her pulse ratcheted up until she could feel it pounding at her temples. "Are you?" she managed to croak out.

"Yes," Brody answered, his voice tight.

She looked to Tate to see him standing there looking so . . . distant. He hesitated for a long second. Then his gaze found hers, and in that moment she saw raw vulnerability.

"Yes," Tate finally said in a voice that was almost too low for her to hear "I do. I have. For a long time."

She opened her mouth, but what could she say? She turned helplessly in Chase's direction. How could she say anything at all? If she denied her feelings for Tate and Brody, she lost them, surely. But if she said anything, what would that do to Chase?

Chase closed the distance between them and gently cupped his palm to her cheek. "Do you remember what I said in the kitchen? Remember that, Zoe. Nothing that happens, *nothing*, will change the fact that I love you."

She looked into his eyes and saw not only acceptance, but something else. Approval? Hope? It was then she realized that she wasn't the only one agonizing over what could be lost here. These guys were friends. Not just her best friends, but each other's best friends as well.

Slowly she pulled away from Chase and turned to face Tate and Brody. She licked her lips and hoped she had the courage to do the impossible.

"I love you too. Maybe I always have. Not just as friends." The admission felt better than she imagined. Weight that she'd borne for days lifted, and she felt lighter and freer. "I don't know what to do, though," she whispered. "What do we do? I love Chase too. I don't want to hurt any of you. I swear I never meant for this to happen."

This time Brody came to her and shushed her with a gentle finger to her lips. His eyes were alight with relief and understanding, but an edge of worry still shadowed his gaze.

"You aren't to blame, Zoe. Neither is Chase, though he seems determined to shoulder it all. I could have said no. I knew what would happen. I also know I don't want to lose you."

She stared helplessly up at him. "Then how?"

Tate and Chase gathered until the four of them formed a loose circle in the middle of the room. Tate stared fiercely at Chase.

"Did you mean what you said earlier?" Tate demanded.

"I meant it," Chase said quietly. "But it's not up to me. It's Zoe's decision."

"What are you talking about?" Zoe asked as she searched each of their faces for some sign of what was going on between them.

Brody touched her cheek again and took a step back so that she was surrounded by the three men.

"It sounded so complicated when Chase brought it up earlier," Brody said. "And now it seems so simple. He was right when he asked me if I would care about anything other than that you had accepted it."

Confusion clouded her mind. "Accepted what?"

Tate stared directly into her eyes. "Us."

Chase's hand slid up her arm and then squeezed her shoulder. "The three of us, baby. We love you. You love us. We don't want to lose you and I don't think you want to lose any of us. What we propose . . . what we want to try . . . is the four of us. We already live together in this house. We've made love to you. We would continue our current . . . relationship. The four of us. You'd be with Brody and Tate. Not just me."

Her mouth fell open, and she turned so she could judge the veracity of his words for herself. He was unsure, but not of his decision. He was unsure of *her*.

"I don't understand," she said faintly. Some of the exhaustion caught up to her. She felt like someone had dropped a brick on her head. She swayed and suddenly Brody was there, gripping her arms as he guided her down onto the couch. "I don't understand," she said again as she sank onto the cushions.

Brody knelt in front of her, his eyes earnest. He framed her face between his hands and brushed the pads of his thumbs over her cheekbones.

"I don't have all the answers, Zoe. I'm as uncertain as you are. But the one thing I do know is that I love you and I don't want to be without you. Right now that has to be enough because it's all any of us can offer with any certainty."

"How does it work? How *can* it work? The three of you accept that I not only love you but two other men as well? What sort of commitment are we talking about here? I mean is this casual? Will you step away from the 'relationship' if you find another woman?"

She was babbling like a moron now, and judging by Brody's expression, he didn't have any liking for her gibberish.

He scowled at her, his eyes fierce. "This isn't casual, Zoe. I won't accept casual. There is no other woman for me. Just because there's more than one guy in this thing doesn't make my commitment to you any less. Or your commitment to me. Yeah, you're with two other guys, but that's it. No others. Period. Even in fantasy land."

A ghost of a smile hovered on her lips. "What if *you're* my fantasy?"

He cupped his hand behind her neck and pulled her into a fierce kiss. His lips melted over hers in a show of possession. He didn't just kiss her. He owned her.

He pulled away, his eyes half-lidded and clouded with desire. "I'd say that's a damn good thing."

She glanced over his shoulder to see Tate in the distance, his head turned as he stared out the window. Brody turned and followed her gaze. Then he sighed and rose to stand in front of her. He extended his hand down to help her up.

The few steps toward Tate had a surreal quality, like she was inside a dream and couldn't shake herself awake. He turned when she stopped just a few inches away.

"Tate?"

He watched her for a moment, his eyes dark and probing. "You want me to respond to that bullshit?"

She laughed, though it sounded strained. "No. Well, maybe. I probably didn't say it like I should have, but I'm still spinning here.

I could use some help. I feel like I'm falling down some hole that doesn't have a bottom."

The corner of his mouth lifted into a half smile. "Welcome to my world. It's the way I've felt since the first time I touched you and made love to you."

She leaned into his body and reached down to take his hand. "Did you mean all of that? All of what they said?"

"I did. I do. And as for that crap you said about casual and other women. Well, it's crap and that's all I really need to say about that. What I feel for you is anything but casual."

She smiled and rested her forehead against his chest.

"This won't be easy for you, Zoe. I don't want to pretend it will be just so we talk you into something we desperately want. We have one person to please. You have three very distinct personalities, each pulling you in a different direction and sometimes at the same time."

She closed her eyes, absorbing the words, the idea that she was loved by three men who meant the world to her. Three men she loved in return. One of whom she already had a stable relationship with. The other two? On the cusp of something new. Still fresh. Feeling their way around. Could they do it?

"I love you, Tate. I do. I need you to know that."

He tugged gently at her hair until she tilted her head up so she could see him.

"I love you too, Zoe. We can make this work. I admit, I had to think about it. I'm still thinking about it. But I want to try. I don't want to walk away, and I don't want to lose you. Can you do the same? Try? For me. For us?"

Her stomach clenched, and instinctively, she turned, searching for Chase. The commitment had to come from her. Had to be her decision. Chase couldn't do it for her. But she had to know she had his support. She had to know he was okay with this.

Tate loosened his hold on her and then leaned down to whisper in her ear. "Go to him. I know you're worried."

She rose up on tiptoe and brushed her lips across his and then backed away and turned to where Chase stood—alone—across the room, hands shoved into his pockets, his mouth set into a firm line as he watched the goings-on around him.

"Chase," she said as she approached.

He opened his arms to her and she rushed into them, relief crushing down on her.

"I don't know what to think."

Her voice was muffled by his shirt, and her fingers curled into his waist in a silent plea. She needed time to process everything that had gone on in the last few minutes. It was easy to say *yeah, okay, great idea*. Nobody would be hurt. Everyone won. But beyond that initial gloss, what then? Would it really work out? Four people in a committed relationship?

"I know it's a lot, baby," Chase murmured against her hair. "I just want you to be happy. I want the hurting and uncertainty to stop. No one's happy right now. We're all miserable. I want you to stop feeling like you can't come home because we're here."

She winced at the accuracy of his assessment.

"Answer me one thing, Zoe."

Slowly she pushed away from his body and stared up into his eyes.

"What do you want? If you could have this work out any way you wanted, how would it go down in your mind? Don't be afraid to be honest. Just tell me what you want."

"I want us to be together," she blurted. "All of us. I don't want Brody or Tate to leave."

Then she realized what she'd said. Her mouth rounded to an O, and her eyes widened as she met Chase's gaze.

"That's what we want too," Chase said softly.

Could it be that simple? Really?

She briefly closed her eyes as her mind raced to catch up. What about . . .

"We can only take it as it comes," she murmured.

When she opened her eyes again, Chase was gazing down at her, his face soft with love.

"That is all we can do," Chase agreed. "I'm going to fight for this, Zoe. For you. For me. I'm not going anywhere. No matter what happens."

She smiled, and the faint stirring of hope flared and blazed higher in her chest.

"We know it won't be easy, Zoe," Brody said.

She turned her head to see Tate and Brody standing a short distance away.

"But we're willing to try," Tate said. "It's going to take work. From all of us. I can promise you that I won't quit."

She sucked in a deep breath, gripped Chase's hand, and then reached across the space toward Brody and Tate.

Brody slid his palm underneath hers while Tate cupped his hand over the top of her hand.

"I won't quit either, Zoe," Brody vowed.

"I love you." She tested the words on her lips. Liked how easily they rolled off her tongue. "I love you," she said again. "I won't quit either."

For the first time, Brody and Tate smiled. Really smiled. She hadn't seen them look so relaxed and happy in a while. Since before . . .

"I'm sorry," she choked out.

Their smiles turned to confusion.

"What for?" Tate demanded.

"That night. Dillon."

Brody shook his head. "You have nothing to be sorry for. We start fresh. Right here. Right now. From now on, any fantasies you want fulfilled, we're your guys."

She smiled. "I can deal with that. I still have lots and lots of fantasies . . ."

Chase groaned, and then they all laughed.

"She's going to wear us out," Chase said.

"And right now my fantasy is for you to love me," she said in a husky voice as she looked in turn at the three men standing in front of her.

"That," Tate said, "might be the easiest fantasy we ever fulfill."

HER FANTASY MEN

SHAYLA BLACK

*Thank you to the incomparable Joy Harris
and all the wonderful readers at* Joyfully Reviewed
*for suggesting that Maya and I do this anthology together.
I had so much fun working on this novella.
I hope you enjoy!*

CHAPTER | ONE

"Which one of you lucky bastards is nailing Kelsey?" Rhys Adams leaned against the back of the sofa, beer in hand, and glanced at the other two men. "It isn't me, and she glows too much to be going without."

Jeremy Beck raised a dark brow. "I assumed it was one of you, since she's put me firmly in the boss category."

Tucker Hall eyed the object of their mutual desire through the window as she bustled around the patio table, setting the last of the party favors in place. She wore another of those long, summery skirts that hid her lush ass. But in deference to the early September heat, she'd donned a little white tank top that hugged the ripe curves of her breasts. Sunlight poured golden over her pale skin and mahogany curls. Kels was like something out of time, one of those women who could have modeled for the masters of oil and canvas long ago. Just a glance at her made his dick stiff. Fantasies of her on her back, legs splayed for him, could make him come in record time.

"I guess Tucker is the lucky winner," Rhys groused.

"Me?" He jerked his gaze back to the other guys. "No. I'm stuck in the friend zone, man. She put me there when we were four, and I haven't been out since."

"At least she's put you two in a category," Rhys complained. "I don't think she knows I'm alive half the time unless she runs out of coffee or needs me to fix her cantankerous bathtub. *Then* she needs a good neighbor."

A collective quiet settled over the trio as they all contemplated the question that Jeremy finally voiced. "Who, then?"

"No one at night," Rhys offered. "I've got sweet views inside her bedroom."

And he didn't hesitate to take advantage of them, Tucker would bet. Unscrupulous but lucky bastard.

"She's always home and always alone," he went on. "Unless you count battery-operated boyfriends."

"You've seen her masturbate?" Jeremy nearly came out of his chair.

Tucker nearly came, period.

Rhys smiled. "Oh, yeah. Our Kelsey has a healthy sex drive." His smile took a nosedive. "She's just not getting any from me, at least not while she's at home. At the office? Nooners, maybe?"

Jeremy shook his head. "No. I keep her busy, half because I can't stand the thought she could get laid at lunch, and I wouldn't be participating."

"The only time she disappears is to go to your place," Rhys pointed out to Tucker, his look expectant.

"I swear, as much as I'd love to lie, we watch action flicks together, but we're not making any action. I've tried a hundred times to think of ways I could bring sex up without ruining the friendship— or having her laugh in my face. So far, I'm striking out."

Silence lingered. Tucker bet that, individually, the trio had often wondered who Kelsey shared that sweet body with. Frankly, his money had been on Jeremy. Tall, dark, handsome, rich, intense . . . What woman wouldn't want that? Except Kels had never been a typical woman. She liked Stallone movies, football, and beer. In the same week, she might also salsa dance, buy a Coach purse, and then attend a lecture at the local college about the discovery of new black holes in the universe. She was always a puzzle.

This was the first time they'd ever discussed their mutual desire for Kelsey. Sure, he'd known the other two were hard for her. Rhys practically followed her with his tongue dragging the floor, and Jeremy watched her with those sharp, dark eyes that missed nothing. Like the others, he'd assumed one of them was Kelsey's lover. Unless someone was lying, this conversation gave him a lot of hope.

"So . . ." Rhys started. "If she's not doing the horizontal mambo with her best friend, her boss, or her neighbor, who the hell is she fucking?"

The answer came to Tucker like a comet through his brain. He drowned the sizzle it roused with a long swallow of beer. Or tried to. Nothing doused his need for Kels.

"No one," he said finally. "She was twenty-one when she lost her virginity."

Tucker remembered it vividly, though he'd really like to forget. Alex the smooth talker had finally persuaded her onto her back by lying about his feelings for her. Kelsey had called Tucker in furious tears when she'd discovered that his feelings only lasted as long as the orgasm and extended to the next coed a week later. His Kels never gave herself easily, and since Alex, she never did unless she was sure. As far as he knew, she'd had only one other lover, David, the musician she'd nearly married. Close call, that. But Tucker couldn't fault her. He'd genuinely liked David, even if he'd been jealous as hell. Kelsey had been the one to decide that twenty-three was too young to get married. David, at thirty, hadn't wanted to wait. They parted, no harm, no foul. She even exchanged Christmas cards with David and his wife.

Many tried to get into Kelsey's panties. She took none of them seriously. He, Jeremy, and Rhys were good examples.

"Yeah, she doesn't sleep around that I can see," Rhys agreed.

"She's never so much as flirted with anyone at the office."

"And that leaves us where?" Rhys asked.

"Fucked, and not in the pleasant way." Tucker sighed. "Plan, anyone?"

Kelsey Rose Rena cast a nervous glance inside the living room. Her guys were talking intently. They'd all been a part of her life for at least the last three years, so they knew each other. Were even friends . . . of a sort. But she'd bet none of them had a clue how she felt about them all. She feared their reaction if they did.

Thank God this party would be under way soon. Let someone else wade through the testosterone in her living room. Once it had started getting thick, she'd had to dash outside. It was either that or overheat.

"Need help, Kels?" Tucker stuck his head out the French doors. That wild wavy brown hair of his made her hands itch to trim it, run her fingers through it. But his blue eyes melted her every time. He had the biggest heart—and the sexiest smile she'd ever seen.

"I'm good. But could you guys find that cooler in the garage and ice down the drinks in the fridge?"

"Will do." He hesitated. "You okay?"

She avoided his gaze. If she looked at him—at any of them—no telling what her eyes would reveal. Jeremy would be furious, Tucker hurt, and Rhys . . . he'd figure it out as he went.

Focused on the plastic flatware she set on her patio table, Kelsey murmured, "Great. When people start coming in, just send them out back."

Tucker sighed. Something was off with him, with all of the guys.

It wasn't football season yet, so no one's favorite team had lost recently. Tucker never let work stress him out. She wondered if he was having girlfriend trouble . . . then decided she didn't want to know.

The door shut, and she breathed a sigh of relief. If she could just make it through the afternoon with those three, then shoo them out after the party, she could escape to her fantasy life. At least four hours to go. Damn! She glanced at her watch and started counting . . .

"Anything?" Jeremy asked as soon as he shut the door.

"Nah, man. She's in her own world." One that didn't include them. Tucker resisted the urge to curse.

"What do you think she wants in a man?" Rhys asked.

"If I were an expert, I wouldn't be telling you. I'd be dating her myself."

Jeremy nodded. "She doesn't seem to care about money. God knows, I tried that route."

"Nope." Tucker grabbed another beer, then headed for the garage, motioning the others to join him. "She's more than comfortable with her ability to make her own money."

"She's also not impressed by anything with a fast engine. I tried that, too," Jeremy confessed.

"Hey, I mowed my lawn shirtless for a month, then struck up conversations with her, hoping she'd look. Her gaze stayed glued above my neck."

Rhys was a fireman and spent nearly all his downtime pumping iron. If Kels was going to be wowed by some guy's body, it would be Rhys's.

Tucker retrieved the cooler, then opened the freezer in her garage and started dumping in bags of ice. The others joined in.

"I've been her confidant, her shoulder to cry on, her prom date when hers dumped her at the last minute . . . None of that did me any good either."

"You knew David. What was he like?" Jeremy spoke in low tones. Always. Yet his voice carried the snap of subtle demand.

"Easygoing. Big sense of humor. Kind of a wandering spirit."

"That leaves me out," Jeremy brooded as he began to toss beers, wine coolers, water, and soft drinks into the cooler.

"But her boyfriend prior to that was a successful guy who owned a few jewelry stores. Flashy dresser. Of course, he was an asshole, too. I don't think she would put you in that mold or you wouldn't be here," he told Jeremy, then wondered why he was trying to make the competition feel better.

Truth was, he liked both Jeremy and Rhys. And it felt good to finally be talking about the elephant in the room.

They finished icing down the drinks in relative quiet, but Tucker's brain was working overtime. A glance at Jeremy—whose brain never stopped—proved Kelsey's boss was lost in his own ruminations, too.

Until he spoke. "Would all of you agree that we'd rather see Kelsey happy with one of us than some bastard who might mistreat her?"

Tucker hesitated, then glanced at Rhys. Finally, they both nodded. Yeah, he'd hate like hell to let her go, but if he couldn't have her, he'd at least be happier knowing that she was with someone who wanted her, had genuine feelings for her, would take care of her.

"Me, too," Jeremy offered. "I think Tucker is right, gentlemen. What we need is a plan."

"Plan?"

Tucker laughed at Rhys's confusion. The firefighter was a great guy . . . but Rhys and a plan combined as well as gasoline and margarita mix.

"We've got to find out what's in her head." And her heart, Tucker decided. But they had to start small. Forever and ever amen, picket fence, and two point two kids was a lofty place to begin. First, they had to know what she wanted in a date, in a lover. Who, if anyone, was on her mind.

"How?" Jeremy asked, getting right to the heart of the problem as usual. "Does she keep a diary?"

"Not that I know of . . . but it's not as if Kels tells me everything." Tucker shrugged, lamenting that fact.

"She might have a journal. No doubt she's capable of writing more than a grocery list," Rhys drawled.

"Kels is a bit private. I'm not sure she'd write her feelings down."

"Maybe because she *is* private, she'd be more likely to pour her feelings out on paper than to another human being." Jeremy pinned his gaze on Tucker. "Or does she have some *really* close girlfriend I don't know about?"

"No. To her, most women like shopping and gossip and those *Grey's Anatomy*–type shows, which she hates."

Rhys frowned. "Yeah. Not Kelsey's style."

"So now what?" Tucker ran his hand through his unruly hair.

"Could you have one of those best friend heart-to-hearts?"

"Yeah." Rhys warmed to the subject. "See if she'll spill."

"Tried that. She blushed and said that talking to me about her fantasies and her ultimate man was crossing the friend line. I told her it was because I was seeking a girlfriend and wanted her advice. She was sure that her wants wouldn't necessarily match anyone else's and ended the conversation."

"Damn."

"Exactly. There must be some way to trip her up or persuade her into a tell-all mood so we can learn what she wants and who she has feelings for," Jeremy murmured.

"Get her drunk?"

Tucker reached over and swatted Rhys on the head. "No, you idiot. Something that won't have her puking or give her a headache. You know Kels doesn't handle her liquor well. I'd rather try something less sneaky."

When Tucker reached down to lift one half of the enormous cooler by a handle, Rhys lifted the other. "I would too, brother, but the up-and-up isn't working."

Jeremy held the garage door open. "He's right."

"What are you suggesting?" Tucker asked. "Seducing her?"

"Tried that." Jeremy sighed as they traversed the house, cooler in hand. "She sidestepped me, then set me up on a blind date with a Barbie who had an equally plastic personality."

"I tried, too." Rhys lowered the cooler by the back door, then glanced out at Kelsey, who stood in the shade, face raised to the sky, eyes closed, basking in the sun. "She giggled and started making jokes about firemen who think with their hose."

"I can't seduce her," Tucker admitted. "First, I'm not a ladies' man, and second, I'd lose her. She thinks of me as someone she can rely on—"

"Which is why you're stuck in the friend zone, dude," Rhys chastised. "You've never tried to make her see you as a man?"

"I kissed her once."

"Yeah?" That got Rhys's attention.

"But we were thirteen, and her comment afterward was that Josh Smith kissed better."

Rhys doubled over with laughter. Even single-minded Jeremy cracked a smile.

"What we need is evidence."

Golden brow raised, Rhys glared at Jeremy. "Spoken like an attorney."

"I *am* one; sue me." The attorney smiled, and something about his eyes reminded Tucker why the guy billed out at two grand an hour. Suddenly, he shot Rhys a cunning stare. "You firemen have interesting ways of gaining access to a house, right?"

Rhys rolled his eyes. "Yes, with all the subtlety of a sledge-hammer."

"I have a key, guys," Tucker offered.

"Give it to him," Jeremy snapped. "I'm going to call Kelsey after the party, make up some emergency. You"—he stared at Rhys—"are going to sneak in. Look around, in that monster closet of hers, through her home office. . . See if she keeps a journal or mementos or has written anything personal on her laptop. Check her correspondence, her voice mails. Scroll through her recent calls and see if she's reached out to anyone."

"I don't know, dude . . . It seems so invasive. What about her privacy? What if she catches me?"

Jeremy's stare lost what little levity it had. He looked as if he were resisting grabbing Rhys by the shirt and shaking some sense into him. "Be careful, and she won't. Just get us some information or we'll all be stuck in this hell indefinitely."

Rhys sighed. "Fuck."

"Call both of us as soon as you've finished your reconnaissance." Jeremy directed. "Then collectively we'll decide the best course of action, regardless of what you find, agreed?"

"Count me in."

Tucker hesitated. He didn't like spying on Kels. He didn't like lying to her or invading her privacy . . . but he also didn't like being cut off from the woman he adored. He hadn't made any progress with her since that chaste tweener kiss. Fifteen years later, maybe it was time to try something new.

Hoping like hell he didn't regret this, he handed Rhys Kelsey's house key.

CHAPTER | TWO

The party had been pure torture. Labor Day festivities, cold beer, and good friends aside, the sight of Kelsey in a bloodred bikini had nearly been Rhys's undoing. The pale swells of her breasts nearly spilling out of her top, that ridiculously small waist above outrageously lush hips and thighs . . . Damn, he got hard all over again just thinking about her.

Too bad he wasn't the only one hard for Kelsey. Rhys grimaced. Tucker's feelings for her were deep and true and abiding, and Jeremy, a man everyone knew played for keeps, intended to make her his submissive. Still, Rhys refused to be strong-armed out of Kelsey's life by loyalty or authority. He burned for her every bit as much as the others.

Soon, he would make her see that. Somehow.

Jeremy might have provided a plan so they could learn Kelsey's feelings. Tucker might have provided the key so they could research what might be in her heart. But Rhys intended to take full advantage of the opportunity to make her his own.

He'd sneaked away during the party earlier and done something designed to ensure that Kelsey would call Rhys tonight after her pretend assignment from her boss, then invite him inside. All he had to do was wait.

Pacing his bedroom, he stared out the window again—straight into Kelsey's. His beautiful neighbor never closed her blinds, thank God.

Finally, she entered the room and stripped off her cover-up. The bikini top came next, then the bottoms—and she stood blessedly bare. And gorgeous.

Rhys wished like hell that walls, windows, and fences didn't separate them. He'd kill to see that beautiful skin up close. Touch it.

But to achieve his personal mission, he had to serve the collective one first. Quickly, he sent a text to Jeremy:

Everyone is finally gone. Call her now.

Less than thirty seconds later, Kelsey jumped, threw the cover-up over her head, and darted back down the hall.

A minute later, Rhys was quiet as he opened her front door with Tucker's key and slipped inside, locking it behind him. Yeah, he should probably wait to see if Jeremy could get her out of the house on this "errand," but impatience chafed. Besides, to leave, Kelsey would have to change clothes . . . which meant she would get naked first. He couldn't bypass the opportunity to see her up close and personal.

Once inside, Rhys heard Kelsey on the phone, pacing the kitchen. The deferential tones she used with Jeremy set his teeth on edge.

"I've had too much to drink to drive to the office tonight, sir, but I promise I'll be in early and finish proofing that brief for you."

A moment later, she added, "I had two more margaritas after you left." Then, "I didn't realize you'd need my help tonight." She sighed. "I realize that's not good for me. I'm sorry, sir."

Kelsey fidgeted. "No, I don't have lunch plans." Another pause. "My job is to help you however I can, sir. I'll plan on attending the meeting with you. Do you need me to make lunch reservations?"

Rhys grimaced at Kelsey's tone. She sounded breathless, almost aroused. Her boss liked to tie women up and order them around. On one hand, it bothered him. *His* independent Kelsey into that? Really? On the other hand, the thought of seeing Kelsey bound and ready to take whatever he wanted to give her excited the hell out of him. He liked the vision better without Jeremy in it.

Sighing, Rhys shoved the thought aside and crept through the foyer, past the living room, circling the back of the dining room, then peeking his head around the corner into the kitchen and den. He was in luck; Kelsey was looking out the French doors into her shadowed backyard, submissively responding to yet another of Jeremy Beck's commands.

Fuck.

He'd worry about her boss later. After all, she might be intrigued by Jeremy, but she hadn't let him touch her. Maybe she didn't have any real feelings for the guy and simply reacted instinctively to the command in a boss's voice. He hoped like hell that deference didn't *mean* anything.

Rhys entered her darkened hallway, then crept to her guest room/home office and shut the door behind him.

Her computer hummed quietly. A quick search of her files revealed nothing more than a few tax records, her playlists, family photos, and mostly work-related e-mails. She was still logged into her Facebook account, but her wall held greetings from a handful of high school friends wishing her a happy Labor Day. Nothing from a lover.

Next, Rhys picked up her cell phone, which sat beside her laptop. He scanned her recent incoming and outgoing calls. Her mother, her aunt, her cousin, Jeremy, Tucker, and himself, period. If she had a lover, she wasn't communicating with him, and that wasn't Kelsey's style.

Shit. Now what? Maybe she kept a journal. He looked around the little room, rummaged through her desk drawers. Other than bills and house papers, they were empty. Maybe the diary was in her bedroom . . .

Tiptoeing across the hall, Rhys could hear Kelsey murmuring something in more of those worshipful tones that made him grit his teeth. Lucky bastard, Jeremy.

With a shake of his head, Rhys slipped into Kelsey's private domain and spied her little red bikini on the pale carpet. His cock hardened in a painful rush. She'd looked fabulous in it, laughing, playing hostess, so natural and unaware of how gorgeous she looked with dancing dark eyes and her riot of brownish-red curls. He knew she looked even better without the bikini.

"No, sir. Really, I'm tipsy. And tired. I promise I'll be in early."

Damn it, Jeremy hadn't been able to get her out of the house. So now his time was *really* limited. Rhys forced himself to focus.

He looked across her dresser, scattered with car keys, jewelry, and other knickknacks. Nothing that stood out. Her rumpled bed was unmade, her tiny nightstand covered by a little lamp, a candle, and what looked like a fairly racy romance. Did that cover have a woman with more than one guy on the front?

As he reached for it, he heard Kelsey say, "Yes, I know you'll reprimand me, sir. Whatever you feel is necessary, I understand." She paused. "Good night."

Then she slammed the phone in its cradle and began stomping down the hall, her footsteps echoing across the hardwood floors.

Hide! He hustled into the shadowed confines of her walk-in closet and scrambled behind her dresses along the back wall, praying she wouldn't find him before he could get out. Otherwise, he'd have to have a good explanation for being here. Which he didn't. And there would be hell to pay.

Kelsey entered her bedroom with a shaky sigh and darted straight for her nightstand. Through the crack in the door, he could see her wrench open a drawer. She withdrew a pair of rumpled paper bags and tore into them. As she extracted the items, Rhys clenched his fists to hold in his groan.

Her battery-operated rabbit and a slender, curved vibrator.

She was going to masturbate. *Fuck!*

Plopping her items on the bed, Kelsey tore off her cover-up, put her iPod buds in her ears, switched the MP3 player on, then lay down. Her skin looked so flawless and fair against the dark sheets. Her breathing picked up, lifting her chest with each inhalation, her hard nipples stabbing the air. Rhys got hard all over again. Yes, he loved watching her through her window, but to be mere feet away from her? Surely, he'd spontaneously combust.

Before moving next door to Kelsey, he'd preferred tall, skinny girls with straight hair and sun-kissed skin. One look at Kelsey and he'd barely looked at another woman. When he'd met her, heard her laugh, experienced her warmth, he'd been a goner.

She closed her eyes, took a deep breath. Time to call the others for a backup plan. It went against his grain to let the others in on her private moments, many of which he'd watched from his bedroom window, dick in hand . . . but he might not get out of Kelsey's house undetected without their help. Damn it.

He hit Tucker's speed dial. Not a second later, her friend picked up. "What did you find?"

"Hang on a second," he whispered, not knowing how loud her iPod might be.

Then he flipped over and dialed Jeremy, who answered immediately. "Well?"

Rhys conferenced the men in together. "I didn't find anything helpful, and now, she's masturbating. I'm hiding in her closet, trying to figure out how in the hell I'm going to get out without getting caught. Ideas?"

"Masturbating?" Tucker choked.

"Yeah. She's naked on the bed with her sex toys. And she looks flaming hot."

"Goddammit," Jeremy growled. "Don't look at her."

"Bite me," Rhys tossed back. "She's ten feet in front of me. Of course I'm going to look."

"Would she hear the phone ring?" Kelsey's boss snapped. "If I can get your eyes off her by calling again—"

"She wouldn't hear it. She's listening to her iPod. But I can't walk past her; she might see me."

Moonlight and the nearby streetlamp filtered light through the slats in the blinds. Rhys watched Kelsey preparing to get down to business. He had to restrain a groan at the sight.

"Oh, hell! She's cupping her breasts." *Her voluptuous, full, mouthwatering breasts.* "And she's pinching her nipples. Damn . . ."

Jeremy groused out a curse. "If you're going to watch this, you're going to share details. Every one of them."

The tone set Rhys on edge. "Fuck off."

"I helped you get into her house with a phone call and a plan," Jeremy argued. "Tucker lent you his key. If such a gorgeous sight is going to fall into your lap, you're going to share with us. Or we won't help you with an exit strategy."

As if he hadn't proven it time and again, Jeremy displayed once more why he was one of the most sought-after attorneys in Texas. The man could flat argue with anyone and win.

"Fine." Rhys ground out between clenched teeth. "She's scraping her nipples with her fingernails."

Rhys could feel their excitement over the phone. He felt the same keen sense of arousal . . . which only multiplied when Kelsey slid a hand across the flat of her abdomen, caressing down to the inside of her thigh. Her legs parted. He swallowed.

"Touch me . . ." she murmured. "Yes."

She dipped her fingers inside her pussy, and Rhys nearly lost his mind.

Tucker choked. "D-did she just beg someone to touch her?"

Fucking hell . . . "Yeah."

"Any idea who she wants doing the touching?"

"Where is she imagining someone touching her?" Jeremy barked.

Before he could answer, Kelsey lifted her fingers from between her legs, and Rhys got a good glimpse. "Fuck, she's wet."

"You see her pussy?" Jeremy demanded.

"That's a terrible word," Tucker chastised.

Jeremy scoffed. "You like *cunt* better?"

Rhys ignored them. "It's her fingers. They're wet."

Tucker swallowed. "She really touched herself?"

"Dude, she does it all the time." Rhys rolled his eyes.

Her friend let out a shaky breath. "I think I'm going to explode."

Easy to relate to that feeling, especially when Kelsey began a slow, rhythmic rubbing of her clit.

"Please . . . " She groaned. "Like that. Oh, yes . . ." Her hips lifted. "I want it . . ."

"Damn it," Jeremy snarled. "I'll give it to her. Relentlessly. Until she begs me to stop. When she does, I'll just give her more."

Not if Rhys had anything to say about it. That would be *his* privilege.

"But I can't," she whimpered. "Too much . . ."

Damn it, who did she picture sharing her pleasure with? What the hell did her imaginary lover do? Say?

A moment later, she grabbed the slender wand, flipped it on, and eased it inside her. Her back bowed off the bed as it disappeared inside her body.

"Oh my God . . ." she cried.

"What?" Tucker and Jeremy both snapped.

"She's using her vibrator."

Kelsey punctuated Rhys's announcement with a cry of pleasure. It filled the room, heating his blood. On the phone, Tucker groaned.

Jeremy's silence had its own sound of careful restraint. He hoped neither of them had taken their cocks in hand. The last thing he wanted was to hear some other guy get off to Kelsey's cries of pleasure.

Though he had to admit, he was tempted to stroke himself in time to her moans.

With one hand, she thrust the slim wand in and out of her hungry body, the sounds of her juicy flesh pushing the edge of his restraint. Finally having a soundtrack to this visual was killing him.

With the other hand, she groped for her rabbit. She found the base first, flipped it on, then clutched the buzzing purple toy and dragged it between her legs, settling it right over her clit.

"Yes! God, yes! I need it! That's so good . . ."

"I can't listen to this and do nothing. I'm coming over there," Jeremy growled.

Everything inside Rhys protested. "Stay where you are, damn it. You're going to help me get out of here when she's done, but this isn't a party."

She gasped. "Please. Oh God . . ."

"I can't take it," Tucker muttered. "What is she doing?"

Flushing. Arching her back. Biting her lip. Clutching her toys. Moaning. And . . .

"Coming."

"I love you . . . you . . . you . . ." Kelsey panted.

Then she rent the air with a sharp, high-pitched cry that went on, became a low growl of satisfaction that nearly had Rhys climaxing in his jeans.

"I'm going to paddle that woman's ass for this torture as soon as I get my hands on her," Jeremy promised.

"You can't hit a woman!" Tucker protested.

Before Rhys could say that he wouldn't mind seeing Kelsey with a pink bottom, her boss answered. "How likely are you to forget the sound of her orgasm? Ever? How many times will you play it in your head the next few days? Weeks? Months? How many times will you masturbate to it and wish to God you were hearing it in person because you'd given her that much pleasure? How many times after your self-induced orgasm will you be bitterly disappointed that you were only torturing yourself with the sound because you don't know who the fuck she's fantasizing about when she brings herself to climax?"

No one said anything for a long minute. Rhys could hear Kelsey panting as she slowly resumed normal breathing. On the phone, her other two admirers each struggled for self-control.

"You're right," Tucker finally said. "I'll never forget that sound. And since Rhys didn't find anything in his search, we still don't know who she wants."

"Or who she loves," Jeremy added. "Are you sure that neither of you knows about another man in her life?"

"We're the only men who ever visit her house," Rhys said. "I have nosy Mrs. MacDermott across the street watch her when I'm at the station, and she always clucks that even her fourteen-year-old granddaughter has more boyfriends than Kelsey."

"She sees no one at work. I intentionally keep her far too busy for an office romance."

"I talk to her folks every other week or so," Tucker said. "They don't mention a boyfriend. Believe me, I ask. And as far as I know, except her dentist appointment last week and grocery shopping, she hasn't been anywhere."

"Maybe her lover is purely imaginary." Rhys winced as he said it. That would pretty much kill their collective hope.

"Or it's one of us, and she just can't say it," Tucker suggested. "I'm wondering . . . Kels and I have been friends for so long, maybe she thinks bringing up sex would be awkward. Or how does a woman tell her boss that she's fallen for him? Or a neighbor she's never even dated? For all that Kelsey is independent, I don't think she's brave with her feelings."

"Another something we have to thank that prick Alex for," Jeremy muttered.

"Totally," Tucker agreed. "So maybe . . . we just have to keep trying individually to reach her."

Jeremy hesitated. "I still think Rhys's idea of getting her drunk would be more effective."

"I won't take advantage of her when she's tipsy." Tucker's disapproval blared through the phone.

"I just want to ask her questions, not tie her to the bed and fuck her all night . . . though that plan has a lot of appeal."

"Kelsey and bondage do *not* belong in the same sentence."

Jeremy snorted. "That's your opinion. Which, by the way, is wrong."

"Look, I know the nasty bedroom games you play, but Kelsey is much too sweet to be aroused by that crap."

The way Jeremy laughed wasn't nice. "Then why is she wet at work all day long? And why does she get wetter the more I command her?"

This argument was going nowhere.

"Stop, both of you," Rhys insisted.

"Let's give it a week or so," Tucker suggested. "We could all question her separately to see what we can learn, then touch base again."

"We can meet at my office some late afternoon when you're both available."

"Won't Kelsey be there?" Rhys pointed out.

Jeremy shot back, "I'll demand she do something in another room."

"Demand?" Tucker clearly didn't like the sound of that.

"I'm good both at being her boss and a Dominant. She'll comply."

"She's not a damn dog."

Rhys sighed. "Stop it! We'll each try to pry the answer out of her separately. We'll meet up at Jeremy's office next week and be *totally* honest about the outcome. I'd still rather see her happily settled with one of us than some loser we don't know who could hurt her."

"All right," Tucker grumbled.

Jeremy's voice was firm. "Agreed."

Tucker sighed. "What do we do if, by next week, we still don't know anything about Kelsey's feelings?"

Rhys paused. Jeremy sighed. Together, they said, "We get her drunk."

The honeyed bliss of release was gone when Kelsey opened her eyes. The tingling in her arms and legs receded, her heartbeat returning to normal. That electric, so alive feeling slowly dissipated, leaving something jagged and empty in its place.

Slowly, she opened her eyes. And she was alone. Again.

Shoving aside her toys, she tore out her earbuds, drew her knees to her chest, and hung her head. How long could she stay in this limbo, desperately wanting three men and having none because she didn't know what they really felt and was too afraid to upset the status quo? Because she couldn't risk choosing one and potentially having the other two disappear from her life?

Tucker she could never live without. He knew her down to her core. He was the first person she thought of when she needed a hug. The only person she'd bared her secrets to had been him. Just as she'd listened in return. His quiet, sexy ways left her breathless. She itched to touch him, discover how much deeper their friendship could be. Doing without Tucker would leave a hole in her heart from which she'd never recover.

Jeremy . . . She'd been working for him for nearly four years. His absence in her life would kill her. Without him, she feared she'd morph from a confident, independent female back to the spiritual equivalent of wallpaper. Her self-assurance soared under Jeremy's hot stares. He'd taught her when to crush opponents and when to show compassion. He made her feel vital, vibrant, needed—and like the kind of woman who could inspire the forbidden. He aroused her as no man had, his commanding streak the stuff of her fantasies. They just . . . clicked.

Rhys often reminded her not to take her life, her job, her problems—or herself—too seriously. He was her positive outlook, her silver lining. He'd taught her that things happened for a reason. Besides preventing her from being too maudlin, he shared her passion for movies with sophomoric humor and was her resident handyman. He was always willing to eat whatever experiment she dished out in the kitchen. And always backed it up with Moose Tracks ice cream. Without him, she'd forget to embrace all her tomorrows and smile gratefully for each new sunrise.

How was she ever going to choose? But how could she keep denying her feelings—and fearing theirs?

Kelsey sighed. She'd had this argument with herself a thousand times. And a thousand times reached the same conclusion: She had to keep her love for them to herself.

Rising slowly, she padded to her bathroom and shut the door. A sumptuous bubble bath might relax her enough to sleep. Of course, she could give herself another orgasm . . . but pleasure without her fantasy men—Tucker, Jeremy, and Rhys—was losing its blush.

And the depression afterward was getting heavier by the climax.

She turned the handle on her temperamental bathtub, praying for hot water. And waited. And waited.

Cold water sloshed over her fingertips. *Damn this tub!*

Groaning, Kelsey closed her eyes. Why now? She had three incredible men to try to soak out of her heart.

Call Rhys or pray for sleep that probably wouldn't come? Kelsey chewed on a ragged fingernail for a moment, then sighed. No contest.

She padded across the hall and grabbed her cell phone.

"Hello?" he answered.

That was it? No *How's my sexiest neighbor?* Or *I never thought you'd call, baby.* Just hello? Even weirder, Rhys's voice on the other end sounded stilted. Shaky.

"You all right?"

He swallowed. "Great."

Sounded more like aliens had overtaken his personality. But if he didn't want to talk about whatever was bugging him, she wasn't going to push it. More than once, she'd been down about her hopeless situation with these great men, and Rhys had encouraged her to confide her troubles in him. But she'd remained silent. She couldn't pry now and expect him to spill if she wasn't willing to do the same.

"Is this a bad time? If I'm interrupting something—"

"Not at all. Just hoping to see you again."

God, she'd love to see him too. And that was so dangerous. She winced. "Even if it's to fix my bathtub?"

"Absolutely. I'll be right there."

Before she could say anything, he ended the call and she heard his knock on her front door. Damn, he must have been walking and talking at the same time. And she was still standing here stark naked.

Throwing on her cover-up, Kelsey dashed down the hall and opened the door. She caught her breath. Rhys stood there in faded jeans and a tight gray T-shirt that clung to every ripped, rugged muscle. The breeze ruffled his short tawny hair. Those green eyes of his were like lasers, fastening on her face, then drifting down in a hot gaze to the zipper secured just above her cleavage. Like he wanted her. Her nipples peaked.

Awareness that she wore nothing beneath a thin bit of white terrycloth was sharp as a blade—and just as disconcerting.

Rhys's narrowed gaze fastened on her breasts. He gripped the door frame and raised his stare to her face again. She'd never seen this side of him. No teasing or laughter. No flirting. Desire broke across his expression, taut, harsh, unapologetic. Though he didn't say a word or make a move, his want detonated like a bomb between them. The explosion rocked her.

She swallowed, shook. Should she let him in? What would happen if she did?

Nothing. She was strong; she had to be. To give him what she wanted—what they both wanted—would upset the delicate relationships she had with all three men.

"Come in." Her legs trembled as she stepped back to admit him.

He brushed against her as he entered her foyer, and she bit back a gasp at the rush of tingles. A flash of dizzy need assailed her.

God, this was a thousand times stronger than any orgasm she'd given herself, and he'd barely touched her.

"Your cheeks are flushed, Kelsey."

I've been stroking myself and thinking of you.

Forcing a shaky laugh, she shut the door, enclosing them in the privacy of her house. "I had a wrestling match with the bathtub and lost. You know how I am when I lose my temper."

The corners of his mouth lifted, but it wasn't exactly a smile. "What's the problem?"

As Kelsey retreated down the hall to her room, hoping the little white garment covered her ass completely, she beat back a rising panic. Nothing was different tonight. She could let Rhys in her bedroom—and had a dozen times at least. He would enter, go straight to her bathroom, fix the problem, flirt, then leave. This was same old shit, different day.

But tonight, he touched his palm to the small of her back, his big body hovering behind her, his chest brushing her back. His scent, like earth and pine, wrapped around her. Kelsey got weak-kneed all over again.

"Kelsey? The problem?"

Right. "I need it hot."

"I'd love to give it to you as hot as you can stand it," he murmured in her ear.

Oh God. His words shivered down her spine. "I meant the water."

His expression said that he didn't believe her. She wasn't sure she did either.

As they rounded the corner to her bedroom, Kelsey drew in a nervous breath. Ten minutes. If he was coming on to her, she could be strong and resist him that long.

"I turned on the water a few minutes ago and . . ." Kelsey risked a glance at him over her shoulder.

He was staring at her bed, at the rabbit and vibrator she'd accidentally left there.

Mortification rushed over her in a hot, sickening wave. *Oh, please don't let him guess that I've masturbated to thoughts of him . . .*

"Fix the water temperature. Please." She pushed him toward the bathroom.

Rhys didn't budge an inch. Instead, he pulled her closer and braced his hands on her hips. She couldn't possibly miss his erection against her belly, hot and pressing. She trembled again.

"Kelsey, baby . . ."

She closed her eyes to avoid his probing stare. "Don't say a word."

"It's all right. You have needs. I want to fulfill them."

Right now, she wanted that too, so badly, she could nearly taste him. He'd be salty and musky and so damn male . . .

"It's complicated."

"It doesn't have to be. I'd never hurt you. I just want to take care of you every way you'll let me."

Oh God, oh God, oh God. She had to stop this now, and she knew one way to scare Rhys off in a heartbeat. He *hated* clingy women. Three had attached themselves to him at last month's community barbecue. He'd cut them all off cold.

"It wouldn't be right for either of us. I'm twenty-eight, Rhys. I want to get married, start having children. You're a few years younger and—"

"Let's do it."

Kelsey's jaw dropped. "Y-you want to get married?"

"To you? Absolutely. I think about you . . . Damn. It's constant. So is my desire." He caressed her cheek. "And my love."

She blinked, drew in a shaking breath, clutched his thick biceps for support. Was he trying to say that he didn't just want her, but . . . loved her. "Truly?"

A smile crept up his lips as his hand drifted to her shoulder. "I know we usually share laughs. But I'm serious. If I thought for a second that you'd marry me, I'd be on one knee with ring in hand, begging you."

Her shaky breathing nearly became hyperventilating. *Oh my God.* "We're friends, Rhys."

"We could be a whole lot more."

"I had no idea you felt that strongly."

"You're it for me, Kelsey."

"How can you know that? I mean, we've never—um . . ." His revelations were so startling, she couldn't form a coherent sentence.

"Kissed? Had sex?" He arched a golden brow. "We can solve that right now."

The bed was in her peripheral vision. They could be on it—together—in the next few minutes. She could have Rhys as her lover, have one of her fantasies fulfilled.

Temptation crashed through her. Her stomach knotted tight. Even the thought made her wet. In the past, he'd subtly suggested that he'd like to sleep with her, wrapped it in a flirtatious joke or double entendre. She'd blown him off. Nothing veiled about his words tonight.

If she turned him down now, would she be doing the right thing? Or would she regret it?

"You're thinking too hard. I want you; you want me. I love you."

He looked at her expectantly, those green eyes shining with honesty. He loved her. Really, truly loved her. Kelsey couldn't lie to him. The moment was too sincere, too raw, for anything else. "I love you too."

"Ah, baby…" He beamed and wrapped his arms around her. "Let's start there. The rest we'll worry about later."

She shouldn't. Kelsey knew that. This would change her relationship with Rhys—and Tucker and Jeremy.

But when Rhys leaned in and settled his mouth over hers in a hungry press, she was gone.

He was like embracing a mountain, big, fresh, powerful, undeniable—a force all his own. At the insistent urging of his lips, she opened to let him inside. The sweep of him against her tongue was a big burst of taste and sensation. Crisp and clean, he filled her with a flash of sensation that swept her with heat and want.

Kelsey threw her arms around his shoulders and lost herself in his touch. He cupped the back of her head, lavishing one heart-stopping kiss after another on her until she was breathless and achy.

Toys had nothing compared to this man, and Kelsey feared that, after tonight, she'd never be satisfied with them again.

"Baby," he breathed against her lips. "You don't know how long I've wanted . . . waited."

"Yes, I do." More than he could possibly imagine.

"Do you think about me when you touch yourself?"

His low voice rasped in her ear, then he pressed his mouth to her throat, her collarbone, the swell of her breast above the cover-up. One of his hands made its way up the back of her thigh to cup her bare ass. Under that kind of assault, Kelsey couldn't be anything but honest.

"I have."

"Jesus," he muttered under his breath. "You don't do for yourself anymore. You come to *me*. Understand?"

It wasn't that simple, and she tried to find the words to explain, but he yanked the zipper of her cover-up down to her abdomen and pushed it away from her breasts.

"Fuck," he whispered. "You're gorgeous, baby."

Kelsey had to resist an instinctive urge to cover her breasts. "They're big."

"Yeah," he said, as if that were the most wonderful fact ever.

Then he cupped one, his thumb brushing her nipple. It was already hard, but his touch pinged reckless pleasure all through her body. She gasped at the electric sensation and felt her sex gush again.

Rhys's mouth covered hers once more, now devouring, heat-seeking, yearning. She melted like a wax on a long-lit candle as he cupped her other breast, rolling the nipple, pinching. Her sex clenched with need.

A long moment later, he tore his mouth away. "When I kiss you, you taste amazing. But I have to taste you everywhere."

Anticipation leapt in her belly, and before she could blink, Rhys bent to her breast, cradling her nipple against his tongue, between the clamp of his teeth. He stung her, then soothed with a suction that made her cry out and clasp him even tighter.

As he moved his head to her other breast and repeated the process, he shoved his foot between hers and nudged her legs apart. A heartbeat later, his fingers stole across her clit, and she mewled at the sweet friction of his touch.

"That's it, baby. You're so wet for me. I'm going to make you feel so good," he said thickly against her nipple before he sucked it in again.

As she stood, trembling, needing, he dropped to his knees and fit his mouth over her. *Eureka!* She'd thought a hundred times about Rhys or Tucker or Jeremy orally pleasuring her. Fantasies had nothing on reality.

At her cry, he sucked her clit into his mouth, toyed with it using his tongue, and plunged two fingers into her slick, clinging entrance.

It was as if the orgasm she'd given herself twenty minutes ago had never happened. Kelsey couldn't ever remember an ache so sharp and unrelenting. And still he didn't let up. He merely lifted her thigh over his shoulder as he swiped his tongue over her again in a wicked caress. She fisted her hands in his thick hair. When he added a third finger inside her and rubbed a sensitive spot that only her little wand had ever touched, all the blood left her head. Kelsey swore she was going to fall to the floor and beg.

She'd missed a man's touch, that hard passion—but Rhys's need stunned her. Desire crashed down on her as he licked her little bud again, teasing her one second, eating her alive the next.

"I-I'm going to come." *Please . . .* She dug her fingernails into his shoulders, clinging to the edge of sanity where she couldn't think, couldn't breathe—and didn't care.

"I'll look forward to that." His fingers hit her sweet spot again. "Very soon. How long has it been for you, baby? You're tight, and I don't want to hurt you."

Kelsey couldn't remember that long ago. "Since David."

Rhys stilled. "Five fucking years?"

She nodded. Robbed of his touch, every nerve ending in her body ached ever more. "Rhys!"

"You'll never have to ask again, baby. You'll be lucky to go five hours without from now on."

Kelsey had barely raised her brows at that statement before Rhys stood and unfastened his jeans. She caught a mere glimpse of his jutting cock, thick and blunt-headed, before he lifted her in his arms, legs spread. A second later, he impaled her, stretching her impossibly wide. Her flesh stung and burned as he burrowed deeper, thrust harder. Euphoria smoldered just under beyond her reach.

Amazement followed. This was happening. Rhys was naked and deep inside her. It wasn't a fantasy or anything in her head. They were making love, and it was finally real.

"Damn, you're mind-blowing. Tight. Warm," he muttered against her throat. "I love you."

In two steps, he reached the bed and lowered her to it, then slammed deep inside her.

The head of his cock flared against her most nerve-drenched spot. She moaned as orgasm pressed close and clamped down on him.

She'd always imagined that sex with any of her men would be incredible—it had fueled her fantasies for months—but this was way beyond anything she'd dreamed up. As he moved against her, their skin grew damp, clung. Breaths synched up as he shoved into her deeply, fiercely, cupping her ass, chanting her name. He plundered her mouth with abandon. As each second passed, he grew harder, his breathing rougher, her pleasure headier.

"Rhys!" She clawed at his back and kissed her way across his corded shoulders, bucking up to meet him.

"I need to see you come for me, baby."

The burn behind her clit swelled, accelerated. Her muscles tightened. Her world stopped.

Then exploded.

She screamed as pleasure detonated through her body. Rhys tensed, his cock swelling as he groaned in her ear. Deep inside, she felt him thick and heavy and hot as he came.

She soared, weightless, timeless. Treasured. And so in love. No way could she live without having Rhys like this again.

As his strokes slowed, he rained kisses on her face. Flinging her arms around his neck, she rubbed her cheek against his, then nuzzled his neck. She felt released, reborn in his arms. To her shock, tears wet her cheeks.

As reality slowly hit her, they became wrenching sobs.

Being with Rhys had been earth-shattering, beyond her every fantasy. What would happen next time they saw Tucker and Jeremy? Rhys would touch her, assume it was now his right. Tucker would be shocked, possibly hurt. Jeremy would be enraged.

She'd lose them both.

And if she pushed Rhys away right now, she'd lose him, too.

Why had she given in to temptation?

"Hey, baby, no tears." Still buried inside her, Rhys brushed her hair from her face. "I didn't hurt you, did I?"

"N-no."

But he'd made her life beyond difficult. Scratch that. *She'd* made it difficult. Rhys had merely given her what they'd both wanted. Now, she had to deal with the consequences.

CHAPTER | THREE

"I didn't give you permission to leave, Kelsey."

She gripped her purse a bit tighter and cursed under her breath. Jeremy Beck, at his delicious demanding best, stood behind her. Usually, he was the consummate professional, the sexual command in his tone so subtle she often wondered if she'd imagined it because she wanted it so bad. Submitting to any man had never occurred to her . . . until Jeremy. She fantasized about it constantly, though he never actually tried to dominate her.

Until this week.

After her Monday night mistake with Rhys, she'd dragged into work Tuesday morning early, hoping to escape the memories by diving into work. Thank God Rhys was scheduled to be at the fire station for the next forty-eight hours. Until his next shift ended, Kelsey hoped that the office would be her refuge from the tangled sheets on her bed that still smelled like sex.

Jeremy made peace impossible. He addressed her with a new

edge in his voice. He stood closer, stared more intently, making her tremble with need.

Tuesday, she'd gone to work, brimming with a thousand recriminations, drowning in a ton of guilt. By the time she'd gone home, her panties had been damp with the desire Jeremy inspired. Today, they were soaking wet, and if she didn't get away from her boss . . . Well, not much escaped his notice. As raw and confused as she felt now, she didn't know what would happen.

After five years of abstinence, she'd taken one lover. Now she wanted another. What was wrong with her?

"It's after six, sir." She closed her eyes, praying he'd have mercy.

She had to get it together or Jeremy would guess how badly she ached for him.

"I can tell time. I'm not finished with you. Set your things down and come to my office." Jeremy turned and crossed the room, entering his private domain.

His words were pure asshole . . . but the tone was so honey-rough. Still, she had to resist—for her sanity and her future.

"Sir, I'm due for a dress fitting for my cousin's wedding. I'm one of her bridesmaids."

"The fitting doesn't start for an hour and a half." He raised a dark brow. "I need you now."

A direct order, boss to subordinate. With a sigh, Kelsey set her things on her desk and followed.

The office was quiet now. Everyone had gone. Lights were darkening in other parts of the building. The air conditioner clicked off. With every step, Kelsey heard her shuddered breaths, the sound of her footfalls on the carpet . . . Jeremy tapping his fingers on the open door.

Her eyes glued to his dark, polished face, she stepped past him. And bit her lip. His gaze burned her. Kelsey's heart stuttered at the sight. He wanted her. For the first time in a long time, he wasn't hiding it. God, why now, when she was feeling so weak?

He shut the door. The subtle click enclosing them in total privacy made her stomach clench.

"Was that Garrison I heard you on the phone with a minute ago?"

Relief rolled through her. *This* she could talk about. "Yes, sir."

Jeremy crossed his arms over his wide chest. "He offer you a job again?"

She nodded. "In Miami."

"And you told him . . . ?"

The same thing she always told Garrison; she enjoyed working for Jeremy and felt far too loyal to jump ship. Even if he was offering more money, it wasn't worth leaving her home, her parents . . . and her men. "No."

Jeremy released a breath, and some of the tenseness left his shoulders. Every day, in little ways like this, he showed that he wanted her with him. That he cared. It had messed with her head. And her heart.

"Very good," he praised. "Now I want to ask you about your behavior this week."

The one thing she *really* didn't want to discuss. "Sir, I—I'm sorry. I'm not feeling well."

His face softened for a moment. "What happened? On Monday night at your party, you looked radiant. Tuesday, you dragged in here looking pale and tired, with your eyes swollen and red."

"I had a hangover."

"That's lasted for two days?"

"Well, then my allergies set in."

"You don't have them." He raised a dark brow at her. "Don't lie to me."

Damn, he was too smart and he always flustered her. "Sir . . ."

"You're distracted. You spilled coffee on an important briefing this morning. You're not eating." She opened her mouth, and Jeremy raised a hand. "Before you say a word, know that I don't want excuses or more lies. I want answers."

She couldn't give them. If she told him that she'd made a wonderful mistake with Rhys, Jeremy would be angry. Even hurt. Nearly four years ago, when she'd told him she didn't take lovers, he'd made her swear that if she ever changed her mind, he would be first, the fact he was her boss be damned.

She'd broken her word.

"I—I've been having trouble with insomnia."

That, at least, wasn't a total lie. She'd been too worried for the last day and a half to sleep much. What would she do when Rhys's shift ended and he knocked on her door? And he would. Already, he'd left her three messages. She didn't know how to answer them.

"Perhaps, but something's caused it. What?"

"N-nothing."

"Do you know what happens to little girls who lie to me?"

Kelsey had a pretty good idea. Ever since learning that Jeremy was a Dominant, she'd been reading erotic romances featuring such men. Her fantasies about Jeremy always involved her boss tying her up, commanding her body . . . with Rhys and Tucker participating in her punishments and pleasure.

"Y-you discipline them?"

"Yes. Do you know what that means?"

Kelsey sucked in a breath. Would he take her over his knee and spank her? Jeremy grabbed her wrist and pulled her close, his stare unrelenting. She read the answer to her unspoken question. Yes, that was exactly what he'd do. Helpless to look away, her insides fluttering, she met his gaze.

"I—I'm sorry. I won't let anything affect my work performance again." Kelsey wasn't sure how she'd keep that promise.

"I'm not worried about your performance at work; you're an excellent employee, which is why Garrison keeps trying to hire you away from me. I'm worried about *you*. But if you lie to me again, I'll have no compunction about disciplining you."

God, why did even his threat make her wet?

"You have no right." She meant to the words to be strong, confrontational. They came out breathless.

"Do you really want to challenge me on that?"

No. Because if he crooked his finger and kept talking this way, she'd melt into a puddle of desire at his feet. How was that even possible? She was still processing her guilt for having sex with Rhys, and now . . .

"Please, sir. This has nothing to do with work."

Jeremy stared hard at her. "Consider yourself off the clock, then. I'm speaking to you as a . . . friend now, not your boss. Are you clear?"

But he didn't sound friendly; he sounded aggressive.

"Yes, sir."

He stepped closer, stalked toward her in the small, enclosed office, forcing Kelsey to back away until her butt hit the edge of his desk. Jeremy's eyes glinted with satisfaction as he braced his hands on the desk, on either side of her hips, trapping her in the cage of his arms. "What happened between your party and your drive to work yesterday morning?"

Here came the barrage of questions . . . and she didn't have any good answers. "It—it's personal."

He hesitated. "Are your parents all right? Do you need help with something? Money?"

"No. My parents are fine. They're in Italy right now. I—I don't need money. Thank you, but—"

"You have no siblings, no pets. No close friends, other than Rhys and Tucker. Did you fight with one of them?"

"No."

Jeremy tapped his fingers on the desk, slow, measured, insistent. "Did you fuck one of them?"

Apprehension bit into her, ran icy in her veins. She'd feared Jeremy would guess the truth eventually, but not this quickly.

"That's a very personal question."

He tightened his jaw as he stepped closer, towering over her. Jealous fury burned across his taut face. "You broke your promise to come to me first if you wanted a lover, Kelsey."

"You're my boss." But she knew it was a bad argument; they both wanted so much more.

"Not right now. I'm a man who wants you, and you're a naughty girl who didn't stay true to her word. You've earned a punishment."

"Jeremy—"

"That's *sir* to you." He grabbed her by the hips and spun her around.

In the next instant, he lifted her skirt above her waist and tore her panties away. She tried to shove her skirt back down, but he grabbed her hands and secured them in his grip at the small of her back. His other palm spread hotly across the cheek of her ass, and Kelsey felt every second of the caress like an electric charge through her body.

"You have a gorgeous ass." He moaned, then smacked her backside—hard.

She gasped. "Ouch!"

"Quiet. For every noise, I'll add another."

"Please . . ."

"You beg me after you've broken your word? No, Kelsey. You knew how much I wanted you. You chose another without coming to me first."

"Sir, I—"

"I didn't give you permission to speak."

"I don't know how to do this," she blurted, tears bleeding from the corners of her eyes.

Jeremy stilled. "Be submissive?"

She gave him a shaky nod. "It scares me."

He wrapped his arms around her. His voice gentled. "There's nothing to be frightened of. You want it."

It wasn't a question; he knew. Again, she nodded.

"Say it. Let me hear it."

"I w-want it."

"What exactly? Be precise."

Kelsey drew in a shuddering breath. "I want to learn to be submissive for you, but Rhys and Tucker—"

"Are irrelevant to this discussion. You want me. I *will* have you—directly after your punishment."

Before she could say another word, he rained a series of whacks across her ass, never in the same place twice, but he showed no mercy. It stung, burned . . . then gave way to a sweet, blossoming heat that had her biting her lip to hold in another gasp.

Why did she like it? No, love it? Shame and desire blended, making her mindless. She clawed the desk, holding in a cry. She wanted to moan his name so badly.

Suddenly, he stopped. Without thought, she thrust her ass back at him, silently begging for more. Jeremy stepped away, and she heard him shed his suit coat, tie, and shirt.

This couldn't happen, not here. Especially not now. She'd already complicated her life with Rhys, but to have sex with Jeremy would completely melt—and destroy—her.

Kelsey worked up her gumption to face him. "Jeremy, I think—"

"Don't. Tonight, thinking is the last thing you should be doing. Just feel."

"I can't. The complications . . . It's impossible."

"So is denying it. I've waited, wanted, agonized. As have you, and don't try to say otherwise. Since you're now taking lovers—"

"It just . . . happened."

"This will happen, too. Repeatedly."

Her heart stuttered in her chest as he whirled her around, pinning her in place with a gentle but forceful hand at the small of her back.

"Don't move."

"Yes, sir."

The next sounds were metallic, the clink of his belt buckle unfastening. She drew in a sharp breath. Her stomach tightened. The rasp of his zipper lowering came next and had her breath rushing out harsh and tight.

"Under my hand, you will learn to submit," he vowed. "I want to adore you as only I can. Pamper and cherish you."

She fisted her hands, wanting that, too. And more. "Restrain me?"

"Yes."

"Use me?"

"Yes. Take off your blouse and bra. Quickly."

He wanted her to remove her protective layers of clothing, bare herself to him until she wore nothing more than a skirt bunched around her waist. *Oh dear God.* Even the thought stripped her psyche down until she felt vulnerable, submissive.

"I'm waiting." And not patiently.

Forbidden desire making her hot and dizzy, Kelsey let out a shuddering breath and unbuttoned her blouse. Jeremy pulled it free of her shoulders, leaving her bra exposed. The hooks were across her back, right in front of him. She waited for him to unclasp it. He didn't move.

Slowly, she glanced over her shoulder to a stunning, well-muscled chest with a light dusting of dark hair and ridged abdomen that attested to his daily gym ritual. He had a scrumptious treasure trail that disappeared into his open slacks and the dark underwear visible through the open zipper. Kelsey couldn't miss the more-than-healthy bulge beneath.

She gulped as she raised her gaze to find his dark eyes burning black fire into her. "Remove your bra. I won't ask you again."

"I just thought—"

"Don't," he cut in. "Follow instructions."

She couldn't possibly undress with her stare all tangled up in his.

Jeremy would see how his commands aroused her. He'd have so much more power over her.

But when she turned her face away, he grasped her chin. "Turn around. Look at me while you remove your bra and show me your breasts."

Fighting back the apprehension and need swamping her, she did as she was told. Jeremy watched her face, his dark gaze never leaving hers until her heavy beige bra hit the ground. Then he reached up to cup one of the soft mounds, and his gaze drifted down to her aching, hard nipple.

"Gorgeous. Lean back on the desk and wrap your fingers around the edge. Leave them there until I say otherwise."

Kelsey's first instinct was to obey. She wanted to please Jeremy so badly . . . But logic kept trying to reassert itself. What about her friendships with these three wonderful men?

"We really shouldn't do this . . . " she murmured. "This isn't smart."

"Either say no and leave or obey me. No vacillating or I'll punish you again."

Could she walk away? Could she give up something—someone—she'd wanted so badly for so long? Kelsey knew if she walked out the door now that Jeremy would let her. But he'd likely cut her out of his personal life, be her boss and nothing more. Even the thought of that made her want to cry. She loved him, looked up to him, craved his discipline.

"Yes, sir." And she complied, gripping the edge of his desk.

"Good girl. I don't use silly safe words. *No* means *no*. But use the word only if you *really* mean it. I won't hurt you. But you must trust me."

"I understand, sir."

Jeremy brushed her hair off her neck and set his lips on the sensitive skin. "Your obedience pleases me."

Kelsey beamed under his praise, which made no sense. She

hadn't done anything extraordinarily difficult. But she sensed he wasn't going to make this easy. She didn't believe for one instant that he was done punishing her for sleeping with Rhys.

Jeremy pressed a soft kiss to her throat, her collarbone, before his lips drifted down to her breasts. He took one in his mouth, his tongue worshipping it before his teeth scraped her nipple. She yelped, the sensation riding the thin line between pleasure and pain.

"Quiet," he reminded.

He heaped the same treatment on her other breast, while he pinched and rolled the first in a tight grip. The sweet bite made her sex clench and weep. Kelsey sucked in a shocked breath. She wanted to beg for more, but suspected that if she did, he'd stop immediately.

"You will not come until I give you permission."

Kelsey closed her eyes and gripped the desk tighter. She knew from working with Jeremy that he could be the most patient bastard on the planet if it got him what he wanted. And she knew without a doubt that he wanted her submission badly.

"Acknowledge me," he demanded.

"Yes, sir," she breathed.

He bit at her bottom lip, then crushed her mouth beneath his. Jeremy's kiss, like his personality, was a force to be reckoned with, clever, masterful. Still gripping the desk, she swayed into him. His kiss made her light-headed. Fresh lust burst through her body, settling into an impatient ache between her legs. She moaned against his mouth, craving more.

This was really happening, her every fantasy about to come to life. Her most forbidden yearning for her boss, her friend, her dominant male, to claim her was becoming reality. The thought aroused her every bit as much as his smooth voice issuing rough commands.

His hands covered hers, ensuring her fingers securely gripped the desk against which she leaned.

"Good girl," he praised as he tore off her skirt, clutched her hips, and lifted her onto the desk.

She screamed as the hot skin of her ass hit the cool black lacquered surface.

He raised a dark brow. "You seem determined to collect punishments tonight."

"No, sir."

"Make one more noise, say one more word, before you're given permission, and I'll add another punishment. Now, turn and face the door."

What was he going to do? Kelsey had no idea as she scooted around on the desk a quarter turn and faced the locked door.

"On your hands and knees."

She hesitated. Here? On his desk?

"You should already be in position, Kelsey. Hands and knees. Facing the door. Exactly as it sounds."

His patience was running thin, and her apprehension soared. Frowning, she turned her body over until her weight rested on all fours. Immediately, she felt vulnerable. Her large breasts hung beneath her, nipples distended. The moisture between her legs began to trickle down her thighs. She closed her eyes.

A rustle of cloth and a few moments later, Kelsey felt Jeremy's hand burrow softly into her hair and pull her head down. She opened her eyes and found him naked, waiting for her, cock in hand. It, like him, was formidable, the angry blue head insistent, slit weeping.

"Suck me."

She licked her lips. Did he know she'd fantasized a hundred times about him commanding her to do just that?

"Yes, sir," she breathed.

As she came closer, she inhaled his scent. The musk of him went straight to her sex, where she clenched in longing. Kelsey licked her lips again.

"You look sexy as hell. Open your mouth. That's it . . ."

Slowly, she cradled the underside of his cock with her tongue.

Jeremy hissed, tensed. She had to open wider to accommodate him. The muscles in her jaw protested. She gasped when he slid all the way to the back of her mouth and bumped her throat.

"Relax around me. Control your reflexes. Breathe through your nose."

Kelsey forced herself to beat back the panic and obey. When she wrapped her lips around Jeremy's erection and sucked, accepting him deep, his hands tightened in her hair.

"Ah, sweetheart. Yes . . ." He hardened even more in her mouth. "I've wanted you this way for so damn long."

Pulling back, she lashed her tongue across his head, lapping up the salty moisture around his slit. He tensed again. And she felt her power. He might be commanding her, but in that moment, she controlled his body, his pleasure.

He was her slave.

Drawing in a breath, she slid her mouth back over his cock, down farther, taking even more of him. He tasted more stunning the second time. Strong, male, an aphrodisiac all his own. She swirled her tongue around his length, laved the head with hard suction, then grazed it with her teeth.

"Fuck," he cursed. "You're trying to undo me, you little vixen."

Could she? The thought made her giddy. Kelsey applied herself again, using slow, strong sucks, dragging her tongue along every inch, tracing the vein on the underside, nibbling on the sensitive tip, tasting the weeping tip time and again. Her pace quickened. His breathing grew labored.

God, she was addicted to the flavor and feel of him, the way every ounce of his attention was focused on her and her alone. She moaned around his cock.

Jeremy's back arched and his hands tightened in her hair again. "Cup my balls. Now."

Kelsey complied without hesitation, fondling them gently, scraping her nails lightly along the tight sacs. He hardened again. Swelled.

Pulsed on her tongue. Began fucking her mouth in hard, rapid strokes.

Ruthless, unrelenting, he held her completely still with his fist in her hair so he controlled the depth and pace of the strokes as he filled her mouth again and again. It was harsh and primal. He was on the very edge of his control, and Kelsey had never felt more feminine or desired.

"I'm going to come. You're going to swallow everything I give you."

She whimpered. The thought of him bathing her mouth in seed was both exciting and scary as hell. She'd never actually sucked a man off. Her forays into oral sex with David had been far briefer and less exciting. This . . . God, she couldn't wait to do it again.

Then his grip tightened on her again and he shouted, "Kelsey!"

His salty release sprayed across her tongue, the back of her throat. She swallowed once, twice, her tongue still moving over him. He gushed into her mouth again, and she drank greedily, her heart pounding as if she'd run a race.

Jeremy's breathing was uneven when he gently pulled away from her mouth a moment later and released his harsh grip on her hair. He smoothed it with the stroke of his hand, soothing her scalp with a tender massage.

His eyes narrowed suddenly, and he wiped a finger along the corner of her mouth, then held it up for her inspection. Another drop of semen dotted his fingertip.

"Open up. I said every drop."

Slowly, she parted her lips.

"Tongue out. I want to watch."

Heat burned through her all over again. Could she get any wetter? Could she want a man any more than she wanted Jeremy?

Eagerly, she stuck out her tongue. He set the pad of his finger right in the middle, and she tasted both the salt of his skin and his seed.

"Suck it."

Immediately, she complied, closing her eyes to savor the flavor of him all over again.

He moaned. "Excellent. How's your jaw?"

"A bit sore," she admitted with a smile. "So are my knees."

"Hmm." His expression was one she'd seen many times. He had something up his sleeve, and she'd never guess what. "I'm not quite ready to move you yet. Stay there."

For Jeremy, a little discomfort was nothing. "Yes, sir."

"So sweetly submissive. You're doing well." He dropped a kiss on her shoulder, her cheek, as he glided a palm down the line of her spine. His other hand dipped beneath her to fondle her breasts. "Look down. Watch me touch you."

She did. Her flesh looked pale against his tanned hands, and the sight aroused her unbearably. Kelsey squeezed her eyes shut tightly, trying to hold in a delicious gasp as he caressed the swells of her breasts with the utmost care, then pinched her nipples roughly. The sensation arrowed straight between her legs.

"You have the most incredible breasts. Many Doms like their subs naked at all times in the privacy of their home, but you need support."

She did. Being bare for Jeremy sounded heavenly, but there was no way going without a bra wouldn't hurt.

"I know what you need. Once I send it to you, you'll wear it when I ask."

Inside, she both rejoiced at his desire and cried at the futility. "Yes, sir."

Again, Jeremy's hand engulfed her breast before he pinched one nipple, then the other, sliding heat through her bloodstream. Then he trailed one finger down her abdomen, dipping into her belly button. With a faint smile, he rimmed her innie a few times. Unable to help herself, she giggled.

"You're ticklish?"

"Helplessly."

As he lifted her chin until her gaze met his, she was struck by the warmth and lingering smile. "Another reason to adore you."

He bent and kissed the tip of her nose, pressed his forehead to hers, and closed his eyes for a heartbeat. She did the same, feeling the reverence of the moment.

"You're beyond my every fantasy. I love you," he murmured against her mouth.

Jeremy never said anything he didn't mean. Her heart stopped as joy and wonder slid through her. Kelsey had hoped, but never dared to imagine he felt this way about her. No way she could deny him anything now. To have this much of him and not the rest would be unbearable torture. No doubt, being intimate with both a friend and her boss would bring trouble, but she'd worry about it tomorrow. She'd waited years for this moment. She wasn't waiting anymore.

"I love you, too."

Peace washed over his face before it darkened again. In that instant, she knew he was wondering how she could have gone to bed with one of her other friends if she loved him. It would only start a discussion that would go nowhere and get them nothing but frustration and tears.

Knowing she had mere seconds to divert him, she reached out and wrapped her fingers around his penis.

Jeremy stilled. "Kelsey . . ."

It was a warning, pure and simple.

"Are you done with me, sir?"

She continued to stroke him, and he drew in a deep breath as he hardened, lengthened in her hand. "Of course not."

Kelsey sent him a saucy smile, then glanced at his erection, now every bit as strong as before. "It appears not."

"Vixen," he muttered. "On your back, hands above your head."

The command came so swiftly, it took Kelsey a moment to process. Jeremy stilled in displeasure, and she scrambled to obey.

Nodding as she arranged herself across his desk, he stroked her belly again. "Legs over the edge, sweetheart, thighs and all."

Ridiculously eager, she quickly complied.

"Good girl. Legs spread. Wide." The frown in his voice was reflected on his face. "Wider."

He tapped the insides of her knees until she opened her thighs to his satisfaction. Her inner thighs burned with the stretch and effort as cool air hit her slick flesh. But nothing could cool her raging need. Hot, ready to burst, she writhed under the dark intent in his gaze. As his palms skated over her breasts, abdomen, her sex, she saw the male craving to dominate and conquer tighten his face.

Jeremy gritted his teeth, then bent to retrieve his necktie. He rounded the desk and approached her, grabbing her hands in his grip. With brisk movements, he wrapped the tie around her wrists, then secured the ends to the metal bookshelf bracket mounted into the wall above her head. Every muscle in his shoulders and forearms strained as he knotted the tie. Twice. No easy fastening, no mere ornament of bondage, this binding would hold until *he* released her.

"Too tight?" His tone warned her not to lie.

"No." Her voice quivered, as did her belly.

She was literally at his mercy now. Rationally, she knew he would never hurt her. But she felt so helpless and hungry. Jeremy could either grant her pleasure or withhold it. A fact he was well aware of, given the predatory smile lifting the corners of his mouth.

"Remember, no coming until I say so."

She had absolutely no practice trying to hold her orgasm back and wondered if she'd be able to.

"Kelsey?"

"Yes, sir."

He ran his knuckles down her throat, between her breasts, all the way to her drenched sex. With a wicked smile, he grazed her clit. Once. Her back arched, and she gasped, staring helplessly at his dark face. There was no question he was enjoying himself.

"Your whole body is trembling. It's beautiful to know I hold you in the palm of my hand. I can give you pleasure . . . or make you wait."

Please, please, give me pleasure.

"Somewhat like you had the ability to choose to give or withhold sex for the last four years."

Uh-oh. Now her real punishment would begin. The spanking . . . a mere warm-up.

"I see you understand. Do you think these last years have been easy for me, Kelsey?"

"They've been difficult for me, too," she insisted.

His strong, square jaw tightened. "But you let Rhys or Tucker end your celibacy."

She opened her mouth to explain. He held up a hand and shook his head.

"I don't want details. You broke a promise, one I took very seriously."

"I didn't plan to," she argued. "Besides, it's not as if you've been without sex."

The reality that she'd all but pushed him into other women's arms suddenly filled her with sick regret. Instead of keeping Jeremy at a distance, she could have been with him.

Except there were her relationships with Rhys and Tucker . . .

"Ever notice how many of my dates are short brunettes with curly hair and lush figures?"

A parade of his previous girlfriends marched through her brain. *Oh my God . . .* "All of them."

He nodded. "I've been substituting, hoping for the real thing, waiting for your feelings and desire to develop, for your trust to grow. I know I'm asking a lot of you . . . Submission, devotion. I wanted you to come to me."

Kelsey bit her lip and tears stabbed the back of her eyes. "I didn't know. I mean, I knew you wanted to sleep with me."

He scoffed. "Did you think I just wanted sex?"

"I—I . . . suppose."

Surprise flared across his face as he planted his palms on either side of her body and leaned over her. "Let me absolve you of that foolishness. I'm going to do whatever it takes to make you mine in every way. My wife, the mother of my children, my everything. I'll be thirty-eight in two months. I've devoted most of my adulthood to my career. Now, I want to devote myself to you."

She looked up at him with wide eyes, and her heart flipped. Words escaped her.

Resolution firmed his expression as he parted her legs wide again. She held in a groan and waited. A heartbeat passed, another . . . Then he caressed the inside of her thighs.

"You're wet. Very."

And he sounded like that pleased him.

His stare was glued to her face as he eased two fingers inside her and teased the front wall of her sex. Oh . . . wow. She sucked in a breath. *That* spot. He'd found it immediately. Then he settled his thumb over her clit and rubbed in torturously slow circles.

Her eyes widened as she watched him watch her, ruthless determination all over his face. He intended to drive her up hard, high, fast.

Kelsey's entire body tensed in the charged silence and she grabbed onto his tie in desperation, spreading her thighs even wider.

"God, you look delicious. You feel incredible, so tight, your sweet pussy clamping down on my fingers, your clit swelling."

No man had ever talked to her like that. Though she couldn't explain why, Kelsey loved it. The rawness of his language, coupled with the wonder in his voice, the tenderness in his eyes.

And those magical, unrelenting fingers.

Orgasm began to close in on her, the ache building between her legs, became a sharp burn that rose and grew. Her cream drenched his fingers, dripped down to her back entrance. She could hardly breathe. The anticipation was overwhelming. Fighting off climax became impossible.

Just when she felt the first stirrings of her womb clench, Jeremy withdrew.

Thrashing, she shook her head in protest. "No. Please . . ."

He dragged the barest touch over her clit, and she lifted her hips to the touch. He pulled away. "Please what?"

"I need you."

"To do what?" He grazed her clit again. "Be specific. Make me believe you want me."

Kelsey stared at him as his eyes drilled her with naked lust. A million thoughts ran through her brain as he slowly grazed her sensitive little bud again and again, keeping her on the razor's edge of pleasure. It was splitting her open, destroying her mind. Every bit of her burned and strained for him.

Jeremy wasn't going to relent or give in. He'd accept nothing less than total surrender.

She swallowed and said two words she'd never said in her life. "Fuck me."

Jeremy rounded the desk, settling himself between her legs, then growled, "No. I can fuck anyone. You're different. Try again."

Frowning, Kelsey tried to puzzle it out. She knew what *she* wanted, but didn't men usually just want to get off?

Since Jeremy loved her and wanted to devote his life to her, clearly not. She'd underestimated the depth of his feeling again.

"Make love to me?"

He seized her thighs, pulled her closer, and gave her a pirate's smile. "Yes. Now and always."

Then Jeremy began easing into her, through her swollen, aching flesh. She burned and hissed as he pressed deep, until he'd buried every bit of himself inside her. Then he leaned over her and canted forward, going deeper still.

Kelsey grabbed the tie with a gasp. She felt him everywhere. No part of her wasn't filled up with him: her sex, her eyes, her heart.

Jeremy groaned, long and low. "Fuck, I'll never get enough of you. So tight. Perfect."

Before she could comment that he felt perfect, too, he withdrew slowly, then rammed home with a power and precision that had her grabbing his tie again until her fingers were numb and she shouted his name.

"Gorgeous. Give everything to me."

As if she could hold anything back from Jeremy.

His thumb brushed her clit again, then he leaned on his elbows, so close she could see the beads of sweat at his temples and dampening his hairline, so intimate that his breath brushed her lips. "You look flushed, needy, that pretty mouth open and ready to beg. I'll look at this desk every day and remember your surrender."

Kelsey looked into his eyes that had gone black with desire and swallowed. She'd look at this desk every day and remember, too. Desire clawed higher, juicing her bloodstream. She was entirely his in that moment—tied to *his* desk, at *his* mercy, filled with *his* cock, slave to *his* seductive words. She cried out as her body raced closer to the pinnacle of pleasure with each thrust.

As she clamped down on him, seconds from orgasm, he backed away, his stare chastising her. "I didn't give you permission."

"I don't know how to stop it! You—ah, God . . . You make me want so bad—"

"That's the way I want you. Could you imagine waiting another four years to feel this?"

No. At Jeremy's first touch, she feared he'd hooked her. She was a pleasure junkie; he provided her fix.

He drove into her again, teeth gritted, shoulders bunching. Her body burned.

"I'll never say no again," she promised rashly. She would do *anything* for the pleasure just out of her reach, for the satisfaction that was so close . . . but so far away.

"You're right; you won't." He backed away and covered her burning clit with his thumb again. "Come."

In that instant, her entire body went up in flames that started with a burst of pleasure between her thighs, then raced down her legs, up her arms, crashing into her heart. Perspiration slicked their skin, blended as they strained together.

He rode her hard through her climax, muttering words that took her higher and higher. "Yes! You're gorgeous when you're this open to me. I'm going to fuck you every day, every night."

The mental image of being his like this with him always simmered in her blood, keeping her aflame. With Jeremy, she didn't feel shy about her lack of experience or her body. She didn't want to cover herself or apologize for having more meat on her bones than she should. Instead . . . she felt possessed. She felt like the most important person in his universe.

His eyes told her that, to him, she was.

"Acknowledge me," he demanded.

Impossible not to when he began to massage her clit again in slow circles that made her breathless. "Yes, sir. Every day. Every night."

"Come again. For me."

Pleasure stacked on top of desire, whipped into a frenzy by his words and touch. It sucked her into its swirl like a black hole, too big, too strong for her to escape. He was still so hard inside her, and her body was strung up tighter than ever. A million sensations cascaded through her all at once, each more stunning than the last, each taking her to a place she'd never been in her life.

"It's too big. Too much."

"It's too much when I say it's too much, Kelsey." Jeremy grabbed her hips in a white-knuckled grip and filled every bit of her sex with his length again. "You're mine—your body, your mouth, your pussy. Even your ass. All mine to take at will. You're going to climax again with me inside you because I want to feel you come all over my cock. Now."

Denying him everything he wanted—she wanted—in that moment was beyond her. He'd restrained her to his desk . . . but inside, she needed to let go, believe that the place he took her was both safe and perfect. She needed to give him her absolute trust.

With a ragged inhalation, she latched onto his stare, withdrew her mental safety net, and gave everything she was inside to him.

His eyes flared with the knowledge that she'd surrendered completely. He drove her body higher until she writhed, incoherent pleadings whispered from her lips until he smothered the cry with his mouth.

And she came.

The pleasure was unlike anything she'd ever known, skin tingling and electric, breathing suspended, her mind and heart clasped around him as she vibrated with pleasure. He shouted and came deep inside her, warm and liquid, marking her as his.

Then her consciousness faded to black.

Moments later, she came to and found Jeremy still naked in his office chair, her cradled in his lap. He'd untied her and settled her head on his shoulder.

She blinked against the harsh overhead lights, then found Jeremy's solemn gaze. The tenderness and possessiveness there took her breath away.

"You know I can never be just your boss again."

"I know." Her voice trembled.

What she didn't know, however, was what to do about Rhys. And what should she do about Tucker.

Kelsey sighed. What happened next?

CHAPTER | FOUR

Watching the sun set, Kelsey drew her legs against her chest and rested her chin on her knees, brushing away the latest bout of tears. Live oaks cast long shadows over the grassy clearing and the little pond a few feet away. The setting was peaceful but didn't soothe the tumult inside her.

At her feet, her cell phone vibrated. Again. She now had fourteen voice mails: four from Rhys, five from Jeremy, two from Tucker, one from Tucker's mother. So she might as well count that one from Tucker too. One from her aunt about her cousin's upcoming bridal shower. And one from Garrison, trying to schmooze her about the Miami job because her life just wasn't complicated enough.

She'd been hiding for two days and she still didn't have the faintest clue what to do.

Wednesday night, after her interlude with Jeremy in his office, he'd wanted her to spend the night in his home, in his bed. She didn't dare. Already dangerously close to agreeing to be his love slave for life, she'd reminded him of her fitting and made up excuses about caring for her parents' animals while they were vacationing. Reluctantly, he'd let her go. She'd driven to Mom and Dad's—and had been hiding since, dodging work with an e-mail to Jeremy telling him that she needed to think. She'd eluded Rhys with silence. Though both knew her parents lived on a ranch outside Austin, neither knew exactly where.

But Tucker . . .

Footsteps behind Kelsey told her that her time had run out. Tucker, of course, had no trouble finding her; his parents lived on the neighboring ranch. Knowing her so well, he'd figured out exactly where she was hiding.

Without a word, he sat beside her, shoulder to shoulder, touching without overwhelming. Tucker always knew when she needed space and when she needed to face the world—even when she didn't.

"Everyone's worried about you, Kels."

She hugged her knees tighter. "I know."

"Jeremy called me. So did Rhys."

Dread pounded her chest, and she squeezed her eyes shut. She couldn't look at Tucker. God, did he know that she'd had sex with both of them? What must he think?

"Tell them not to worry. I'm fine."

"If you were, you wouldn't be hiding here."

In his gentle, insistent way, Tucker shot her the straight truth. Kelsey drew in a bracing breath. "I don't know what to do."

"Avoiding reality isn't the answer."

Something in his voice made her pause. "They told you what happened."

Beside her, she felt him shrug. "I'd rather hear it from you."

Look at one of the men she loved and tell him that she'd slept with the other two? But the only alternative was to lie. She had to, for lack of a better term, man up. Besides, Tucker was her best friend. She'd always confided in him. Even if he didn't love her romantically, he cared about her as a friend. He'd be hurt if she cut him off.

She swallowed. "I had sex with them, Rhys on Monday after the party, Jeremy on Wednesday after hours."

Tucker tensed. "And now you're torn between them?"

Something in Tucker's choked tone gave her pause. "If I chose one of them to date or marry, how would you feel?"

He plucked at the grass between his booted feet, those hands that made such beautiful custom furniture brown, strong, and steady. "I'll be honest, Kels. I'd still be your friend—I always will be—but at more of a distance. If I were a better man, I could watch one of them make you happy, shake his hand, smile. But I love you too much to look at another man's ring on your finger and not be jealous as hell."

"You w-want me? As more than a friend?" She'd wondered . . . but to hear him admit it shocked her.

With a gentle finger beneath her chin, he urged her to look at him. His so-blue eyes surrounded by that thick fringe of dark lashes pierced her with sincerity, honesty. Devotion.

"I've known for twelve years that you're the girl for me. Guess I kept hoping that you'd figure it out too."

Twelve years? "We were sixteen."

"Yeah. Remember when Katie Benson broke up with me? I wouldn't go to a stupid kegger party with her, so she told me that I was dull, then hooked up with some football jock."

"I remember. You looked so down."

"No, confused. I'd chased that girl for four months. I should have been devastated when she dumped me. I felt oddly relieved. When you found me making my mom that rocking chair on the porch, I was trying to figure out why. You came over and took my hand. You told me then that I deserved the best in life, someone who would love me exactly as I was. I realized in that moment that you'd always loved me. And I'd always loved you."

Kelsey remembered that night vividly. That was the first time she'd felt a romantic pull to Tucker. But they'd never done anything about it.

"You didn't say anything."

"At the time, you were dating Mike what's-his-name. I couldn't tell you that he was no good for you—you had to figure it out on your own. But then, you went off to college. Mom encouraged me to move on, and I tried."

"You got quite a reputation as a ladies' man." She winced.

"I woke up at twenty-one and realized that I'd had a lot of sex but never loved anyone the way I loved you. By then, you were dating Alex."

"The slime. Ugh! Don't say his name to me. Talk about a regret." She bit her lip. "I wish . . . If I'd known how you felt then, I would have never been with Alex."

He dropped his gaze. "And that's *my* regret. I didn't think I could compete with a rich, sophisticated guy like him. He drove a damn Porsche. My blue pickup has seen better decades."

"I don't care what you drive! Your truck has character. It's . . . you."

He shrugged. "I was young and insecure. In my head, Alex could give you the flashy cars and diamonds I couldn't. I thought . . . I'd never be good enough."

"You dated the prettiest girls, always outgoing and thin and—"

"And never half the woman you are. Whatever happened with Rhys and Jeremy, I still love you. When you choose one, I'll just love you from farther away."

She grabbed his face, willing him to understand. "Please don't. I love you, too. That's my problem. I love all three of you. I should have resisted Rhys, refused Jeremy. But I didn't. Couldn't. Now, I want to be wrapped in your arms so badly, and I know I have no right . . ."

Leaping to her feet, Kelsey raced toward her parents' house.

Tucker must think she'd indulged her hedonistic needs without regard for anyone's feelings but her own. God, she'd made a mess of everything, screwed up one of the best friendships in her life and ruined the chance for the relationship to become more.

Seconds later, Tucker was right behind her. "Kels!"

Hot tears ran down her face as she sprinted for the house. Damn it, she never cried—except this week. And she was so tired of it. It didn't solve anything, and she needed to work on salvaging what she could of her relationships, especially with Tucker.

But nothing she said or did could take back the damage she'd already done.

Kelsey made it as far as the sunporch before breathlessness and tears caught up with her. So did Tucker. As she threw open the door to the little room, Tucker was on her, covering her body with his own, pressing her to the doorjamb. She had nowhere to look but right into his earnest blue eyes.

"You love me?" His voice cracked.

She didn't have words for how much she loved him. So she just nodded.

Tucker grabbed her shoulders and crowded closer. His size hit her then. He'd always been a tall boy, playfully teasing her about her short stature, but he'd become a big man, six-three, as solid and permanent as the trunk of a redwood.

"You know I'm not a fighter, Kels. But I'll fight for you. Whatever it takes to make you mine . . ."

Before she could tell him that a part of her would always belong to him and beg him not to make her choose, Tucker cradled her face in his wide hands and lowered his mouth to hers.

She'd imagined Tucker laving her breasts, touching her sex, sliding deep inside her. Since their thirteen-year-old experiment, she hadn't thought much about his kiss. He'd learned a *whole* bunch since she'd compared him to Josh Smith.

The way he took her mouth left her breathless. Firm, seductive, and cajoling at once, Tucker kissed like a man who knew what he wanted and could coax her into giving it to him.

Kelsey wrapped her hands into the shaggy waves of his dark hair and hung on. He lit up her body until she felt as bright as Austin's Sixth Street on a Saturday night. His tongue dipped deep in her mouth. He tasted of beer and something spicy he'd probably eaten for dinner. On him, the flavors were captivating. The man smelled like well-sanded wood and grass. Everything about him combined to put her on sensory overload.

In about ten seconds, she went from bereft to wet and clinging. How did he do that?

How could she?

Kelsey ripped her lips from his. "Tucker . . ."

His jaw hardened like granite as he shook his head. "A chance. That's all I'm asking. Spend one night with me. We'll do whatever you want. If it's not sex, that's fine. But don't shut me out before you've considered how much deeper our friendship could be and how damn much I love you."

"Even though I've . . . been with Rhys and Jeremy?"

"Especially because you've been with them. You have to give me a chance. We could have so much more . . ."

Staring up at him, trying to control her harsh breaths, she suspected Tucker was right. Even her parents had always said that the best relationships started as friendships. She and Tucker had been there for each other since he'd moved next door shortly after they'd both turned four. There was no one in the world she trusted more.

If she walked away now without giving him a chance, it would be unfair and irreparably damage their close-knit bond.

Slowly, she nodded. Then grabbed fistfuls of his T-shirt and jerked it up.

The heated relief on his face slipped from her view as his shirt left his body and revealed his gorgeously muscled torso. Not bodybuilder beefy like Rhys, not leanly elegant like Jeremy, Tucker was between. Tall, substantial, quietly powerful. Wide shoulders narrowing into a sinewy midsection, complete with a six-pack, all covered in golden skin since he built so much of his furniture outdoors.

In a word, Tucker was gorgeous. How had she resisted her feelings for him for this long?

He grabbed her hands. "Kels, this will change our friendship."

The gravity in his tone made her swallow. "It will."

"I think we'll have something better."

Kelsey hoped he was right, especially when he lowered gentle hands to the buttons of her blouse and began to undo them one at a time, looking into her eyes like she was the only woman in the world.

Once he freed the last button, he peeled her shirt off her shoulders, his gaze dropping to the swell of breasts above her sturdy bra. Suddenly, she felt ridiculously glad she'd picked the black one with low, lacy cups.

"Oh my . . . Kels," he breathed.

His breath and palms worshipped her breasts, cascading, sliding, caressing over them. She shivered.

"I dreamed of you a million times . . ." He cupped her breast in his hand. "You're even more gorgeous than I imagined."

Kelsey actually felt herself blush at his words. "I'm not as sexy as the other women you've dated."

"That's your opinion, not mine. Sex with them meant nothing. With you, it's going to mean everything."

In the past, Tucker's girlfriends had looked more like Victoria's Secret models than the average hometown girl. They paraded through her mind, and she fidgeted. "I'm afraid of disappointing you."

He took her face in his hands, arousal on the back burner behind his concern. "How could you think you ever would? I've never cared this much about a woman. I don't want you to be whatever you think I expect. I just want you to be you."

God, how could a girl feel anything but loved?

Tucker wrapped his palm around her nape and pulled her closer. And stared. Hunger and longing darkened his eyes. Need gripped her unmercifully, and she swayed against him, fingertips against his hard chest, feeling the *thump, thump, thump* of his heart against her palm.

With a groan, he melded her lips to his own, stealing her breath. Capturing a part of her soul. Thoughts ceased. He brightened her, like sunlight in winter, warm and welcome and necessary.

She clutched his shoulders, head thrown back, as his palms slid down her spine, making her shiver. His hands pressed tight, following the indention of her waist, flaring with the curve of her hips. He pulled her so close, there wasn't a breath of air between.

This was her friend. Her *best* friend. Before, she'd looked at him and seen her sounding board, her rock, her hand to hold. Now she saw all man. A passionate lover. She burned and arched into him, as he nuzzled her neck, making her tremble.

"God, you feel so perfect," he whispered.

So did he.

He captured her lips again, sinking ever deeper into her mouth. Kelsey pushed her fingers through his thick hair, moaning, losing herself in everything that made him the Tucker she'd always known . . . yet revealed a man she'd never seen. God, how badly she wanted him.

As if he read her desire, he picked her up, cradling her against his chest, and smothered her protest that she was too heavy with a fierce kiss.

Moments later, he eased down to the sofa and sat, positioning Kelsey across his lap. As she straddled his hips, their lips melded, tongues mated. His tight grip crushed her breasts against his chest. His woodsy scent rose up again, driving her mad. Then she became aware of the thick heat of his erection pressing against her sensitive, swollen sex.

She moaned into Tucker's mouth, falling heart first into heady desire. In that instant, she pictured them naked, panting together as he buried himself inside her, those big, creative hands guiding her hips down to take him deep.

The very thought made her sex clench hungrily.

He swept his palms up the bare skin of her back and unclasped her bra. It fell down her arms, and he flung it away. Goose pimples rose all over her flesh. Her nipples tightened under his gaze.

"You're so pretty and soft, honey." He cradled her breast in his palm, thumbing her nipple with teasing brushes. "Do you know the number of times I've fantasized about how you'd feel? So damn many."

"Oh . . . Tucker," she gasped.

"Hmm, you're so . . ." He gently pinched the sensitive tips of her breasts. "Perfect."

Her flesh sizzled. Friendship turned to fire and burned in her blood.

"Kelsey, honey, I want you so bad. Tell me you want this too . . ."

His whisper cascaded over her, warm with caring, passion. How could she ever say she didn't want him? Impossible.

"I do. Don't stop," she gasped, then laid her lips over his and sank into his kiss. "Please . . ."

His blue eyes blazed at her, even as he stroked her hair with tender hands. "I'm going to take such good care of you."

Kelsey bit her lip against a rush of need. "Then love me."

"Always have."

His answer made her even more certain that tonight was right. "C-can I touch you?"

Tucker moaned. "Anywhere you want, honey. Anytime you want."

Smiling, she scooted back onto his thighs and whisked a finger down the hard ridges of his abs. He rippled wherever she touched. She smiled—and did it again, this time going lower and running a finger over his jeans, down the length of his cock. And down, and down, and . . .

"Oh my God," she blurted, blinking at him. "Seriously?"

He repressed a smile. "I won't hurt you, Kels."

"Not on purpose, no. But that's *way* beyond average."

"You're good for a guy's ego." He laughed.

"You can't tell me you've never heard that before."

"I have," he admitted, then rubbed a hand down his face. "Could we not talk about other people right now? I'm trying really hard to focus on just us."

And not think about the fact she had recently had sex with Rhys and Jeremy and loved them. *Good call.*

At least she had a thousand gorgeous sights to distract her. Golden, bulging shoulders rife with leashed power. Tucker was usually really relaxed. Now, she could see the tense set of shoulders, the flexing of his arms as he gripped her, realized he was holding her a bit too tightly, then releasing her . . . only to repeat the process. His pectorals, firm and ridged, not man-boobs as she'd heard them called. Just the natural state of a male body well versed in physical activity. His abdominals, even his obliques—muscles she knew only because she'd tried a million exercise videos and classes—were more defined than something in a dictionary.

He'd won the testosterone lottery.

But her pull to Tucker wasn't his physical beauty; it was that she knew—and loved—him, all the way to his soul.

Running her hands down his torso, she met his gaze. "You're gorgeous."

He rolled his eyes. "I'm a guy. We sweat, forget to cut our hair, think WWE is quality entertainment—"

"You're thoughtful. You've never forgotten a birthday. You called faithfully, even when I was away at college. You criticized my bad decisions in the most diplomatic ways possible. You never let me cry alone." At that, tears started again, rolling down her face. Tucker was a treasure, and she had to make sure he knew she was grateful for him. "How did I look for love for years and not see you right in front of me?"

He wrapped her in his arms. "Honey, we've both made mistakes. Yesterday isn't important; we can't change it. Tomorrow we'll face together. Right now, we have to embrace the moment and make the most of it."

The man was so right, as usual. Wise in a way she needed. And she loved that about him.

Throwing her arms around his neck, she covered his lips with her own and crashed inside, greedy for more of his taste, for the comfort and passion of his embrace. He held back, let her lead, followed her tempo, pressure, duration. But she sensed him holding back.

"What's wrong?"

"I'm trying to control myself. What I feel, Kels, it's . . ." He scrubbed a hand across his face, then sighed. "It's a wildfire. I don't know how much longer I can contain it."

He wanted her that much? Inside, she was doing one hell of a happy dance.

"Then don't."

Tucker paused. "I want our first time to be gentle. I want you to know that I love you, that I won't hurt you."

"I want it to be what you need it to be. I trust you."

His breath blew out in a rush. "You're throwing kindling on an inferno."

Kelsey leaned in, nipped at his ear with her teeth, then whispered, "Let it burn."

She didn't get to take even half a breath before Tucker took her mouth, invading, plundering—owning. Passion sizzled in every second of that kiss, and she felt it all the way to her soul.

His mouth was still on hers when she realized she was dizzy and wet and aching. *Goody.* A few times she'd wondered if the fantasy of Tucker was better left to her imagination, if kissing him would be like kissing her brother. That was *so* not the case.

Seconds later, he devoured her mouth again and seized her breasts in hot, calloused hands. His thumbs strummed the beaded peaks, sending a fresh wave of tingles across her skin.

Then he bent his mouth to her and sucked one.

Her senses rocketed, jackknifed. Pleasure burned in her belly. God, she was getting wetter by the second.

Tucker gently scraped her nipple with his teeth. She cried out, arched to him, before he moved to the other and repeated the process. Then he did it again. And again. Kelsey clawed at his shoulders . . . then realized it would be far more productive to rip his pants off. Whatever it took to get him closer, deep.

Thankfully, Tucker had similar ideas.

As she attacked the button and zipper of his jeans, he hooked his thumbs into the waistband of her shorts and pulled them over her hips, down her legs, until they were an afterthought on the floor.

"Oh, damn, honey." His gaze blistered her with heat as his hands roamed from her waist, down her hips, over her bare thighs. "You're killing me. Matching black panties?"

"You know I like things to . . . coordinate."

He caressed the curve of her hip again, hesitating over the little satin ties of her panties. "So damn sexy. And so gone."

With a pronounced tug on one bow, then the other, the panties fell away from her body. He tugged the scraps out from under her and tucked them into his jeans.

"I need those back!"

"No." He grinned. "You don't."

He was going to take them, like a trophy? They matched her bra, damn it. Those were fighting words.

Kelsey crossed her arms over her chest, intentionally plumping her breasts. His eyes bugged and glazed over.

"Then you don't need your underwear, either."

"I completely agree with that."

And with her still straddling his lap, he bridged his thighs off the couch and whisked his pants down his hips. Kelsey wriggled away to assist, and soon all his clothing was on the cozy little throw rug—and she got her first look at Tucker naked.

Oh my God, so worth the wait.

But he was big, no denying.

With a tentative touch, Kelsey gripped his erection and squeezed. She did her best to encircle him, but her fingertips didn't quite touch as she stroked up and down his long length.

Kelsey gulped.

Tucker groaned. "Damn, Kels, I've wanted your touch for so long."

He thrust into her grip and shuddered. As he groaned in her ear, Kelsey felt every bit of his passion, and it aroused her more. Tucker was big and far more experienced, but at the moment, he was completely with her. He wanted her. He loved her.

The thought gave her confidence and warmed her at once.

"As great as your touch is, that isn't how I want you tonight. Lie with me."

He reclined on the sofa, then fit his chest to her back, his erection prodding her buttocks and lower back. When he pillowed her head on his shoulder, she turned to look at him in question. He took her mouth in a drugging mating of lips and tongues.

A daze of need descended, and she only felt dizzier when his hands began to roam her body. He plumped her breast, toyed with her nipple, skimmed her abdomen . . . then delved between her legs and caressed her clit.

Though they weren't facing each other, he could discern every time she tensed or caught her breath. He'd feel her skin heat against his. The position was lip-bitingly intimate.

About ten seconds later, she knew her best friend was going to give her a killer orgasm. She sucked in a harsh breath.

Tucker lifted his head, panted against her neck. Shivers raced through her. He drove her higher . . . higher as he worked the slick bundle of nerves under his fingers. Sensations climbed, quickly and mercilessly.

"The way you tremble in my arms is killing my self-control, honey. Your whole body is blushing pink. You're swelling to my touch." He cupped her sex. "Damn."

Orgasm was about to steal away her sanity. Tucker knew her so well that, without ever having touched her, he *knew* her body.

"Yes," she whimpered, nearly begging.

He grabbed her thigh and placed it behind her, over his own, opening her sex to him. Then he plunged his fingers deep.

Kelsey clawed at the sofa as the tension ramped up higher. He teased her with his fingertips, rubbing at her most sensitive spot. She arched to get closer to the touch.

"Are you ready?"

Frantically, she nodded. "Now, please . . ."

Her orgasm burned right under his fingers. He rubbed insistent, lazy circles around her clit, eased off her G-spot. With a keening cry, she shook her head. "Tucker!"

"Let me build it, Kels. Let me make it really good."

She wanted to tell him that it already was, but impossibly, the pleasure grew, firing through her body, holding her captive as she burned. She dug her nails into his forearms and clung like it was her only grip on reality.

"You look so hot, all glowing and wet."

Kelsey had the passing thought that she was happy Tucker liked what he saw, but . . . "Damn it. I need you now!"

"Burn, honey? Ache?"

She nodded desperately.

"Yeah, that's how I feel for you. Sometimes, I only have to be in the same room with you for a handful of minutes and I'm dying."

Even now, she could feel his erection against her backside, the base nestled between her cheeks as he gyrated into her in time to his caresses.

A sheen of sweat broke across her skin as they moved together, her pleasure burning like a fever.

"As soon as you come, honey," Tucker whispered gruffly in her ear, "I'm going to work inside you, feel all those sweet little after-pulses before I drive you up again."

One thing about Tucker: He was as good as his word. She groaned, the need for release, to feel him so deep inside her, breaking her down to a pleading mass.

The ache between her legs tightened until it nearly became pain. His fingers toyed with her, just above her clit, around it, under it, awakening every nerve between her legs. She panted, clawed, aware that he balanced his head on his hand and watched her come undone. Kelsey feared how much her face revealed to him as she lost herself to pleasure, but he just smiled, his eyes burning blue fire.

Then he skimmed two fingertips right over her clit. The biting pleasure converged and exploded. She screamed his name and grabbed blindly for him, her body no longer her own. In that moment, she was completely his.

As the last of the liquid satisfaction wound through her body, Tucker rolled her to her back on the long sofa. "You're gorgeous, Kels. I've wanted you forever."

Automatically, she parted her thighs for him, and he settled in between, sliding the first few inches of his erection inside her.

"Hurry!" She barely breathed the word before she felt him slide deeper.

"Oh . . . Kels. God. I feel you pulsing all over me, honey."

He looked nearly cross-eyed, and she smiled. "Good?"

Tucker sighed. "I've never felt anything better. Hold on to me. Getting all the way inside you may take some doing."

An understatement. She'd had no idea that her best friend had been blessed with such amazing equipment. She knew he'd do his best not to hurt her, but she still tensed.

"You have to relax. I won't be able to fit myself in if you don't.

Tucker grasped her hips and tilted down to her. As he squeezed his way inside her one agonizing inch at a time, the friction scraped her sensitive flesh, and that quickly, her arousal was on the rise again. Though he moved gently inside her, easing in with caution, he stretched her mercilessly.

As he pushed farther inside her, she sucked in a shocked breath at the raw pleasure. Her eyes flew wide open. Every muscle taut, she stared straight into him. "Tucker . . ."

He gritted his teeth. The jolt of connection was getting to him too. "Relax, honey."

Kelsey forced herself to take a deep breath, funnel relaxation through her body as she exhaled once, twice.

Tucker slipped in another few inches. She moaned, a long, throaty growl.

"Damn, you're so sexy." He pushed another inch into her, infusing her body with another heavy deluge of desire. "Almost in . . ."

"Do it. Now."

"I don't want to hurt—"

"Do it!" she demanded, grabbing his face and pressing her mouth to his.

When she arched up, Tucker gripped her hips tighter, sank deeper into her, kissing her like a man possessed, all hint of gentle and friendly gone.

Teeth bared, he reared back, put his strength behind his body, and pushed all the way inside. She hissed in a shocked breath. Kelsey felt him deep, prodding the very end of her channel, stretching her with his girth until she burned and gasped.

She loved it.

"Oh hell . . ." he muttered. "You're incredible. Did that hurt?"

"In a good way," she panted as he pulled back. "Don't stop."

"I couldn't if I wanted to." His voice sounded strained as he braced his forearms on the sofa near her head and used his weight to thrust inside her again.

The sensations were indescribable. Like melted chocolate, the best bubble bath, the most tropical vacation, and the tastiest margarita all rolled into one pleasurable thrill—then multiplied by a thousand. It wasn't just that he filled up every bit of her sex and rubbed all the sensitive spots inside—he did—but the fact that it was Tucker inside her. He was a man of his word, was so good to her, had always cared and always would. Utter safety enveloped her carnal delight to create an experience she'd never before known. And could never again do without.

Tucker kissed his way up her neck, then nibbled on her lobe as he pressed against her womb. "You don't know how many times I wanted to be with you like this, feeling your hot skin against mine." He reached between them and cupped one of her breasts, rolling the nipple between his thumb and fingers. "How many times I wanted the right to touch you, take you whenever I wanted. To hear you scream *my* name."

Until today, no. And he likely knew that his verbal seduction was destroying her, breaking her down into fragments, that between his words and his long, slow thrusts, he'd pushed her to the pinnacle again.

Kelsey dug her nails into his back, reveling in the friction of the hair dusting his chest against her breasts, the plunge of his cock so deep inside her, they felt like one being. It was . . . perfect.

"You ready to scream my name, honey?" He swiveled, twisted his hips, dragging the head of his cock right against her most sensitive spot and prodding it relentlessly.

In seconds, her orgasm went from approaching to inevitable. "Yes . . ."

"So tight. So amazing. Reach between us," he breathed into her ear. "Rub your clit for me. I want to watch you."

Normally, Kelsey was shy with her body. The thought of touching herself to please Tucker thrilled her. She pushed her hand between them, and he rose to his knees to give her room.

The second her fingers made contact with the hard, wet little button, she tightened, her channel squeezing him even more. He gripped her hips and lifted her to his every slow, deep thrust. They both groaned.

"That's it, honey. So sexy to watch your reserve and your need clash. Keep it up . . . Yeah."

Unbelievably, she grew even more sensitive. The ache tightened, blazed right under her skin, spreading through her like a wildfire. She arched, lifting her hips to him in offering.

"Harder, Tucker," she whimpered.

"Patience." But as he held back, he looked as if he was in pain. "You look so pretty with my cock sliding inside you, all slick with your juices. I'm not ready to end it."

"You're driving me insane!" She clawed at the sofa cushions.

He grabbed her hand and put it back on her clit. "We'll go crazy together. Touch yourself."

This time, she couldn't stop for anything. She swirled her fingers around the needy little bud as Tucker drove into her, harder, deeper than before, again and again. She gasped as the pleasure balled, condensed, burst deep inside her.

"Tucker!" she wailed at the top of her lungs. "Yes! Yes! *Yes!*"

"Kels . . . Love you. Oh God!" he shouted, then came, his body spasming as he emptied inside her, leaving her warm and wet and supremely sated.

Panting, he smiled, eyes warm and blue, and Kelsey swore she could see all the way to his clear, gentle soul. "Kelsey Rose Rena, would you do me the honor of marrying me?"

CHAPTER | FIVE

She was going to have one hell of a hangover tomorrow.

Kelsey closed her eyes to block out the ugly motel room and ignored the ringing of her cell phone again. It would be one of her fantasy men—and she couldn't face them right now, not until she figured out what the hell she was going to do.

They all loved her. Just . . . wow. Never would she have imagined how much Tucker wanted her, how serious Jeremy was about a future, how deep Rhys's feelings for her were.

On Friday evening, she and Tucker had fallen asleep on the couch after making love. She'd awakened to moonlight streaming into the sunporch, Tucker's light snoring, and confusion whirling in her head.

She was going to have to choose between these men.

Holding in a sob, she'd extricated herself from Tucker's embrace, grabbed her purse, and thrown herself in her car, driving to . . . hell, she wasn't sure where. Vaguely, she remembered checking into a low-budget motel, thanking God she had enough cash to avoid using her credit card. Jeremy and Rhys both had enough contacts to track her down if she put herself "on the grid." The little town had been way off the interstate and had an old Dairy Queen and a ragtag collection of mom-and-pop restaurants. After the sun had fallen and the sky opened up in a downpour, Kelsey had figured here was as good as anywhere.

Along the way, she'd acquired a bottle of wine and a half-stale sandwich. After sleeping all night and most of the day, Kelsey had awakened—and still had no clue what to do. The wine had been a bad solution. Now, she wished she'd eaten the lousy ham on rye before chugging the Burgundy.

No, she wished she hadn't complicated her life by sleeping with all three of her fantasy men. Nothing would ever be the same again.

Downing another hefty swallow of the tart wine, she glanced at her phone again as it rang. Tucker. Five minutes ago, it had been Jeremy. Rhys about ten minutes before that.

Staring at the faux-wicker headboard and cheap plastic nightstand, Kelsey sighed. What the hell was she going to do?

She picked up her phone, fondling it. Then she pressed her lips together. She'd have to face them at some point. Maybe . . . maybe they could find some way to forget the sex and just go back to the friendship.

After accessing her voice mail, Kelsey held the phone to her ear, her stomach jumping and stuttering. She had twenty new messages since last night.

"Kelsey, baby," Rhys's voice coaxed, making her remember him naked and passionate and perfect. "You okay? I'm home and would love to see you. I was hoping we could call my parents together and tell them about our engage—"

Delete.

"It's Jeremy. Avoiding me by sending e-mails to explain your absence is unacceptable. That's a punishable offense, and I definitely have something in mind." Kelsey remembered very well, and hated herself for the arrow of heat that pierced her. "If something troubles you, tell me. As we speak, I'm looking for the lingerie we discussed. I've cleared tomorrow to shop for engage—"

Delete.

"Where are you, Kels?" Tucker's concerned voice wrenched at her heart. "I woke up and you were gone, honey. I know you're scared and confused, but it's going to be fine. I can't wait to tell our parents that we're engage—"

Delete.

Shaking her head, Kelsey closed her eyes. Utter disaster. They all thought she was going to marry them. It kinda followed, right? They apparently loved her—who knew?—and she loved them. She'd made love with each of them, and they all knew she wasn't the kind of girl who could give her body without giving her heart. Of course, each assumed she was going to marry him.

"Kelsey Rena, you're being a bad girl, disappearing like this," Jeremy snapped . . . but he sounded concerned, almost desperate. "Call me. This silence isn't like you, and—"

Delete.

"Baby, I'm on for another forty-eight starting Sunday night." Rhys sounded choked. "I, um, talked to Tucker. He told me . . . everything. I still love you. Guess you're confused. We should talk and—"

Delete.

A heavy sigh she immediately knew belonged to Tucker came through the phone, then, "Kels, you can't keep avoiding me—us—forever."

Delete.

Yeah? What would happen if she didn't? If she tried to resume her life, nothing good would come of it. She didn't have the strength to resist them all, and if she picked one . . . the other two would tempt her, pull on her heartstrings. She'd hurt them already far too much with her behavior, and that wasn't acceptable.

Damn, why had she let passion get the better of her and thrown such caution to the wind?

"Kelsey, honey, this is Aunt Mary. Do you have a punch bowl we can borrow for the shower? Mine has a crack in it, and I don't know that I'll have time to find another."

Frowning against her headache, she deleted the message and made a mental note to run her punch bowl over to her aunt's house.

"Ms. Rena, this is Dave Garrison."

Again? She sighed. Why couldn't any man in her life take no for an answer?

Because you'd actually have to say no first.

"I'm going to call you every day until you say yes," he vowed. "This Miami job is a great opportunity. I'll give you run of the office. You can organize it however you like."

Kelsey's lifted her finger over the delete button . . . but lingered, rather than pressed.

"Whatever Beck is paying you, I'll increase it by twenty-five percent and pay ten thousand dollars of your moving expenses. I need you here yesterday. I know Beck is easier on the eyes, but I'm less of a bastard to work for." He hesitated. "Call me. Day. Night. You have my number."

Biting her lip, Kelsey deleted that message too.

"You fucked Tucker too!" Jeremy roared two seconds later. "You'd better get your pretty ass back here so I can paddle it and remind you who you belong to. When I'm done, you'll know—"

Delete.

More voice mails followed from all the guys, all angry and confused. Hurt. She hit delete.

What was she going to do? Naturally, they'd all want any woman they cared about to themselves. She'd been raised to believe one man, one woman. Marriage. Together forever.

The feelings she had now tested all that—to the limit.

After she finished deleting all the voice mails and hung up, Kelsey took another swig of the wine and paced. She had to make decisions, and fast. Her men—scratch that; Rhys, Jeremy, and Tucker—deserved answers.

She glanced at the time. Nine-twenty. An hour later in Florida.

Kelsey chewed on a ragged fingernail. Her life had come to the fork in the road. Now she had to find the right path.

With a deep breath, she picked up the phone.

The sun cast long shadows when Kelsey drove up her street and pulled into her driveway—next to Jeremy's Jaguar and behind Tucker's blue pickup.

They were all here.

Her headache would have to take second fiddle to talking to the guys. She owed them an explanation. Time to grow a spine and stop hiding in a motel room like a fugitive.

Kelsey parked the car, sighed, then climbed out. Dread pitted her stomach. Yes, she needed to do this, but it was going to be a long evening, no doubt.

As soon as she opened the car door, they all rushed out of the house, Rhys using his physical prowess to dart to the front of the pack. Jeremy barreled right behind him, jaw clenched, fire in his eyes. Tucker hung back, giving her a bit of space. He paused halfway up the sidewalk and held up a hand in greeting.

Swallowing a lump, she waved back—right before Rhys grabbed her up in his arms.

"*Oomph!*" she grunted as he crushed her against his hard body and pinned her to the side of her little Honda. In his bear hug, she felt his caring surround her. Kelsey clutched his shoulders, almost afraid to let go.

"You're going to crack her damn ribs." Jeremy elbowed Rhys,

who quickly released her. Her boss snapped her up, pulling against his taut body. "Definitely another spanking," he whispered hotly in her ear. "Do you know how worried I've been?"

Yeah, she had a pretty good idea, and it just made her feel guilty all over again. She probably didn't deserve this sort of caring from not just one, but three wonderful men. Shame slithered through her. She'd shared herself with each of them—bad enough—but then she'd run off without explanation.

Time to do the right thing.

"Thank you for your concern. I never meant to worry you."

Jeremy pierced her with dark eyes that vowed all kinds of sensual torture once they were alone. He followed it up with a wild kiss. Instantly, he sank deep, all the way to her heart, her soul. The male flavor of him, now so familiar and dear, cascaded over her, igniting the yearning inside her.

With a sob, she wrenched away and ran toward the house. Tucker blocked her path, but he stood open, waiting. On any other day, she would have run right into those arms and sobbed against his chest, but now . . . she knew every contour of that chest, the way he felt deep inside her. Their strictly platonic friendship was totally over, because she couldn't look at him as anything other than a virile lover—her lover—ever again.

Instead of rushing to him, she cupped his cheek and tried to repress her tears as she made her way to the front door.

"Come inside." Her voice trembled. "All of you. We have to talk."

"Damn straight." Rhys looked at the other two, then back to her. "Why, Kelsey? Why did you do it?"

Do *them*, he meant.

Jeremy was on her heels a second later. "To say I was unhappy that you took Rhys as a lover before coming to me is an understatement. The fact you slept with Tucker afterward makes me wonder if you just don't feel a damn thing for me."

Valid questions. How the hell could she explain this tangle of love, lust, yearning, need, comfort, and fear?

"Why was I last, Kels?" Tucker spoke so softly, she almost didn't hear. Almost. In a way, she wished she hadn't, but she'd created this situation. Now she had to stop taking the coward's way out.

"Because you were last to find me during my weak moments. That didn't make it any less special to me. At all." Damn it, she could barely hold back the tears. "Come inside. I'll explain everything." *Somehow.*

On shaking legs, she mounted the steps and dragged herself into the house. Instantly, she saw they'd kept vigil here. A pizza box with one slice left sat open across the kitchen table. An empty bottle of scotch explained the extra glare in Jeremy's expression. A dozen crushed cans of beer sat in the recycle box beside the counter, with a few more on the counter. Someone had left a pillow and blanket on the couch, and she'd bet money her two guest beds were rumpled beyond recognition.

"How long have you been here?"

The guys all exchanged glances before Rhys spoke. "Since yesterday at noon. I checked your house earlier—"

"You had no key." But Tucker did. She sent him a questioning stare.

He shrugged. "We were worried, Kels. When you left your parents' house. I had no way of knowing if you were okay."

She sighed. It was true. For all they knew, she could have been in a car accident. God knew her driving as she'd fled Austin to her little two-bit hideaway hadn't been great. Hard to see through a downpour of both rain and tears.

If she was going to be mad at anyone, it was herself.

"Thank you all for caring." Slowly, she sat at the kitchen table. The headache from her hangover tried to reassert itself.

When she rubbed at her head, Rhys grabbed a bottle of water and handed it to her. Tucker followed with two ibuprofen and a frown.

"You have that look like you've been drinking wine," Tucker muttered. "It always hurts you."

Bless him for knowing and caring. God knew she didn't deserve it after the way she'd behaved.

Before she could say anything, Jeremy slid behind her and rubbed his talented hands up the tense muscles of her neck and shoulders. She groaned.

"Those little noises are giving me a hard-on, sweetheart," he whispered.

She noticed that Rhys and Tucker had edged closer, too. And she was sitting in the corner with no escape route. The testosterone overload was about to bowl her over.

"Sit," she barked at them. And didn't say a word until they'd all complied.

Jeremy was the last to do so—no surprise since he was used to giving the orders. But finally they all sat around her little round table, so close she could reach out and touch any of them. So far away she felt as if she'd never touch them again.

"I can only say this once." Damn it, her voice was already beginning to shake. She drew in a fortifying breath. "I love all of you. Rhys, your teasing and helping hands with anything that breaks in this house got my attention. You about killed me with the physical fitness kick, but I feel so much better now. You cared enough to keep badgering me. I love our movie nights and the way you make me look forward to every day. You've really taught me the true meaning of turning negatives into positives."

"I love you too, baby. I just want to marry—"

"Let me finish." She turned her gaze to Jeremy . . . and melted under the flare of those blazing dark eyes. "You were lust at first sight for me."

"Same here."

Kelsey had known that, but acknowledged him with a nod. "I assumed, though, that I'd be working for a demanding womanizer and it would be easy to fall out of lust. I got the demanding part right. But you were also surprisingly patient, teaching me more than I would have ever learned about the law otherwise. You praised me when I got it right, pushed me harder when I didn't. Somehow, over the years, you made me embrace myself and my curves. I gained confidence and loved sparring mentally with you. I'm richer for knowing you."

Jeremy stood. "Goddammit, that sounds like a good-bye speech. You can't just leave. I've never allowed myself to love anyone until you."

And the fact he'd admitted that in front of Rhys and Tucker told Kelsey exactly how serious he was. Her stomach clenched again, and she fought off fresh tears.

She took another deep breath, then turned to Tucker. "I could never describe all that you mean to me. The quickest way to tell you how much I value you is to say that I've known all my life that if I fell, you'd catch me. No hesitation. No questions asked. You know me all the way down to my soul and still like what you see. That's worth more than anything in this world."

Tucker tensed. "Kels, don't go. We can work this out."

"We can't," she argued, then dissolved into a sob. "I've wronged all of you. And still, you want me to choose among you. I can't do it. All of you mean the world to me. If I tried to choose one, I—"

God, how could she confess her worst nightmare—and her greatest fantasy?

"You're saying you couldn't be faithful?" Jeremy quirked a dark brow, seething just under his unreadable façade.

"I'm saying I can't give up two of you in favor of one. It's unfair to all of us. If I committed to one of you, you'd always wonder about my feelings for the others. You're all stubborn, so I know the two I didn't choose would have a difficult time moving on."

"I'd respect your decision," Tucker vowed.

But he looked like the words alone cost him so much pain. To stand by if she married Rhys or Jeremy . . . no, it would destroy a lifetime of friendship now that they'd become so much more to each other.

"I don't want to put you in that position. Or me. I'm weak where you're all concerned."

"Fuck!" Rhys yelled. "That's so damn unfair, Kelsey. I made love to you first. That's got to mean something."

"It means you were first to catch me at a moment too vulnerable to say no. Since I first started fantasizing about you all, I feared it was only a matter of time before I couldn't say no anymore. And I was right." She sniffled. "So, on the way home today, I called a real estate agent, who's coming later to talk about the possibility of listing my house. I'm flying to Miami to talk to Garrison tomorrow."

"No!" Rhys and Tucker shouted.

"Goddamn, Garrison!" Jeremy snarled.

The job was hers if she wanted it. For as long as Jeremy's rival had been trying to lure her away to work for him, they all knew that.

"Kelsey, just leaving us makes no fucking sense," her boss argued. "You're going to make us all miserable instead of making one bastard happy?"

"Don't you get it? You'd *all* be miserable. If I married you, would you let me be alone with Tucker again for five minutes? Ever?"

She saw the answer in his face. He wouldn't allow such a thing in a billion years.

"See." She stood. "You'd have a difficult time trusting me—not that I don't deserve it. And being forced to cut the other two out of my heart to pacify a jealous husband would eventually change who *I* am and crush the marriage."

"I'd never make you choose," Tucker said.

"Then it would be your mistake," she spit out in brutal honesty. She turned to Rhys and Jeremy. "Correct me if I'm wrong, but neither of you will give up easily or soon, even if I married Tucker, right?"

"I'd have to take my last breath in order to give up." Jeremy crossed his arms over his chest, his challenging gaze spearing Tucker.

God, he looked ready to fight, here and now.

"I'd never back down," Rhys promised. "You may see me as your laid-back neighbor with the big sense of humor. But about you, I'm deadly serious."

"Which only proves my point. I *knew* better than to give in to my cravings for any of you . . ." She buried her face in her hands. "I feared you'd be hurt. I knew I'd be confused. I don't see a way out of it except to leave."

Tucker grabbed her hand. "Kels, no—"

"Don't do this!" Anguish thundered across Jeremy's face.

Rhys, the closest, grabbed her face and planted a hard kiss on her mouth. "I'm not letting go without a fight."

Kelsey had known this scene would be difficult, painful. Even she hadn't been able to foresee that turning them all away and ending everything between them would shred her guts and heart. Their expressions said she was doing the same to them. She slapped a hand over her mouth, watching them with a watery gaze.

The doorbell rang, cutting through the tense despair in the little kitchen.

"The real estate agent?" Jeremy snapped.

Likely so. She nodded.

I'm so sorry . . .

Her only consolation was that she was ending their relationships now. If she stayed and tried to choose one or go back to the way life had been . . . No. There were too many feelings out in the open now. She knew how they felt inside her, about her. Going back was impossible.

Before they could stop her, she darted past them and into the foyer, wiping away her tears. After brief introductions and a short tour of the formal living and dining rooms, she returned to the kitchen nook with the sharply dressed woman. By then, the guys had cleaned up the pizza box and beer cans, stashed the trash can, and folded their blankets. Their eyes were grim. Rhys clenched his fists. Jeremy ground his jaw. Tucker's cajoling speech was on the tip of his tongue—and all over his face.

Kelsey introduced them to the agent. The fifty-something woman looked confused by their presence, and the resulting silence quickly became awkward.

"Can you guys excuse us? I need to show Barbara the house."

Another long pause, and Kelsey wondered if they were going to argue with her, despite the agent's presence. Finally, Rhys gave her a sharp nod and stormed out of the room.

"Call me, honey." Tucker's voice was a plea. "Please."

And where would a phone call lead except deeper under his spell?

Jeremy saved her from answering. "This discussion isn't over."

It was, and that fact was killing her. Jeremy knew it was over, too. He just didn't concede defeat easily. That was one of the reasons he was so successful.

"Good-bye."

Kelsey wanted to sink into the couch and wail out her heartbreak, but Tucker would use it to draw her into his arms, and Jeremy would find some way to use her weakness to his advantage. She didn't dare succumb to tears now.

"Let's see the backyard, Barbara."

The agent nodded, clearly glad to be away from the men. Together, they went outside. When Kelsey returned with the other woman a few minutes later, the guys were gone.

With a crushing sense of sadness, she wondered if she'd ever see them again. If she was smart and wanted to keep from breaking everyone's hearts, the answer must be no.

CHAPTER | SIX

By some unspoken agreement, all three men found themselves in Rhys's house. Probably so they could stare out the window and see when the real estate agent got in her Lexus and left. And they could all storm back over to Kelsey's house.

Jeremy wasn't, for one minute, ready to let this go. As the beers and scotch dwindled over the next two hours, Rhys and Tucker also made it clear they didn't subscribe to the if-you-love-something-set-it-free theory.

He slammed his bottle on Rhys's table. "Both of you knew I wanted her. I made that perfectly clear."

Rhys snorted. "You may be used to people giving you what you want in legal negotiations, but she is a woman. I wanted her every bit as much as you. More, even."

"That's not possible," Jeremy assured. After nearly twenty-five years of sexual activity, he could say without a doubt that he wanted Kelsey with an enduring intensity that he'd never felt.

"I've known her my whole life," Tucker groused. "I always

hoped that our long-standing relationship would count for something . . ."

Silence descended, and they all downed more alcohol. Diluting it with dinner would probably be a good idea, but it might also temper this angry buzz he had going, and right now, Jeremy wanted to feel how badly he'd fucked up. Miscalculated. He did his best thinking when he was furious.

Rhys stood and paced. "Damn, I have to report for duty in six hours, which means I have to stop drinking."

But the fireman eyed his beer as if sobering up were the last thing he wanted to do.

"To do that," he continued, "I need to find some clarity. Let's look at the facts."

"Fact one: She let each of us fuck her," Jeremy said brutally. "You on Monday, me on Wednesday, and Tucker on Friday."

"She didn't do it to be malicious," Tucker argued. "But because she says she loves all of us."

Jeremy sighed. "That's fact number two."

"Maybe . . . we're making this about sex, and it isn't," Tucker suggested. "Maybe it's just about her heart. She's being honest when she says she loves us all, and we're arguing about who's sleeping with her."

"Of course she's being honest. But where the hell does acknowledging that leave us?" Jeremy scowled. "There's three of us and one of her. What the fuck are we supposed to do?"

Tucker raked a frustrated hand through his fashionably shaggy hair. "We're tearing her apart."

"No shit." Jeremy knew the sarcasm wasn't helping, but seriously, did Tucker think he hadn't realized that?

Suddenly, Rhys froze. "I got it."

"Got what?" he and Tucker both snapped.

Rhys rolled his eyes. "The solution! We *share* her."

The words went off like a bomb. After the explosion, eerie silence reigned for a full dozen seconds.

Then Tucker pushed back in his chair. "Pass her around like a lap dog?"

"Let her leave my bed to crawl into yours?"

"Look, do you want her to move away?" Rhys demanded.

Jeremy tried not to grind his teeth. "No."

"Of course not," Tucker muttered.

"Then get over your own fucking egos." The fireman started pacing again. "She says she can't choose. So we don't make her . . . at least right now. Maybe she just needs more time with each of us to make a more educated decision, so for now, we share her. Take all the pressure off."

Tucker's fist tightened around his beer can. "How would that work?"

Rhys blew out a breath, clearly clueless about the practicalities. The fireman was big on ideas but short on details. "I think we have to let her choose who, when, where . . ." He sent a pointed glance in Jeremy's direction. "Give her all the power."

Jeremy tensed. That went against every instinct he possessed as a Dominant and a man. But as Rhys had so ineloquently pointed out, this wasn't about his ego, and Kelsey would leave them permanently if they continued to press her before she was ready to make a decision. She had to relax and really experience him as a man, a friend, a life partner, before she could commit.

"I don't like it," Tucker crushed the aluminum can in his grip. "But it makes a perverse sort of sense. We've all taken our relationships with her from platonic to intimate in the span of a few days. I asked her to marry me—"

"Me, too," Rhys admitted.

What the fuck else can go wrong? Jeremy poured more scotch down his throat. "Make that three."

"So she must be incredibly confused," Tucker concluded. "She went from having a friend, a neighbor, and a boss to juggling three potential fiancés in a handful of days."

"Too much too fast," Rhys reiterated with a nod.

As much as Jeremy hated it, they were right.

Then again, he'd never feared competition, and he wasn't about to start now. He could weed Rhys quickly out of Kelsey's heart. She'd met the fireman last and leaned on him as a handyman; how deep could her attachment really be?

Tucker would be more challenging to eliminate. It seemed possible that she felt guilty because her friend had confessed to deeper feelings that sensitive Kelsey wouldn't want to eschew. She hated to hurt anyone. In time, Jeremy was certain he could make her see that her feelings for the other man didn't extend beyond friendship. Mentally, he began a to-do list that would sweep Kelsey off her feet. All he had to do was whisk her away for a romantic trip to Paris, give her lots of attention, and plunge her into life as the sexy, perfect submissive he knew her to be. By then, he'd have her all to himself.

No need to tell the others that.

"I agree," Jeremy asserted. "I'm in."

"As demanding and possessive as you are?" Tucker's jaw dropped. "You're the last one I would have imagined agreeing to this."

"Part of being a good negotiator is knowing which battles you can successfully fight, how far you can push them, and when to fall back. As we've already stated, she's hurting, scared, and she'll leave unless we find a way to help her relax so that she has the proper time and information. I want her to be absolutely certain when she finally chooses, and rushing her is counter to that goal. I don't love this plan, but I see its wisdom."

"Exactly." Rhys spun to face Tucker. "What he said."

Tucker glared at the fireman. "How will you feel, knowing he's tying sweet Kelsey up and spanking her for his perverse pleasure?"

Rhys frowned, then shrugged. "Well, bondage isn't . . . *all* bad. I think her ass would look pretty pink."

Jeremy couldn't resist the dig. "It does."

Tucker shot to his feet and lunged at Jeremy. "Damn you! If I find out that you hit her again—"

"You mean paddled her ass just right so that she came for me? More than once?"

"Lucky bastard," Rhys murmured.

Jeremy smiled. He had a partner in crime, albeit a temporary one. And Tucker had just given him the means to eliminate Kelsey's best friend from the running. While he had a hell of a good time doing it.

"I wouldn't worry about what I do with her, if I were you," he drawled as he tossed Tucker a challenging gaze. "I'd worry about how you're going to keep up in the orgasm count."

"I'll do just fine," Tucker assured. "After last Friday night, I have no doubt. And Kelsey will end up mine."

Game on.

"I have no doubt she'll be *mine*." Rhys smiled like he was the most confident bastard on the planet. "May the best man win."

Kelsey stared at her suitcase, pondering the two suits she'd laid out for her meeting with Mr. Garrison tomorrow afternoon. At least if anyone had seen her, that's what they would have thought.

But the truth was, she couldn't focus on tomorrow's job interview because she couldn't get her mind off her men.

Lifting the glass of wine to her lips, she took a deep swallow. Yes, she'd pay for this in the morning, and her flight would likely be miserable. Being tipsy would solve nothing. The idea, however, that she might never see the guys again—never mind hold or kiss them—made her stomach reel and her head spin. Why not give it a little alcohol-induced kick?

She glanced at the clock. Nearly nine P.M. Sighing, she mentally reviewed the contents of her refrigerator. Eating would be good . . . especially since there was so much wine left in the bottle, and puking it all up before she had a really good buzz going would be a shame.

Turning her back on the suitcase, she made her way to the kitchen and looked everywhere for something edible. Then she saw her sticky note on the freezer: GO TO GROCERY STORE. Which she hadn't done. Damn!

Laying her forehead against the freezer door, she closed her eyes. Rhys, Tucker, and Jeremy were all there in her thoughts, laughing, passionate, loving. Snatches of their time together flitted through her mind. The best times of her life. Now that they were gone, she realized she'd never felt more protected or more loved for who she was than when she'd been with them. How stupidly she'd taken all that caring acceptance for granted. Giving them all up would kill her.

But it might save their hearts, and that's what mattered.

Wiping away her tears, she looked around for her phone book to find a pizza joint when she heard someone insert the key in her front door. The lock jangled. The door swept open.

Tucker!

As she rounded the corner, she didn't just come face-to-face with one of her men, but all three. Wide-shouldered and tall, and determined—a wall of testosterone.

Kelsey's knees went weak. She was dangerously happy to see them. *One last time, just a few minutes . . .*

"Guys . . ."

"We're going to talk," Jeremy said in that commanding voice that made her shiver.

"As soon as you've eaten," Rhys said as he shouldered his way into the kitchen and set a plate on the table.

"I'll take that." Tucker grabbed the wine bottle and frowned at it. "After this morning's hangover, you don't need another. And we'd rather talk to you when you're sober."

They were melting her with their gruff caring and good food, because whatever they'd brought smelled damn good. Their kindness was wrenching her heart . . . and weakening her resolve.

"Eat," Jeremy demanded, hooking an arm around her waist and leading her to a chair at the table.

Tucker poured the rest of the wine down the drain.

"Hey!" she protested.

He shook his head. "Saving you the headache, honey."

Annoyance wrapped around her nerves, which was actually a bit of a blessing. "You're my friend, not my daddy."

Calmly, he filled a glass with ice and water, then snagged a coaster. He set both on the table with a smack, then looked her right in the eye. "I'm your lover."

Kelsey swallowed. Tucker almost never got angry. But he was riding the edge of his temper right now. Still . . .

She shook her head. "It's over. It has to be. Don't you see? I'm doing you a favor—"

"One we didn't ask you to do," he pointed out.

"Eat," Jeremy commanded again. "Don't make me repeat myself or I'll paddle your ass red."

"You're not touching my ass again."

Jeremy only raised a dark brow at her. "I wouldn't take that bet if I were you."

Rhys took the foil off the plate and put something on the fork. "Open up, baby."

She'd open up all right, to set Jeremy straight. Instead, Rhys forked the most tender, buttery angel hair into her mouth. She chewed, swallowed . . . and damn near had an orgasm from the flavor. "Where did you get that?"

"Franco's," Jeremy advised. "I picked it up fifteen minutes ago. While you eat, we're going to talk."

Kelsey hesitated. So that was the plan: talk her out of moving. Why? Certainly, they could see her rationale.

But then again, they were three packages of stubborn masculinity. This conversation required a solid, logical argument. Unfortunately with them so close, logic was the last thing on her mind.

Shaking her head, she grabbed the fork from Rhys's hand and dove back into the pasta, then nibbled on her crisp salad, deep in thought.

"You're not leaving." Jeremy stood over her, hands on hips, as if his word were law.

If the whole situation weren't so disastrous, she'd be tempted to smile. He was a give-an-inch-take-a-mile sort. He'd make assumptions and demands and act as if she would follow. But he knew it didn't always work that way.

Tucker gritted his teeth at her boss. "Way to go, steamroller. Why don't you let Rhys and me talk?"

Jeremy tapped his toe for a long moment, then gave them a sharp nod. Kelsey stopped chewing to process his response. Wow, Jeremy had given quarter. That *never* happened. Whatever they had in mind, he wanted it badly.

Or he just wanted *her* badly.

Shivering, she set her fork down. She shouldn't do this. Their visit had *train wreck* written all over it, but . . . "I'm listening."

Rhys and Tucker looked at one another. Her neighbor shrugged. So this wasn't rehearsed?

"What if . . ." Rhys said finally, "we didn't make you choose between us?"

Kelsey frowned, trying to puzzle what he meant. "Two of you are voluntarily walking away?"

"No!" they all thundered at once.

She leaned back in her chair at the decibel level. "Okay. Then what?"

"What if we all continued seeing you?" Tucker elaborated. "If we . . . had no expectations of you choosing among us until you're ready to?"

"I'm not choosing among you."

"Not until you're ready," Rhys vowed.

"You mean be a girlfriend to all of you? At the same time?"

Tucker hesitated, then nodded. "Basically."

Kelsey burst out laughing. "That's a joke, right?"

"This proposition is as goddamn serious as my face is right now," Jeremy spat.

And since his face had all the levity of a grave, she surmised that they really meant it.

"I don't understand." She bit her lip. "I'd . . . be with all of you? How?"

"In part, that's up to you," Tucker explained. "We want you to feel comfortable. Not rushed. You set the tone, the pace, the schedule until you're ready to decide."

Kelsey frowned. The Twilight Zone had nothing on this idea. "So, in theory, I could go to a movie with Rhys on a Saturday afternoon, have dinner with Jeremy that night, then invite you over for dessert?"

"Yeah."

She sent Tucker a skeptical stare. "And if the movie included a blowjob, dinner was accompanied by hot sweaty sex, and dessert morphed into breakfast the next morning?"

Tucker's jaw tightened, but he nodded. Rhys rolled his shoulders, then nodded as well. She shot Jeremy a look that suggested he get real.

"We're checking our jealousy at the door." He didn't growl . . . but it came close. "This is about you, not our egos."

"We want you to feel comfortable, get time to truly know us," Tucker explained. "And not feel like you have to change the way you behave with any of us because the others won't like it. You have to experience each of us as potential mates for more than a few days in order to choose. We understand that."

"In other words, this is my real-life episode of *The Bachelorette*?" Were they serious?

"You can do anything you want in order to choose who will make you happiest. Just don't move away." Rhys grabbed her hand and squeezed.

They were dead serious. Oh. My. God. Three boyfriends at once? She took another bite of pasta, chewing slowly. How would she make this work?

Could she?

No. Too far-fetched. How patient could she expect them to be? What if it took her six months or a year to choose one to marry? Tucker would be hurt. Jeremy would never check his jealousy at the door. Rhys's competitive nature would likely drive her insane.

But she wouldn't have to give them up right now. She wouldn't have to leave her house, her job, her parents, her hometown, or the men she loved most in the whole world. The decision could come naturally, in time. It was possible that she'd naturally grow apart from one or more of them over the months, and there'd be no painful breakup.

Kelsey bit the inside of her cheek. And she might be stretching reality, but . . . their offer was *so* tempting.

How sincere was it?

She took another bite of salad, washed it down with water, and studied the guys' expressions. Tucker looked earnest. He really wanted her to accept. Rhys squeezed her hand and smiled hopefully. Jeremy gave her a hungry stare that made her belly do flops.

"So . . ." she began, thoughts running through her brain at a hundred miles an hour. "What if I did this?"

Kelsey turned to Rhys, grabbed his face, and planted her mouth on his. As soon as their lips met, the others' shock sucked the air out of the room. She still pressed on.

Rhys caught on quickly, then nudged her lips apart, twining his tongue with her own, the kiss physical, finessed. Like her experience with him on Monday, he made her head spin as quickly as a whole bottle of wine.

But she had to stay focused.

Abruptly, she broke the kiss and stood. Tucker and Jeremy both looked tense, but to their credit, neither said a word.

Raising her chin, she brushed her body against Jeremy's as she slid around the table and approached Tucker. She slid a hand under his T-shirt, fingers brushing across that incredible six-pack, and then she stood on her tiptoes and slanted her mouth over his.

He threw his arms around her and kissed her with a fervor that made her breathless. Before Friday night, she would have never believed he could be that intense. But now she knew, and she wanted more. With a moan, she plunged deeper into his mouth, and he met her, allowing her everything she wanted. When he pressed against her, she felt his enthusiasm for the embrace—all those mouthwatering inches of it.

Still, she couldn't afford to be distracted.

She drew away and whirled to stare right at Jeremy. He watched, breathing hard. They all were, in fact. The irregular cadence of their exhalations sharpened the silent tension gripping her nipples and squeezing. Her sex clenched.

Without a word, Kelsey reached for Jeremy. He met her halfway, plowing into her mouth and pulling her against him in one tense moment. As he gripped her hips, she felt his erection press insistently against her. She writhed against him.

Achingly aroused now from kissing all of them—something so close to her fantasy—she looped her arms around her boss's neck and threw herself into the kiss. The heat of his mouth mesmerized her. With a hand pressed firmly to the back of her head, he gave her no chance to escape, but continued his onslaught as the endless seconds ticked away.

Suddenly, a wave of male heat shimmered behind her. A hot palm landed on her shoulder, and harsh breath on the back of her neck clawed through her body, all the way to her clit. Tucker.

Another blast sidled up on her right, and she felt a male hand grip her own. Rhys. Even that little touch set her ablaze. They were touching her, somewhere—all at once. Her body sang chorus and verse of *Hallelujah!*

Then Rhys's other hand cupped the side of her breast.

She gasped into Jeremy's mouth, and he used the opportunity to sink deeper into her, while Tucker edged closer and laid his lips on the back of her neck. Incredible, the heat, the need . . . She melted, her knees literally losing the ability to hold her up.

Gasping for air and sanity, she broke free of Jeremy's mouth and shot a startled glare at Rhys. He didn't say a word . . . just brushed his thumb across her taut nipple. The sensation pinged through her body. Jeremy watched, hissing in a breath. God, she'd have thought he'd rip Rhys's hand off, but instead he looked . . . aroused.

Holding herself steady with a grip on one of Jeremy's shoulders, she turned a tentative gaze behind her at Tucker. Definitely aroused. She almost didn't recognize him—wild eyes, heaving chest, every muscle in his body tight. No longer her easygoing pal.

With a savage yank, he pulled her around, dragging her against his body again. His kiss came hard, fast. Breath left her, and she felt swollen everywhere. And incredibly wet. Then it was Jeremy's lips on her neck, nibbling, watching her surrender her mouth to Tucker. She felt his eyes on her. That realization, along with his scorching-hot stare, sent a bolt of need through her.

Rhys pressed against her side, his lips at her ear. "You look so fucking sexy."

Jeremy sandwiched a hand between her and Tucker to cup her breast and pinch her nipple. "Are you wet?"

Tucker tore his mouth away. "Are you, honey?"

She looked at them—all of them. They must know . . .

"Yes." She was barely able to choke the word out over her lust.

"Good." Tucker smiled, then cradled her other breast.

Dear God, she had two men's hands on her aching mounds at the same time? A fantasy to be sure, but she'd never imagined it could ever be a reality. And it was heaven.

"Please don't tell me I'm dreaming," she whimpered.

"You like this? You want us?" Jeremy growled.

"I've fantasized about this for months."

"All of us, all together?" Rhys asked. "Like the book on your nightstand?"

Tucker and Jeremy stared, panting, hanging on her answer. Her stomach pitched and rolled. Her heart hammered loudly in her ears.

Lord, this was crazy, impetuous. Also the most dizzyingly pleasurable moment of her life.

She clenched her thighs together, but nothing was going to ease this ache except her men. "Yes!"

Tucker flicked the nipple of the breast Rhys cupped and took her mouth in a ravaging kiss. When he finally lifted away, he was breathing harder than ever. He looked at Jeremy and Rhys in question. Was this all unscripted? Whatever he saw on their faces made him relax.

"Let me see you kiss him." Tucker pointed at Rhys—and reached for the buttons on her shirt.

CHAPTER | SEVEN

Heart racing, Kelsey leaned left. Plunging his fingers into her hair, Rhys dragged her mouth to his. With an urgent press of lips, he devoured her.

Rhys's hunger bled into her and burned. She melted against Tucker with a gasp, her fingers clutching his shirt.

"You like that," Tucker whispered. It wasn't a question. She *did* like it—loved it.

She moaned, and his fingers made quick work of her buttons until he shoved the garment off her shoulders. It had barely cleared her body when he cupped her lace-clad breasts, plumping her nipples with his fingers. Behind her, Jeremy attacked her bra's hooks and dragged the straps down her shoulders. Tucker ripped the cups from her body, exposing her to their ravenous gazes.

Rhys broke away, panting, and stared. Jeremy covered her right nipple with a slightly rough palm. She shivered. A fresh ache bloomed there. Craving his touch, she arched into his hand.

And into Tucker's waiting mouth.

Her best friend lifted her left breast until his hot tongue swirled around its nipple, teasing, flicking the sensitive bud. Then he drew her flesh deeper with a gentle suction that brought her to the tips of her toes and the edge of her self-control. She keened out at the dizzying rise of pleasure.

Then Jeremy repeated the motion with her right breast, taking the crest into his mouth and lavishing it with attention, a caress of tongue, a rough scrape of teeth.

As Kelsey looked down, her breath caught. A man at each breast, both dark heads moving as they worked her tender flesh, mouths pulling at her nipples that seemed attached by a thin electric wire to her clit. The sensations engulfed her, tearing through restraint and composure.

"Yes. God, yes!" she cried out. "More . . ."

"You look hot getting your nipples sucked, baby," Rhys murmured against her lips as he caressed her ass. "Are they arousing you?"

Jeremy turned blazing dark eyes up at her as he drew the hard tip of her breast between his lips again, dragging it between his teeth. Her fingers tightened in his hair. Tucker sucked at her with strong pulls that deepened her ache unbearably. They made her breathless, wet. Wanton.

Forming words at the moment was beyond her. She whimpered and nodded.

"Wow," Rhys murmured. "Your cheeks and chest are beautifully rosy. I wonder if the rest of that pretty fair skin is all flushed too."

"Find out," Tucker whispered against the curve of her breast.

Rhys hustled behind her and dug into the snap of her jeans. It came apart in his hands. Her zipper fell next before he manipulated the denim and her little panties down her thighs.

This was dangerous, the three of them touching her at once. So overwhelming. She should put a stop to it. Three alpha males like this would never be able to share her—separately or all together—

even temporarily. But how the hell was she supposed to reject something she wanted so badly? Even find the words, when she was so overwhelmed by their touch? How could she not experience her most persistent, recurring fantasy?

The second her jeans and panties cleared her hips, Jeremy knelt and pushed them to her ankles, then raised each foot so he could lift them free. He raked a fingertip through her wet slit, lingering over her needy clit. Every one of his exhalations brushed her slick flesh. Tucker swallowed her gasp with his kiss. Rhys reached around her body to toy with her nipples, so sensitive now they felt tight and burning.

Overloaded. Overwhelmed. Overboard. And she loved it.

"Let's get her to the bed," Jeremy murmured.

"Hell, yeah," Rhys breathed on her neck as he cradled her breasts, thumbing her nipples.

Tucker hesitated, his mouth hovering above her own, his blue eyes watching her carefully as if searching her willingness.

"Talk to me," he whispered.

Kelsey bit her lip. She was likely going to hell for loving three men so much and begging for this. She feared what sex would do to her relationships with them . . . but fighting their pull and her heart was impossible.

"I want this," she whimpered. "All of you. It's what I fantasize about every night. Please . . ."

Tucker looked over her shoulder at Rhys, then nodded sharply. "Her bed. Now."

Her belly clenched at the resolution in his words. She had no time to think about the fact that her most searing fantasy was about to become reality before Tucker pushed her back into Rhys's arms. The beefy fireman lifted her effortlessly, charged past the others, and dashed down the hall. He kicked the door open and stormed in. Jeremy fanned out beside him and ran to tear the pillows, quilts, and top sheet from the feminine bed. Nothing to impede them from ravishing her.

"Set her in the middle, legs spread," he ordered.

Without a word, Rhys did as Jeremy commanded. Their stares were all over her, and she couldn't help but arch up in offering. Rhys leaned over her, focused on her nipples beading right under his lips. Jeremy crawled up the foot of the bed, taking an ankle in each hand, his hungry gaze between her legs. Tucker hovered just inside in the doorway, tearing at his shirt, his blue gaze ensnaring hers.

Kelsey looked for something to cover herself so she could catch her breath, make sense of this fast-moving train. But Jeremy, in his usual ruthless fashion, ensured she had nowhere to hide, no way to escape the blistering intent in their eyes that told her they were going to push her to her limits and beyond. She trembled.

No clit stimulators here that she could adjust to the speed and pressure comfortable for her. No slender vibrators she found easy to insert . . . and forget. They were going to consume her, ramp her up and up and up, have no mercy, push and shove her into endless pleasure until they were good and done.

Swallowing, Kelsey opened her mouth, besieged by second thoughts. Individually, each of the guys devastated. Together . . . what if she couldn't handle the reality of her fantasy?

"Whatever you're about to say, don't." Jeremy knelt between her parted thighs, his wide shoulders ensuring that she had no way to close them. "This is your fantasy, and we're going to fulfill it. Be woman enough to take it."

"Feel us," Rhys whispered as he knelt, lowering himself over her breasts.

"Surrender to us," a shirtless Tucker added, coming to the right side of the bed, opposite Rhys.

Their words made her swell and ache. This evening wasn't

planned, she knew, yet they seem to have some unspoken unity. Each man had a mission he was ready to perform.

"Maybe . . . some fantasies are better in my mind. I've never done anything like this—"

"You'd rather that we leave you to those sex toys I caught you with so that you can masturbate to thoughts of us, instead of actually having us?"

At Rhys's challenge, she bit her lip.

"I don't think so, Kelsey," Jeremy growled and raked two fingers through her sopping slit before plunging them deep inside her.

At the involuntary surge of pleasure, her back arched, her hips lifting to his touch. She cried out for him.

"That's a good girl . . ." His tone praised, seduced.

At her left, Rhys eased closer, his cock straining against his jeans. "Will that little vibe you use fill you up the way we do? Will you come harder for it or us?"

"Fuck! She just clamped hard around my fingers," Jeremy hissed, then sent a scorching stare her way. "This is turning you on, vixen."

He didn't ask; he knew.

"Of course it is," Tucker ran a soft hand down her belly. "Look how flushed she is, how hard she's breathing. You worry that we can't handle this and that you'll hurt us. But what kind of lovers would we be if we put our feelings above your needs? You want us all together. We'll give it to you."

They were right . . . at least according to her lust-heavy brain. Tomorrow, she feared she'd feel differently.

"Get ready for a hard night," Jeremy vowed.

Oh God.

Rhys's hard breaths on her nipples made her breasts heavy and tight. Tucker's hand sweeping across her skin fired nerve endings that made her entire body leap and tingle. Jeremy's fingers rubbing ever-so-slightly against the most sensitive spot inside her body forced her to writhe and mewl.

Why not live her fantasy this once?

"Yes! More . . ."

Rhys didn't hesitate; he simply swooped down and took her nipple in his mouth, hard sucks followed by soft sweeps of his tongue. Tucker opened her lips beneath his. He didn't ravage, but rather took her apart breath by breath, kiss by kiss, accompanied by his palm sweeping up the curve of her stomach and cradling her other breast. Then Jeremy joined in, his tongue rasping against her clit before he sucked the responsive bud into the brutal heat of his mouth. She lifted to him, silently begging.

The sensations were like nothing she'd ever felt—or dreamed of. She thought she'd imagined what their collective touch would feel like. But she'd been so very wrong. More intense than a tempest, more fiery than a thousand suns, this belied everything she'd ever thought pleasure was, eclipsed all she'd experienced before.

"She is so sweet on my tongue." Jeremy murmured harshly against her thigh.

"She is," Rhys concurred. "And when she comes for you, it's heaven." He turned his attention back to her breasts and moaned. "Your plump nipples are swollen. They sore, baby?"

Though not hurting from overuse yet, she suspected that would come later. And she didn't care. Now they throbbed. Insistently. Even with his mouth and the attention of Tucker's fingers, it wasn't enough to ease her. Instead, with every touch, they made her hotter, more restless. And Jeremy's hands on her hips, his mouth feasting on her pussy, took her so close to the pinnacle, she whimpered.

When this was over, would she have any sanity left?

Kelsey closed her eyes, but the sensations kept bombarding her. Tucker laid a gently insistent kiss on her mouth, as Jeremy's lips tugged on her clit. Then came the rustle of cloth. She opened her eyes to see Rhys kneeling beside her on the bed completely naked, cock in hand . . . guiding it to her mouth.

Those green eyes of his were like magnets, hot. Luring her in.

Silently demanding she suck him. And Kelsey wanted to. She licked her lips.

But what would the others say? Do? Yeah, they said they'd checked their jealousy at the door, but now that she was going to touch one of them, would that hold true?

Biting her lip, she turned her stare to Tucker, who was bending to her right breast. He captured the little bud between his lips and sucked.

Her breath caught. "Tucker?"

He paused, took in the situation in a single glance. Blue eyes darkened, mesmerizing her. "You want to suck his cock?"

Even hearing Tucker ask the question drove her closer to the brink. She nodded.

"Answer him. Out loud," Jeremy demanded, brushing his knuckles through her wet slit, providing an electric friction where she needed it most.

She grabbed what she could of the fitted sheet, straining closer to the pleasure. "Yes."

"Yes, what?" Jeremy prompted, those dark eyes endless and hot as he shoved two fingers deep inside her again.

Her body clenched.

"Tell us exactly what you want, honey." Tucker seconded.

God, they were going to make her say it aloud. "I want . . ." She panted for her next breath. Then another. "I want to suck Rhys's cock."

"Open pretty and wide," Jeremy demanded. "Take him deep."

"Yes, sir," she responded automatically to his dominant tone.

Rhys sent her a naughty smile, then took her neck in hand and lifted her to his waiting cock. The mushroom head was blue and distended, his length heavily veined.

"Slowly," Rhys commanded.

Kelsey licked her lips, parting them, leaning in. He fed her the first inch bit by bit. She nearly howled with impatience. Then the curved head of his cock rubbed against her tongue, hot and slightly salty, tip wet.

Groaning, he slid the next inch into her mouth. Kelsey sobbed. She wanted more. Now! He restrained her, teasing her. Dissolving her.

"She's clamping down on my fingers again," Jeremy bit out.

Rhys gathered her head in his palm and inched another fraction into her mouth. "This is the tightest, silkiest mouth . . ."

"It's lethal to your self-control," Jeremy agreed.

"Damn, she looks so hot. I want some of that . . ." Tucker's fingers tightened on nipples.

She warmed at their words and wrapped her tongue around Rhys's length. He tensed, hissed.

Kelsey sensed Jeremy and Tucker watch her every move. Felt them want her more.

"You're a fucking goddess," Rhys breathed as he fisted his hands in her curls and finally eased completely into her mouth. "So gorgeous. I could almost come just looking at you, baby."

Their desire permeated her with a confidence she'd never had in her body. Tonight, instead of wanting a thinner figure, she rejoiced at the lush breasts Tucker worshipped with caresses that left tingling paths and hot suction that set her clit ablaze . . . where Jeremy worked her with relentless skill, his tongue leaving behind a fiery need. He massaged her plump thighs, praising her womanly curves without a word. Rhys's heavy cock on her tongue melted her with stark sensuality as he slid in and out with a torturous moan. The need was too big to keep in, too much to hold back.

Euphoria swam inside her. Her fantasy—her most cherished dream—was coming true. She didn't have to choose between her men tonight. In this moment, they were all devoted to her. And she could give herself completely to them without reserve, without fear of hurting anyone. How lucky she was. Yesterday, she'd been certain life as she knew it was over. Now, she prayed this was a new beginning. As love and gratitude welled inside her, Kelsey vowed she'd hold nothing back.

"That's it, vixen. Squeeze on my fingers. You're so deliciously wet and getting wetter by the second. You're going to come for me, aren't you?"

"Mmmm!" she moaned around the hard flesh in her mouth.

Jeremy sent her a stare heavy with desire and demand. It singed away the last of her resistance with the silent order to come.

Pleasure flowed from all over her body, converging between her legs. The ache at her clit swelled, grew more desperate. She fisted the sheets again, sucking Rhys harder as need ramped up inside her. Kelsey filtered her hand through Jeremy's hair. She burrowed her other in Tucker's dark waves. Arching, she offered all to her three amazing men.

A second later, orgasm rocketed through her, casting her into the stratosphere. Rhys eased away as she screamed, her body flying into white-hot bliss. Here, there was no worry or trepidation. She felt only Rhys, Tucker, and Jeremy, not just their touches but their love for her.

The orgasmic torment lasted for a small eternity, a relentless press of clenching heat and gasping need. Finally, Kelsey became aware of her surroundings, heard the echo of her cries in the bedroom, felt the scratchiness of her throat left over, a remnant of her screaming. Her heaving breaths punctuated the silence.

From between her legs, Jeremy sent her a dark, lascivious smile as he shucked his shorts. "Now, *that's* what I want to hear when you come."

"Hopefully in the next five minutes. I think I'm addicted to that sound." Tucker stood on her right and ripped off his jeans.

Oh God, one glance and she wanted him inside her.

"Fuck, that was hot!" Rhys said as he eased back onto his heels and stroked his cock.

He looked so sexy touching himself. Kelsey wanted nothing more than to take him in her mouth again, savor him until she gave him the kind of release he'd helped to give her. Smiling, he teased her lips with the head of his cock, but then shared a glance with Jeremy. A second later, he backed away. She moaned in protest.

Uh-oh. She cast a glance at her boss, now lover, as he then silently communicated with Tucker, too. What was going on inside that razor-sharp mind?

An instant later, Tucker nodded, then nudged her closer to Rhys, stretching out in the space she'd just vacated. Without a word, he lifted her over his body so that she straddled his hips. Then he was easing that large cock inside her wet flesh one burning inch at a time.

Up, up, up, Tucker pushed inside her until she was stretched so tight, the sensation nearly bordered pain.

His face was tense with concentration. "Trying not to slam you, honey. But I want to be buried completely inside you so badly."

And he wasn't yet? Wow . . . He felt even larger in this position. But if he wanted her this way, she wanted to give it to him. Whatever he needed to feel satisfied sharing her with her other two lovers.

Kelsey wriggled her hips, easing up and down . . . and was quickly barraged with the scrape of his erection against the one place designed to break her into a million pieces. Eagerly, she worked him deeper, heedless of anything except giving him the lightning-hot pleasure he gave her.

"You can take him, vixen." Jeremy's voice shook behind her.

"Damn, baby . . ." Rhys looked at her like she was his everything and ran a palm over one of her swaying breasts. "Gorgeous. I didn't think I'd get off on watching you get fucked but I'm a step away from losing it."

Tucker looked close too as he started to move inside her, at first in gentle strokes, probing, testing her body's ability to take those final inches. As her lubrication spread over his cock, her body finally adjusted to fit him.

"I'm in." He swallowed. "Don't know how long I'm going to last. Fuck . . ."

His thrusts lengthened, strengthened, hastened. Soon, Tucker pounded up into her, shoving her hips counter to his, maximizing friction, sending her reeling. Just as pleasure scrambled her body and she felt crazy-dizzy with need, he stopped.

"No! Please . . ." she begged him.

"We're not done, Kels," he whispered. "I swear."

A glance up proved Rhys was still slowly stroking his cock and staring hungrily at her mouth. Behind her, Jeremy crawled up on the bed and . . . What the hell was he doing?

She didn't have to wonder too long. Suddenly, something cool and slick touched her back entrance.

Kelsey gasped. "Wh-what is . . . Oh my God!"

Jeremy leaned over her. "Has anyone ever made love to this gorgeous ass?"

Anal sex. Her breath whooshed out. *Wow* . . . She'd read about it, fantasized about her fantasy men taking her there. Still, she had to admit that fantasizing and doing weren't the same, and she was suddenly nervous.

"N-no. I've never been touched there."

She could practically feel Jeremy smile. "I want to, Kelsey. Right now. Be the first. I'll make sure you enjoy it. All you have to do is trust me."

"I do." *Without hesitation.* She just hoped it didn't hurt like hell.

The words had barely cleared her lips before his finger surged deep inside her. With her pussy already filled to bursting, his finger felt enormous.

"How can you possibly fit? I feel stretched to the limit."

Jeremy withdrew and caressed her spine, softly stroking until he reached her ass again. His palm worshipped her curves, and she began to relax under his touch. "We'll fit."

If he said so . . . she believed him. Kelsey sent him a shaky nod.

A moment later, he filled her again, this time with two slick fingers dripping moisture. As he did, Tucker stroked his enormous length inside her pussy again, deep, slow, mind-bending. The dual sensations rolled over her, and ecstasy raced through her blood, aching to be set free.

Jeremy added a third finger and parted them wide, stretching her more. New nerve endings awakened to blossom with sensations she'd never experienced. Savage, unrelenting, they melted her. She tensed, gasped.

"Relax," he breathed against her neck.

Kelsey released a deep, shuddering breath and consciously unclenched her muscles.

"That's it," he crooned, as he pumped his fingers inside her back entrance.

Fire ripped through her blood. "Jeremy!"

"Intense, isn't it, vixen? Just wait until my cock is here, and Tucker and I are fucking you at the same time. You're going to come utterly undone for us."

"I can't wait." Rhys smoothed a hand over her hair. "This is so hot."

Tucker grunted as he filled her again.

Sensations were building to a crescendo, one so loud, she feared her body would shatter. But she held on, grasping Tucker's shoulders, anchoring herself on Rhys's blistering stare. When Jeremy's fingers left her, Kelsey knew what was coming next and breathed deep so she didn't tense up.

The head of Jeremy's cock probed her untouched entrance, then began to push in. Quickly, he encountered resistance, and she bit her lip against the sudden pain.

"It won't fit." She grimaced.

"Shh." Jeremy stroked her hip, kissed her neck. "It will. Relax for me. Push back. Embrace that little bite of pain."

If he had demanded her acquiescence, she would have balked. But his tenderness was her undoing. She yearned to feel him, please him, take everything he wanted to give her.

Letting out a shaking breath, she released more tension from her body. Thinking of him deep inside her, every bit as deep as Tucker, revved her blood. Despite her fear, she *wanted* him there, both of them completely enveloped by her body. Wanted to give them every part of her.

With a moan, she pushed back on Jeremy. He gripped her hips, and he pushed against the tight ring of muscle, gentle but determined. Her resistance was no match for him. With a pop, he broke through.

She gasped as he eased in deep. Slow, measured. Calculated. A thread of pain clawed at her, but as quickly as she felt it, the burn became pleasure, and she cried out.

Jeremy advanced until his balls nestled against her, until his back lay over hers. Until she felt so full and wild and ached for both men to fuck her. Until she screamed at the pounding need just beyond her reach.

"Oh, damn," Tucker muttered. "You're so tight, honey."

Jeremy's hands on her hips tightened. "The friction. Damn it . . . You ready, vixen?"

She sent them a shaky nod.

Quickly, Tucker and Jeremy began working together in a rhythm of thrust and withdrawal that singed her every nerve ending. She felt both taken and adored. Reveling in the new feelings, but cocooned in the arms of the men she loved, Kelsey soared. Beyond her darkest fantasy, they catapulted her to the precipice of ecstasy in moments, especially when Jeremy rubbed her clit and whispered, "It's sweet to be the first inside you here. Watching you come undone for Tucker and me is the sexiest thing I've ever seen. You're panting. Need it?"

She sent him a wild nod. "So bad . . ."

Someone groaned, and she looked up to find Rhys's hand moving ever-faster over his cock. His hard grip over his turgid flesh made her belly pulse with fresh need.

"I am *so* getting off on watching you, baby."

Just like she was enjoying watching him touch himself. "I have to taste you again."

He stilled, and she opened her mouth. Kelsey didn't have to ask Rhys twice.

The weight and flavor of him on her tongue was its own slice of heaven. The head of his cock was slick with salt and fluid. She lapped it up, taking him as far into her mouth as she could. He hissed out his approval and fisted her hair until she took him deeper.

The four of them moved together in perfect synchronicity. Advance, retreat. Push, pull. Gentle, rough. So deep, so good, so hot. Pleasure poured over her like the hottest rain, and Kelsey wasn't sure she could survive the buildup that kept climbing and climbing in her system. She tightened, whimpered, grabbed them. And still the ache grew, multiplied, until it overtook her. Sweat popped out across her skin. Breathing turned erratic and short. Her heart pounded like a tribal drum.

Then the world exploded. Heat washed her as her whole body bowed. Colors popped behind her eyes. She moaned, drawing in a sharp breath, sucking Rhys's cock harder, pulsing all over Tucker's and Jeremy's. As she soared into the ultimate bliss, they followed with staccato groans and curses, tense bodies and tight grips. Hot fluid splashed inside her body, on her tongue. She absorbed it gladly, reveling.

Then, boneless with satisfaction, she melted into a satisfied puddle, feeling more loved, more complete, than ever before. Their touch had felt so right. *This* was what she wanted in life—the love of the three men who were her everything.

Rhys slid from her mouth and kissed her forehead. "You're amazing, baby."

She felt amazing. With an exhausted smile, she slid down onto Tucker's body, and he wrapped his arms around her. Jeremy withdrew and hovered over her, carefully caressing her back, her hip, the curve of her ass.

"Thank you for your trust," he murmured, dropping a kiss on her shoulder.

It had been entirely her pleasure. Tonight had been beyond her wildest desires—and hopes.

In the back of her mind, she wondered . . . Was it a portent of things to come or a fantasy that couldn't last?

CHAPTER | EIGHT

The second Kelsey opened her door to him, Tucker spilled inside her little house and pulled her body into his embrace. She'd been in Miami for only thirty-two hours, and it felt like forty million.

He couldn't stop himself from covering her red bow mouth with his own, barging in to connect with her in any way she'd allow, taste the flavor of her kiss.

Instead, he tasted wine. *Shit.*

Brushing curls from her cheeks, he stared into her dark eyes. Troubled and uncertain. His stomach pitched, dropped. "Talk to me, honey."

"Garrison offered me the job."

Tucker tried not to panic. Instead, he closed her front door and took her hand in his, leading her to the sofa. He sat and pulled her into his lap.

"I'm too heavy for you!" She tried to sidle off.

He held firm. "You're perfect. Stop."

The fact that she'd been offered a job fourteen hundred miles away disturbed him. The good news? She didn't look happy.

"You're not surprised," he murmured, stroking her hair. "The man's been trying to lure you away for a while now."

Kels nodded, looking tired, much too pale. "He's offering me a lot of money and professional freedom."

"Jeremy would give you the same if you wanted it."

She shook her head. "He can't. In his office, his senior partner's wife heads up the paralegal team, which is the job Garrison is offering me. Jeremy has given me all he can."

Tucker's stomach plummeted. He knew better than to offer her whatever she thought she lacked financially. Kelsey had always been ridiculously independent. She'd want to do for herself.

"You don't know a damn soul in Miami."

"I don't," she said miserably. Tears welled, and her red eyes told him this wasn't the first time today she'd cried. "My family, my roots, my friends are here. But this job represents all I've worked for professionally. Garrison couldn't have been kinder or more enthusiastic if I'd written the script. He introduced me to everyone in the office, and they're clearly wonderful. Then he and his wife invited me over for dinner. I told him my vision for a great paralegal team, and he wholly embraced it . . ."

The disquiet in Tucker's gut slid closer to terror. "Don't do anything hasty, honey. I love you; you know that. I'm not the only one." As much as it pained him to admit it, he would do or say whatever necessary to keep her in Austin. "You know Rhys and Jeremy have strong feelings for you, as well."

"Yeah, and I love you all. I don't want to leave any of you." She bit her lip. "So I feel like I have to choose between my aspirations and my heart. It hurts. Sunday night . . ." Her lashes fluttered, and the expression in her chocolate eyes looked so earnest. "I don't know how you felt about it, but it was everything I'd ever hoped for and more."

Tucker drew in a deep breath, trying to process the barrage of desire and fury that pelted him at once. Yes, he'd known that she'd been thrilled at the fulfillment of her fantasy, but it had been more than a check mark on her sexual to-do list. In her every arch, gasp, and touch, he'd felt her love for them all. Watching her suck Rhys off while buried deep inside her, feeling the slide of Jeremy's dick on the other side of the thin divide of her flesh . . . Damn! He scrubbed a hand down his face.

There was no denying that the mere memory of that night made him harder than hell. He wanted to take Kelsey to bed again, spend hours inside her until she surrendered every bit of herself to him . . . and the other guys. Sunday night had roused something primal in him. Out of control. He'd never been so goddamn aroused.

Or pissed off. Two other men were touching the woman he loved, wanted to marry and fill with his seed. And instead of being ridiculously jealous and fighting them for exclusive rights to her, he'd indulged every hedonistic instinct he'd ever repressed and fucked her with them.

When had he become so twisted?

In her little kitchen Sunday evening, when they'd first broached the possibility of collectively making love to her, he swallowed his initial jolt of desire. He'd merely been doing this for Kelsey, so he wouldn't lose her. She had to get this fantasy out of her system before she could choose the man she wanted to spend her life with, right? He lied to himself that he wouldn't like a damn thing about it.

Then she'd kissed Rhys right in front of him. Something inside him had snapped. Anger surged, yes, but desire smashed it all to hell. Watching her be touched and aroused had done something to his brain, to his sense of right and wrong. Suddenly, it hadn't existed anymore. He'd only known that he needed to get naked with her and watch her come apart . . . and not necessarily be driving her to orgasm alone.

He'd grabbed her, kissed her, getting even more aroused watching Jeremy pinch her sweet little nipples. Fondling her other breast at the same time had given him the sort of sick thrill he'd never imagined he would respond to. Shame and excitement was a terrible, addicting combination.

By the time her boss had put his mouth to her pussy, and she'd arched and mewled, Tucker had known he'd found a new thrill he wished he never had. But one he couldn't give up. Seeing and feeling Jeremy tunnel into her ass, and absorbing her response—there was no way he could give that up.

Fuck.

Even now, he was shaky and excited. Sure, he'd love to have her alone. Making love to Kelsey was a sublime experience. Watching her dissolve into a puddle of feminine need between the three of them had been the most mind-blowing experience ever.

He cursed.

"I know Sunday night was your fantasy." He swore silently when his voice shook.

"Did you hate it very much?"

Lie or truth? How could he admit to loving the view of other men touching her? But how much lower would he be if he was dishonest?

Before he could untangle his thoughts, her cell phone rang. She pulled it out of her purse. "Hello?"

"You home from Miami, baby?"

Rhys. Tucker recognized his voice, though she had the phone pressed to her ear.

"I'm here. Walked in the door fifteen minutes ago."

"I've missed you."

She cast an anxious glance at him. "I missed you too."

"Mind some company? I want to hear about your trip. I just got off duty and showered."

Tucker's dick tightened. Kelsey hesitated.

"Um . . ." She bit her lip uncertainly as she looked his way. "Tucker is here."

"Yeah? He touch you yet?" Rhys sounded every bit as excited about that prospect as Tucker was.

Kelsey licked her lips. Her breaths got faster. Damn, she liked it too.

He clenched his jaw. Neither of these two was going to help him fight what he so sickly, desperately wanted.

"No, he just arrived." Her voice had dropped, taken on a husky tone.

"Would you like him to touch you, baby? You aching?"

Through her shirt, her nipples hardened. Her cheeks flushed. Her lashes fluttered. Tucker got hard imagining exactly what he might to do her—with the fireman's help.

Need torqued in Tucker's gut. God, he was going to regret this . . .

He slid a hand over her taut breast, thumbing its tip, and grabbed the cell phone from Kelsey. "I'm touching her now. Her nipple is burning my palm. Get your ass over here."

Tucker ended the call and threw her phone onto the nearby living room sofa. Then he turned his hot stare back to her.

Kelsey's jaw dropped. "Of the three of you, I thought you'd regret Sunday night the most and refuse to do it again but . . . You want Rhys to come over and—"

"Don't make me goddamn say it." He clenched his jaw. "Just unzip that little skirt and lose the panties. I need to get my mouth on you now."

She blinked a few times, looking slightly dazed and so fucking sexy. Tucker swallowed, his patience ebbing in the face of blistering desire.

Finally, Kelsey reached behind her. The zipper rasped in the silence and she took it down. Then the garment fell down her hips, revealing black lace panties. His entire body tensed, his heart thumping, as he fell to his knees and ripped them away.

Pale and pink and bare except for a few curls on the mound right above her clit. He spread her flesh with his thumbs, staring. Wanting. But sampling her taste as she stood . . . it just wasn't going to work. He wanted to feast on her and needed to lay her out.

Tucker ripped her blouse away in one broad sweep, then picked her up and laid her across the living room carpet. Following her down, he crawled between her thighs and parted them.

"Tell me you want this, Kels."

She only hesitated an instant, but the wait nearly killed him.

Nodding, her voice husky, she murmured, "I want this. So much. I'm thrilled you're okay with it."

Tucker swallowed and looked up her body, to her face. "Seeing you happy and well pleasured was the biggest turn-on ever. I want to give you that every day."

"Thank you. I can't choose . . ."

Discussing it seemed pointless. The desire just was.

He raked his tongue through her slit, and she stopped speaking. Satisfaction pumped through him, and he thumbed her little bud of nerves, feeling it grow hard under his touch.

"Damn, you taste good." So addicting and unique, he couldn't resist another lick—and didn't try. Instead, he lowered his head to her again, inhaled her scent, nostrils flaring. Then he fixed his mouth over her once more, laving her with an open-tongued swipe that made her writhe.

She grabbed fistfuls of his hair. His scalp stung with her urgency, and he groaned.

"God, yes! I love you, Tucker."

His heart and dick both swelled. "I love you, too. And I love making you come."

Rhys burst inside the house. "Where is she?" As he got an eyeful, he stopped. "Fuck me, that's hot."

Slamming the door, Rhys began closing the distance between them. Tucker turned his full attention back to Kelsey, but the rustling of cloth told Tucker that Rhys was shedding clothes with every step. The big fireman quickly dropped to her side, holding her hand, watching as Tucker eased his arms under Kelsey's ass and hooked them back over her hips, dragging her even closer to his waiting mouth.

"That's it, man," Rhys groaned. "Isn't she fucking sweet?"

Damn, he'd had no idea . . . And he wasn't going to lift his mouth away to answer.

Rhys took the hint or got too impatient for a reply. Instead, he took one of Kelsey's hands in his and swept the other up her abdomen, to her bare breast. "That feel good, baby? Is Tucker going to make you come?"

She whimpered, tensed, and Tucker sensed her nodding. At his touch, she heated. Under his tongue, she swelled. Her moisture gathered, pooled. He lapped her up hungrily, wanting everything she had to give. Beneath him, she dug her heels into the carpet and lifted her hips. He held her to the ground, making her take one lash of his tongue after the other. His blood burned when her clit hardened even more.

A shadow fell across Kelsey's body, and he glanced up to see Rhys cup a big hand around her neck and kiss her red mouth with a blood-burning hunger. Her nipples tightened and her skin flushed even rosier.

God, he couldn't wait to get inside her.

Tucker lapped at her with renewed fervor, her body telling him she was close. He wanted to demand that Rhys suck her nipples, but refused to take his mouth away from her sweetness. Thank God the fireman read his mind and his mouth drifted down her neck, nipping then devouring her soft skin, before his lips closed around a pert tip. Kelsey cried out, arched her back. Tucker seriously wasn't sure how much longer he could take this torture.

He had to be inside her.

"You have any experience with anal sex?" he asked Rhys.

The other man lifted a tawny brow and smiled. "Love it."

"Get to it," Tucker barked.

Rhys rubbed his hands together. "Fuck, yeah. Be right back."

The fireman ran out of the room, and Tucker stood, doffing his shirt with an impatient jerk.

"Wait," Kelsey murmured, lifting her hips again and lowering her hand to rub herself. "I'm burning up. Please . . ."

Shoving his zipper down, he speared her with a hot stare. "Oh, we're going to make you come, honey. Don't you doubt that."

Tucker couldn't get his pants off fast enough. He yanked them down his hips, to his ankles, and kicked them away. An instant later, he covered her body and crushed her mouth under his, parting her thighs with his own. He curbed his impulse to plunge into her sex in one thrust. He refused to risk hurting her. Instead, he guided his cock to her wet opening and pushed slowly.

Her body sucked him in, tight, clasping, scorching. His every muscle tensed, and the urge to come began to broil in his balls. Kelsey slammed his self-control and enveloped his heart. Everything about her—softness, scent, sensuality—called to him.

Writhing against him, Kelsey tried to take all of him. Tucker felt her body stretching, parting for him slowly, like a curtain parting to reveal a masterpiece. Impatience chafed, but he gritted his teeth and restrained his urge to rush her. Instead, he let the exquisite torture of her tight flesh wrap around him, zapping his spine like lightning.

Most of all, he liked being bare inside her. He was well aware of the fact he'd never made love to her with a condom—and that she took no birth control. He was ready for whatever happened and had to believe she was too, or she would have insisted on latex all around.

"Tight fit?" Rhys whispered as he returned to their sides, bottle of baby oil in hand, watching their every move. "You feel good, baby?"

"He burns . . ." She threw her head back, arched, lifted to him again.

Her mewling need and bright pink cheeks turned him on like nothing else . . . as did knowing Rhys watched them with hungry eyes.

She threw her arms around Tucker's neck and kissed him desperately, and he couldn't hold back. He heaved forward, sliding in completely, now bathed in her heat and cream, drowning in molten desire.

With Rhys about to join them, things were going to get a whole lot hotter. Damn, he wasn't going to survive with his sanity intact.

Rolling to his back, Tucker took Kelsey with him, her legs bent and braced on either side of his hips. Suddenly, she was on top, and he was sliding deep, rubbing the head of his cock over that one spot that always sent her reeling. Inches away, Rhys opened the little bottle, poured some of the clear liquid in his palm, then applied it on his cock, fisting it in hard strokes. Kelsey reached out to wrap her small hand around Rhys. At the sight, Tucker's cock jumped. He thrust up harder.

She gasped, tightened. He could tell as she grabbed his shoulders, bit her lip, moaned long and low, then tightened unbearably, that she was on the edge.

Rhys escaped Kelsey's grip and caressed his way around her body until he stood behind her bent form. He crouched, watching as Tucker plowed into her body, one hard stroke after another.

"You were made for us to fuck you, baby." The fireman grabbed her hips to still her.

Tucker slammed his eyes shut, bracing against the grip of unfulfilled ache broiling in his veins. "Hurry up."

"Don't want to hurt our girl," Rhys chided, holding back, tormenting them.

Staying still, not plunging into Kelsey's snug heat, was a torture rack, ripping him apart, mind and body.

Finally, he felt Rhys ease into her, push past her tight ring, then slide down, down. Beneath him, Kelsey's dark eyes widened and she let out a keening cry.

"It hurting you, honey?" If it was, he'd make Rhys stop or rip him a new one.

Then the other man sank in completely, laying his body across her back and caressing her breasts. Her lashes fluttered shut, lips parted. Her pleasure was the single sexiest thing he'd ever seen.

"No," she whispered. "Incredible . . ."

Over Kelsey's shoulder, he caught Rhys's eye, and the other man nodded. By unspoken consent, they started to fill her slowly, alternating strokes. Like Sunday night, the heat and pressure was breath-stealing. Literally. As he gripped Kelsey's hips and drove up, she screamed, clawed, tightened . . . Behind her, Rhys flattened her body with his own, pushing her into Tucker's chest as he thrust deep. Tucker kissed his way up her neck to capture her mouth as Rhys's fingers circled the bud of her clit, his lips on her shoulder.

"You're close, baby."

"So close," she breathed.

Tucker groaned as he kissed her again, tongue plunging deep when his cock did. He was damn close too.

"Faster," Rhys demanded.

They turned up the speed, like the pistons of an engine, advance and retreat, in perfect synchronicity. He focused hard to keep the rhythm, to scrape her G-spot with the head of his cock, to swallow all her sexy little cries.

Then Kelsey pulsed around him, clamped down hard, tearing her mouth from his with a scream. Her face and chest glowed a deep rosy shade, nipples peaked, face lost to passion.

Holding his orgasm in became impossible, and Tucker let go of his self-control with abandon, releasing everything to Kelsey—morality, heart, soul. If she needed all three of them to be satisfied for the rest of her life, he'd happily oblige.

In the background, he registered Rhys stiffening and tossing his head back with a shout as he came undone, too.

A moment later, Kelsey slumped across his chest, lashes fluttering shut.

"Thank you," she whispered.

Tucker wrapped his arms around her, and above her, Rhys smiled and withdrew.

This wasn't the happily-ever-after he'd envisioned with Kelsey, but in the span of a few short days, he'd realized that it was one he could willingly embrace—if they could keep the four of them all together and prevent her from moving to Miami.

Twenty minutes later, Tucker kissed Kelsey's lips softly and left to pick up a pizza. Rhys followed suit, vowing to return with sodas and salad and chiding her for her bare pantry.

As soon as they left, Kelsey haphazardly pulled on the remnants of her blouse and panties. In a minute she'd find the energy to put on a robe, but for now, she was sated, kissed, cuddled—and utterly euphoric.

Except the niggling fact that she hadn't heard from Jeremy since Sunday night.

Frowning, she rose to her feet, in search of her cell phone. She'd just bent to her purse on the side table in the living room when the front door opened. She whirled. Her blouse slipped off, exposing her breast. Jeremy's gaze went right to it, a tote bag tight in his grip.

His jaw tightened, his flared nostrils. "They've already been here, fucked you."

Fury stamped his face. Her stomach jumped nervously.

"Yes. Jeremy, you know I can't pick between and you said—"

"I didn't give you permission to speak."

Hot anger rushed inside Kelsey. She stiffened her spine. "That might work in the bedroom and in the office, but you don't tell me what the hell to do otherwise."

Jeremy slammed the door and stalked closer. "You are *mine*. Sunday night was a mistake. I never planned on sharing you again. So for you to fuck them—"

"First, I never said I was yours exclusively." She thrust her hands on her hips. "Second, I choose who I sleep with and when. And third, they did not, as you so ineloquently put it, fuck me. They *made love* to me. They missed me. So what the hell . . . You just come in my house and start yelling at me?"

He paused, drew in a deep breath, then bowed his head. "I'm so used to thinking of you as mine. I did miss you. I wanted to be the first one—the only one—to welcome you home."

"You all agreed to leave your jealousy at the door."

Wincing, Jeremy hissed in a breath. "I'm finding it harder than I anticipated."

All along, Kelsey had known that Jeremy was possessive and demanding and difficult, but after Sunday, she'd hoped they'd settled this matter.

"That night, you directed a lot of the action. You were just as aroused as I was. You—"

"Thought it was a onetime event."

"That's not true." She poked his chest with her finger. "I told you I couldn't choose. You all vowed to work together. Tucker and Rhys have."

"I'll bet," Jeremy dropped his bag, grabbed her elbow, and dragged her closer. "Tucker worked his way right back into your pussy, didn't he? Possession is nine-tenths of the law, sweetheart. Don't think Tucker isn't imagining that you're mostly his."

Was Tucker counting on that? She didn't think so but . . .

"He and Rhys shared willingly."

Jeremy lifted his chin, anger stamped on his face. "And I'll bet Rhys wasn't satisfied with another blowjob. Did he fuck that pretty ass? My ass?"

"God, you just don't learn. It's *my* ass, and I happily gave it to him."

Suddenly, Jeremy buried his hands in her loose curls, bent to her, and inhaled her scent at her neck. "I don't like the thought of them touching you. I don't like lacking the right to keep you for myself. It's ripping me up, the fear that you'll never be mine."

Kelsey's anger deflated. "I am yours. I'm every bit as much yours as I am theirs. I wish I could change how I feel. God, you don't know how many times I've wished that! It would be so much easier if my heart could choose one—and if your hearts wouldn't be broken if I did. But none of that is reality. So we have to deal. Together."

"Just give me a chance." His voice was choked, raspy as he pressed his forehead to hers. "They don't understand what you want like I do. I'll give you what you need."

As she swallowed, trepidation made Kelsey's heart stutter. Yes, he knew one thing she craved, just as she knew he could deliver. That taste of his domination less than a week ago sparked both flutters and fears deep inside her.

She licked her lips. "Jeremy—"

"Shh." His cheek rubbed hers, five o'clock shadow gently abrasive, as he made his way to her mouth and covered it with a seductive kiss that pressed and teased and made love to her.

Against her will, her anger melted, and when he cupped the back of her head in his hand and sank deeper into the kiss, Kelsey felt her hold on her self-control begin to slip away.

Kissing his way down her cheek, he smoothed his palm over her collarbone, toward her shoulder, taking her tattered blouse with it and tossing it to the floor.

"Yes, that's my beautiful girl. Pretty bare breasts for me."

He bent and lifted the bag at his feet onto the sofa and opened it with one hand. Then he sucked her nipple into his mouth and cupped her breast with the other. His hot suction jolted her all the way to her toes.

She'd been happy, satisfied, before his arrival. With a single kiss, he made her itchy, hungry, achy.

Her fingers curled in his dress shirt. "Jeremy . . ."

"I know, sweetheart. I'm going to make it better," he vowed as he sucked her nipple again, laving it.

Then he lifted his hand to her, put something over the hard point. With a smile, he adjusted and fiddled with it. She couldn't see around his hands, but she could feel him. Something gradually tightened around her nipple, firm, then taut, then pinching to the point of pain. She gasped.

"Gorgeous," Jeremy breathed, then kissed the tip.

When he pulled back, Kelsey looked down. An adjustable ring. With little weights. The sensation of tightness, heaviness, slammed her. She gasped for a breath, then looked at him in shock.

"Stunning, isn't it? I love that you love it."

Oh, God, she did.

When he bent to the other nipple and repeated the process, another wave of heat invaded her. Twice as big, twice as powerful. She staggered, turning to brace herself on the back of the sofa.

"Mmm," he hummed against her ear in satisfaction as he wrapped his arms around her waist, palms flat on her belly. "You're so fucking sexy. I knew the moment we met that you were everything I need." He caressed his way up her torso, and she arched for him. "That's it. Feel me . . ."

Gently, he tugged on the little rings. Her clit flashed electric. Her pussy clenched. She dug her fingernails into the cushions.

"Yeah, you like that. I've got more to give you."

He reached into the bag again and pulled out something so quickly, she couldn't discern what. Until he grabbed one of her arms and bent it behind her back . . . and something cold and metallic snapped hard around her wrists.

He was handcuffing her.

"No, Jeremy. You can't—"

"Shh." He caressed her free arm.

Kelsey was tense, but under his touch, her muscles slowly relaxed. His palm soothed her, gentled her. His lips feathered across her shoulder, the back of her neck, nipped at her lobe. Desire flaring inside her, she tossed her head back, resting it on his chest. She thrust her ass against him, and he pressed against her, hard as granite.

"I'll give you everything." Jeremy wrapped his hand around her throat and whispered in her ear, "But I'll make you beg before I give it to you."

Kelsey couldn't find words to reply. He offered her the dominance she'd secretly craved since first becoming aware of her sexuality. And he didn't want to just tie her down and issue orders. He understood and sought to satisfy her most forbidden fantasies.

She loved him so much. He'd always been possessive, and expecting him to lose all sense of jealousy in a few days was unrealistic. One day at a time . . .

In the meantime, he'd made her crave this—him. Only he could deliver the pain-touched pleasure she hungered for.

So when his palm skated down her free arm again and he wrapped warm fingers around it, easing it behind her back, she didn't struggle.

A second later, the cuffs tightened around her other wrist. She was well and truly bound.

"Damn, that's the sexiest thing I've ever seen, sweetheart, you in my cuffs."

He was breathing hard now. So was she.

Then his lips made their way up her neck. He reached around her to cup her cheek and turn her head toward him. Their mouths met, his open, devouring, relentless. Heat permeated her everywhere, and as he dragged his teeth along her bottom lip, she moaned.

"That's it . . ." he encouraged, his voice low. "Just submit."

A moment later, he cupped her shoulders and guided her to bend over the back of the sofa. With her hands cuffed behind her back, she was helpless when he dragged his palm up her spine, then filtered his fingers into her hair and gripped. The tinge of pain in her scalp blended with the discomfort of having her hands bound behind her, then mingled with the delicious, constrictive weights dangling on her nipples. The conflicting sensations bombarded her, overloading her body.

Then he smacked her ass. Hard.

She yelped. The sting and heat spread. She moaned.

"You know the rules, Kelsey. Quiet unless you're coming, and only then when I give you permission."

She bit her lip hard, nodding.

"Good girl. I reward obedience. Let's try it again."

Another smack, this time on her other cheek, higher up. She tensed, but smothered the sounds by pressing her lips together.

"Very good," he praised, cupping her breast, tugging on her ring.

Kelsey sucked in a sharp breath, but kept her gasp inside.

"Such tight little nipples. I can't wait to suck them."

Damn, she'd come right then and there if he did. Everything between her legs had become a burning ache, her clit actually throbbing in time to her heartbeat. Her blood was on fire, and she felt so empty without him. With her wrists cuffed, she was powerless to remove her shirt or panties or touch him. She wasn't even allowed to say a word.

Totally at his mercy. Kelsey mentally railed against it . . . yet burned for more.

"Are you as aroused as your nipples suggest?" His fingertips grazed her abdomen in a straight line down to her curls, then slipped into her slit to caress her clit. "Ah, look how wet you are."

He held up his fingers in front of her face, confirming what she already knew: She was soaked.

"You like me bending you to my will," he rasped in her ear. "And it makes me fucking hard to do it."

Kelsey breathed erratically, dying for whatever Jeremy did next. She needed to come so badly . . .

Once more, the flat of his hand connected with her ass, firing the skin. Then he repeated the slap on the other cheek. Again. And again. And again. She wriggled, not sure if she arched away from his spanking . . . or into it. Every time she moved, the friction of her wet folds nearly made her lose her mind. Her blood rushed to her ass, her pussy, collecting, engorging, arousing her.

The spanking wasn't brief—or easy. With each smack, he picked up intensity and speed.

She tossed her head back, wriggled, arched. But his hand in her hair ensured she didn't move much.

"You're going to come." It wasn't a question.

He knew her body so well.

"Yes, sir."

"Not until I tell you." The spanking ceased, his hands moving almost reverently down her ass. "Luscious and glowing. I want to see your ass this way every day."

Oh, God. Her womb clenched hard, releasing more moisture. She was a breath away from orgasm.

Suddenly, she didn't care what punishment he invoked, as long as he ended this torment. "Help me."

Guiding her to stand, her back to his chest, he murmured in her ear, "You're not to speak."

Then he swatted her right cheek again.

Her breath stuttered in her chest, and heat washed over her skin, melting her pride. "But I need you. I need . . ."

"For me to fuck you?" he growled.

"Yes. Please, yes. Now."

"Hmm, begging. I do love that. I'll forgive you for speaking this once. Tell me what you want."

"Everything!" She rubbed her ass against him, and the abrasion of her sensitive flesh against his slacks nearly undid her.

Low laughter rumbled in her ear. "Let's get these panties off."

The air conditioner kicked in, and cool air blasted her nipples. He grazed his knuckles across them, and she gasped, clenching impotent fists at the small of her back.

Jeremy hooked his hands into the waistband of her panties and tugged them halfway down her thighs—and left them there. Before she could protest, he turned her, then lifted her against his body with a hand under her ass. Her nipples rubbed across his starched shirt, her wet sex against his zipper. She was about to go out of her mind.

Walking around the sofa, Jeremy set her down, unzipping his pants as he watched her face. She leaned in to suck the tempting hard steel length inches from her mouth, but he sank down on the sofa beside her, grabbing the bottle of baby oil still resting on the carpet in one hand. A second later, he had it open and in his palms, rubbing the oil with a harsh fist all over his cock.

Kelsey's stomach clenched.

His head snapped up and he sent her a laser stare. "What am I going to do to you?"

She swallowed hard. "Fuck my ass."

He nodded. "And you want me to, don't you?"

"Yes," she whispered.

With a grim smile, Jeremy brought her against him and cradled her across his chest, one arm beneath her bent knees. The hand supporting her back disappeared for a moment, then she felt the head of his cock pressing into her back entrance.

In this position, she was utterly helpless. Besides cuffing her hands, he now held her legs together as he slowly sank into the deepest recesses of her body. The tingle that spread over her felt as if someone dipped her in pure electricity, one inch of her body at a time. She gasped, tensed, her breath shuddering, faltering. And still he pressed in and in and in.

Until he was balls deep and she swore she was going to break in half. He felt enormous in this position. And with her cheeks still on fire from his spanking, sensation drowned her.

"And now I'm going to fuck you. Hard. You're going to take me, come for me, and feel how damn much I want you."

Kelsey had no time to comment before he lifted her with his strong arms up and down on his cock. The friction boggled her mind and senses as he slid hotly into her. Every inch seeming to forge deeper than ever, especially when his hips surged up to meet her body, and he slammed home.

She tossed her head back, hovering on the edge of orgasm. "Please! Oh . . . oh!"

"Beg sweetly," he demanded between clenched teeth. "What do you want?"

"Harder," she whimpered. "Let me come. I need it . . ."

"I can't wait to see you come undone for me."

He lowered his head and popped her nipple in his mouth. Combined with the little ring, the sensation was almost too much. When he released her knees and caressed his way between her thighs, fingers circling her clit, Jeremy barely had to touch her before she exploded, a kaleidoscope of colors behind her eyes. She bucked, convulsed, as pleasure erupted under her skin. She screamed until her throat hurt, until she ran out of breath, until tears ran down her eyes. And still the ecstasy drowned her, scraping her raw, leaving her trembling and gasping.

Instead of slowing down, Jeremy lifted her and set her down on her knees, face in the armrest. Again, he grabbed her hair, thrust his cock deep in her ass, then unleashed the flat of his palm on her ass again and again until she screamed with another agonizing release, and he came on a long, hard groan.

"No more fucking Rhys and Tucker without my permission. Who do you belong to?" His fist tightened in her hair. "Tell me."

Kelsey opened her mouth to refute him . . . somehow. She never got the chance.

"Not you, asshole."

Tucker!

Suddenly, Jeremy was ripped away from her, and Kelsey spun around to see Tucker slam his fist into Jeremy's jaw. "Don't you ever fucking touch her again."

CHAPTER | NINE

Kelsey's heart stopped when Tucker's punch slammed into Jere-my's jaw. Her boss's head whipped around, and he staggered to one knee.

For an endless moment, tension sucked the air from the room in a soundless gasp. Everyone froze. Silence deafened.

She broke it.

"Stop! Oh my God." She scrambled off the sofa, arms still cuffed at her back, panties clinging to her thighs, to glare at Tucker. "You *hit* him?"

After rubbing his offended jaw, Jeremy fastened his pants and turned to Tucker. Rage boiled in his eyes. "Kelsey is *mine*. I took her, as is my right."

"Wait a minute!" Kelsey protested, glaring at Jeremy. "I never said that."

Tucker pushed her behind him protectively and leaned toward Jeremy, pressing the advantage of his slightly greater height. "She's not a possession. And you have no right to beat her."

Beat her? Kelsey's jaw dropped. How could both of these men who felt so right in her life have gotten the situation so wrong?

"*She* is right here," Kelsey pointed out. "And this is ridiculous. Somebody uncuff me."

Tucker hooked an arm around her waist and slid her to his side. She could feel his critical gaze on her backside. "My God, what did you do? Not only are her hands bound like a criminal, but her ass is bright red."

"Her skin takes a spanking beautifully. She's gorgeous bound. And she *enjoyed* it." Jeremy's voice sounded like he was grinding glass with his teeth.

"Not fucking possible." Tucker shook his head. "She's too independent to want to be your doormat."

"Dude, I think Jeremy is telling the truth," Rhys cut in as he approached Kelsey and put an arm around her. He surveyed her naked body, lingering between her legs. "Her pussy is soaking wet."

She closed her eyes as mortification and dread slid through her. What the hell was the matter with everyone?

"Someone uncuff me!" she demanded. Maybe then, she could straighten this out. Because right now, this train was on the fast track to disaster.

Jeremy and Tucker both moved in her direction, but Rhys was already fishing the cuff key out of Jeremy's bag of tricks.

"Ask questions before you throw punches next time. You might find out that she was perfectly willing."

Both Jeremy's words and tone were reasonable.

Until he hauled back and delivered a right cross to Tucker's jaw that sent her friend-turned-lover reeling.

Kelsey screamed. "What the hell are you doing?"

Jeremy turned a hard stare on her, his chest rising and falling with swift, harsh breaths. "Not letting anything or anyone come between us again."

"Stop it!" she demanded.

As Rhys finally came to the rescue with cuff keys and unfastened them, she rolled her shoulders, grabbed a sofa cushion to cover herself, then turned to Tucker. "And you? What are *you* thinking? Did you imagine this fight would thrill me? I didn't ask you to defend my honor." She looked at them both. Neither looked contrite exactly, but they winced. It was a start.

"I told you that I can't choose one of you," she went on. "You all said you understood and would stifle the jealousy. My first mistake was in hoping you could. No, I take that back. My first mistake was falling in love with three men. Being unable to choose was the second. But you can rest assured I won't make any more mistakes."

Quickly, she unhinged the little rings from her nipples and threw them at Jeremy. Then she cast an accusing glance at Tucker and stormed out of the room, slamming her bedroom door—and locking it.

What the hell was she going to do now?

Stupid, stupid, stupid. On Sunday afternoon when she'd returned from small-town Motel Hell, she'd feared that a relationship with all or one of them wasn't going to work. No, if she was being honest, she'd known it. Still, she'd allowed herself to be seduced by them, by her fantasy of being happy with them all. They'd been on their best behavior, not because they'd worked their differences out, but most likely because they'd agreed to temporarily buried their jealousy so she would reject Garrison's job offer and stay in Austin.

Chewing a ragged fingernail, Kelsey sat on her bed. Great group sex aside, what had changed since she'd downed the bottle of wine and acquired the unfortunate hangover?

Nothing. No, that wasn't quite true. The jealousy had escalated.

Jeremy was still dominant and possessive. And Tucker abhorred the way he treated her, despite the fact something inside her *needed* it.

And as Jeremy guessed, Tucker had mentally slotted himself as her man. Clearly, he shared her physically because it turned him on.

A shock to her. Probably even a shock to him. But not for one second did she imagine that he wanted to share her emotionally.

No way could Rhys be expected to play referee all the time . . . assuming he'd even want to. Even before they'd become lovers he'd been displeased if he didn't get enough alone time with her.

Could she possibly ever please them all? Make them secure enough in her relationship with each of them individually to end the resentment and fighting?

Kelsey sighed. Her fantasy of the three men she loved had turned into a nightmare.

In the last nine days, she'd leapt into the emotional pit. Her situation had morphed from difficult to truly fucked up.

Could she ever work alongside Jeremy again and not remember exactly how desirable and submissive he'd made her feel? Could she ever invite Rhys over for a friendly movie again and not dwell on the feel of his mouth on hers, him deep inside her? And Tucker, he could no longer be her rock-solid friend who always helped her through trials and tribulations. Now he'd forever be her alpha lover in her mind, working that thick cock of his into her . . . and directing Rhys to do the same.

The fact that her relationships with them could never be what they'd been nine days ago was entirely her fault. The men . . . they were who they were, and it was her fault for hoping they could accept this. Or thinking she could change them.

At this point, she could see only one course of action—and the mere thought crushed her heart. Tears stung, fell.

"Kelsey?" Rhys called softly from the other side of the door.

So he'd either volunteered or been appointed to draw her out. Not happening until she was good and ready.

Instead of answering—he'd never give up if he knew she was listening—she dragged herself to the bathroom, lugging the suitcase she'd packed for her Miami trip, and turned on the shower. Thirty minutes later, she put the finishing touches on her lipstick, grabbed her suitcase again, and, with a deep breath, marched out her bedroom door.

The three men lingered there, Rhys sitting, Tucker nervously tapping his thumb on his thigh, and Jeremy pacing from one end of the living room to the other. As soon as she stepped into the hall, they all turned her way—and ran to her in one huge wall of testosterone.

"Kels, please don't be angry." Tucker stood in front of her, blocking her path. "I only wanted to protect you."

"And keep you from me," Jeremy pointed out. "From what we both need, sweetheart."

Rhys elbowed Tucker aside and took her face in his rough hands. "Please, baby. Let's talk. We can work this out."

"No." She shook her head. "We can't. It's my mistake. You're not built for this sort of relationship, even temporarily. At this point, I'm not even sure I am. Since I can't choose between you and I created this mess, it's up to me to fix it. And that's what I'm doing."

Tucker glanced at the suitcase she rolled behind her. "By leaving?"

"Do you see another alternative? Because I don't. I can't live with just one of you, and you all clearly aren't going to be happy sharing me. Everything between us has changed, and we can't go back. Tell my mother I'll call and explain. Jeremy, I'm resigning, effectively immediately. Rhys, please water my yard until the house sells."

Jerking free of their touches and wiping away fresh tears, Kelsey fought the urge to hug and kiss them good-bye. Would she ever see them again? Could she be in the same room with them again and not fall into a lovesick puddle at their feet? No, and she'd best leave here now before she lost her resolve and forgot how much she was hurting everyone instead of remembering how much she loved them.

Jeremy grabbed her arm again.

Kelsey looked back, knowing her shattered heart was on her face. "Please. Let me go . . ."

A long moment passed. He reluctantly released her.

Biting her lip, Kelsey ran down the hall, dragging her rolling suitcase. She grabbed her purse and opened the front door. *Go. Leave!* she told herself. She couldn't do it without looking back at them one last time.

They looked devastated. Tucker's heartbreak shone from his eyes. Desolation swept across Jeremy's dark face. Rhys clenched his jaw and his fists, looking a breath away from real tears. Her gut clenched. Her knees buckled. She'd done this to them. Now she had to leave so the healing could begin.

"I'm sorry it couldn't work. I love you all." She swallowed. "Be happy."

A week dragged. Then another. And every time Jeremy walked out of his office and saw his temporary paralegal sitting at Kelsey's desk, anguish pounded him all over again.

Damn it, he wasn't sleeping. Or eating. Or focusing on anything except Kelsey.

Where the hell had she gone? Of course, he'd called Garrison the next morning to ask if Kelsey had accepted his job. Bastard refused to say, but his smug tone told Jeremy all he needed to know. Or so he'd thought. But his quick trip to Miami a few days ago and a thorough search of Garrison's office had netted no proof that Kelsey worked there. Or planned to. The job his rival had interviewed Kelsey for had been filled by another paralegal. But Jeremy felt down in his gut that Garrison knew exactly where Kelsey was.

Jeremy had no fucking clue. None of them did. Unfortunately, she'd changed her cell phone number. Deleted her e-mail account. He'd used every contact he knew to see if Kelsey had started a new paralegal job. And according to Tucker, her parents weren't talking, either. Rhys had used some of his cop and PI friends to try to find her. All to no avail.

She'd well and truly left them. Jeremy couldn't avoid the truth that he was largely at fault. Fuck, she'd warned them all along that she couldn't choose . . . and they'd refused to believe that they couldn't use time, money, sex, and love to force her. He'd been a jealous bastard and driven a wedge between them.

Now, he regretted it like hell.

A dull headache beat between his temples. Jeremy looked at his watch. Eight P.M. He'd been at work for the last fourteen hours, eaten next to nothing and accomplished even less. But why the hell should he go home to an empty condo, even with his views of the lake, and take stock of just how fucking empty his life was without Kelsey Rena?

A knock on his door made him look up. Rhys and Tucker both stood there. He hadn't seen them since the terrible evening Kelsey had left them. He'd spoken to each once—long enough to extract a promise to call him if she contacted them and for them to secure a promise in kind.

"Have you heard from her?"

Tucker rubbed his hands nervously. "Yes. When she knew I'd be working and away from my phone, Kels left me a voice mail. She's due in town for her cousin's wedding this weekend. She's asked to see us all at ten o' clock on Saturday morning at her house." His shoulders dropped on a big sigh. "She was very clear that we should not assume this means she's coming home to stay or wants to resume a romantic relationship with any of us."

Jeremy clenched his jaw. That was Kelsey, unflinchingly direct when she chose to be. "So what *does* she want?"

Rhys shrugged. "Other than maybe wanting another chance to read us the riot act, I don't know."

"Me, either."

A long, silent moment ensued, and Jeremy turned that last evening with Kelsey over in his mind again.

"What happened that night? Really?" He glared at Tucker. "You couldn't think for even a second that I'd actually hurt her."

Tucker's jaw dropped, suggesting to Jeremy that he'd surely lost his mind. "What the hell else would I think? You'd restrained her so that you could *hit* her. Where I come from, that's abusing a woman, and I wasn't going to stand there and watch."

Had the asshole never heard of BDSM? "Rhys verified that she was very much enjoying herself."

"I don't see how." Tucker shook his head. "Her ass was bright red. I clearly saw your handprint on her fair skin. She had tears running down her face, for fuck's sake."

"From coming so hard! Are you that blind? That unaware of what it means to be dominant with a female?"

"Hey, I'm plenty alpha."

At Tucker's objection, Jeremy shook his head. "Not the same thing."

"It's not," Rhys supplied.

"What, are you on his side?" Tucker snapped.

"I'm on the side of whoever can figure this shit out and get her back here," the fireman pointed out.

"So stop being sanctimonious," Jeremy snapped. "I saw how you looked at her. You were pissed . . . but you were also hard."

Tucker's eyes narrowed. "She was naked. I was furious, not blind. Don't you dare suggest that I'd get off on hitting a woman."

"Punching her, no." Jeremy shrugged. "Slapping her ass and watching it turn red for you, yeah, I think you might."

"You're wrong," Tucker insisted.

"I don't care about Tucker's kink or lack thereof," Rhys cut in. "The truth is, something happened that night and none of us handled it well. She'll be back in three days and wants to see us. This might be our last shot."

Rhys's words shot dread through Jeremy, but damn it if he wasn't right. "I'm assuming we are all still in love with her?"

"Yes," Tucker confirmed.

Rhys nodded. "Damn straight."

Jeremy swallowed. Now reconciling got difficult. But if he didn't embrace her wants and needs over his own, didn't love her enough to man up, she'd come and go on Saturday, perhaps never to appear again.

If it was within his power at all, he needed to ensure that didn't happen.

"Good," Jeremy asserted. "Until we fucked up, she wanted all of us. Kelsey doesn't change her mind or heart that easily, so let's work from the assumption that's still true."

Tucker nodded. "And you're now okay with that?"

"Being without Kelsey is far, far worse than sharing her. If she needs us all . . ." He sighed. "I want her happy and need her in my life. Since we all still love her, we're going to have to learn to work together, get along."

Rhys's jaw dropped. "Wow. I wasn't sure you'd ever get there. You really do love her."

"Yes."

The fireman slanted Jeremy a challenging stare. "If she agrees to stay, you know that means we're all going to fuck her, probably every day. And you're going to have to deal."

"I know." Not that he loved the fact. But it was reality. "Her happiness is most important, and I know you'd never hurt her."

"Wish I could say the same about you." A deadly note crept into Tucker's voice.

"Goddammit, you thick-headed cowboy! Dominance isn't about beating a woman into submission; it's about earning her trust. It's a Dominant's job to understand his submissive's deepest desires and give them to her. Part of doing that means he rewards the compliant behavior and punishes the undesirable. She grants trust, and he exercises it, proving he's worthy, so he earns more and can get to the deepest core of her needs."

"He's right," Rhys concurred.

"How do you know?" Tucker whirled on him, brow furrowed.

The fireman shrugged. "I did the D/s thing with a girlfriend in college. Loved it."

Tucker rolled his eyes. "Is there anything sexual you haven't tried and haven't liked?"

Rhys thought. About two seconds later, he shook his head and smiled. "Nope."

"I don't get it." Sighing, Tucker scrubbed a hand across his face. "But I'll try to."

"Think with your dick and not your Southern gentleman upbringing." Some of Jeremy's anger drained away. "I pushed Kelsey's boundaries, and she proved to me that she was every bit ready and happy for more."

Tucker didn't say anything for a long minute. "I'll try to be okay with that—provided she even gives us another chance. I don't know . . . I'll at least promise to ask questions before I hit you again."

Jeremy laughed, feeling lighter than he had in weeks. "That's a good start, and I'll do the same . . . but I think I have an idea, too."

CHAPTER | TEN

Kelsey smoothed a hand down her skirt for the tenth time in the last five minutes, then pressed a hand to her fluttering stomach. She tapped her toes in a nervous gesture. The guys were due here any moment, and it was all she could do not to lose the contents of her stomach.

How would they react to what she had to say? She'd run a thousand scenarios in her mind but still didn't know. The next hour could be the longest of her life.

At precisely ten o'clock, the doorbell rang. Her stomach jumped, cramped. Drawing in a deep breath, she tried to find a Zen moment as she approached the door and opened it.

On the other side stood three wonderful men. God, they were all stiff and quiet, their faces silently yearning. Tucker's expression held so much regret. She'd never seen Rhys this somber. Jeremy looked flat exhausted. He'd never been one to reveal his emotions, but today he wore his heart on his sleeve.

Kelsey closed her eyes for a moment. Finality resounded inside her like a death knell. This was going to kill her.

"Good morning." She stepped back. "Come in and . . ."

The living room had too many memories. Bad ones. Every time she passed it, all she saw was punches thrown. She heard the echoes of hurled threats and insults.

No, not here.

"Let's go to the den," she murmured.

They followed in silence. Rhys was right behind her. Funny how she knew his musky scent so perfectly. Tucker followed. The way he shuffled when he walked was distinct. Jeremy fell in last—a surprise. She'd expected him to barge in first and demand the most. What was up with him?

Once they reached the family room, she purposely sat in the room's lone recliner. The men all stopped in front of the sofa and sat reluctantly. Without a word, they knew that what she had to say was going to change everything.

"I know you're wondering why I called you here."

"Wait." Tucker leaned forward, looking like he'd burst if he didn't get to speak. "I'm sorry for everything. I thought before I acted—"

"Thank you. But it doesn't change anything."

"Actually, we hope it does," Rhys replied. "We've talked. We know we fucked up bad."

She sighed. "It wasn't just the fight."

"You're worried about everything behind it; we understand," Jeremy assured.

Then her former boss rose to his feet, crossed the room. Kelsey watched, wide eyed, as he came closer.

"Don't," she protested.

She didn't have the strength to resist him—any of them.

"Shh. I won't . . . touch . . ." Sighing, he dropped to his knees at her feet. "Please. Just hear us."

The toughest, most go-for-the-jugular attorney in Texas begging? She didn't know what to say. She swallowed. The ice around her heart was already cracking. How the hell could she stop it when Jeremy looked at her like she held his heart and soul in the palm of her hand?

"I know whatever you're going to say is . . . final." Tucker folded his hands in his lap. "You've got that look on your face. But before you say it, we'd like to try to set things right—"

"It won't work. I can't—won't—choose, and you can't share, even temporarily. So let's just . . . not hurt each other more."

"I know you won't choose. We won't make you try," Jeremy vowed.

"Eventually, you would. Especially you."

"You're not just mine," Jeremy blurted, taking her hands in his. "You're *ours*. I was putting my demands above your happiness. I know now that I can't. I've never shared well." He shrugged and sent her a tight smile. "Only-child syndrome, I guess. But you looked . . . radiant when you were with all of us, and I'm sorry I thought I could take that from you. If you'll give us a second chance, I will never come between you and the others again."

She sucked in a breath. A stunning promise. Huge. Her heart jumped with possibilities . . . before reality crashed in. "It's easy to say . . . and hard to do. You'll tell me whatever you think I want to hear now, but you don't really mean it. Like last time—"

"Last time we all made love to you at once, I was thinking that I would grant you this one fantasy before I claimed you for my own. Now, I know better."

Did he? Really? "But when our situation tests you—"

"Test us now," Jeremy insisted. "As long as you love me, I can deal with anything."

He looked *so* honest that Kelsey did a double take. "And this isn't some ploy to make me choose eventually?"

He shook his head. "I swear."

"This is us wanting to love you, baby," Rhys supplied. "However you need to be loved. As long as you'll love us back."

Seriously? Had they really talked about what had gone wrong?

Maybe she shouldn't get her hopes up. She knew she wanted a lot from them. And they still had more barriers between them.

"What about you, Tucker? Can you accept what I need from Jeremy?"

Something crossed his face as it tightened. Resolution. He stood tall, squared his shoulders. His caring blue eyes hardened as he looked at her with demand.

"Stand up. I'll show you exactly what I can accept, honey."

Tucker? No denying the command in his voice made her pulse race, echoing between her legs.

Slowly, uncertainly, she stood. "What is it?"

"Faster next time. Now lose the skirt."

Her eyes nearly popped from her head. *That* order had come from her sweet friend Tucker? And his tone . . . deep, snapping like a lash, insistent.

Kelsey felt herself go damp, but forced herself to rein in her desire.

"I don't know where you're going with this, but we have really important things to—"

"Lose. The. Skirt." Tucker took a heavy step toward her, his expression hot and impatient.

They'd planned this. Kelsey understood that now. The three of them really had talked about the problems between them and each tried to accept responsibility. Jeremy swore he would share her, Rhys vowed they'd love her however she needed, and now Tucker had adopted a dominant mantle to please her.

She bit her lip. Was it possible they really meant to make it work?

No. She'd been there, done this with them. But her resolution wavered. She'd been so damn miserable the past two weeks. A few mornings ago she'd awakened in an unfamiliar city in an unfamiliar apartment with an unfamiliar job and bawled her eyes out. Then she'd received more shocking news and . . .

What was the best course of action here? Cut them off before anyone else got any more hurt? Or listen and hope that, by some miracle, they could all get it right?

Kelsey knew herself. If she got up and walked away now, she'd forever regret not hearing them out, especially when there was so much at stake.

Swallowing, she reached for her zipper and lowered it. As soon as the skirt cleared her thighs and revealed her little white lace thong, Rhys hissed, Tucker panted, and Jeremy cursed.

Her legs went weak.

"Good," Tucker praised. "Next, the shirt."

She was crazy. Certifiable. But with a few words and their rapt, scorching gazes, her breasts had become heavy, her nipples hard. Masturbating to thoughts of them did nothing for her anymore. She needed to *feel* them.

Whipping the shirt up over her head, she revealed the matching lace demibra, the swells of her breasts pushed up high.

"Yeah." Tucker's word was a long caress, and she responded, her body tightening.

"What next?" Her voice shook.

"Sir," Jeremy cut in. "You call him *sir*. Are we clear?"

God, that made her sex clench. Now she was really wet. "Yes, sir."

"Rhys, finish undressing her," Tucker demanded.

The fireman rose from the sofa, his cock tenting his shorts. He wore a lascivious half smile, then stared Jeremy's way. "You know I'm going to touch everything, put my mouth everywhere."

Jeremy nodded. "I'm waiting."

This was surreal. Jeremy sat at her feet. Tucker stood halfway across the room, issuing demands. Rhys strode across the room with every intent to . . . what? Strip her? Fuck her? While the others watched?

Her knees nearly gave way.

Rhys placed a simple, reverent kiss on her lips. "I missed you, baby. I'll cut my heart out and give it to you, if that's what you need to be happy."

His words staggered her. And humbled her. They didn't think she needed that, did they?

Then again, she'd asked for a great deal. When they'd been unable to give it to her, she'd left abruptly. Angrily. Maybe they could have worked it out . . . and she'd been too afraid of being caught in the middle and destroying all their relationships to try.

"Just love me," she whispered. "That's all I need."

He smiled, his green eyes dancing with mischief as he cupped her shoulders. "You have no idea how well loved you're going to be . . ."

Before she could process the comment, he caressed his way down her back. A minute later, her bra hit the floor. Rhys's hands were instantly beneath her breasts, supporting, lifting. He sucked in her nipples one at a time, laving, scraping, swirling.

Kelsey grabbed his hard shoulders for support, feeling Tucker's and Jeremy's gazes on her. Tucker looked aroused; she expected that. Jeremy watched with a dark, enthralled stare. He wasn't ready to kill Rhys? Really?

A moment later, thoughts scattered when Rhys gently twisted her nipples in his grip and his mouth drifted across her neck.

As she shivered in Rhys's grasp, Tucker stepped closer.

"Now the panties."

Rhys stepped back, and they all stared, waiting expectantly, wanting her naked. So they could . . . what? Kelsey didn't know, but whatever it was, it felt damn good to be with them, have them get along, even if temporarily, swearing they understood her needs. It may not last, but they sought to prove something to her . . . and she didn't have the will to turn away.

Hooking her thumbs in the strings across her hips, she wriggled her panties down and off.

"Give them to Jeremy," Tucker demanded.

So he could feel how wet they were? Turning ten shades of red, she complied.

Immediately, Jeremy lifted them to his nose and inhaled. "She's ready."

"Good." Tucker looked at her with approval. "Spread your legs. Jeremy is going to watch Rhys make you come."

Shaking, she looked over at Jeremy. Could he really handle this or would he feel compelled to grab her, sink deep into her, and warn the others off with bared teeth and a growled threat?

If he could watch and not interfere—and not assume he'd never have to share again—it would be a huge step forward, a definite door to new possibilities.

Stomach clenching nervously, she sank to the chair, butt perched on the edge, and spread her legs. She was breathing hard now; Jeremy peered at them over her thigh, his face less than a foot from her wet folds. He licked his lips—but nothing more.

Instead, Rhys settled in front of her, crouching between her thighs. Jeremy held his breath, waiting. Hell, she waited breathlessly too. But Rhys didn't keep either of them in suspense for long.

He parted her folds with his thumbs and dropped his mouth over her aching clit, licking and sucking at her, not like she was a treat, but the most precious person on the planet. He'd never been so tender. Always fun. Always physical. Always ready. But this . . . He worshipped her with every breath, movement, and touch.

Her back arched and her eyes misted.

Rhys took her hips in his hands. Kelsey threaded her fingers through his. Hands linked, they moved together, as tension and pleasure rose with every heartbeat.

"Come for Rhys, honey," Tucker directed.

No way she could refuse that request. A second later, she bucked, shuddered as desire climbed then burst open, leaving her floating and serene. Rhys continued to lap at her gently, as if reluctant to leave her.

Across the room, Tucker's demanding voice cut into her haze. "Make love to her."

Rhys pulled her off the chair, nodding. His green eyes met her questioning stare. Right here? As she lay back on the carpet, she cast a nervous glance at Jeremy, now a mere six inches away.

"Are you happy?" His dark gaze connected with her as Rhys shed his clothes.

Kelsey soaked in Jeremy's beloved face, searching for any sign of distress. "Not if you're miserable."

"Do you love him?"

"I love all of you. You know that . . ."

"If he makes you happy, I'm happy. I just—" Jeremy choked. "I can't lose you again."

She wanted to ask how he knew that tomorrow or the day after he wouldn't reconnect with his jealous tendencies. But Rhys climbed between her thighs and probed for her wet opening.

"Wait," Tucker snapped, then regarded Jeremy. "Kels doesn't look convinced of your sincerity yet. You need to take a more active role in helping Rhys fuck her. Sit behind her, put her head in your lap. Like that. Good. Now grab Kelsey's legs and hold them apart. Watch them."

The request was shocking, taking the idea of sharing her to a whole new level. Jeremy was supposed to assist someone else in having sex with her? Inside, she knew she should be scandalized, maybe even horrified. Instead, the arousal Rhys had sated with his mouth leapt to new life, flames of need scorching behind her clit all over again.

Especially when Jeremy did as Tucker instructed, holding her legs at the knees and pulling high, opening her wide.

A moment later, Rhys began feeding her hungry body his cock, one granite inch after another at the slowest, most maddening pace. She clamped down on him, and Rhys hissed, holding himself above her on his elbows.

Feeling flushed and full of tingles, Kelsey tipped her head back to search Jeremy's expression. He watched Rhys tunnel into her with an intent gaze.

Then Jeremy looked down to meet her stare. "You're flushed."

"I'm aroused," she admitted.

"And you're happy?"

Before she could answer, Rhys drove home—hard. She gasped as he filled her in one burning stretch of flesh, then ground against her, pressing against her clit.

"Yes!"

"Yes you want more, or yes to Jeremy's question?" Tucker snapped as he knelt beside her.

"Both." She could barely gasp the word out as Rhys withdrew with an agonizingly slow tilt of his hips, then rammed home again.

He unleashed weeks' worth of pent-up lust on her in a series of pounding, rhythmic thrusts that had her holding her breath, chanting his name, hovering on the brink of orgasm more quickly than she would have thought possible.

Tucker ducked under Jeremy's arm and took her nipple in his mouth, sucking hard.

At the pain-tinged pleasure, her body drew up tight. As she clenched around Rhys's cock, the friction awakened pleasure everywhere in her body. Her heart, already so in love, had no way of resisting them. She fluttered, cried out, then released with a shudder that matched Rhys's as he came inside her.

A moment later, she realized she'd reached above her head and now clutched Jeremy's thighs.

Her former boss breathed heavily, his every muscle tight, his stark gaze a blistering demand for her body. Still, he said nothing, merely released his hold on her legs as Rhys withdrew, kissed her abdomen, then left the room, returning a second later with a wet washcloth.

As Rhys cleaned her gently, she felt the caring in his touch, saw it in his eyes. She melted all over again.

God, what was she doing? Letting them do? Jeremy was exercising enormous self-control . . . but what if he snapped? What if Tucker's boy-next-door upbringing overwhelmed his common sense next time Jeremy dominated her? This could so blow up in her face at a moment's notice. She really ought to put a stop to this now.

"Guys," she began.

"Wait," Tucker demanded. "Let us make sure you understand."

After cleaning her, Rhys pulled away, then donned his underwear and sat back on the sofa with a satisfied grin.

"Get on your hands and knees, Kels," Tucker demanded again in his darkest voice, the one that reached inside her and, amazingly, reignited her ache.

"Yes, sir."

Slowly, uncertainly, she rolled to her belly, then propped herself up on all fours. And found Jeremy's face inches from hers. Still he watched her, his gaze hard and unwavering. A moment later, she felt Tucker behind her, the front of his thighs against the back of hers.

Then she felt something cold against her back entrance . . . just before his fingers slid deep. She craned her head to watch more resolution solidify on his face.

"You're going to take me here," Tucker told her. "All of me."

"You're big," she protested automatically.

"And if it hurts, you'll tell me. I'll adjust. I've never done this. Jeremy is going to talk me through it. And only talk."

Seriously? Kelsey turned back to Jeremy. He looked equally resolved.

"I am."

Her insides quivered as Tucker pumped her with one finger, then another. Amazingly the desire she'd felt sure Rhys had utterly sated kindled again into a needy flame.

"Okay," she finally whispered.

"It wasn't a request, and I'll only fuck this gorgeous ass after I spank it."

"What?" she asked, turning back to him.

Tucker pressed a hand to the small of her back and forced her back down, all the way to her elbows, so her ass pointed up. He cast a glance at Jeremy. "Hold her down."

Jeremy smiled, then clamped his hands over her shoulders. "Absolutely."

Kelsey's eyes widened and she shot at him, "You're enjoying this?"

"He's going to make your ass bright cherry red, vixen," Jeremy informed her. "Hell, yes, I'm enjoying it. If you're not careful, I'll add to it myself before I fuck you."

"You, I believe. But Tucker? Is he really going to spank—ouch!"

His slap against her ass resounded in the room. She hadn't been prepared for it. Her cheek didn't really hurt so much as sting. But as soon as the blood rushed in, it throbbed.

She turned back to Tucker, and he was looking directly at her ass.

"Amazing," he breathed. "I can actually see my handprint on her fair skin."

"Arousing as hell, isn't it?" Jeremy taunted.

Tucker sent him a shaky nod—then whacked her across the ass again. "That's for leaving us without giving us a chance to make it right. We worried like hell about you. Jeremy went to Miami, looking for you. Rhys used his contacts." *Whap.* "I camped out at your parents' house."

"You're—you're punishing me?" Even the possibility of Tucker administering a punishment boggled her mind.

"Yes," he bit out, then smacked her ass again. "That's for disappearing off the face of the earth without telling any of us where you were."

"No point," she eeked out over the tingles and heat and pleasure-pain. "We were over."

"We weren't," he snarled—and lit up her ass again. As she gasped, he continued, "We love you. People in love don't just give up; they work it out. That's what we're going to do, now and always. Got it?"

Smack! Slap! Thump! Again and again. High, low, left right, Tucker never struck the same place twice, but soon, her ass was on fire.

"Yes . . . sir," she panted. Oh dear God, she was seconds from coming.

"If you return to us for good, there's no turning back. No playing favorites."

Another series of slaps had her overheated, melting. Jeremy's searing gaze on her face turned up the temperature even more.

"You understand? Love, acceptance, devotion—nothing else." His palm landed on the top of her ass, her hip, high on her thigh. Then he reached around to slap the pad of her pussy.

Oh God, yes! She gasped, hanging onto her composure by the barest threads.

"Please . . ." Kelsey wiggled, squirmed, silently pleading.

"Understand?" he repeated.

"Yes, sir," she shrieked.

"Excellent." Suddenly, his hands stilled.

"No!" she protested.

Tucker ignored her, then addressed Jeremy. "Now what?"

"You liked it," Jeremy accused.

After hesitating, Tucker nodded. "Loved it. I felt her need in a way I never had. I knew I was giving her something she wanted mentally and physically, and it was a massive turn-on."

"Exactly." Jeremy's smile was downright bad. "Spread her cheeks with your hands and ease your dick into that little hole just a bit. It will burn and sting. Watch for her tensing, hissing, scratching. Any could be signs the pain is too much. Arching, gasping, or begging, and you've got a green light. Press slowly to make sure you don't hurt her. It's a killer to your self-control, but by the time you're balls deep, she'll nearly be ready to come."

Kelsey sucked in a breath. Jeremy had just . . . laid it all out, told Tucker exactly how to take her in this most forbidden way. And he'd done it without fighting or growling—or even blinking. In fact, he looked almost satisfied.

Then she had no more time to marvel at this turn of events when she felt the head of Tucker's cock part her and begin to sink into the tight little opening. An exquisite pain. Burning. Overwhelming. She loved it.

Gasping, she dug her hands into the carpet. "More!"

"It's going to hurt, honey."

"I know." She pressed back against him, wriggling, trying to take him deeper.

Grabbing her hips, he eased forward in a controlled press, one torturous inch at a time. God, the way he stretched her. Nothing like it. She panted, trying to absorb the riot of sensation bombarding her at once, the heat, the ache. She closed her eyes and melted into the carpet.

"She's there with you," Jeremy assured. "Fuck her now."

The seductive demand in his voice made her shiver. Tucker didn't waste any time complying.

Using his palms to pull her cheeks wider apart, he sank inch after relentless inch into her ass, filling her up and up, until she cried out when pain overwhelmed pleasure.

"Hurt, honey?" he asked, pausing.

She whimpered and nodded, reaching around to dig one of her hands into his leg, sending her nails deep into his skin.

"That's okay. Take it out on me if you need." Kelsey felt his regard shift to Jeremy. "She can't take more."

"She can," Jeremy argued. "I've seen a woman's pain threshold. She isn't at hers. Go on. Get deeper."

Jeremy lifted her head to his and kissed her mouth slowly, then pushed the hair back from her damp face. "Take more of Tucker's cock. We're almost there. Do it. For me."

Kelsey drew in a deep, shuddering breath. It hurt. Really hurt. Yet she felt oddly . . . euphoric. And she wanted to take all of Tucker. Needed to know he was deep inside her in whatever way he wished to be. She yearned to please Jeremy.

She nodded. "I want all of you, Tucker."

He leaned over her, his chest to her back, then rubbed lazy circles around her clit. "Good. Let Jeremy kiss you and make the pain go away."

As she turned her face up to Jeremy again, he dedicated his lips to her pleasure alone, and Tucker pressed inside her, slowly, ruthlessly. She screamed into Jeremy's mouth, and suddenly felt Rhys at her side, brushing soft fingers across her diamond-hard nipples and the soft swell of her abdomen.

"He's in," Rhys whispered in her ear. "You look gorgeous and so aroused."

"And so damn happy." Jeremy's voice cracked, and Kelsey opened her eyes to find him looking her with a mixture of arousal and devotion that made her heart and pussy clench at once.

Then Tucker pulled back to the tight ring of muscle, brushed her clit with his fingertips, then tunneled in again, one long inch after another. On and on, deeper and deeper, until she grasped at the carpet again, mewled, writhed.

"We could have this forever," Tucker whispered seductively. "We could give you pleasure and push your boundaries."

"We could protect and support you, baby." Rhys leaned in and kissed her shoulder. "Every single day."

Jeremy pressed his mouth to hers. "We could show you how much we love you in every way. Every night."

It was too much—to ignore, to bear, to fight.

As Tucker withdrew, then plunged deep again, his fingers grazing her swollen clit, she exploded in a supernova burst, seeing white starbursts behind her eyes, her body following in a detonation of pleasure so extreme, she screamed until she could no longer see or breathe . . . or distinguish where she ended and her men began. They were all with her now, in spirit, in body, in heart.

As the peak smoothed into satisfaction, love coalesced inside her. Tears ran down her face. She kissed Jeremy one last time, longing and thanks on her lips. Then she angled her body to Rhys, giving him the same dose of her devotion. Finally, she eased up onto her knees. With Tucker still deep inside, she pressed her back to his chest, then turned her head over her shoulder to meet his waiting lips, holding him to her mouth as he moaned and came deep inside her.

He withdrew, and she sank into the carpet in a boneless heap.

Moments later, she roused to find herself in Jeremy's arms. He set her on the bed, pressed another warm washcloth to her, then smoothed her damp curls away from her face, his body brushing its way up hers. His erection slid home inside her wet sex in one easy stroke.

She gasped as he filled her up.

"God, I've missed you, sweetheart."

"Missed you, too. All three of you."

"Let me love you," Jeremy whispered.

She smiled tiredly. "Only if you love me back."

"Forever?"

"You've really worked through this, haven't you?" She asked Jeremy before her gaze slid to Rhys on one side and Tucker on the other.

"We have," Jeremy promised. "Seeing you glow like this, knowing I'm a part of making you this happy . . . it's all I need."

Complete joy sank into her. This morning she'd awakened dreading this day, fearing it might be the last time she saw all her men together in one place, knowing the information she held close to her heart could tear them apart for good . . . now she prayed it was a fresh beginning, a new hope for tomorrow.

"Forever," she whispered, stroking his midnight hair and wide shoulders.

A huge grin broke across his face, until ecstasy overtook her and had her crying out and shuddering in passion. Jeremy followed quickly, panting against her neck, whispering with every other breath how much she amazed him, how much he loved her.

"Ah, vixen." He kissed her mouth softly, then pulled away. "Damn, you really are glowing."

"Funny you should mention that . . ." She bit her lip.

Would she get the reaction she now dared to hope for? Or would jealousy consume them again?

"Glowing?" Rhys looked puzzled.

"Yes. I actually had you meet me here today to tell you a few things."

"Like where you've been?" Rhys pouted.

She nodded. "I can start there. About a week after I left, I called to accept Garrison's job offer in Miami, but he'd already filled the position. So he offered me another job at his office in Palm Beach. So . . . I went up there and stayed in his vacant apartment and looked for a place of my own. I'm supposed to start work Monday."

"Did you like it there?" Tucker asked carefully.

Kelsey could tell he was holding his breath—and his opinion of her move. She loved him all the more for it.

"Hated it. It just wasn't home."

"Home is where we are." Tucker smiled, then folded her hand inside his.

Jeremy raised a dark brow at her. "Garrison is a smarmy bastard who doesn't deserve a star employee like you."

Not subtle, but he hadn't demanded that she return to work this instant. "There are definite perks to being your submissive—I mean subordinate," she teased. "I could probably be persuaded to come back to work for you . . . with a raise."

"Sweetheart, I'll do you better."

"Of course, because Garrison isn't doing me at all!"

Jeremy laughed. "I meant to say that I'd talked to St. John," he said, referencing his senior partner. "His wife has decided to go into business for herself, and I even gave her a few accounts . . . so her position heading up the paralegal team is vacant. What do you say?"

"Very tempting." Then she turned to Rhys. "But I have another issue. Well, two actually. The first is that I have this very hunky neighbor who's fabulous in bed."

"Damn straight, baby." Rhys nuzzled her neck.

"But I don't want him for a neighbor anymore. I want him as a lover who lives with me every day and night. Just like my other lovers do."

"You got it," he assured.

Jeremy and Tucker quickly agreed.

"What's your other issue?" Rhys tucked a curl behind her ear.

Kelsey drew in a shuddering breath. Now came the hard part. What would they say? How would they feel? Happy feel-good vibes and teasing of the last few minutes aside, this was serious stuff that could make or break them.

"Honey?" Tucker picked up on her tension and squeezed her hand.

She glanced at all three to see that they were hanging on her every word. *Now or never . . .*

"I'm pregnant."

For a long second, no one said a word. Her heart careened out of control, thumping madly against her chest. Damn it, any minute they'd start fighting about who would marry her and who had fathered the baby and—

Rhys gave a whoop of joy. Tucker smiled and rubbed his hands together in a gesture of adorable arrogance. Jeremy caressed a hand along her belly and pressed his mouth to hers.

"You're sure?"

Cautiously optimistic, she nodded. "I went for a physical for my new job. They told me I'm pregnant, just a few weeks. I'm due early in June." She sucked in a shaky breath. "I don't know which of you . . ."

"If you're happy, I'm thrilled," Jeremy assured her.

"If you stay and let us be the baby's fathers, you'll make us the happiest men ever," Rhys vowed.

"Agreed," Tucker put in. "Marry one of us? Legally, anyway. Privately, we'll—"

"No." She backed up, drew a sheet over her nudity. "I'll agree to a private ceremony marrying you all. I want to be yours always. But legally . . . I told you I won't choose."

They were quiet a long moment, and she could see them turning the idea in their minds. They didn't look thrilled, but she knew that eventually they'd see the wisdom of her decision.

"I understand there are legalities with children involved. When the baby is born, we'll have a paternity test. The baby's biological father will be listed on the birth certificate. All other legalities, we can work out from there." She turned to Jeremy. "I know you'll be able to help nail it all down."

He looked tense, uncertain. "And that will make you happy?"

"Yes. But what about *you*? It doesn't work if you're not happy too."

He pressed his lips together, clearly formulating his next words. "I'm almost thirty-eight. What if this baby isn't mine? I can share you with them. You have enough love to go around, and I was a fool not to see that. But someday, I'd like to be a father."

Her heart melted. "If this isn't your baby, with a little cooperation from Tucker and Rhys . . . we'll just make sure the next one is."

"Next one? You'd do that for me?" He looked amazed all over again.

Did they think this "oops baby" was the end of their family? "In my heart, I want to be a wife to all of you. Like any marriage, we'll have challenges and disagreements. But you've already compromised so much to make me happy. I'd be thrilled to have your baby. In fact, I think three children sounds great."

Jeremy hugged her tightly against his chest, then pressed his lips to her forehead. "Thank you so much. I love you."

"I love you, too."

He released her to Rhys's waiting arms, who pressed a hot kiss to her lips. "Hmm. A little girl with my eyes and your spirit. I'd love that."

"We'll work on it." She winked.

"Looking forward to it already."

Then Tucker wrapped his arms around her. "You amaze me. Thank you for coming here to tell us about the baby."

"I refused to take the chickenshit way out and tell you over the phone . . . and I guess part of me hoped we'd work everything out."

"I'm so glad you did. Now, honey, understand there's no more running off like this. If there's a problem in the future, we talk it out, right?"

Resolved and blissful, she nodded. "Absolutely."

He flashed her a naughty grin. "Though you could pretend a

little . . . walk to the end of the block or something. Give me a good reason to spank you again."

"Yes, sir." She laughed. "Though I expect I'll do plenty over the years to warrant lots of punishment."

"We're counting on it," Tucker said.

"We're also counting on a lifetime of love," Jeremy added.

"Damn straight." Rhys smiled.

"Me, too." She sniffled, happy tears springing to her eyes. "Always."